C.A.RUDOLPH

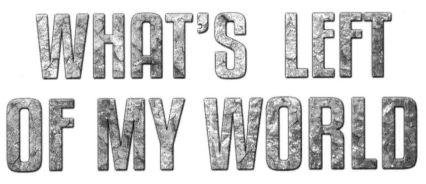

WHAT'S LEFT OF MY WORLD

BOOK ONE OF THE WHAT'S LEFT OF MY WORLD SERIES

Copyright © 2016 All rights reserved.
Cover Art: Deranged Doctor Design
Formatting: Deranged Doctor Design
Editing: Sabrina Jean, FastTrack Editing

ISBN-13: 978-1530974405
ISBN-10: 1530974402

DEDICATION

For Emma

Despite several personal failures in the parenting department for varying reasons, in 2008 God decided to permit me another chance at being a dad when He gave me you. From the moment I first saw your eyes gaze into mine, I swore to myself that I would be the best dad I could be or I would die trying. I hope that I haven't let you down.

I feel as though I've taught you a lot about this world and about life and I cherish the closeness we have and the moments when we talk. I hope that what I have managed to teach you goes a long way into making you an amazing woman someday. Even as young as you are as I write this, I know for certain you are off to a great start.

You are the inspiration for everything I do every day. You were the chief inspiration for me writing this book. Always stay true to yourself. Always be strong. Never stop fighting. Keep stoking the fire that's burning inside you. Never forget how beautiful you are to me. I love you.

— Dad

PREFACE

A S A SELF-EMPLOYED CONTRACTOR FOR many years, I was fortunate enough to be able to maintain a very close proximity with my home and my family. Due to financial reasons several years ago, I was forced into the unfamiliar world of career change. My new profession provided me with a solid weekly paycheck and all the accoutrements of working for a profitable company in a highly technical field, all of which I was more than grateful to have. I was provided with a company vehicle—the caveat of which was that I now began travelling anywhere from one to two hours from home, either to my office or any one of many different job sites, most of which were located in the very populated metropolitan areas around and within the District of Columbia. I never realized just how much I had taken for granted being so close to home until acquiring a job that kept me so far away from it, and so distant from those I loved the most.

With all the added time I was spending on the road, I wanted to come up with a way to use the time constructively, so I began listening to audiobooks. As an avid backpacker and outdoorsman, I started with books about hiking and the Appalachian Trail and before long, progressed to classic works by Henry David Thoreau and John Muir; where I found a new appreciation for the outdoors in general.

One day, I read an article that regarded a book in a completely different genre. The article intrigued me enough that I downloaded the book and listened to it, and it forever changed the way I viewed my life, the lives of those I cared about the most, and the world we all lived in and enjoyed. It made me realize just how fragile things really were. That book was *One Second After* by William Forstchen.

After listening to *One Second After*, I began listening to other audiobooks with similar post-apocalyptic storylines, such as *The Survivalist Series* by A. American and *The Borrowed World Series* by Franklin Horton, as well as many others. Listening to these audiobooks inspired me to begin thinking long and hard about what my family and I would do if placed into a similar or even an identical catastrophic situation. I quickly came to the conclusion that we didn't have anything even remotely close to a plan. As such, we needed to get off our butts and start preparing.

What you are about to read was written based upon my somewhat limited familiarity of such a disaster, my intermediate knowledge of the outdoors, and the simple understanding of the true virtue of family. My expertise, while not nearly as technical in nature as the previously mentioned authors, relies on personal experience and my relationship with the characters, some of whom are based on my closest friends, family members, and people who have left a lasting impression in me over the years. I feel, that the will to fight and survive can exist in anyone, in any situation, regardless of age, knowledge, or training.

This book and the books that will follow it are about what I personally believe a fairly well prepared and equipped family would do if suddenly placed into a situation that changed their lives forever—and were forced to make decisions as a family that had been separated from their husband and father, and him from them. I hope you enjoy reading *What's Left of My World* as much as I enjoyed writing it.

C.A.Rudolph, December, 2016

CHAPTER 1

"Our most basic instinct is not for survival but for family. Most of us would give our own life for the survival of a family member, yet we lead our daily life too often as if we take our family for granted."
— Paul Pearsall

Big Schloss Spur Trail
George Washington National Forest
Hardy County West Virginia
Present day

THE BRISK WINDS BLEW LAUREN Russell's hair across her face occasionally. Her feet were sore and achy. Her calves burned almost as much as her shoulders did from the weight of her backpack. She had just reached the peak of a steep mountain approach trail she had been hiking on for the past thirty minutes or so. Not long after crossing a familiar wooden bridge, she scrambled to the top of a large rock outcropping, and did so rather enthusiastically, in spite of the nagging pains. Taking in the view, she rested for a moment to gather herself and to catch her breath. These hikes were a part of what had become her daily routine and she truly enjoyed the physical workout almost as much as she enjoyed the solitude. An experienced hiker, she wasn't an athlete by any means, but she welcomed the rise in heart rate and the exercise-induced endorphins that made her feel invincible. She had been following this routine ever since her family had moved to the cabin earlier on that year. Her stamina had gotten better over time and she noticed. The paths she followed in this area were very rocky, like most trails along the Appalachians, and in spite of her experience with them, there were times when she would stumble or otherwise injure herself inadvertently. She did so especially in her earlier travels. The more trail time she got, the more predictable the trails were to her, and she knew what to look out for and when to tread lightly. She was to a point now where she felt she could almost hike them blindfolded.

Lauren had been a trail junky since she was a child. She seemingly had no choice in the matter, since her family practically lived in the outdoors and brought her up to do the same. Her dad was an avid outdoorsman and had been a hiker and backpacker since his youth. Her mother had followed suit since marrying her dad, but growing up in the mountains of Germany, it came naturally to her. It seemed as though just about every weekend, there would be an outdoor adventure for the family to go on. It was camping and day-hiking mostly but on occasion, her dad would plan an overnight backpacking trip and sometimes an excursion that lasted a week or more, and that was what she truly loved. There was something amazing to her about being able to go anywhere she wanted to go, carrying everything she needed on her back. Her dad had taught her just about everything she knew about the outdoors. Other skills had been self-taught. She thought often about her first backpacking trips with him. She remembered how he used to insist on holding her hand on the more rough and treacherous trails. If she tripped, he was always there to stop her fall. If she fell, he would pick her up, dust her off, and encourage her to continue. Her world had changed so much. Things were indeed different now. On these hikes she was on her own and had to be cautious with every step she took. One wrong move could mean injury, and depending on the circumstances, even death. There was no one there to hold her hand now.

Lauren's favorite thing of all were the views that the mountain peaks provided. In addition to the solitude, it helped take her mind off of things and send her thoughts to better places. It was the only thing that worked to clear her mind. Where she was standing today provided one of the best payoffs, in terms of the vistas she had seen with her own eyes, in all of her hiking and backpacking career. It was a true panorama, and it was breathtaking. As she surveyed the landscape below her through the conifers and leafless trees, Lauren took mental photos of what she saw, especially noting if anything had changed since she had last visited. Today, things looked normal to her—or as normal as they could be for the times. There wasn't even the tiniest bit of human-generated noise. The only thing she could hear was the sound of the wind whipping through the trees and the trees dancing with one another when their branches would rub together. She pulled out a pair of small binoculars from the waist pack that hung over top of her backpack's hip belt and had a look around. Below her on the west side of the mountain was Trout Run Valley, the area which her family and the small community within considered home. On the other side of mountain was a small valley in the Virginia side of the George Washington National Forest, followed by Little Sluice Mountain, and after a few more hills and valleys to the east was the town of Woodstock, Virginia. This was where her grandparents lived and a place she'd called home for a short time before moving further west. The town was blocked from her view by the mountains, but she knew it was there.

The sun was starting to show itself over the horizon. She was a true early-riser and had been since childhood, leaving the cabin before dawn nearly every morning on her hikes. It used to take her a few hours to get from the cabin to the top of Mill Mountain, using the switchbacks of a steep game trail, but her times had truncated as her speed and stamina increased. Without a wristwatch or any true method of telling, she would estimate time using the sun's position. It was the middle of autumn and the days were beginning to shorten. From what she remembered, the sun would usually rise around 7 o'clock and set around 5 o'clock this time of year. She assumed it was around 7am, but there really was no way of knowing exactly. Time didn't seem to matter much anymore. There was morning and there was evening; day and night.

This was how Lauren's days began and it had become a steady routine for her. The hikes she took were special journeys to her, and in addition to allowing her a temporary escape from reality, they served a very important purpose in the current world she and her family now lived in. That purpose was reconnaissance. The area they lived in was sparsely inhabited. The individuals that she and her family knew as their neighbors were for the most part, a compassionate, hardworking people, and they looked out for one another. They all had families of their own to provide for and protect. They were a very self-sufficient people, and that trait had unfortunately made them targets. Areas surrounding them were now peppered with *takers*. Takers were people who survived by taking what they wanted, most often by force, from others whenever it suited them. Shortly following the events that occurred a little over a year ago, now known to many as *the collapse*, groups began migrating out of the densely populated areas heading west to the mountains, thinking they could find what they needed to survive there. It was understandable—they simply had no other choice, and desperation was their fuel. No city was capable of supporting its own population. No store contained more than three days of food at most, and when the deliveries stopped, it didn't take long for inventory to disappear from the shelves. When food began running out, they were forced to look elsewhere. As densely populated as the area was in Northern Virginia and the nation's capital, it wasn't long before the takers began migrating into the rural areas to the west, soon ending up in the territories that surrounded Lauren's home.

For unknown reasons, the belief of nearly every city-dweller, suburbanite, and the like was that the woods were full of plenty and there was enough for everyone, even though nothing could've been further from the truth. Technology had been the only reason that people in large populations were able to live and thrive like they had. The populations were forced to learn over time that this was indeed the case, and without that technology, they slowly met their demise. Anyone who relied on technology for survival had perished a long time ago. Most of those who had survived to this point, had done so by practicing subsistence as a part of their normal lives before the collapse, using skills that most generations had forgotten long ago. Survivalists and those known as *preppers* that had set aside supplies during good times, in order to prepare for the possibility of bad days ahead, were also able to find ways to sustain life without technology. Finally, there were the takers—the people who took what they wanted because they could. Most of their victims were chosen specifically because they had no way to defend themselves against an opposing force. Lauren's family was learning to subsist and live off the land. They had begun their plight as fairly well-equipped preppers, thanks to decisions made by her father over the years. Her family and other members of their community had come in contact with takers before. The confrontations had always turned deadly, and her family and neighbors were lucky to have survived. She knew that one day they would certainly meet some of these people again. It wasn't a matter of if, it was a matter of when.

With the lack of communication outside of the local community being the new normal, one of Lauren's motives for her early-morning travels in and around the mountains was knowledge of the outside world, or at least the area that surrounded her community. Her community had chosen to isolate itself, in the name of safety during the first summer after the collapse, by setting up a barricade on their southern border. Takers had come in from the more populated Virginia side of North Mountain and something had to be done to prevent that from happening again. This offered some protection, but being knowledgeable about the area around them and what was going on within it served to keep them all alive, and that required patrolling it on a regular basis. Lauren felt she had a tremendous responsibility now to herself, her family, and in a broader sense, her community. She was so aware of this fact that it was literally tattooed to her soul. Each member of her family had a responsibility to each other now. Each family had a responsibility to the community. They had to work together or they would not survive these hard times. There was safety in numbers—no single person was capable of protecting his or herself now. At eighteen years old, Lauren had more responsibilities than she had ever dreamed—they just weren't the responsibilities of a typical eighteen-year-old. It wasn't about getting good grades in school, getting accepted to a good college, and finding a lucrative career anymore. It wasn't about popularity or social status. It was about staying alive. It was about survival.

After getting a decent magnified view of the area, Lauren placed the binoculars back into her waist pack and zipped up the outer zipper to secure them. She unzipped a side pocket, pulled out a small bag of deer jerky and removed a couple pieces out of the plastic bag before returning the bag to the waist pack. She placed both pieces between her teeth to dangle as she decided to take a load off and rest her tired feet and knees. In order to do this, she made some quick adjustments and lifted her AR-15 carbine over her head, after loosening the sling and placed the rifle on the rock just beside her, making certain to keep it within her reach. She then reached behind around to her back and unsnapped the belt of her waist pack, laying it just to her right. She unbuckled the hip belt of her backpack and then, slid it off of her shoulders to the ground with a slight thud. As she did this, she giggled a bit, knowing how heavy it was. Lauren's pack seemed very large compared to her slender five-foot-six-inch stature. She always carried more than she needed in there, just like her dad always did. His belief was that it was better to have more than you needed than to not have what you need in any situation. His belief became hers, just like so many others.

Her eyes took in the view as she took a seat on the enormous slab of cold white sandstone that made up the peak known as Big Schloss. She had guessed she was sitting on the part that was geographically located in West Virginia, but was not completely certain as the border with Virginia arbitrarily divided the area. Lauren had been to Big Schloss many times growing up on day hikes with her family. It was one of her dad's favorite places to hike. She knew it was around three-thousand feet in elevation and got its name from German families who had settled in the area in the 1800s, some descendants of which still lived in the valleys below to this day. Some of those families were her neighbors. She chewed on the deer jerky slowly and took a couple sips of water from one of her Nalgene bottles that she kept in the outer pockets of her backpack. The air was cold and crisp and the view was breathtaking to her. It was hard for Lauren to believe how bad things had gotten in the world she'd known while looking down at nature's beauty. It was nearly unfathomable to her that in such a small amount of time, her entire world had been turned upside-down. As usual during times that she was alone, her memories began hitting her hard, and she drifted away into a daydream.

* * *

CRACK! The .22 long rifle round's distinct report sounded as Lauren's young finger pulled the trigger on the Ruger 10/22. She had put every one of the five shots she had taken so far on the paper at fifty yards. She fired again, hitting very close to dead center. She then emptied the 10-round magazine with the final four rounds hitting within an inch of the fifth shot.

"Nice, L. Now, click over the safety, and set her down," Alan Russell said to his little girl. "Let's go see how well you did." It was obvious he was more than proud of her. He had been viewing the target with a spotting scope, so he knew how well she had done already, but Lauren was using the iron sights and had only a vague clue.

She did as he said and jumped down from the shooting bench enthusiastically.

"If I did really good, can we show it to mom and maybe frame it?" Lauren asked.

"Absolutely," Alan replied. "This is your first time shooting a rifle. It's important to display your accomplishment."

They walked up to the target stand where Lauren got a chance to see the holes she had put in the target. At first glance, she noticed a few wild ones on the edges of the paper, but was elated to see the five holes in the center ring. She reached up and pulled the paper from the thumbtacks to give it a closer look. She produced a large smile that displayed a few of her missing teeth.

"Can we shoot some more, Daddy?" she asked.

"Of course we can," Alan replied. "We have all day for you to practice—and I want you to at least try every rifle we brought. After this, no more BB guns for you."

"I LOVE GUNS!" Lauren exclaimed. Her father looked at her and she drew back, thinking maybe she had been a little too eager. "I mean, I really like them. A lot."

Her father laughed and she smiled brightly. Lauren's enthusiasm was always so readily available and easy for her to express. She always seemed to be able to find joy in most things in life.

"Well, me too," he said with a smile. "Let's get some more targets up and put a few more down the pipe with the sights, then we can try a red-dot sight. We also have a couple rifles with scopes that you can try."

"You brought your Granddad's gun?" she asked. "Your Granddad Oliver?"

"Yes, I did. How did you know that?"

"That's the one with the scope I remember most," Lauren replied, "and it has real wood, not plastic like some of your new guns."

"Interesting that you'd remember that," Alan said as he put his hand on his daughter's shoulder and the two began walking back to the shooting bench. After they arrived, Alan began reloading magazines. Lauren picked up one and began to reload it as well, watching her father closely for guidance. The two said nothing for a few minutes and only smiled at one another occasionally. Lauren finally broke the silence.

"Daddy, can this gun kill someone?" Lauren asked. She placed her hand on the stock of the Ruger and looked it over, her grin no longer apparent. Her emotion had definitely changed, as if she had been thinking about this in her silence.

"Yes," Alan responded, almost immediately. He paused. "Honey, all guns can kill. Even your BB gun can kill if it's used properly."

"But I don't want to kill anyone," she said innocently.

"That's good. Me neither. In most situations, it's not something that needs to happen. But that being said, there are times that require it say, in cases of self-defense. The world can be a wonderful place, L. But it can also be a dangerous place. We don't want to think about it, but there are people out there that aren't nice. They will take from you and they will hurt you and they don't care. Having a gun is a good deterrent and if needed, can stop someone from hurting you or taking something from you that isn't theirs."

Lauren removed her hand from the rifle and looked up at her father inquisitively with her blue eyes.

"You're scaring me, Daddy," Lauren said as she turned away and her eyes welled up. Alan reached for her and made her face him.

"Look at me," he said.

Lauren looked up to him and began to cry. She always wore her heart on her sleeve. When something bothered her or upset her, she was always just a second away from showing her emotions.

"What have I told you about crying?" he asked, placing both hands on her shoulders.

Lauren sniffled and wiped her tears, then said, "Turn it into something else."

"That's right. There are people, like your mom and me, that it's ok to cry in front of. But there are other people out there who will use the tender heart and strong emotions you're gifted with as a way to hurt you. You need to find a way to turn it into something else."

"I'm trying," she said quietly, a little embarrassed that she had seemingly disappointed her father.

"Listen—I'm not trying to scare you, L. I'm trying to prepare you for some harsh realities. You know I always tell you the truth about everything. I always have—and these are things a little girl doesn't need to know too much about—that is, unless you want me talk to you about it. If you do, just ask me. Ok?

"Yes, Daddy," she said. Her tears were now beginning to dry up.

"Your mom and I are more than capable of protecting you. All I want you to worry about is being a kid," he said.

"Ok. Can I still keep learning to shoot?" she asked.

"Of course," he replied.

Her smile returned. Alan kissed her on the forehead. She reached for him and he lifted her up into his arms, hugging her tightly. After a moment, Lauren jumped down and returned to her seat at the bench, placing another ten round magazine into the rifle, and snapping it into place. She then set it on the pad as she'd been shown before, making sure to keep the muzzle pointed downrange, pulled back the bolt, and loaded a round into the chamber.

Alan turned around just in time to see his wife Michelle walking up behind them with her shooting glasses and a pair of pink earmuffs on. He smiled at her and noticed her closely monitoring their daughter as Lauren pushed off the safety on the Ruger 10/22 and began steadily firing.

"What do you think?" Alan inquired.

"Huh? Can't hear you," Michelle said. She pointed at her earmuffs with a sarcastic grin.

"Never mind, wasn't important," he said as he turned away, playing along.

Michelle quickly closed the gap between herself and her husband. She came up from behind him and gave him a big hug. Alan turned around and hugged her in return, kissing her on the forehead. He then turned around to watch his daughter shoot, placing his arm around Michelle's waist.

"She's doing well, huh?" Michelle said.

"Yes, she is," Alan said. "I'm very impressed with her."

"For what it's worth, I'm really glad she's learning to shoot, Alan," Michelle said. "I didn't like it when you first started teaching me, but I grew to really enjoy it."

"You were scared because you didn't understand guns," Alan said. "All it takes is education and proper training."

"Yep. And now I'm a better shot than you," she said.

"The hell you are," he retorted.

Lauren finished emptying the magazine, clicked the safety on and set the rifle down on the bench. Turning around, she noticed her mother had joined them and quickly ran over to her and her father, reaching for them.

"Group hug! Group hug!" she yelled.

Alan and Michelle lifted their daughter up, each with one hand, and pulled her close into an embrace.

* * *

Lauren snapped out of her daydream. She shook her head and sighed heavily. A tiny tear had rolled from her right eye and she wiped it away quickly with her hand. She shook her head and opened her eyes wide enough to revisit reality. She didn't want to cry, but she really felt she needed to when she thought of her dad and how much she missed him— and she missed him deeply. He had been right about so many things. She wished he was here, so she could at least thank him. In spite of her sudden sadness, she tried hard to turn it into something else, just like he always told her. It was time for her to move.

Deciding her respite was over, Lauren stood back up and shouldered her pack. She then wrapped her waist pack around her and snapped it into place, leaning down to sling her rifle over her head and left arm. The sling was set in a single-point configuration, and it allowed her AR-15 to hang directly in front of her, where she could ready it if needed in a pinch. She carried two full thirty-round magazines in her waist pack, and had four others located inside her backpack. In addition, she carried a sidearm, a Glock 22, hidden in the concealment sleeve of her waist pack. There were two extra fifteen-round magazines in the waist pack, and a spare box of hollow point ammunition in her backpack. At one point, this would have been considered overkill for most hikes but in these times, she felt it was just approaching adequate. She knew there was always a possibility of stumbling into someone whenever she was away from home, and anyone she didn't recognize could be a threat. She felt confident that she could defend herself if necessary. She had spent a lot of time training for something like that. She always tried to remain in close proximity to home so that if she did have to use a firearm, it wouldn't be long before someone would be en route to render aid, having heard the shots. There was no guarantee, however, even though the sound of a gunshot in these hills carried for miles. Her family and those they trusted were not known for running from the sound of trouble, and that was reassuring to her.

As Lauren began to descend from the peak to the bridge below that crossed a large chasm on Big Schloss, the unmistakable sound of rapid gunfire caught her ear. As it came from the east side of the mountain, she turned and quickly ran back up the trail and pulled herself onto the top of Big Schloss. Down on one knee and lifting her rifle to her cheek, she adjusted the magnification of her scope to get the widest field of view, then brought it to her left eye and began to swivel north to south, looking for any visual evidence that might help her see where the sounds were coming from. Then she heard another, and another, and then another burst of gunfire. And yet another, then finally a loud explosion. Her heart was beating through her chest—both from the run back up the trail and having to pull herself back onto the rock outcropping, and from the shock of hearing what she was hearing. She had swept back and forth twice and still couldn't see any visual indication of the blasts as they echoed throughout the valley. She assumed it had to be coming from the other side of Little Sluice Mountain, possibly in the valley that followed or maybe even over the next hill from there, which would put it in or near the town. Either way, it was blocked from her view and there wasn't anything she could do about it from this location. She lowered her rifle and sighed loudly. The hike from her current position to get to a vantage point to view that area was several miles, through areas she hadn't visited in a while—and with that she didn't feel fully safe to travel, especially by herself. It was nearly a half-day's trudge with what she was currently carrying. She knew no one at home would agree with her going there alone. It was too far from help if she needed it. She also knew that if she went home first to tell the others that the return trip back up the mountain and over to Little Sluice Mountain would take exponentially more time—possibly time they didn't have. She closed her eyes and thought hard for a moment. She needed to know what was going on sooner than that. Something inside her told her that she needed to see what was going on. She felt that if she didn't go now, that what was happening would eventually affect her family at their doorstep. And that, is why she decided to go.

She re-slung her rifle and hopped back down to the trail, moving swiftly downward across the footbridge and down the approach trail back to Mill Mountain. As she began heading north, she heard a few gunshots echoing in the distance. She pulled back the charging handle of her AR-15 slightly to verify that a round was chambered, checked the safety, and then marched north. In her heart she felt afraid, but her will was undeterred. This was after all, her chosen responsibility now. She had to protect herself. She had to protect her family. She had to protect her community.

CHAPTER 2

"Family isn't always blood. It's the people in your life who want you in theirs. The ones who accept you for who you are. The ones who would do anything to see you smile, and who love you no matter what."

— Unknown

The cabin
Trout Run Valley
Hardy County West Virginia
Present day

MICHELLE RUSSELL AWOKE AND FOUND herself staring up at the ceiling in a thick pile of blankets and pillows. Taking a moment to rub the sleep out of her eyes, she slowly pulled herself up and out of bed. The sun was brightening the sky and the light was starting to shine through her bedroom window. This was her indication that it was time to get up and start yet another day of preparations for the incoming winter months. She went to her closet and pulled a thick camouflage hoodie from a hanger, quickly putting it on to ease her shivers. She was always cold in the morning. She went to her dresser and pulled out a pair of Carhartt work pants and slipped them on one leg at a time over her base layer thermals, which she hardly ever took off. She grabbed a pink camouflage fleece beanie from her dresser and put it on, tucking her long, curly brunette hair into a pony-tail and securing it with a hair tie.

She then reached over to the nightstand and opened the top drawer where her holstered Glock 23 lay dormant, attached to a thick padded tactical belt with a double magazine carrier on the other side. She wrapped the belt around her and snapped it closed, then adjusted it a bit downward, just below her waist. She grabbed some merino wool socks and pulled them over her feet, and then slipped her feet into a pair of open-toed Birkenstock house shoes.

Looking into a small circular mirror mounted to the wall on the side of the door, Michelle cocked her head, taking a visual snapshot of her face. She smiled at herself at first, and then produced a slight frown.

"I really do miss makeup," she said with sigh.

She opened her bedroom door and walked down the hallway of the ranch-style log cabin that her family now called home. The old hardwood floor creaked with every step. As she passed the next bedroom, she noticed that Lauren wasn't there, and was not surprised. It would've been a surprise to see her there, but knew full well that Lauren usually left the cabin before the sun came up. She was always outside in the mornings—milling about around the valley and gathering intelligence of the area. That was her chosen duty, her responsibility to her family, and Michelle recognized that. She just didn't like it. Although she was never at peace, knowing her baby girl was not home, she knew there was simply no point in arguing with her. Lauren was headstrong like her father, and always had to be doing something to keep herself occupied. She would obsess on a particular task and not want to be bothered until she was done figuring it out. Michelle passed the next bedroom on the right and knocked on the closed door. A voice from inside the room groaned and then she heard a fart. She smiled.

"Boys," she said quietly to herself. Then, she raised her voice to a speaking level. "Get up, Lee...rise and shine! We have water to gather and firewood to split."

There was a pause, then a voice from inside the room said, "I'm so sick of living in the woods..."

"Tell you what...forget the water and firewood and just go back to sleep. But we might get thirsty soon. And we might start getting cold. Oh yeah, and without water or firewood we can't cook, so we'll start to get hungry before long," Michelle said.

"Ok—ok. FINE," Lee said aggressively.

"I knew the mention of hunger would get your attention," she joked.

"Yeah, yeah," Lee uttered. "For the record, I'm getting up, but I don't have to like it."

"No, you don't. Wake up your dad too, once you've wiped the crap out of your eyes. I'm going to relieve your brother. I'm sure he's dead tired," she said as she continued down the hallway to the kitchen and living room.

She turned right and headed for the front door, then opened it and walked outside as the old door creaked back into position. She stepped out onto the front porch and looked to her left where John was sitting in an outdoor rocking chair, his short blonde hair sticking nearly straight up, as if being pulled by static electricity. She was somewhat surprised to see him as wide awake as he appeared. In one hand he had a book, and in the other he had a cup of coffee. Michelle assumed the coffee's warmth had dissipated a long time ago as no steam rose from the mug in the early morning cool outdoor air. A Mossberg pump-action shotgun was lying in his lap. John closed his book, looked up at her and yawned, lifting his arms high in the air to stretch.

"*The Shining*," John said. "Stephen King. I've read it like ten times. Never gets old."

"With the limited library we have, we're lucky that you're easily entertained, John," Michelle said. "Good morning."

"Yeah...so far it's a good morning," John replied. He grinned and then yawned again. His eyelids narrowed over top of his eyes, which were as blue as the morning sky.

"Any idea how long ago Lauren left?" Michelle asked.

"A couple hours ago, I guess. Just before dawn. She looked ready for yet another mission," he said.

Michelle paused. "I take it that she was dressed for the occasion..." she said.

"I don't necessarily mean what she was wearing, it was how she *looked*. Today, she just had a different look in her eyes."

"Is it something that we need to worry about?" Michelle asked, somewhat jokingly, but mostly with concern.

John shifted in his chair and stood up, slinging the Mossberg over his right shoulder. He walked up closer to Michelle, smiled and kissed her on the cheek, leaning over in order to do so. He was about foot taller than she was.

"With Lauren, every day is something different," he said and he walked past her into the house, tossing the cold coffee out of the mug and into the yard.

Michelle nodded. "She's always been like that, I guess," she said. "I think she just likes being unpredictable." She paused. "I know I'm not telling you anything you don't already know—Lord knows you probably know her better than I do now."

"No...not really. Sometimes I think I do, but then other times she really throws me for a loop," John said. "She's been like that, especially since we moved here." He turned and started heading down the hallway to his room, banging on Lee's bedroom door with his fist. "Get up, dickhead!" he yelled.

Michelle walked closer to the edge of the porch and pulled a slightly smashed pack of cigarettes from her hoodie pocket. They were showing some wear as she had been trying to conserve them, and they had been in her pocket for the better part of a week. She knew that eventually there would be no more to smoke, so each opportunity she had to smoke one became a special ritual all to itself. She enjoyed every single puff to the bitter end. She pulled a BIC from her pants pocket and ignited the cigarette she'd slid between her lips.

"Just another day in paradise," she mumbled.

From behind her, she felt a strong hand touch her shoulder. She didn't even need to turn around to know whose it was. In a world full of unknowns, it was one of the more familiar things that she had become accustomed to.

"Good morning, Norman," Michelle said. "Just an FYI—your son is being a pain in my ass again."

"Which one?" Norman asked quizzically as he walked just past her, turning to face her.

"The usual."

"Ah, the eldest. Want me to beat the crap out of him?" he joked. He coughed a few times, turning his head away and covering his mouth and in the process, covering his rather shaggy goatee. Norman preferred to maintain the same look he'd had since before the collapse. His hair was always kept as short as possible. With the exception of his goatee, he was always clean shaven, and he was as proud of his facial hair as he was his enormously thick stainless hoop earrings—which he never took out.

"Actually, I would just like some firewood split...and maybe some fresh water brought in from the creek. That would make my day," Michelle offered.

"Well, let's get that fun stuff done first, and then I'll beat the crap out of him," Norman joked again. "Just so you know, I'm probably going to do some hunting later. I have a hankering for some meat and I think we're running a bit low."

Michelle smiled. She had grown familiar with the early-morning witticisms between her and her best friend, and truly looked forward to them. It made life so much easier to have extra hands around in these hard times, and it was just as comforting to have the added personalities. Norman had filled a huge void in her life. His skills came in more than handy after the move to the cabin, and their less-than-ideal surroundings made those skills essential. He and his sons had become part of the family in spirit a long time ago. When the final decision was made to evacuate their home, it had come when her husband was not around. She knew it would be extremely difficult if not impossible, for her to do it on her own. She knew very little about primitive skills and had no idea how to live off the land, other than with her gardening knowledge—which she knew wouldn't be enough. It was far easier and safer to have more people around, and she knew that Norman would come if she asked him to. He was a man of honor and there wasn't any way he'd allow her to take her family into the wild by herself. This was the primary reason that he and his sons had been involved in their family emergency plans that Michelle and her husband had established years ago. She knew that Norman considered them his family. He treated them as if they were his own.

Norman's son John was a shoe-in for the move. He and Lauren had been literally inseparable since they were kids. Their love for each other had grown over the years, but like her father, Lauren was staunchly independent and with that, had no need for his companionship all the time. John knew she was a loner and was content waiting for her, never knowing what to expect from her on any particular day. If Lauren needed him, John would come and remain by her side until she pushed him away. He had always been patient with her. Regardless of her idiosyncrasies, Michelle knew that wherever Lauren went, John would follow. They were good for one another. Love was something rare and precious in the world they lived in now.

Michelle finished her cigarette and walked back inside just as Norman was literally dragging his older son Lee out the door with him, with Lee's forearm in one hand and an AK-47 rifle in the other. It was a bit of a struggle for Norman, since Lee outweighed him by about fifty pounds.

"We need water for washing up, too," Michelle said with a barely audible giggle.

"We'll take care of it," Norman said.

Lee was in protest with his father, but this was not a new thing. He always ended up listening and doing what was needed, he just constantly needed to be coerced. It had been like this for as long as Michelle could remember. She had known Norman and his boys for many years and their collective behavior had become a part of her family ties. They were indeed a family now, after all. Each of them had responsibilities to this new household they had created. Each of them had a skillset essential to the family's survival. In this new world, Michelle knew that they all needed each other, now more than ever. She would do whatever it took to keep them all together and safe, even if it meant risking her own life in order to do so.

Michelle walked back to the hallway and turned down the staircase to the basement, which was little more than a cellar; surrounded by a formidable stone foundation lined with concrete. It stretched the entire length of the cabin and most of their provisions were kept there. As well, the cellar was also where her step-daughter Grace had set up her sleeping area. She had done so not long after the family moved, in order to 'escape the testosterone', as she put it. Michelle grabbed a headlamp that hung by a nail on the wall as she went down, and turned it on to illuminate her way. At twenty-four, Grace was the oldest of the younger generation in the cabin, and preferred to have an area all to herself. The cellar was cold and musty, but that didn't seem to bother her. The past year's events had hardened her quite a bit. Michelle could remember when Grace used to be petrified of just about everything. Since moving here, she had learned many new skills and had matured well beyond her years. She had become a distinguished homemaker and had learned how to handle firearms and defend herself. During the day, she was Michelle's companion when everyone else was off doing their chores.

Michelle turned the corner and from behind the blanket that hung across the cellar ceiling, that Grace had hung for privacy, she saw that Grace was already up and getting dressed. She had a headlamp on and was lacing up her hiking boots. Grace looked up at her, and Michelle held her hand over her eyes as the headlamp Grace was wearing temporarily blinded her.

"OH…um sorry," Grace declared, "I didn't mean to blind you."

"That's ok. I was just coming down here to see if you were ready for another day—"

"In paradise?" Grace interrupted. "Yes. I believe so. Don't have much else planned. What's on the agenda?

"The guys are out splitting wood and getting our water supply replenished. Norman said he would probably go on a hunt after that."

"Really? YUM. I am so tired of eating rice and beans and canned meat," Grace said.

"It'll definitely add some variety to our pantry. I'm sure he'll smoke some, but we can make jerky with the rest of it," Michelle said.

"We should just make jerky with all of it," Grace said with a smile.

"Good point," Michelle agreed, "we all love Norman's deer jerky."

"Well hopefully, he'll bag something today," Grace said. "The woods aren't as plentiful as they used to be. With hunting seasons not enforced and everyone hunting for food, it's only going to get worse."

"We're lucky to live in a remote area, Grace. There's a lot of land out there for our community to use. It's not nearly as bad the areas closer to the city, but you're right. The chances of us finding wild game will become more remote as time goes on if we don't exercise some conservation," Michelle said. She turned off her headlamp, seeing that there was no need to have two of them burning in the same room. "It's the nature of the beast. I know it's not going to get any easier—I'm just trying not to dwell on that."

Grace smiled and stood up, reaching to the ceiling to stretch. She tossed her waist-length brunette hair over her shoulder, deciding today not to braid it or put it into a pony tail like she usually did. She then reached down to the foot of her bed where an outside waistband holster lay with a Glock 27 pistol secured in it, and snapped the holster to her pants. Grace pulled the pistol, press checked it, and secured it back into the holster. She slid an extra magazine into the left rear pocket of her pants. She went to the corner of her room where a tan colored AR-15 carbine was leaning in the darkness, then picked it up and slung it over her left shoulder.

"You know—since deer are the animal everyone is trying to hunt, maybe he'll have better luck hunting bear. I could eat that right about now," she said, taking a deep breath and feeling her stomach growl. "I could eat just about anything right now."

Michelle laughed inside at Grace's words. She had indeed changed so much. It wasn't long ago that she wouldn't have even considered to eat any type of wild game, even the most common ones.

"I don't think we have a gun big enough for a bear," Michelle said.

"He's got a knife, doesn't he?" Grace quipped.

They both walked back to the staircase and ascended back to the hallway where there was just enough natural light to see. Grace turned off her headlamp and stowed it in her pocket. Michelle returned the headlamp she had to the nail on the wall in the staircase.

"So, I guess Lauren is out on a walkabout again?" Grace pondered.

"Yes. She left earlier this morning, according to John."

"I worry about her, Michelle," Grace said, "don't you?"

"I worry about her all the time—but worrying never fixes anything, Grace. I have to let her be who she is. What she is doing provides us and our neighbors with good information," Michelle said.

"Yeah. I don't know. She's just like—some kind of soldier now," Grace said, imagining her sister as one of the camouflage-laden girls carrying an AK-47 in the movie *Red Dawn*. It made her somewhat proud, as well as apprehensive.

Michelle gave her a glance, then turned away and started remembering Lauren's childhood in pieces. "Lauren has always been a bit of a soldier, Grace," she said. "Of course, it's been much different since the collapse."

Grace walked into the kitchen, unshouldered and propped her rifle against a half-wall that divided the kitchen from the living room, and began going through the cupboards. She pulled out a large can of pancake mix and set it on the counter, and then reached into a shelf on the island and pulled out a medium-sized cast-iron skillet.

"I'll get some breakfast going. I am absolutely starving," Grace said as she busily began stuffing kindling into the kitchen stove. "Maybe some food will help me stop worrying about her."

Michelle smiled. She never had to ask Grace to do anything. She just always knew what needed to be done, and always knew when to do it. Grace had been visiting with them for the weekend at their home in Winchester, Virginia when things went bad. She was a product of a relationship comprised of Michelle's husband and old girlfriend that Michelle grew to know as a friend, later on in life. Grace had been born long ago and had lost touch with her father, only to get to know him as a teenager and a young adult. As her relationship with her father had grown, she had become very loyal to the family. She was especially close to Lauren whom she developed to know as her baby sister and with that, nurtured her. Grace was a confidant and an eternal advice-giver and had helped Lauren find her way through life on more than one difficult occasion. She was also very daring, assertive, and a complete smartass—the latter trait making it apparent to all who met her, who her father most definitely was.

On the day that things went south, Grace had a choice to make that wasn't easy for her. She could chance going it alone and attempt to make it back home to her mother and her other family, or she could join her second family in their plans to bug-in for as long as they could hold out. Knowing full well how dangerous the world was becoming and the fact that anyone going it alone who wasn't properly prepared for such a task would eventually meet their demise, the decision, although a difficult one became obvious to her. People had become desperate; even diabolical after the shock of what had happened hit them. It became even worse when food began running out. Grace knew she had zero chance of making it on her own if she chose to leave, and that her best chance for survival was staying with the Russell family, even if it meant forsaking those who were closest to her.

With the morning activities well on their way, Michelle walked back outside to the front porch and closed the front door behind her. She closely surveyed the wooded front yard of their property, including the driveway that stretched a few hundred yards to a metal gate mounted to a very old wooden fence, reinforced with stone. Just beyond the gate was Trout Run Road, a two-lane asphalt road which led south through the George Washington National Forest to Wolf Gap and the Virginia/West Virginia state line. This was where the community had barricaded the road using explosives a few months ago, in order to isolate themselves from dangers that existed on the eastern side of the mountain where the population was much greater. Unless travelling by horse or on foot, the road was impassable. On the northern end of what they considered their community, the road ran through the small village of Perry, West Virginia. Perry was little more than an old store and a defunct animal petting zoo that had closed a decade ago. There were a few houses there, some of which sat empty before and some that had been abandoned after the collapse. Not everyone had prepared adequately and had decided to leave to search for better options. Some of the homes were nothing more than weekend retreats for some families. The road ended ultimately just outside the town of Wardensville, over ten miles away. Fuel was extremely limited and most vehicles didn't run anymore, so it was a rare occurrence to see that type of traffic on the road. The ones that still ran just didn't get used that often. Some of their neighbors had all-terrain vehicles that they used only on rare occasion. People had become very fuel conscious and had chosen to preserve it as a precious commodity that could not be replaced or replenished.

The old Chevrolet Suburban that had brought Michelle and her family to the cabin had only a quarter tank of gasoline left in it. Norman's crew-cab Dodge had in it, about the same. Both sat beside each other behind the shed on the rear of the property. The only time either would run was when Norman would start them on occasion, to keep the engines and batteries maintained. The family had no extra gasoline in their stock of provisions. It was one of a very few things that the family didn't plan for, and Michelle thought about it every day, and more than regretted the oversight. They were lucky enough to have three Honda Rancher four-wheelers with full gas tanks locked up inside the shed, which was situated on the other side of the creek from the cabin. It was accessible only by a small wooden bridge that crossed a deep ravine where Trout Run ran through. They had a case of additive in there as well, and it was added to the tanks on occasion to keep the gasoline from going stale. While they were nice to have, it had been decided long ago that the ATVs were to be used only as a last resort, since they had no way to refuel them.

For normal transportation to and from their trusted neighbors, to meetings, and occasionally into Perry to barter with other inhabitants of the valley, each member of the family had a mountain bike. This kept their operational radius very limited. Wardensville had once been a meeting place for most of the communities in the region, as well as most of Hardy County. It was nearly an hour away on bike and wasn't the safest place to be in these times. The local authorities had lost control of the town over the summer, during a raid on supplies and it was rumored to be completely lawless now. Stores and businesses had been looted and burned. The pharmacy, restaurants, and even the schools had been ransacked for anything that the takers deemed necessary for survival.

Many people who had lived there had been killed and their houses burned to the ground. The proximity of the town of Wardensville to their location was something that Michelle worried about every day.

It took a while for Michelle to become accustomed to living in such a rural area so far away from what she considered 'civilization', but she felt she had adapted and with that, was beginning to love being here. Most of her neighbors did not seem affected much by the collapse. They had practiced subsistence as a part of their everyday way of life, even before the lights had gone out. The closest supermarket was over twenty miles away and it just wasn't in their nature to depend on the system, living in such rural surroundings. Everyone had woodstoves in their homes and several winters' worth of seasoned firewood. Everyone had gardens and some had livestock. To them, the only thing that made life harder was lack of electricity, but they soon overcame it, and were now doing their best to thrive without it.

Their land was situated between two mountains; Long Mountain to the west and North Mountain range behind the cabin to the east. It was a formidable location and even though rocky and wooded, one could see from one end of the property to another, all the way to the foothills of each mountain with the naked eye. In order to trespass, one would either have to trudge over the mountains to the west or east, which was no easy task, or travel Trout Run Road on foot for many miles. The barricade at Wolf Gap reduced most threats from the other side of the border and eliminated the possibility of vehicle traffic. Takers had come from Virginia into the valley and had caused the community some trouble earlier on that year, and they needed to prevent that from happening again. From the outside of the gate, the cabin was well camouflaged and nearly hidden from the road. The land that surrounded them provided them with just about everything they needed, including a consistent supply of fresh water as Trout Run was fed mostly by mountain streams and springs. Trout Run itself was aptly named as it was full of tasty and very edible river and brook trout. The West Virginia Department of Natural Resources had done a great job of stocking it before the collapse, and most of the fish population remained today. Small and medium sized game were abundant, due to the lack of population in the area currently, and hunting was therefore a mainstay of finding food, which helped them further ration their provisions. The rear yard near the creek had some of the most mineral-rich soil that Michelle had ever seen, and her first gardening experience here had been an amazing success.

Their initial time spent here was full of trials and tribulations, which they were fortuitously able to overcome. Michelle felt that they had been more than fortunate. If things remained this way, she knew they could live safely and thrive here for many years. She also knew, in the world they lived in now, that the chances of this were slim and with that, their current comfort level was finite. If thriving here was to continue, they would eventually need to defend what was theirs.

CHAPTER 3

"You gain strength, courage, and confidence by every experience in which you really stop to look fear in the face. You must do the thing which you think you cannot do."
— Eleanor Roosevelt

Tuscarora Trail
George Washington National Forest
Shenandoah County Virginia
Present day

LAUREN HAD BEEN HIKING THE trail in front of her for what seemed like hours and her breathing sounded more like panting. Even in the cool, sharp air that an autumn day in the mountains sometimes offered, especially in the mornings, she was sweating profusely, due to the effort she was exerting. Mill Mountain Trail heading north wasn't an exceptionally difficult trail to hike, as elevations hovered around the three-thousand foot mark and most of the trail was therefore fairly level. It wasn't the difficulty level of the trail though—it was the pace that she had chosen that was taking its toll on her. The trail was very secluded and didn't offer any view, in spite of how tall it was, and the lack of distractions allowed her to keep a steady stride. Lauren wasn't concerning herself with the lack of scenery today. She only cared about reaching her destination and investigating what she had heard.

Upon reaching an intersection, she followed the Tuscarora Trail to the east, which through this corridor shared space with a rocky old wagon road, and was very wide, compared to most of the trails in the area. The trail's width and openness concerned her. It was at one time, used for much more than just foot traffic. What made it most disconcerting was the feeling of being out in the open, so she forced herself to stay very alert of her surroundings. She constantly monitored the ground below her for fresh tracks or evidence of foot travel, but didn't notice any. The Tuscarora, or the "Big Blue Trail" as some knew it, led her down into a small saddle and back up to Sugar Knob, then back down into another valley and finally back up steeply to Little Sluice Mountain. Upon reaching the peak of Little Sluice, she veered from the trail which continued northeast, and began trudging downward on a thinly visible side trail to the peak of White Rock Cliff, which would offer her a grand vantage point of the valley below. The trail, which was marked by two rock cairns on either side was overgrown, rarely used, and very narrow. While not very steep, it was as treacherous as any trail in the area could be, and after the long hike to get here, her sore feet were not enjoying the trip.

While on her way here, she had stopped at Sandstone Spring to refill her water bottles and fill her hydration bladder, which she normally left empty on her morning patrols, in an effort to lighten the load on her shoulders. Sandstone Spring was a year-round fresh water source on the ridgetop that seemed to emanate out of pure sandstone. The area around the spring was unmistakably sandy, almost as if a beach existed in the middle of the woods. A similarly sandy campsite sat adjacent to the spring. Lauren could remember spending more than a few nights with her family there, while backpacking the National Forest. Her first time here had been a trip she and her dad had taken together, just the two of them when she was younger. She remembered how magical this place had seemed to her then. The water was cold and as pure as could be in such a remote area. The spring waters ran down the west side of the mountain and became one of the many tributaries of Trout Run, where her family and neighbors sourced their water in the valley below.

Against her better judgement on this trip, Lauren had decided to sling her rifle over her shoulder, in order to free her hands and utilize her trekking poles, which normally remained strapped to her backpack. With her rifle on her back, she felt a bit on edge, but she kept telling herself that being on a trail as remote as this, the most likely danger she would encounter was the type that couldn't fire a gun. She knew this well, but was also knew that she could very easily transition to her Glock, which was always only a second away if she needed it.

In spite of having all four limbs working for her, Lauren was truly exerting herself. She had found herself nearing exhaustion on more than one occasion and had taken several breaks to combat it, but the pauses were short-lived. She hadn't heard any more sounds of gunfire, since beginning her jaunt several hours ago. The curiosity of what had happened earlier kept her moving. Wanting to get back home by nightfall, Lauren did her best to stay aware of how much time her extended hike was taking her. She needed to get this done as soon as humanly possible. As best as she could estimate, it was nearly lunchtime or possibly just after. She gauged the time, partially by looking at the high southern hemisphere sun, but mostly due to the noises that her stomach was making.

As tired and sweaty as she was, Lauren was warm and relatively comfortable. In lieu of the hundreds of things a backpacker must remember, in order to remain safe and survive in the backcountry, this was paramount to her, especially now when the weather was beginning to get cooler. She knew, having heard it many times from both parents, that wearing the wrong clothing in the wild in any weather is a recipe for hypothermia. Amidst her deep breaths, she occasionally unzipped her insulated jacket, in order to vent the buildup of body heat from underneath. She tugged on her base layer as well which was nearly saturated with sweat, and just touching it and feeling the soft texture jarred her memory. She remembered when she had gotten it on a trip to REI with her dad, just before going on a two week backpacking trip in Dolly Sods Wilderness. She had nothing but fond memories of that trip, and remembered learning a host of outdoor survival skills there. It was the longest she had ever spent outdoors in a single span before. Though unsure of how she'd fair in that environment for an extended amount of time, and as well a bit bothered that she'd go that long without a shower, the trip turned out to be one of the most rewarding things she had ever done. The skills she had learned on that trip were necessary then, and had become absolute in today's world.

After lumbering down the decline for some time, the trail began to level off as she was finally nearing White Rock Cliff. She slowed her pace a bit as she passed a large campsite on her right, and began making a serious effort to control her breathing. The campsite, which had two large fire rings and logs fashioned into benches, was just as vacant as she'd expected it to be, even though she hadn't been certain. Looking ahead of herself down the trail, she began anticipating what she would be able to see from the outcropping. It was possible that the view from the top of this ridge would let her see what had been the cause of the blasts that she heard earlier this morning. The anticipation increased her pulse as well as her anxiety. She moved off the trail just before reaching the rock scramble and dropped her trekking poles to the ground. She then unslung her AR and set it carefully against a tree. She unsnapped the sternum strap and hip belt of her backpack and slid it off gently, laying it on the ground. She then adjusted her waist pack to ride on her side and picked up her rifle once again. Tossing the sling over her head and holding the rifle at low-ready, she continued to the top of the overlook, occasionally using her hands to carefully move across the rocks.

Lauren peered over the eastern side of the mountain with her head low and rifle ready. The view was magnificent, and she smiled slightly as she took it in. She pulled the rifle stock to her cheek and looked into the scope with her dominant left eye while keeping her right eye open to watch around her. Looking downward into the valley below she pivoted, first to the farthest south that the view allowed, and then northward. About three-quarters of the way through her pivot, she noticed a very small column of smoke rising from the forest in the valley directly below her. This seemed peculiar to her. A small column usually meant a campfire and seeing one this close to where she was located was certainly cause for some concern. Stumbling onto people in the middle of nowhere wasn't as safe as it used to be. With everyone in survival mode now, it was downright dangerous and was to be avoided if possible. She did her best to mentally estimate the proximity of the trail to where the smoke was, but it wasn't easy. Lauren could recollect that a small settlement of homes, including an old colonial-era farm was located in that same area and that the smoke could just as likely be coming from someone's woodstove. She continued her pivot northward and saw nothing, so she elevated her view and rotated southward again to see yet another plume of smoke, this one considerably larger and much darker. It was coming from the other side of the next mountain to the east of the valley below. Lauren couldn't remember the range's name, but to her at this moment it was insignificant. In her mind, this had to be the remnants of what had caused the noises she'd heard echoing throughout the valley earlier that morning.

Lauren lowered her rifle and sighed, blowing a burst of breath into her bangs that fell in front of her face often. She looked down at the rifle and began remembering all the times she had trained with it, along with her dad. She remembered how apprehensive she'd been when she had first fired it, and how much she'd grown to like it. As she used her sleeve to wipe some grime from the upper, she closed her eyes and drifted into reminiscent thought.

* * *

Lauren sat nervously on the ground, a blindfold wrapped around her head. Pieces of a disassembled Smith and Wesson M&P 15 were scattered about her. After stripping it down, her father walked over to a shooting bench and picked up a revolver, checking it to make sure it was loaded.

"Can you hear me ok, L?" he asked. Lauren nodded that she was able to hear his voice through her earplugs. He continued, "Ok. When you hear the shot from my revolver, it's time to move. Assemble the rifle as fast as you can. Once you feel it's operable, stand up and remove the blindfold. Acquire the targets as fast as you can and take them down, but remember—no rush. Your eyes will be adjusting to the brightness, so things will be blurry at first."

"You might want to lay down, so I don't accidentally shoot you, Dad," Lauren joked.

Alan smiled. "Are you ready?"

"Yeah, I guess so," Lauren uttered.

Alan considered pulling the trigger immediately, but backed away from the notion. He waited about a minute, long enough for Lauren's anticipation to spike. He then fired. Lauren cursed loudly as she began fumbling around her, identifying the pieces of the dismantled rifle. She placed the lower in her lap, quickly checking to see what pieces were missing. She noticed that the trigger group was intact, but the buffer and buffer spring weren't. She felt around her on the ground until she found them, and installed them as quickly as she could. She then found the upper and set it in her lap, pushing her finger into it to verify that the bolt carrier group was indeed not there. Finding all the pieces, she quickly seated them, struggling mostly on the retainer pin. Alan watched her closely. This was the part he fought with all the time, even without a blindfold on. Lauren soon overcame it and finished assembling the rifle. She quickly found a loaded magazine and sent it home while she stood up and pulled off her blindfold. She charged the bolt as her vision began to clear, and began looking around her and finally downrange, where several steel silhouettes stood. The closest was about twenty feet away with the furthest being about fifty yards. Lauren brought the rifle cleanly to her shoulder, slapped off the safety, and began firing. She smacked each target with at least two shots, the steel targets reporting the hits. After hitting each of them, she lowered the rifle and flipped the safety back on, turning to face her father.

"That was pretty damn good," he said. "What did you think?"

"I think I want to try it again," Lauren said with a smile.

They ran the exercise several more times. Each time, Alan tried to trip her up by placing the parts in different locations and changing the level of disassembly. Lauren would get stumped, but eventually was able to overcome. The day ended with the two walking side by side back to the car to load up and head home.

* * *

Lauren snapped out of her temporary slumber upon hearing the sound of a twig snap on the trail just below her. She turned around quickly, pulling her rifle to her shoulder and snapping off the safety just as she had always been trained to do. Just in front of her, stood a young girl. She had long matted blonde hair. She was filthy and her clothing looked as if it hadn't been washed in months. Lauren shuddered a bit, feeling the shock of the situation as she studied her. The girl lifted her hands into the air close to her chest, just as another figure walked up behind her, wrapping her arms around the little girl. She wasn't carrying a weapon, but did have an old plastic bag hanging from her wrist that appeared half-full of whatever was in it.

"Please don't shoot," the woman pleaded. "We don't want any trouble."

Lauren moved her sights back and forth between the two, which appeared to her to be mother and daughter. The mother had the same tangled hair, and was in just as much disarray as the little girl's was. Having no idea what their intentions were, Lauren had no choice other than to keep them at gunpoint for now.

"I don't want any trouble either," Lauren affirmed. "Did you follow me here?"

"We saw you on the trail below," the woman said, seeming slightly ashamed of her dirt-covered face. "We don't see people on the trail very much anymore."

"Do you live here?" Lauren asked curiously, as she continued to study her. The woman didn't answer immediately. She was wearing clothes that didn't fit her and a pair of canvas shoes that were covered in patches made of duct tape. She did not appear to be carrying a weapon. The situation was a curious one—if they saw her walking on the trail below, they certainly had seen that she was carrying a weapon. Why they would willingly follow an armed stranger down a dead-end trail didn't exactly make sense.

"In the valley below," the woman said quietly.

The girl looked up at her mother and said, "Mommy, aren't you going to ask her if she has any food?"

The mother, seemingly mortified, placed her hand on her daughter's face.

"You followed me for food?" Lauren probed, glancing at the bag that the woman was now attempting to hide from her. "What's in the bag?"

The woman reluctantly opened the bag and with her hand pulled out what appeared to be a mushroom of some type, which the mountains here were full of, especially in the early mornings. Lauren nodded to her, satisfied with the simple answer that the woman and her daughter spent their mornings foraging. From the looks of their emaciated bodies, she guessed this had been their method of survival for quite some time. The woman placed the mushroom back in the bag and tied a knot in the top.

"We'll be on our way—sorry to bother you."

The woman and her daughter turned and began descending the rocks, walking back down the trail. The little girl was in protest with her mother, but was being told to hush. Lauren noticed the little girl's shoes now, and even though well-worn and dirty, she could tell that they were the kind of sneakers that had blinking lights in them that flashed each time a step was taken. They weren't nearly as bright as they'd once been, but still worked. Lauren lowered her rifle and reached into her waist pack, pulling out several pieces of pemmican about the size of golf balls.

"Wait!" she said, raising her voice just enough for the woman to hear her.

Lauren held out the pemmican as the woman turned to face her.

"It's pemmican. Our neighbor makes it with venison, walnuts, and red raspberries," Lauren explained. "I don't have much, but you're welcome to it."

Upon seeing the food offering, the young girl ran up onto the rocks without fear, directly to Lauren. She grabbed the pieces in her hands and immediately placed one to her mouth, taking a bite without hesitation. She smiled as she chewed. Her mother began to crawl back up the rocks to her, but stopped when she noticed Lauren's backpack leaning against a tree beside the trail. Lauren looked up from the pemmican-devouring child and noticed her mother was eyeing her backpack. She immediately brought her rifle to a fighting position in the woman's direction.

"Please don't mistake my kindness for weakness," Lauren ordered. "I suggest you take what I can give you—and nothing else."

"I'm sorry," the woman said as her eyes darted back and forth between Lauren's rifle and the backpack. "We're just so hungry. I'm—I'm really sorry."

"Everyone is hungry," Lauren said.

"Some more than others," the woman declared in a stern voice, taking another hard glance at Lauren's backpack. "My husband died last month. We're doing all we can to stay alive."

Lauren nodded, seemingly unconvinced. It was true, people were hungry and therefore, desperate. So much so that they would say or do just about anything to stay alive. Her husband may have died, or maybe he was below them on the trail with a gun. She didn't think that was the case, but readied herself regardless. She said, "Does that include stealing?"

The woman's pale face started to show some color underneath the dirt that covered it. She pursed her lips.

"We do what we have to," she said. "We have nothing now—it's all been taken from us." She paused and stared deep into Lauren's eyes. "We do what we have to do."

The little girl noticed the tension and ran to her mother, dropping a piece of the pemmican on the ground and picking it up in turn. Her mother placed a hand on her shoulder.

"Look, mommy—food! I got us some food," the little girl said.

"I see that, baby," the woman said glumly, looking down at her daughter with a genuine smile. Her gaze soon returned to Lauren, who held her rifle, ready to defend what was hers if she had to. Lauren knew very well that there was just no way possible to help everyone that needed it. There was nothing wrong with being compassionate, but in the world she now lived in, she knew that compassion could just as easily get you killed.

"You best be on your way," Lauren said. "I'd like to help more—but I can't. I'm sorry."

"It's ok. We're sorry to bother you," the woman said with a nod. "Thanks for the food."

She turned away and led her daughter across the rocks and down the trail beside her, turning around several times in the process. They soon disappeared from sight. Lauren hiked down the trail and grabbed her pack, truly glad that she had it and even more glad that she didn't have to shoot someone in order to keep it. She counted herself lucky in more ways than one. If the woman had possessed a gun, or if she wasn't as innocent as she'd pretended to be, the situation would have had a completely different ending. She would need to be more careful now, and that meant no more daydreaming.

Once Lauren felt comfortable enough to let her guard down slightly, her thoughts returned to the real reason she was here. She would never forget what had just happened and truly hoped that they would manage to survive, but inside she knew it was unlikely. The food she'd provided them was only postponing the inevitable. It made her sad to think about it, but this new world was a sad place, full of tribulations. She began to recall the task at hand, her curiosity and her sense of duty both beginning to reach a level she had never experienced before. She looked down into the valley at the smoke columns in the distance, desperately wanting to know where they were coming from. She could still almost hear the sound of the gunfire and explosions in her mind that she had heard earlier, and began imagining what the source could be. She knew that the Tuscarora Trail would take her steeply down into the valley, alongside Cedar Creek and end up about a mile outside the area of Van Buren Furnace, where it would meet a forestry road that was little more than an ATV trail. It would eventually lead up and over the hill where the larger smoke plume was coming from. The ATV trail was a better option overall. Although traveling it would be more precarious, it was nowhere near as steep as the Tuscarora, and would get her to where she wanted to be sooner, as it crawled through a gap in the mountain. Following this route would provide her with an opportunity to recon all of the areas in question. It was just three more miles to get there, which meant it was six miles to get back to where she was. She had gotten this far already and the last thing she wanted to do was turn back.

Lauren had so many thoughts in her mind at the same time that at this point, she couldn't sort them or assign them priority. She knew she could make it there, but it would be well past evening before she could get back to where she was, and even if she made it back here by then, it would be a very long hike back home, all in the darkness of night. She had brought enough gear and food with her for an unintended overnight stay in the woods—possibly two, if she rationed appropriately. This had happened to her before when had she had misjudged trail distances on one of her first patrols, after moving to the cabin. She knew that if she made the decision to continue on instead of returning home, that her family would end up being very worried and would quite possibly come to look for her. She knew that her mom would be worried, but mostly just pissed off that she had gone so long without contact. She knew that Norman would be her advocate and as well, the last one to truly worry. He had made a habit out of being steadfast when doubt was abundant. The others, of course would worry as well—and that didn't bother her much.

Then, she thought of John. Lauren began thinking about how she had always treated him so unfairly after the collapse, and had pushed him aside on more occasions than she could count. She knew she loved him and she knew that he adored her. If anyone would come for her she knew it would be him, even though he knew she wouldn't want him to. Lauren believed in her heart that she was more than capable of doing this on her own—even if no one else did. If only there had been a way to communicate to her family where she was and what her plans were. There would only be concern, without fear of the unknown. In this world she lived in now, that was an impossibility.

Lauren pulled off her fleece beanie and wiped her eyes with it as they had begun to tear up. She didn't want to worry her family, but finding out what was going on in the world around her was the driving force in her life right now. Attaining information and learning what was going on, outside of the confines of her community, was her priority. If this was a real threat, information like this would help them prepare and in turn, keep them all safe. Her imagination, combined with the fear of the unknown was painting pictures in her mind of the worst case scenario. That could not be helped. She needed to know the truth.

Knowing what she had to do, Lauren stood up confidently with her rifle to her side, in spite of her aching muscles, which were beginning to annoy her. She shouldered her pack, snapping the straps around her waist and sternum and re-slung her rifle over her head and left arm once again. She then began the hike downhill back to the Tuscarora Trail, all the while, watching the woods around her for any sight of her previous visitors, or any other surprises.

Pushing as many of the negative thoughts aside as she could, she struggled to confine herself to the task at hand. She kept thinking of her dad and how safe she felt when he was around. She could see him holding her hand like he'd done when she was half her age. He never let anyone near her. He seemed to always be in control and was constantly fixated on protecting her. Lauren missed him and wished he was here more than anything else in the world. She took a deep breath and slowly exhaled, feeling the need to cry, but fighting the feeling with all she had. *Turn it into something else* he would say to her. *Turn that shit into something else.* It was like he was still there sometimes.

Lauren looked up at the sky. "Dad, I don't know where you are—but if you're listening, I really could use your help right now," she muttered aloud, almost incoherently. She knew there wouldn't be a reply. She exhaled, checked her rifle, and continued on.

CHAPTER 4

"People glorify all sorts of bravery except the bravery they might show on behalf of their nearest neighbors."

— George Eliot

Trout Run Valley
Hardy County West Virginia
Present day

NORMAN WALKED INTO THE CABIN and closed the door behind him. He unslung the AK-47 he had on his shoulder and removed his jacket almost immediately, which was sporadically covered in sawdust. He placed the rifle next to the door and hung his jacket on the coat rack mounted to the wall. Michelle had stoked the main woodstove to bring up the temperature in the cabin, that had lowered quite a bit overnight. It wasn't unusual for the temperatures to drop below forty degrees in the valley this time of year. With the kitchen stove burning as well, the added heat was nearly unbearable, while wearing outerwear of any sort. He wiped the sweat from his forehead with his shirt sleeve and began removing his boots, which were wet and covered in mud. He then re-opened the door to vent some of the heat buildup outside.

Grace eyeballed him from the kitchen where she had just gotten done with a large batch of banana pancakes, which she had just set on the small dining room table.

"Um, yeah. Don't you dare walk any further with those on," she griped.

Norman looked up at her as he slid his boots from his feet one at a time, neatly placing them on the mat near the front door.

"I hadn't planned on it, Grace," he said.

"You've done it before," she quickly responded.

"Just once. And I remember the backlash all too well. That's why it won't happen again," he said.

Through the open door, Michelle entered with an armload of dry firewood. She kicked her boots off fairly close to where Norman had placed his, and walked over to the hearth where she dropped the pieces of wood, making sure they didn't roll off onto the hardwood floor below.

"You guys did great with the wood this morning, Norman," Michelle said. "Thank you."

"Sweetheart, you don't have to thank me," Norman offered. "It's what we do. I just wish we had more gas for the chainsaw. My body wasn't made for swinging an axe."

"I know. I think about that oversight every day," Michelle said. "Gas nowadays is worth more than gold."

"I know, I know, nothing we can do about that. I'll just suck it up," he said as he lifted his arms to the ceiling to stretch. "I'm guessing we have about a few days to a week's worth of wood with what Lee and I split today. At that pace, we shouldn't fall behind this winter."

Lee staggered inside, carrying two five-gallon food-grade buckets full of water. Norman took them from him as Lee continued huffing and puffing. He bent over and began untying his boots, eventually just sitting on the floor while doing so. As Norman carried the water to the kitchen, Lee pulled his boot off of his left foot and used it to push the door shut. He then removed his right boot and pulled himself up onto his knees and finally, back to his feet. He walked to the table, grabbed a seat and plopped down, while exhaling loudly.

"Damn—it's hot in here," Lee said.

"That's why we left the door open, genius," Grace jeered. She watched Norman for a moment and then said, "Looks like you got yourself quite a workout."

Lee looked up at her with red cheeks and eyes that were nearly bloodshot. His large chest was expanding and contracting with every deep breath he took. He reached behind him and opened the door once more.

"I'd like to see you come outside and split some wood, smart ass," he said, "oh, and carry a hundred pounds of water all the way here from the damn creek."

"I'm afraid you'll be waiting for a very long time to see that," she said. "Did you get water for the toilets as well?"

Norman looked at her and back at his son, absolutely flabbergasted with their exchange.

"Some of us aren't privileged enough to just have to worry about cooking every day," Lee retorted.

Grace didn't hesitate. In a slightly raised voice, she said, "Privileged? Really? Well, maybe you're not privileged enough to eat my pancakes— so guess what? You can make your own!"

Michelle quickly inserted herself before the conversation escalated any further. "That's enough you two. Lee, go wake up John and let's all get some breakfast in our stomachs," Michelle said.

Lee just looked at her dumbfounded and paused for a moment, as if not knowing what to say. "Whatever," he finally said, as he stood up and reluctantly trudged down the hallway, dragging his feet as he went. Michelle took a seat at the table to the right of where Lee had been sitting.

"Idiot," Grace said in a very low tone.

"Whatever happened to you guys?" Norman asked, "I thought you two were closer than that."

Grace gave Norman a look that made him move back a step. Knowing he was pushing a button that didn't need to be pushed, he backed off, turning his head away and holding both hands palms outward in surrender.

"Never mind," he said solemnly. "Never mind."

Norman touched the cooking surface quickly to make sure it was still hot, then lifted the coffee percolator to find that it was empty. He was curious why an empty percolator was sitting on the cook stove and started to ask Grace why there was no coffee made, but decided it best not too. Shaking his head, Norman placed the percolator down on the cooktop and then hefted one of the buckets of water and began dumping it into the group water filter he had built when the family had moved into the cabin. It was constructed using two food-grade five-gallon buckets stacked on top of one another. The top bucket had four water filter elements installed into it and was marked "raw water." The raw water bucket had a lid and beneath it was a pre-filter made of an old t-shirt that helped keep dirt and debris out of the bucket. It sat on top of another bucket which had holes drilled into its top that allowed for the clean-side filter elements to be inserted. The bottom bucket was marked "clean water" and had a spigot at the very bottom where water was drawn. Water would flow from the raw water bucket, through the filters and into the clean water bucket. After the clean water bucket was full, more water could be added to the raw water bucket without the worry of overflow. The group easily went through five gallons of drinking water each day, so new water had to be pulled from Trout Run or one of the nearby springs at least every other day. The cabin had internal plumbing, but without electricity to pump the water from the well, it had to be done manually.

Lee appeared from the hallway and returned back to the chair he had been sitting in before. Rubbing his eyes, John also appeared and sat down at the table. Both of them began grabbing pancakes and putting them on their plates as Grace rolled her eyes and turned around to see Norman laboring with the water filter.

"Sorry I didn't make any coffee, Norm," she said. "I don't know why…I guess I forgot."

"Baby girl, don't worry. I can make the coffee," he said assuredly. "I certainly don't expect you to do it all."

"Well, it appears some people do," Grace said as she turned to look at Lee who was devouring his pancakes. "Want something to drink to wash all that down, Lee?"

Lee looked up at her with a mouthful of food and nodded. Grace rolled her eyes again and lifted his glass from the table, then turned on her heels to the filter, opened the spigot and filled the glass to the top. The glass immediately began showing the signs that the water was very cold. She set it down gently in front of Lee.

Lee nodded and whispered, "Thank you," in a very muffled voice, due to the amount of food he had in his mouth. Grace picked up the remaining glasses and began filling them up and placing them back on the table in front of the others.

John nodded to her when she placed his glass of water in front of him and Grace smiled back at him. It was a well-known fact that Grace and John had never had a harsh word spoken between them. He was normally a very quiet person and had no problem keeping to himself what he wanted to say. His expressions as well as his strikingly blue eyes were usually all that was needed to convey a message. Grace, in spite of her name, on the other hand was very assertive and occasionally argumentative with just about everyone, except John.

John finished swallowing a bite of pancakes and washed them down with his water. "So, I take it that Lauren won't be joining us for breakfast today?" he said, "again."

Michelle took a sip of her water and set her glass back onto the table. She reached out and forked over a couple pancakes onto her plate. A lump formed in her throat as she couldn't help but start to worry again about her daughter. She swallowed and continued on.

"Looks that way. We've been trying to make breakfast come a bit later on in the mornings to accommodate her schedule, but the later we serve it, the later she stays out," Michelle said.

"I'd like to know where the hell she goes all the time," Lee said brashly. "I think she's crazy for going out there all by herself, and she never tells us where she's going."

"She patrols the property and the areas around it, Lee," Michelle replied. "Then, she follows that steep deer trail up Mill Mountain and usually goes to Big Schloss. She can see the entire valley on both sides of the mountain from there. I suppose, in the grand scheme of things, seeing what's going on outside our little community makes it worth it."

"Big Schloss. I remember the first time you guys took me there. That trail sucked," Lee said as he placed the last bit of his meal in his mouth.

"We took you guys up the cutoff trail on the other side of the mountain. Compared to the game trail she takes from here, it's a piece of cake," Michelle offered.

"Whatever," Lee said dismissively.

After finishing filling everyone's glass including her own, Grace sat down at the table. She placed a couple pancakes on her plate and turned to hear the percolator bubbling on the stove, not long after Norman had set it up to brew some coffee.

"Can you make me a cup please, Norman?" she asked.

"Of course," he said. "Black?"

"Is there any other way?" Grace said rhetorically, knowing full well they were rationing their sugar supply, and they had run out of creamer a long time ago. She and everyone else was forced to like unflavored and unsweetened coffee.

Norman smiled as he took a mug and poured the coffee from the percolator into it, handing it to Grace. She took it willingly and blew onto the top before taking a sip. He then poured himself a cup and sat down at the table with everyone.

"Now that—that's what I'm talking about," Grace said, practically elated with her beverage.

"It tastes ok—I just need the caffeine," Norman said, "always have."

"That's because you're the fool who used to drink thirty-two ounce coffees two or three times a day," Michelle said with a smile. "You can't kid anyone at this table, we know you."

"Yeah, that was me. But this is the new me," Norman said jokingly.

The group got a small laugh from the exchange and continued their meals until every last crumb of pancakes had been consumed. Norman lifted his cup of coffee and took a sip, then offered it to Michelle who held up her hand.

"No thanks," she said.

"That's fine. More for me."

"And me," Grace said as she stood up to get another cup.

"Are you guys ready to hear today's agenda?" Michelle asked trying to get the group to focus. Everyone nodded and Grace sat back down a few seconds later.

"I'm spending the day hunting, that's all I know," Norman said. "Small game, big game—hell, any game would be nice."

"Absolutely. Some meat would definitely help things. Grace and I are going to inventory food and supplies. Winter is right around the corner and I know we're getting low on a few things. Lee, I'd like you to inventory weapons and ammunition. We haven't done that since we moved in and I want to know exactly what we have."

"No problem. That's a job I can do sitting down, so I don't mind," Lee joked. "We have so much of it, I doubt we'll run out anytime soon."

Michelle paused and looked at him sternly. The rest of the group said nothing.

"What?" Lee asked, noticing her stare and the silence around him.

"I don't know the future, Lee. Do you?" Michelle asked.

"Well, no," he replied.

"I know we have a lot of ammunition. But, one day could change all that," she said.

"I know—I get it. I just think with so many things to worry about, it's nice to know that's not one of them," he said.

"Lee, ammunition is finite just like the food we have. We can't go to Wal-Mart or a sporting goods store to get more. If we need more, we have to find someone who has it and with that, is willing to barter for it," Michelle continued as everyone listened intently. "Which brings up a good point—we need to inventory our bartering supplies. I don't think we have much more than a few cartons of cigarettes, a case of whiskey, coffee and ultimately, the fuel in the ATVs."

"Well, I'm putting my foot down right now. No way in hell are we bartering the coffee," Norman said. Grace held her cup up to his and they toasted.

"Seconded," Grace said with a smile. Norman smiled back at her.

"We can't trade the fuel in the ATVs either," John said finally breaking his silence. "That is our only way out of here if we need to leave, or head further west."

Everyone nodded in recognition. John stood up and walked back to his bedroom where he spent his time napping on and off during the day, due to his nights spent on watch. Almost at the exact same instant that he closed the door, everyone at the table jumped when a gunshot was heard outside. Norman quickly placed his coffee down and moved to the door, picking up his AK-47 and opening the door. Grace nervously stood up as well and reached for her AR, which was still propped up on the wall in the kitchen. She followed behind Norman to the door as the sound of another gunshot echoed through the woods. As Michelle got up and walked to where her boots lay, Lee stood up and went to the back of the hallway where the gun safe stood, and began turning the combination dial. He opened the safe and pulled out two chest rigs, one for himself and the other for his father. Each chest rig had several extra magazines in them, as well as a host of other gear stored in the pockets. He then pulled out another AK-47, this one with synthetic furniture, loaded a magazine and charged the bolt.

John literally flew out of his bedroom with his shotgun and a bandolier of mixed 12-gauge shells over his shoulder at the sound of the third shot. As he and Lee ran to the front door, they passed Grace who stood guard just inside, and exited to the porch to see their father down on one knee with his right hand held upward in a fist, signaling the group to stay low and stay behind him.

"It's coming from the south a bit closer to the road," Norman said, as Michelle peered outside the door where Grace was standing.

"The Ackermann's?" Michelle questioned. "That's the closest house to us in that direction."

"Possibly," Norman said.

"Jesus, I hope it's not them," Grace said. "They're in their eighties and they have livestock on that farm. Takers are probably raiding them." She pulled the charging handle back a bit on her rifle to verify a round was indeed in the chamber, and checked the safety.

Another gunshot erupted and then, a flurry of them followed. Several shots back to back.

"I've counted two, possibly three different guns going off," Norman said confidently.

"Yeah, Dad, I think you're right," John agreed.

"Well, hopefully, some of them are coming from Mr. Ackermann's gun," Lee said as he looked around with his AK at low-ready.

"Mr. Ackermann was in the Korean War, Lee," John uttered. "He's an old-school warrior. I guarantee at least one of those guns we're hearing was his."

"They all sound the same to me," Grace said with a look of extreme apprehension on her face. She gripped her rifle tightly.

"There's one in particular—if you listen for it, you'll hear it. It's more powerful than the others—a large caliber rifle probably. I'm guessing 30-06. Probably an M1 Garand," John said.

"John—how the hell could you possibly know that?" Michelle began as she looked at him questioningly. John looked back at her and smiled. Michelle shook her head and looked away with a smirk.

"I'm going to head that direction," Norman said. "It's not far...about a quarter mile." He took his chest rig that Lee handed him and put it on while Lee held his AK for him. "We need to investigate this and see if they need help."

"I'm going with you," Lee said.

"Me too," John agreed.

"Oh great. Just great," Grace said nervously. "You guys be careful, please."

"We'll guard the fort," Michelle said, "but you guys might consider putting on some footwear before you head off." She pointed to Norman and both of his sons, who were standing on the front porch in sock feet.

All three of them shook their heads and smiled, then went back inside to get their boots.

"And maybe a jacket while we're at it," Norman joked.

Norman and both sons grabbed and put on their boots and their jackets, got into their chest rigs and headed off with weapons ready. John reached down beside the door and picked up a small olive drab daypack and slung it over his shoulder.

"Grace, let's go inside and stay low until they get back," Michelle said as she walked back inside and past her.

"Gladly," Grace said as she closed the door. She walked back down the hallway quickly to the open gun safe, grabbed two additional magazines for her AR and closed the safe. "Do you think Lauren heard the shots?"

"I hope so," Michelle said.

As Norman and Lee both approached slowly toward the small farm that could be seen just on the other side of the edge of the woods in front of them, they slowed their pace to a crawl and got down as close to the ground as possible. They had decided on a route through the forest, to take advantage of the cover the woods provided them. John was adjacent to them, just in view, but was walking the road in plain sight with his Mossberg shotgun at ready. Norman had protested his choice of route a couple of times along the way, but John only smiled softly and ignored him each time it was brought up.

The three hadn't heard any more gunfire, since leaving the cabin around twenty minutes earlier. Once upon the edge of the woods, Norman got down on one knee and held his right hand up in a fist and Lee knelt down just behind him. They both scanned the area and didn't see anything out of place at first. Lee tapped his father's shoulder and pointed to John, who had already walked onto the driveway through the open gate.

"Two on the ground—looks like they're dead," John said rather loudly as he pointed to the front yard of the two-story farm house in front of him with the muzzle of his shotgun.

"Who's dead?" Lee asked his father.

Norman sighed and stood up and Lee followed him. They stepped out of the woods and onto the rather unruly yard, which resembled more of a field since it had not been mowed in a very long time. Approaching where John now stood, they noticed two late-model Harley Davidson motorcycles parked side by side, in between them and the house. There were two large men lying on the ground. Both had what appeared to be several large caliber bullet wounds. The men were both wearing black boots and each had on matching leather vests, which was typically indicative of a motorcycle club or gang. One man had been hit at least four times and was on his stomach with a lever-action rifle laying just beside his right hand. The other was on his back with a large gaping hole in his neck and had what appeared to be a .357 magnum revolver in his grasp. Both men were obviously dead and were now laying in pools of their own blood which was warm enough to show steam, rising into the cool late morning air.

John nudged each man a couple times and then kicked both men's guns away from them. He then poked the muzzle of his shotgun at the patch on the back of the man who had died on his stomach.

"Marauders M.C.," John said, reading the patches.

"Who the hell are the Marauders?" Lee asked.

"I've never heard of them," John added.

"I've never heard of them either," Norman responded. "I'm guessing they aren't a friendly club by the looks of them."

"No, they look like bad mofos to me," Lee said nervously.

"They just look like another brand of taker to me," John uttered with a look of disgust.

John began rifling through the first dead man's pockets and then the other's. From the first man's pockets, he pulled out a couple cigarette lighters, some rolling papers, and what appeared to be a small bag of marijuana. He lifted it up to show his father, who nodded in recognition. From the other man's pockets, he found a few extra rounds of .357 magnum ammunition, and a baggie full of pills. He nudged the man's vest and noticed a patch that read "VICE PRESIDENT," which had fresh blood splattered on it.

"Shit—this can't be good," he said, pointing to the patch.

Norman noticed the patch and shook his head. "I don't care if he's the damn emperor of China, so long as he's dead," he said firmly. "What else do you have there?"

"Just the weed, and some pain killers," John said.

"You didn't find any crack?" Lee jested rhetorically as his brother began stuffing the items as well as the revolver into his backpack. John shook the bottle of pills and noticed it was half-full of small round tan-colored pills.

"Looks like Oxys," he said, "or something similar."

"Cool! Give me one," Lee jested.

Norman raised his eyebrows and looked at John as he slid the baggie of marijuana and the bottle of pills into one of his backpack's outside pockets. John noticed the look and smiled.

"For medicinal use," he said with a grin. "We'll put it in the first aid kit at the cabin."

"Of course," Norman said with a smirk.

Just then, an elderly man kicked open the screen door of the house in front of them, stepped outside and pointed a large rifle at the three. Norman dropped his rifle to the side and held both hands up, as did Lee. John stayed right where he was at, on one knee with his hand on the pump grip of his shotgun. He slowly moved it in the man's direction.

"Easy—easy, Mr. Ackermann!" Norman yelled. "It's your neighbors—Norman, Lee, and John. Don't shoot!"

The old man slowly noticed who he was aiming his rifle at and lowered it slowly. His face was grim and sullen, and he appeared to have been crying. Norman noticed he had blood on his hands.

"If they're not dead, shoot them until they are, please," Mr. Ackermann said solemnly in a barely detectable Bavarian accent.

"They're dead, sir," John replied. "As dead as dirt."

"Good," Mr. Ackermann said. He turned around slowly and walked back inside his home with the screen door slapping the threshold behind him.

John stood up and took notice of all of the bullet holes in the door. He also saw that several of the downstairs windows had been shot out, almost as if the raiders had just rolled up and started unloading on the house, even before they'd dismounted their motorcycles.

"These guys must've been high on the stuff we found," John said. "To roll up on a house like this in broad daylight and open fire is pretty stupid."

"Weed makes you hungry. Pain killers make you tired and docile," Lee said. "I don't buy it."

"Maybe they weren't high. Maybe they came here specifically looking for something—like food," John said.

"Or maybe they were high and looking for food," Lee said.

"They definitely wanted something," Norman added. "But they got something else entirely."

Norman walked up to the porch of the house and turned around. "You two watch the perimeter of the house. Keep an eye out for any more of these guys that could pop up looking for their buddies. Shoot anyone that you don't recognize. I'm going to go find out what Mr. Ackermann knows," he said.

John and Lee both nodded. Norman then opened the screen door and entered the house. Upon walking inside, he saw a gruesome scene and realized quickly that he was nowhere near prepared for it. Mr. Ackermann was kneeling down on the ground, and just beyond him was a body. There was blood splatter on the wall to his left. Norman knew immediately that it must be Mrs. Ackermann, and that she had been shot during the attack. Norman walked closer and placed his hand on Mr. Ackermann's shoulder as the old man broke down in agony.

"We've been married for fifty-five years," he said. "I always told her she'd outlive me. I guess I was wrong."

The old man trailed off into tears. Norman couldn't speak. His eyes welled up and tears began rolling down his cheeks. He wiped them with his sleeve and knelt down beside Mr. Ackermann, putting his arm around him to allow him to completely let go. Norman got a closer look at the damage that several bullets had done to the old man's wife. There were two bullet wounds to her head, one of them had landed on her well-aged but still pretty face. There was no doubt what the old man was feeling now, these men hadn't just killed the love of his life, they'd managed to disfigure her permanently. Norman turned away, deciding he had seen enough, but this was a memory that could never be erased.

Several minutes went by, but it seemed like an hour. Norman finally stood up beside the now broken old man, noticing that the rifle he had was indeed an M1 Garand. He also noticed that the stripper clip was gone, and the rifle was empty. Had Mr. Ackermann attempted to open fire at him and his sons, he would've done so in vain.

"Mr. Ackermann, did you know those men?" Norman asked, trying to sound as compassionate as possible. "Have you seen them before?"

After a long pause, he responded. "No, I don't. I've never seen them. Erika had heard a knock at the front door. I hollered at her to not open it, but she did. I came around the corner with my rifle and that's when it happened. She looked at me and started backing away and that's when the bastards started shooting. When they saw me with my rifle, they ran outside and headed for their bikes and I unloaded on them. But by then, it was too late," he said slowly. "My Erika was dead. They killed her."

Outside, Lee and John were on guard, walking around the house and keeping an eye out for anything they deemed suspicious. After circling the house a few times, John walked over to the motorcycles that were still standing upright on their kickstands to take a closer look. Both bikes had saddle bags. He nudged them one at a time with the muzzle of his shotgun and could feel that they were full of something. Moving his shotgun to one hand, he opened the first saddle bag. Inside, he saw a few boxes of 30-30 rifle ammunition, some MREs, and a few cans of unopened Budweiser beer.

"Oh, my dear God," John said slowly, his voice showing signs of mild disbelief.

"What? What is it?" Lee asked curiously.

"Beer. It's beer!" John said in a raised voice. He reached down and picked up the partial six-pack of Budweiser, each can still clinging to each other by the plastic can ring.

Lee ran over to where his brother stood and looked into the saddle bag he had opened. John handed the beer to him and Lee placed them in his pack.

"I'll be damned," he said. "Looks like this bike belonged to Mr. face-plant over there."

"Did the rifle ammo give it away?" John quipped.

"Shut the hell up," Lee said. He walked to the other side of the motorcycle and opened the other saddle bag. Looking inside, he noticed it was half-full of jewelry. There was an assortment of rings, necklaces, and bracelets. They were mostly gold, but there was silver mixed in. Lee ran his fingers through the bounty and also saw some coins, and noticed that some of the rings had very large diamonds in them.

John peered over to see what Lee was doing. His eyebrows lifted at the sight of all the jewelry. "Looks like these two have been busy," he said. "Killing folks and taking their valuables."

"Yeah. Pretty sad, actually," Lee said solemnly. "I wonder how many people they stole from to get all this crap."

"What's makes it really sad is how useless gold is right now," John elaborated. "I mean, you can trade it, but what is it really worth? You can't eat it—it can't protect you…"

Lee removed his hand and closed the top to the saddle bag. He then walked to the other motorcycle and opened one of the two bags it had attached to it. Looking in he said, "More MREs, a box of .357 magnum ammo, a poncho, a mini Maglite, some patches..." He paused as he opened the other saddle bag and simultaneously took a step back with his hand over his mouth. "Oh—shit," he said slowly.

John walked over to see what made Lee react the way he did. Looking inside, John saw what it was, then staggered backward.

"Oh my god—what the hell?" John exclaimed. His expression showed nothing but utter disgust.

Lee took a closer look. "Dude, are those really fingers?" Lee asked.

John swallowed a few times to rid himself of the need to regurgitate. "Looks like an assortment of—trophies," John said.

"Trophies? No. Those are fingers, dude—human fingers. These Marauders are some sick bastards," Lee said.

A moment later, Norman appeared on the front porch and walked down the steps to where his sons both stood near one of the motorcycles. As soon as he approached, he too saw the grisly contents of the saddlebag. He turned his head away for a second, then looked back; morbid curiosity taking him over.

"Mother of god," Norman said, totally repulsed.

John picked up a stick from off the driveway and used it to stir up the hideous contents of the saddlebag. "Looks like there's some clothes in there too—looks like women's underwear," John said. "They're pretty ripped up."

"I don't want to know what these guys were up to," Lee said. "But I have a pretty good idea."

"It doesn't paint a pretty picture, that's for sure," Norman said.

"It's just a sign of the times," John said grimly.

The three stood silently for a moment.

"What else did you guys find?" Norman asked his sons.

"Some ammo, some MREs, and the other bike has a saddlebag full of coins and jewelry," John said.

Norman and his sons looked at each other a few times and then back at the motorcycles. It didn't take long to register to them what the two dead men had been doing lately, and it sickened each of them.

"Let's get this area squared away and get back to the cabin. We need to make the girls aware of what happened here," Norman said. "God knows, it won't bring them any peace, but they need to know."

"Not just the girls—we need to inform everyone about this," John said. "The whole community needs to know. What about the jewelry?"

"Take it, I guess," Norman replied. "It's pretty useless to us, but it may have some barter value down the road. I'd like to get it back to the original owners but from the looks of things, they won't have much use for it."

"What about the bodies? And the bikes?" Lee queried, "It would be amazing to have the motorcycles to use for getting around."

Norman thought for a moment, wanting to agree with his son but he couldn't. "We're going to have to hide the bodies in the woods, along with the bikes," he began. "Eventually, someone is going to come looking for them and the guys that were riding them." He pointed at the dead biker with the Vice President patch and said, "Especially that one."

"It's hard to tell how many more of these guys are around. If they see this, they will be looking for some payback."

"This sucks," Lee said as he kicked one of the tires. "I've always wanted a motorcycle."

"Have you always wanted to be dead?" John retorted at his brother.

"No," Lee relented.

"We can walk the bikes over to the old abandoned cabin up the road and camouflage them. It's pretty thick and overgrown there. As far as I'm concerned, the bodies can go there too," Norman said. "We can come back another day and siphon the gas from the bikes."

"Agreed. God knows, these guys don't deserve a burial," John said. "We'll let nature take care of that."

"What about Mr. Ackermann?" Lee asked.

Norman kicked at his heels and looked at his son. "We'll check in on him in a couple days. He's got some things he needs to deal with on his own."

CHAPTER 5

"The greatest faith is born in the hour of despair. When we can see no hope and no way out, then faith rises and brings the victory."
— Lee Roberson

The cabin
Trout Run Valley
Hardy County West Virginia
Present day

SITTING AT THE TABLE ACROSS from Norman, Michelle took a sip of her tea and held the mug closely between her hands. Grace stood silently with her arms crossed, leaning against the kitchen counter. Her AR was still slung over her shoulder, and she was staring at the floor. Both women were silent. Norman, Lee, and John who were also seated at the table had just finished going over with them what had happened at the Ackermann's, and what they had found. They were deeply saddened when they had heard that Mrs. Ackermann had been shot to death. Both worried about how Mr. Ackermann would be able to survive without his wife of so many years. When Norman began explaining to them about the Marauders and what they had found in their motorcycle saddlebags, the women became deeply disturbed. Grace was especially sickened by it and it showed on her countenance. Lee stood up and walked past Grace, reaching for a glass on the counter, and then filling it with filtered water from the bucket.

Michelle stirred. She set her mug down on the table and cleared her throat. "I'm not surprised at this," she said nervously while staring down at the table. "I'm not surprised at all. I knew it would only be a matter of time before we ran into another group of takers."

Grace was becoming very flustered. Her method of dealing with stress was never subtle. "I'm not surprised either, but this is fucking freaking me out," she asserted. "I mean—where did they fucking come from? We barricaded the road at Wolf Gap. I don't remember ever hearing engine noise on the road recently, so they had to have come from the south. With the road blocked, how in the fuck did they get here?"

"I guess it's possible they made it across somehow. Either that or they've been here all along," Norman said as he interlaced his fingers and placed his hands on the back of his head, leaning back in his chair.

"I'm sorry—*made* it across?" Grace barked. "How is that even possible? We blew the fucking road up."

"That's true, Grace. But to my knowledge, no one has been up to the barricade in a while," John said. "I won't say it's impossible that it hasn't been breached because I don't know that for sure." He paused as Grace met his eyes with hers. "If someone had the equipment and wanted to open it up, it's completely possible."

"Well, who has that kind of equipment?" Grace asked.

"Grace, you know what's going on over there," Norman said. "The populated areas are like war zones. If the feds are involved like we assume they are it's easily explainable. They have those kind of resources."

"I thought we were dealing with a motorcycle gang, Norman. Not a convoy of black DHS Humvees and shit," Grace retorted. "I'm confused."

"I know—and for what it's worth, it makes no sense to me either," Norman said.

"If the barricade is compromised, we need to do something about it ASAP," Michelle said. "It's the only way we can keep most of the craziness in Virginia out of our valley."

Everyone nodded in agreement. Lee said nothing and raised his glass to his mouth and began taking large gulps of water.

"I suggest that we bring this up with everyone on Sunday at the community meeting," Norman said. "Whatever is going on here, we need to make sure that everyone in this community is aware. If the barricade is an issue, we need to find out now and do something about it."

"We should probably not fail to mention the killer motorcycle gang," Grace interjected. Norman looked at her and nodded, somewhat getting a kick out of her insistence.

"We could blow the bridge," Lee finally opened up. "The bridge at the bottom of the hill that crosses Trout Run."

Michelle gave Lee an odd look. The rest of the group followed suit. "Wonder what our neighbors would think about that?" Michelle said. "I'm not sure they'd like it very much."

"They don't even have cars that work," Lee said. "Everyone is either on foot, or has horses or ATVs or bicycles—all of which can clear the creek. You don't need a bridge, unless you have a vehicle that needs it to cross."

"I don't think that's an option, retard," John said to his brother. Lee lifted his middle finger at him as he continued. "We need to verify what's going on with the barricade. We also need to be ready because when these two dickheads don't come back to their roost, their buddies will come looking for him. My guess is they won't be looking for an explanation when they do. They'll be looking for blood—and there's no way of knowing how many of them there are."

"This is insane," Grace said as she shook her head nervously, "as if we don't already have enough to worry about."

Michelle took a sip of her tea and again placed the mug back on the table. "Ok—let's not let this get us off track. We all still have jobs to do. We have a ton of things to get done in order to prepare for the winter, so let's get it done. What happened today doesn't change that. In the meantime, we need to be on high alert, and I do mean high."

"Agreed," Norman said as John and Lee both nodded. "We'll bring it up Sunday and let the community decide what to do about the biker dudes as well as the barricade. I would like to offer one suggestion— you ladies are not to be alone from here on out. Ever."

"I'm perfectly fine with that," Grace said as she held up her hand. "And by the way, Norman—tomorrow is Sunday."

Everyone looked at each other and smiled, some with raised eyebrows.

"That's a pretty important point," Norman said jokingly.

"We need to arm ourselves to the teeth, also," John said. "Everyone carries a rifle, a sidearm and extra magazines at all times. We need to have a guard outside at all times, not just at night."

Once all of the details were worked out, the group small talked for a few minutes and traded jabs at each other in an effort to add levity to an uncomfortable conversation. At a point where the conversation died down, John mentioned the fact that Lauren had been away for what seemed like a very long time today. Instead of allowing the group to jump to conclusions, Michelle mentioned the time that Lauren had accidentally made a mistake in distance and ended up spending a night by herself in unfamiliar territory by accident. Everyone offered their thoughts concerning how worried they had each been that night, and remembered seeing Lauren trudge up to the front porch the next morning as if nothing had happened, even though the conditions for her overnight stay were less than cozy. Michelle specifically mentioned how she hadn't gotten a single wink of sleep that night, not that it was different than any other night for her.

At the conclusion of the discussion, Norman retrieved a scoped rifle from the gun safe, donned a pack and went hunting as he had offered to do earlier that morning. A sentry at heart, John offered to stand guard outside on the porch and watch the property as had been decided. Grace and Lee gathered themselves and their weapons and went to the cellar to begin inventorying supplies. It was nearing mid-afternoon and Michelle began putting a few food items together to develop a plan for dinner.

Grace was counting the buckets of beans and rice and other assorted canned foods while Lee was going through the stockpile of ammunition they had stored underneath the staircase to the cellar. They had brought a lantern down with them and it was barely enough to illuminate their surroundings. Lee had donned a headlamp in order to better see what he was doing.

"We have so much ammo, it's not even funny," Lee said as he fumbled through an open .50 caliber ammo can full of assorted rounds.

"Good," Grace said, "we can use it to kill all those fucking, sick assholes who like raping, stealing, and cutting peoples' fingers off." She paused. "I mean, what kind of person does something like that?"

"Yeah," Lee said. "Trust me, it was pretty gross seeing that."

"I don't need another mental picture, Lee," Grace said, "the one I have is bad enough."

"Sorry," Lee said. "It's not like we couldn't tell you guys."

"I know. I get it. It just sucks that we all have to go into defensive mode again. I was actually starting to feel safe here. Now I feel like we're back where we started...or last summer—or back in Woodstock or Dad's old neighborhood or whatever. No matter what, we just can't be left alone anymore."

"I agree this new world sucks," Lee offered. "But it's all we got, Grace. We are all we have."

"Fingers. Absolutely unbelievable." Grace hissed.

A few moments went by without a word being spoken.

"By the way," Lee said, "it's been awhile since I've heard you mention your dad."

"So?"

"I didn't mean anything by it…just an observation."

"I miss him, Lee. What else do you want me to say?" Grace barked. "I came to visit him and got to see him for all of a couple hours, then the next day he never came home." She paused. "It really sucks."

"What about your other dad?" Lee asked.

"My adopted father? He's not my dad. It's that simple. Alan has always been my real dad. Our relationship didn't start until I was damn near a teenager, but he did everything he could to make up for lost time. As soon as that happened, my adopted father decided it was time to disappear from my life."

"Guess he got a dose of butt-hurt," Lee said with a smile. Grace looked over at him and shielded her eyes from his headlamp. Lee noticed the beam was aimed at her and turned it away. He could see that she was smiling, and that was a good thing for her. After a few seconds, Grace turned her head and went back to what she was doing.

"Did you guys find anything else on those guys or was it all just jewelry, fingers, and granny panties?" Grace asked with a smirk.

"Actually—we did find a few things worth mentioning," Lee said. He stopped separating ammunition and turned to face Grace. She noticed him walking up to her.

"What?" she asked. "What did you find?"

"Beer," Lee said quietly.

Grace's eyes opened wide and she produced a look of disbelief before saying, "Are you kidding me?"

Lee smiled. "Nope. Four cans of Budweiser."

"Gross. I mean—it's beer so I'll deal, but still. Budweiser?"

"They're bikers, Grace," Lee pointed out. "What else do they drink?"

"I guess that's true," she said, "and I probably shouldn't judge."

Lee walked up the staircase and could be heard rummaging around upstairs. He returned after a minute with the four unopened beer cans still dangling from the plastic six-pack beer rings. He was attempting to hide them under his shirt, in an effort to surprise her. He pulled them out as she studied what he held for a second before reaching out and pulling one of the cans from the rings. She cracked it open and almost immediately, foam shot out from the top. Placing it to her mouth, she took several long gulps of the frothy beverage. She pulled it away from her mouth and swallowed one last time, this time letting out a burp.

"Holy shit," she said, wiping her mouth with her sleeve. "I never thought I'd say this about Budweiser—but this is heaven." She then offered the open can to Lee and he held his hand up in refusal. He then pulled a can off the ring and set the others down on the floor. He cracked it open and it began to foam over a bit. Grace offered hers up and he toasted with her, then took a long pull from the beverage. Grace did the same.

"It's warm, but it's damn good," Lee said.

"It is absolutely grand," Grace said taking another sip.

"I should probably feel guilty, drinking this without dad or John," Lee said. "But for some reason, I really don't at the moment."

"Courtesy, I think goes right out the window here, Lee," Grace stated. "I gotta say that this was something I needed desperately. Besides it's ok to be selfish—sometimes."

Lee smiled and took another sip. He then said, "We found other stuff, too."

Grace looked at him, her curiosity showing.

"What else did you guys find?" she asked. "No way it could be better than this—unless it's moonshine, that is." She finished her statement with a slight giggle.

"It depends on what you consider to be better."

"Well then, do tell," Grace said.

"One of the guys had a small bag of weed on him," Lee explained as Grace's eyes grew wide. "He also had a full bag of pills. Pain killers."

"Oh, wow. Well, the pain killers we should definitely hold onto for..."

"Pain?" Lee interrupted. "Yeah, I'm not trying to get addicted to that shit. But the weed however..."

"Lee, I think you just became the best post-apocalypse friend I have," Grace said with a deep smile.

The two stood there and spoke for a while, as if nothing bad was happening around them and the danger to their livelihood didn't exist. Once they finished their beers, they opened the last two and took a seat on the edge of Grace's bed, sipping on them and enjoying what was a rare occurrence in these times, a temporary escape from reality.

Their reprieve was interrupted when they both overheard a loud whistle from upstairs. It was one they had heard before, and they both knew it was John alerting those inside the cabin that they had company. They stood up and quickly ran up the staircase almost running into Michelle, who had her pistol in her hand. Grace immediately noticed that both she and Lee had forgotten their weapons in the cellar. Michelle noticed too, but said nothing and continued on to the front door. She opened it and walked outside to the porch, immediately seeing a group of people standing in the driveway. It was their closest neighbors, Fred Mason, his wife Kim, and their sons, Chad and Mark. John was already off the porch and was in the process of shaking their hands as Michelle, Grace, and Lee walked out. Michelle quickly holstered her weapon upon recognizing their visitors. She couldn't help but be a bit on edge.

The Mason family lived directly across the road from the cabin. Both homes were about a half-mile from the old St. James Church where the weekly community meetings were held. It was well-known throughout the community that Fred was an avid survivalist, prepper, and firearm enthusiast. He held a Federal Firearms license and at one time, was the area's main source for firearm and ammunition purchases. He ran his business from his own basement, which was completely legal and way cheaper than having a separate storefront. It was a very lucrative business for him and his family, and in addition to Fred's pension, it afforded them many benefits of life that other families in this area could not afford, up to and including a rather sizable home and large plot of land spanning several hundred acres. They owned a fair share of vehicles that still ran, including an armored M35 Deuce and a Half, as well as two military surplus Humvees, each complete with gun turrets for mounting a belt-fed weapon.

Fred was a veteran and had seen action both in Iraq and Afghanistan. He had spent several tours as an Army Ranger and finished his career as a well-decorated Sergeant Major. Despite being honorably discharged and suffering combat-induced PTSD, he had managed to deal with life on the home front as best he could. He found that being around firearms, military surplus and other familiar equipment made him feel at home the most and kept him calm. In the world after the collapse, he was the one who united the residents of the valley and thus, became the community leader. He was a tall, muscular man with chiseled features and a quick temper. His voice carried a higher volume than most people. The members of the community respected him, and for good reason. Fred had known Michelle's husband and his parents before the collapse—their cabin being literally right across the road from his home. Knowing that Alan had not made it to the cabin with his wife and daughters after the collapse, Fred and his family checked on them often, and were always ready to lend a hand if needed.

After shaking John's hand, Fred looked up to see Michelle walking toward him. He shouldered his Springfield M1A and nodded to her. His sons stood on either side of him and his wife just behind him.

"Howdy, Michelle," Fred said with a smile that showed a couple crooked teeth.

"Hello, Fred," she responded. "Hi, Kim. Hello, boys."

"Hi, Michelle," Kim said with a smile and overbearing accent that could only be described as West Virginian, being born and raised in Hardy County.

Both Chad and Mark nodded to her in recognition. Being brought up in a strict military family, they typically did not say a word unless their father told them to. Both were carrying rifles that were slung over their shoulders. Kim didn't appear to be carrying a weapon, even though she hardly went anywhere without at least a handgun.

"Have you all been doing some target shooting today?" Fred asked inquisitively. "Heard a bit of gunfire earlier."

"We weren't target shooting. There was an issue down at the Ackermann's this morning," John spoke up.

"What kind of issue is that exactly?" Fred asked John, his voice sounding like a drill sergeant grilling a cadet.

John took a minute and explained what had happened earlier on in the day at their neighbor's house down the road, in detail. Fred became more and more interested as the story went on. As John and Fred continued to talk, Kim walked up to the porch and gave Michelle a hug. She told Michelle how sorry she was to hear about Mrs. Ackermann. They both then went inside, as did Grace. Lee remained on the porch while John spoke with Fred. Fred looked down at the ground at times and shook his head. His lips pursed and eyes grew wider as the story went on. His disgust was building.

"It's a shame about Mrs. Ackermann. But Marauders? A motorcycle gang in the valley? You have got to be shitting me," Fred said.

"Have you heard of them?" John asked.

"Hell no, I haven't," Fred exclaimed. "Sounds like a fantastic group of guys, though. Too bad I didn't have a chance to meet them and kill them."

Both Chad and Mark snickered at the comment. They respected their father, but sometimes the things he said, and perhaps the way he said them were just too amusing to ignore.

"Shut up, you two retards," Fred said to his sons. They both stopped snickering, and did their best to conceal their smiles. Fred turned his attention back to John. "How the hell did they get into the valley? Aint heard no engines running lately—especially Harley Davidson engines."

"That's what we can't figure out," John said. "We were planning on bringing it up tomorrow at the meeting."

"Damn right, we need to bring it up. We need everyone down here armed and ready to cull the herd," Fred said. "Their buddies will be back soon looking for them. We'll need to be ready for that. The last time we had trouble down here, we weren't dealing with killers. From the sounds of it, these guys most certainly are killers."

"To be honest, we were surprised that no one else heard the shots and came our way," John said.

"We've been in our basement all day inventorying supplies," Fred said. "We heard a few shots, but just assumed it was y'all target shooting or something. Are you guys good here? Need anything? Where's your dad?"

"He's hunting," Lee said, still standing idle on the porch. "We're running low on meat."

"So are we," Fred said. "If I could get these two nitwits to shoot something other than a fuckin squirrel, we'd be much better off than we are." He motioned to his sons who had all but stopped grinning.

"If we get more than we need, we'll send some your way," John said. Fred nodded. "Much obliged."

As if too impatient to wait any longer, Lee opened up with, "Why isn't Megan with you guys?" Lee was referencing Fred's daughter who was Lee's age and who almost always accompanied the family everywhere they went, as Fred never let her out of his sight. It was also common knowledge throughout the community that Lee had quite a crush on her. Fred didn't seem to mind much, but he took every opportunity to debase Lee, whenever the chance presented itself. It was all in good fun though, and this time was no different. His attention then turned to Lee.

"Megan is at home," Fred affirmed. He squinted and noticed that Lee was a bit pale and expressionless. "Boy, you look like someone just gave you a reach around. I can almost see your corneas…what've you been drinkin?"

Immediately, John turned to his brother and Lee noticed John eyeballing him. Without saying a word, Lee knew that John guessed exactly what in fact he had been drinking, and wasn't pleased.

"Son of a bitch," John said as he shook his head.

"We'll see you all tomorrow at the meeting. We need to get this situation squared away," Fred said. "Come on, Kimmy! We're done here."

The door opened and Kim walked out, waving goodbye to Michelle and Grace.

"See yall," she said.

Fred nodded to John as he and his sons turned around and began walking back up the driveway, Kim in tow. Fred turned around quickly and shot a look at Lee, grinning and winking at him. Lee lowered his head. John walked back onto the porch and up to his brother.

"You asshole," he said.

Lee, realizing his brother was quite pissed, said nothing as he turned and walked back inside the cabin.

CHAPTER 6

"Danger, if met head on, can be nearly halved."
— Winston Churchill

Shenandoah National Park
Madison County Virginia
Several years earlier

A FTER A VERY LONG DAY of backpacking in the summer heat, Alan Russell dropped his pack from his sore shoulders onto the mossy ground of a primitive campsite near the Staunton River. Michelle dropped hers as well, and their daughter Lauren did the same not long after. The campsite they had chosen, more or less chose them. It had manifested itself at the right time, as all three had found themselves exhausted after hiking ten miles over varied terrain that day in the Shenandoah National Park. After seeing their fair share of waterfalls, switchbacks, steep ascents, and precarious descents, the three were more than ready to set up camp and relax for the rest of the evening. They had a full day of hiking to get back to their vehicle tomorrow and they were all looking forward to some rest.

Alan began immediately setting up the family's tent. Michelle was stringing up a clothesline from one tree to another over the top of the fire pit. After a day of hiking, she would wash the family's sweaty, smelly clothes in a nearby water source if available, and then hang them over the fire. Any wet clothes hung over the fire would quickly dry, even in the most humid environments. They would of course, smell like smoke, but would otherwise be clean and dry. Lauren was walking around the woods, picking up sticks of assorted sizes for the campfire. Not taking much time to set up, the tent was staked down in a matter of minutes and Alan had already pulled everyone's inflatable mattress pads out and was in the process of inflating them while sitting partially inside the tent. Lauren walked over to the fire pit and dropped an armload of kindling near the stone fire ring. She then went back out to gather more.

On her return trip to the camp, Lauren noticed two men hiking up the trail a good distance behind her. She turned around a couple times to get a glimpse of them and tried to do so without them noticing. Both had backpacks on and were carrying fishing poles, and didn't seem to be in much of a hurry. This didn't seem strange to her as the trail ran beside the Staunton River, along the edge of the National Park and was well-known for its abundance of rainbow trout, especially in the spring and early summer. There was still a fair amount of daylight left and she didn't feel threatened in the least by their presence, so she continued on to the camp and dropped the firewood on top of the existing pile.

"There's a couple guys coming up the trail," she said.

Alan popped his head out of the tent and turned to look down the trail, which descended gradually down and along the river bank.

"Fishermen?"

"Yeah, Dad. It looks like it," Lauren said. "They both have packs on and they're carrying fishing rods."

"Trout season," Michelle stated as she grabbed some articles of clothing that the family had taken off and approached the riverbank with a small bar of soap in her hands.

"Next time, we should bring some rods do some fishing ourselves," Alan said as he pulled himself up from the tent, finished with inflating the sleeping pads. He walked over to the edge of the riverbank and took off his outer layer t-shirt and tossed it at his wife. Michelle caught it and gave him a stern look, then smiled.

Lauren had stacked the kindling in a lean-to formation inside the fire ring. She squatted down and pulled her knife and began to cut small slivers of wood from a dried birch branch to make a pile of tinder. Alan watched closely as his daughter did so. Once the pile was a decent size, Lauren pulled a flint and steel from her pack and began striking them together. After a few strikes, a spark ignited the tinder. She got down as close as she could to the tinder pile and blew on it, just enough to cause the small ember to ignite the tinder. She then scooped up the tinder and placed it under the lean-to of kindling. After giving it a few seconds to catch, she blew on it again and the fire engulfed the lean-to. She then began adding more kindling to the pile.

Alan smiled. "Where the hell did you learn to make a fire like that, little girl?" he asked.

Lauren looked up at him and smiled. "My daddy taught me," she said, trying to emanate a backwoods accent. Alan laughed and Lauren turned back to her fire. Under her breath, she said disparagingly, "Little girl—please, Dad."

The men that Lauren had seen coming up the trail had just appeared and walked past the campsite. Alan looked over to them and held his hand up, waving in recognition. The two looked at each other, and then to Alan. They both smiled and waved. They both were missing some teeth but otherwise seemed like nothing more than local guys on a fishing trip. After turning away and walking just past the campsite, they stopped again and turned to face the campsite. Alan noticed immediately.

"How are ya'll doing?" he said trying to sound like a country boy himself. Growing up on a farm had helped him tremendously, but he had to admit to himself, he wasn't as country as he was pretending to be. Sometimes in the forest when meeting locals, it was better to pretend you were a local too. If you were too city they would usually pick up on it and admonish you for it, depending on how far away from civilization you were.

"Oh—we doin just fine," the taller man said with a smile. One of his eyes was squinted more than the other.

"Just doin some fishin," the other, shorter man said.

Both men had camouflage pants and t-shirts on, as well as black leather combat boots that were very well-worn. Their skin was tanned and both had stubble beards. Their backpacks were Ozark Trail brand, signifying they did their shopping at a local Walmart.

"Must be fishing for rainbow then," Alan said. "Good time of day for that."

"Yeah," the taller man said. His smile diminished and he turned away and spit a large glob of what appeared to be tobacco juice on the trail.

"Well, we're headed up yonder to catch us some—rainbow," the other said. "Might be back by later."

"Take care then," Alan said.

The two turned away and continued up the trail in a very slow manner. Every so often, they would turn around and look back at Alan and his family. Lauren finally stood up, satisfied with the fire and the way it was building.

"Finally," she said. "Now I can get out of these gross tights and put on some shorts."

"L, put on pants instead, please," Alan said.

"Dad, mosquitoes don't bother me," she replied with a mocking look.

Alan paused and looked back at her, taking his eyes off of the two men for a moment. Lauren noticed his gaze and it did not appear he was kidding with her.

"Do as I tell you, please," he said firmly.

"Fine."

Michelle walked up from the riverbank and over to her husband. She reached out and put her arms around him as Lauren got inside the tent with her pack and zipped the door closed.

"Mmm...sweaty husband. Everything ok?" she asked.

"Yeah. Our beds are ready, the fire is going, and Lauren is changing."

"Great. Almost time for dinner then," Michelle said.

"Yeah. Just so you know...there's a good chance we may be having guests for dinner, baby," Alan stated.

"Guests?"

Alan went on and told Michelle about what had happened while she was at the river washing clothes. Michelle was immediately spooked, but he assured her that if they needed to act, they had the means to protect her and Lauren. Until it got to that point however, they would be cordial and treat these people normally as if they weren't suspect, even though to him they were. Michelle was uneasy with that decision but agreed anyway, trusting that her husband was more than capable of protecting his family if needed. While talking with his wife, Alan reached down near his backpack and picked up his waist pack. It was well-known by those closest to him that this was where he kept a concealed Glock handgun when camping or backpacking. He snapped it around his waist and returned to the hug that Michelle always had ready for him in any situation.

After a few minutes in an embrace with her husband, overlooking the round pool below a small but splendid waterfall, Michelle began working on dinner. She pulled out a large packet of freeze-dried beef stroganoff from her pack, which was the family's favorite, and put a pot of water directly over the fire, resting it on two sticks. After a few minutes, the water began to boil. She poured the water into the large foil packet and set it aside to rehydrate and cook. Lauren finally unzipped and exited the tent. She had put on a down jacket and a pair of hiking pants, per her father's request. She had her long hair pulled into a ponytail and was wearing a pink Mountain Hardwear beanie on her head. The fire had died down a bit, so she added a few more sticks to it.

"I should go out and get more," she said, looking at her father for support. He shook his head, not giving her any.

"Stay right here where I can see you," he said. Lauren nodded and noticed that he had his waist pack on. She sat down in the dirt beside the fire and held her hands out over it, warming them.

Alan followed her by seating himself, as did Michelle. Michelle pulled out some ultralight plastic plates and handed one to each of them, keeping one for herself. She pulled out some utensils and passed them around, using hers to spoon out a serving of steaming hot stroganoff to Alan, then to her daughter, and finally herself. All three began eating as the woods around them began becoming immersed in darkness. The three chatted intermittently about the day's events and some of the things they had seen while hiking the trails.

As Alan placed the last spoonful of the hot dinner into his mouth, two flashlight beams came into view. Michelle noticed them not long after, but said nothing. Lauren watched both of her parents as they became instantly fixated on the company headed their way. It seemed as though they had just seen them, but it had actually been well over an hour.

"Oh, shit," Lauren said.

"Watch your mouth," Michelle remarked. Lauren immediately apologized and sat back against a large stone. She spooned the remainder of her dinner into her mouth as a typical backpacker would—like it was the only thing she had eaten in a long time.

As the men came into view, the three immediately noticed that it was the same two men who had visited them earlier. Before waves could be exchanged or nods could be seen, the two men impulsively walked right up to the campsite, within a few feet of Alan and his family. The taller man looked closely at the fire and the other held up a stringer with three large rainbow trout hanging from it.

"Y'all want some fish?" the shorter man asked with a smile. "Got ourselves a good catch…we'd be happy share some with ya."

Alan was annoyed at how impetuous the men were. He felt immediately threatened by their presence, but put on his best poker face. "Sure!" he said. "Take a seat." Michelle gave him a cross look, but it left her face as fast as it had appeared. She turned to the men and smiled at them charmingly.

"We appreciate it," the taller man said as he took a seat beside the fire, directly opposite from where Lauren was. The other man sat down beside him. "I'm Shane," he continued. Pointing at the other man with him, he said, "This here's Ronnie."

Ronnie lifted his hand up in recognition of being introduced. Shane did nothing but watch the fire. Occasionally, his eyes lifted over the flames to look at Lauren, who was oblivious.

"Good to meet you both," Alan said. "I'm f-bomb."

Shane and Ronnie both gave him a bewildered look. Alan continued, pointing at Michelle and then at Lauren, "My wife over there is half-cocked, and my daughter here is little bear."

The bewildered look continued on both of their faces, but soon changed to a faint smile on Shane's face. Ronnie looked at Shane and saw his expression change and in turn, changed his own.

"What the fuck kinda names are those?" Ronnie asked with a sly grin.

"Trail names," Alan offered promptly, in an effort to eliminate contestation. "We backpack a lot. We don't hand out our real names. It's trail etiquette—you understand, of course."

Ronnie nodded and smiled. Shane's smile turned into a smirk. He sucked his teeth for a second, then said, "Yeah, mister. Trail names. Of course we understand." His backwoods accent was becoming more and more evident, but he suddenly began annunciating some of his words with more clarity. It was easy to tell he was a tad annoyed.

Ronnie took his pack off and reached into it, pulling out a good sized grate just big enough to lay over top of the stone fire ring. He laid it on top, then tossed the fish directly over the flames, still attached to the leader. He moved them around the grate with a stick as he looked at Lauren and smiled. Lauren turned her head away from him and hid her expression behind her arms, which were crossed over her knees.

"Y'alls fire is dying down," he said. "I'll go fetch some more wood." He then stood up and walked out into the darkness. Shane didn't move a muscle. He just sat there watching the fire and every so often, eyeballed Alan, Michelle, or Lauren. Every time Shane's eyes went to his daughter, Alan could feel the adrenaline rise and fall in his veins as his anger went from moderate to nearly uncontrollable. He did manage to keep his cool, but it wasn't easy.

"You guys caught some beauties," Alan said. "Didn't take you long either."

"Well," Shane began, "we know a good spot just up the river from here."

"You guys do a lot of fishing?" Alan asked, noticing that Shane wouldn't look him in the eyes.

Shane nodded and again looked over in Lauren's direction. "If it wern't for fishin' and hunting, we wouldn't have much to eat around here," he said.

Alan nodded and said, "I completely understand."

"Well…it's been a long day. How's about a drink?" Shane said as he reached into his backpack and pulled out a mason jar full of clear liquid. He opened it and took a long sip from the jar, wincing as he swallowed. He then offered the jar to Alan who at first hesitated, but took it and smiled. He had a feeling that if he chose direct refusal, it would most likely cause an immediate conflict with this man.

"I'd be happy to join you," Alan said, doing his best to keep the situation civil. He took a small sip from the jar and immediately coughed as his eyes teared up. The distilled concoction, whatever it was, was some of the strongest he had ever consumed. After getting it down and regaining his vision, he realized quickly that doing what he had just done could've have provided these men with the window they needed to do whatever it was that they intended to do. He felt lucky so far that they hadn't. His guard would not go down again.

Shane smiled and snickered. Alan handed the jar back to him and Shane grabbed it forcibly. He offered it to Michelle and then to Lauren, both of whom smiled and held their hands up in refusal. Shane just offered that same devilish smile that he'd been showing all along.

"Gotta admit there, Mr. f-bomb, I don't feel real welcome right now," Shane said as he unscrewed the jar again and took a large sip. Gulping it down, he said, "Hard to find good people in the woods to drink with, I guess…no offense to you there, Mrs. half-cock and miz little bear, you little cutie bitch you."

Alan postured himself. He had had enough. The tolerance switch inside him rocked the other direction and the bright mental LED was blinking red. If you give an unjust person enough time, they will eventually show their true intentions. These men were now presenting themselves for who they really were and were no longer welcome.

"The thing is, Shane, you in fact, *have* found good people," Alan asserted, completely dropping his faked accent and articulating his words clearly. "We have been welcoming and completely nice to you and Ronnie up until this very point. I suggest you pack up and head out. You've worn out your welcome."

Shane put the jar down on the ground. He spit a mouthful of moonshine into the fire over the fish and the fire flamed up quickly, causing Michelle to jump.

"You got somethin' to say to me, city boy?" Shane said as Ronnie came out of the woods with an arm load of wood. He dropped it at the fire pit and noticed Shane's mood had changed, as well as everyone else's.

"Everything ok, Shane?" he asked.

"Yeah. We were just leavin'," Shane said as he stood up and grabbed both his backpack and the fish from the grate over the fire. Ronnie grabbed his backpack and stood behind Shane.

"We'll be seein' y'all," Shane said as he took another long pull from the mason jar.

The two walked away from the campsite, turned on their headlamps and headed back down the Staunton River trail. Once they were out of site, Michelle stood up and took a deep breath.

"What the hell was that, Alan?" she asked.

"Luck," he said.

"Luck? Are you kidding?" Michelle responded.

"Dad, I'm really freaked out right now," Lauren said.

"I know, baby. You guys pack it in and try to get some sleep. I'll keep watch tonight and we will head out at first light."

Michelle and Lauren both nodded and Lauren stood up, walked to her mother and hugged her. Michelle kissed her forehead and the two walked to the tent and got inside. Alan could hear them getting into their sleeping bags and zipping them up. Flashlights flickered on and off from inside the tent but eventually, everything went dark.

Alan sat beside the campfire motionless with his eyes to the trail. He reached into his waist pack and pulled out the Glock and racked the slide, placing a round into the chamber. He then checked the pack to verify that there were two spare magazines inside and he was content to find that he didn't forget them. He pulled out a small plastic bag of caffeine pills and placed two of them on his tongue, choking them back with a gulp of water from a Nalgene bottle in his pack.

"Next time, Alan, invest in some night vision," he said to himself. The fire died down and the sounds of the forest overtook the night.

The next morning, just as light began to infiltrate the forest, Alan began packing up camp. He unzipped the tent and reached inside to nudge Michelle and then Lauren, who were both startled by his actions. "Let's get moving," he said.

Michelle got out of her sleeping bag quickly and Lauren followed, showing signs of hesitation. The two eventually joined him outside and began helping pack up. Michelle reached into her pack and pulled out a few Clif bars, handing one each to Lauren and Alan.

Lauren's raised her eyebrows and said, "Yum. Breakfast."

"I wish we had time for oatmeal and fruit," Michelle said. "Sorry, toots."

Before long, the camp had been completely packed up. Alan pushed the grate aside that the men had left there last night, placed some stones on the campfire embers, and donned his pack. Michelle and Lauren had already snapped their packs on and were adjusting their trekking poles for the steep uphill climb on the Jones Mountain trail. The three then set off, soon finding the trail intersection and following it up the mountain.

Not long after they began their ascent, Lauren looked back and noticed that they were being followed.

"Dad—they're back," she said.

Turning around to notice, Alan stood just off the trail and allowed his wife and daughter to hike by on the next switchback. The trail had been very steep for the past quarter-mile and they were all out of breath and completely exhausted. He held a trekking pole in his right hand and a Glock handgun in his left. He watched as Lauren trudged past him quickly with her trekking poles in hand, and then looked back down the trail over several switchbacks they had just ascended. A ways below the hill were the two camouflage-dressed men that had joined them in the backcountry at their camp the night before along the river. They were looking up the hill and pointing in Alan's direction with smiles on their faces. One of them had a machete in his hand. Neither was carrying the backpacks they'd had on last evening and were therefore, able to move a bit faster than Alan and his family.

"Is it them?" Michelle asked in between deep breaths.

"Yes," Alan replied. "And it looks like Shane has a machete."

"Dad...let's drop the packs and run. It'll help us move faster. Maybe that's all they want," Lauren said.

Alan turned to follow his wife and daughter up the steep trail. He pointed up the trail.

"Keep moving. I know what they're after and it's not our backpacks," Alan said in a serious tone while trying to catch his breath. "You should know better than that, L."

"What the hell is wrong with people?" Michelle queried rhetorically. "One minute they seem decent and the next minute, they're the damn devil."

The three continued trudging uphill to the next switchback and the next, doing what they could to keep distance from the pair of camo-clad men that were pursuing them. The pace was becoming unmanageable.

"Those guys kept staring at me last night, mom," Lauren said. "I didn't say anything because I didn't want the conversation to get out of hand."

"I saw them," Michelle said. "After Shane pulled out the moonshine, I knew things were headed downhill. It was good not to antagonize them, Lauren."

"You two continue on," Alan said as he stopped and dropped his pack.

"Dad—what are you doing?"

"Just keep going. They aren't going to stop until they get us and they are moving faster than we are. Cut across the next few switchbacks and hide behind one of those large rocks."

"Dad..."

"Lauren, go now! Don't question me!" Alan barked as he tried to catch his breath.

Michelle said nothing. She snapped her fingers at her daughter and pointed to a large rock about a hundred feet up the trail from them. Lauren sighed and reluctantly followed her mother up the mountain, going against "Leave no Trace" protocol and cutting across the switchbacks. Alan reached into his waist pack and pulled out a full magazine of .40 caliber hollow-point ammunition. He placed the magazine in his pocket and got down on one knee, making sure to stay in a spot where he could see the two men until they were in range. He held his pistol close to his body at low-ready with his finger alongside the trigger guard.

Michelle and Lauren made it quickly to the large rock and dropped their packs, finding cover behind it in a thick area of mountain laurel. They both could see Alan below them, and they could barely see the two men who were making their way quickly up the trail to where he waited. Lauren watched her mother as she dug into her pack, pulling out a small handgun and racking the slide, chambering a round. Michelle placed a finger over her mouth, signaling for them both to keep quiet. They didn't want to expose their location. Lauren placed her hand over her mouth and her eyes opened wide when she saw the men turn the corner of the switchback where Alan waited on one knee. As they came into view, he raised his pistol in their direction. One of the men, the one they knew as Ronnie, raised his hands. Shane was indeed wielding a machete. He did nothing but smile and spit out a wad of tobacco juice. They both had evil, drunken grins on their faces, the same grins they'd had the previous night—the kind that would make just about anyone feel uncomfortable or even endangered.

"Hey, now," Ronnie said, "I thought we was friends."

"We are not friends," Alan said authoritatively. "My suggestion is for both of you to turn around and go back the way you came." A pause followed before a reply was heard.

"My suggestion is fuck your suggestion," Shane said.

After last night's events and confirming it with today's, Alan could easily tell that Shane was the alpha, and with that, most likely the killer. Ronnie seemed to just be the follower, capable of killing, but more capable of just following orders. Both had strong backwoods accents and it was easy to tell that neither had much education. He assumed they had come from the one of the villages in the foothills of the mountains they were in, and stumbling on unsuspecting hikers in the National Park was a hobby of theirs. Perhaps they were after money, food, or gear, or something else much worse. It was impossible to tell how many times they had done this, but it was obvious it wasn't their first time.

"Just so we are clear, if you come any closer, I will kill you," Alan said as he brought his right hand around to support his left which held the Glock tightly.

"Hey man, we're on a hike just like you guys are," Ronnie said. "We have just as much right to be here as you do."

"Yes, you do. But you don't have a right to scare people, pursue them, threaten them, or attack them with a weapon," Alan said.

"Ain't nobody done no attackin'—yet," Shane said sternly. "But now that you have a fuckin gun in my face, I am seriously considering it."

Alan remained as calm as possible, but he could feel the adrenaline hit his bloodstream. The alpha was a dangerous person and it was blatantly obvious. He didn't move and didn't falter. Deciding he was the biggest threat, he lined up his sight picture with Shane's center mass just over the front sight of his Glock. If this man moved, he would be the first one that Alan would shoot.

"Where's that purty piece of ass that was with ya?" Shane said as he spit another pile of tobacco juice from his mouth.

"Both of them are purty, Shane," Ronnie said to his cohort.

"Shut the fuck up, fuckstick," Shane said. Turning his attention back to Alan, he said, "A good daddy should know better than to let his teenage daughter prance around the woods in leggins."

Shane swung the machete around his body at a bush in disgust, easily slicing off a small branch about an inch in diameter. He kicked the ground beneath him with the toe of his black leather combat-style boots which were loosely laced. His boots were one of the many things that had clued Alan and his family in quickly that these two were not the usual day hikers or backpackers they'd normally cross paths with in the woods. The previous night at the campsite had started out well and had ended with Alan telling the two men to leave, after they had said some things that made him and his family very uncomfortable. It was now escalating.

Alan was about to explode and he was on the border of killing both of these men without any further provocation which he was certain would happen. The fuse that held his composure together had blown. He knelt there and tried to push thoughts of doubt aside. If it was going to be him or them, it would be them.

"You gonna answer me, city boy?" Shane pressed.

"I'm no city boy," Alan said, "and my family is not your concern."

"We'll see about that," Shane said.

He began walking toward Alan and Ronnie was on his heels in an instant. They were twenty feet away from Alan when he stood up and fired a warning shot in their direction, hitting the ground just in front of them. Shane raised his machete over his head and launched it at Alan. Alan ducked and lifted his weak side arm upward defensively to prevent the blade from hitting his head. It landed true, on the outside of Alan's right forearm as he lifted his Glock and began to fire. Three shots hit Shane center mass and he dropped on the ground in a lifeless heap, dust from the trail rising around him. Alan looked at his forearm which was beginning to inundate with blood, just as the other man lunged at him in a fit of sudden, unexpected rage, after seeing his accomplice fall. Alan fired his Glock again, this time a double-tap, one round hitting the man in his chest and the other taking a chunk of flesh out of his neck. Ronnie fell to the ground a couple of feet from where Alan stood. Blood poured from the carotid artery in his neck onto the ground.

Michelle and Lauren were on the trail in an instant, running toward Alan as fast as their legs could carry them. When they got to him, he was nursing a large wound on his right forearm and blood was pouring from under his lacerated shirt sleeve.

"Jesus Christ, Alan," Michelle said in a mild panic as she reached for shears and a wound dressing in her first aid kit.

"Amen," he said, unusually calm after the trauma of what had just transpired.

"Dad…Daddy," Lauren said as she embraced him from his left side. Alan wrapped his arm around his daughter, still gripping his pistol.

"L, do me a favor and pull the magazine from my back pocket and replace the one in the Glock with it."

"Ok, Dad."

Lauren did as he asked. She took the handgun from him and dropped the half-empty magazine from it, replacing it with the full one. She then placed the half-empty magazine in her right back pocket, and slid the Glock into her left back pocket. She then returned to her embrace under Alan's left arm that he wrapped around her neck. He kissed her on the top of her head. Michelle was busy stopping the bleeding on his slashed forearm. After she cut the lower portion of his sleeve off, she pulled out a bag of hemostat and emptied the powder on his wound, making him jump from the sudden pain.

"Holy shit, that burns!" he said as his arm shook.

"You're lucky you're not dead," Michelle countered. "I have no idea why you felt the need to talk to those guys…you should've just shot both of them and been done with it."

"Sorry, I thought I was doing the right thing by giving them a chance to back off," Alan said sarcastically. "Next time, I'll shoot first and ask questions later, momma."

Michelle just shook her head. The hemostatic powder stopped the bleeding rapidly, and she then placed the dressing over the affected area and secured it with tape.

"We need to get out of here and get you to a hospital," Lauren said. "How far are we from the car?"

"About six miles. After we get to Bear Church Rock, it's mostly ridge-walking from there. I'm guessing about three to four hours," Alan replied.

After gathering themselves, Alan reached down and shouldered his backpack, then all three began the hike back up the trail to where Michelle and Lauren had stashed their packs. Following his wife, Alan noticed the handgun in her back pocket.

"Nice, momma. Glad to see I had some backup," Alan said.

Michelle smiled and looked back to her husband.

"Stop looking at my butt," she said.

"Can't exactly help myself right now," Alan joked.

"You guys are gross," Lauren said as she shook her head.

After gathering their gear, the family continued up Jones Mountain Trail to the top of Bear Church Rock, which offered a beautiful view and wasn't too far off the trail. During the twenty-minute hike, Lauren didn't say much and Alan was worried about her being traumatized by what had happened. Once on the rock outcropping, Alan dropped his pack and pulled out his cell phone to call the Park Ranger emergency number and report the incident. Lauren walked out to the edge, held her hands outward meditatively, and took in a deep breath. She loved overlooks like this. Michelle took off her pack, took a seat and began sipping on a water bottle.

"Everything ok, L?" Alan inquired to his daughter.

"Yeah, Dad. Yeah. I'm ok."

"You understand, I had no choice back there," he said.

"I understand that. Yes," she replied. "You've always told me that people like that are out there and to never let your guard down—and I didn't. My heart told me there was something about them…and no matter how nice they seemed at first, I kept my guard up."

"That's good situational awareness," her father said. "Being aware of possible dangers, no matter where you are, who you're with, or what you're doing is paramount. But there will also come a time when you will need to take action. It goes without saying that if you or someone you love is threatened, that you must choose to act. It's unfortunate, but sometimes the only thing that can stop a violent act is—violence."

"I know, Dad. I know," Lauren said.

"I'm not proud of what I did, L," Alan offered, "but I'm proud of you."

Lauren turned to him and smiled. "I'm not proud of it either, Dad," Lauren said. "But I'm glad you did it. You protected us like you always do. I just hope that if I ever have to do it someday, I'm able to think—and act."

"You will," Alan assured her, "you will know it when the time comes. You already have good instincts. I'll make sure that you're ready. We'll train together. And it goes without saying that I'll protect you guys. You two are my world."

Michelle put down her water bottle and wiped her mouth with her shirt sleeve. She began to dig for her sunglasses in the brain of her backpack. "All things considered, I'm just glad they're dead," Michelle said. "People like that don't deserve to live. All they want to do is hurt other people. For that reason alone, I don't have any remorse for them."

Lauren turned away from the overlook and walked to Alan, reaching out to hand him his Glock handgun.

"Keep it," he said. "You may need it someday."

CHAPTER 7

"None of us knows what might happen even the next minute, yet still we go forward. Because we trust. Because we have Faith."
— Paulo Coelho

Tuscarora Trail
George Washington National Forest
Shenandoah County Virginia
Present day

T HE SCENE THAT SHE JUST observed would probably give her nightmares for the foreseeable future. Lauren had finally reached the area where all the commotion she had heard earlier on in the day was sourced, and it was far worse than she could have imagined. The first thing she noticed upon reaching the area, to go along with the putrid smell of burning plastic and metal, was a sport-utility vehicle that had been completely destroyed. It was riddled with bullet holes and the entire rear of the vehicle had been split open like a clam shell. As she cautiously approached the vehicle, making sure to stay near the forest edge, she noticed two bodies lying face down on the ground. They were ripped apart and burned as if they had possibly been inside the vehicle when it had exploded. They each had an execution-style gunshot wound to the back of the head. The vehicle had no markings that she could detect and wasn't displaying tags, so positively identifying it was impossible for her.

She could only guess where it may have come from. The bodies had been charred beyond recognition, and the vehicle itself was still smoldering.

Lauren wished she had a working camera with her so she could have taken as many pictures as possible to record what she was seeing, and show the others. Instead, she did her best to take mental photographs. She had a feeling that what she was seeing now, would be pretty hard to forget. After a few minutes, Lauren began to feel nervous being there and decided to make her stay brief and soon headed back the way she had come. Not long after returning to the wagon road and heading downhill, she noticed a blood trail on the right hand side and began to follow it. The blood was sporadic and relatively fresh. She immediately knew that there had to be another person who had survived this, and that person was possibly still alive and therefore, still a danger to her and others. She continued down the trail back into the valley under the tree cover, noticing that the blood had veered off-trail and gone into the woods, just before reaching Cedar Creek. She began to smell smoke, but it wasn't the same scent as had come from the burning truck. It was the familiar smell of wood smoke—possibly from a campfire.

After crossing the old white forest road gate that marked the end of the backcountry and what could be the beginning of some sort of civilization, Lauren looked through the trees to her right and noticed immediately, what the source of the smoke she had been smelling was. Just a short walk down another forestry road and before yet another gate and a bridge over Cedar Creek, was a small primitive campsite right on the bank. From here, she could see a man sitting down and a small column of smoke rising from the ground near him.

Lauren moved slowly in the direction of the campsite, making sure not to break the cover of the thick foliage that helped keep her presence a secret. The man was sitting down, leaning against a tree and had a fire pit dug into the ground deep enough that the flames could barely be seen. He was wearing a black uniform and she could see the patch on his left arm had the letters "DHS" and the word "SECURITY" on it. Lauren was well aware that the Department of Homeland Security was one of their enemies in this new world, and their presence was one of the reasons that her family had decided to move further west. She scanned the area and couldn't see any weapons anywhere near him. All she could see was the man, the smoke rolling from his in-ground campfire, and several pieces of wood in assorted sizes strewn about near him. He was breathing shallow breaths and was holding his leg with both hands, occasionally letting out a moan, signifying to her that he was indeed injured. She assumed the blood trail she had seen belonged to him.

Lauren continued scanning the area. It appeared to her that he was totally alone. His black uniform was ragged, ripped, and dirty, like he had been in the woods for a long time. He was younger, possibly in his mid to late twenties, with short hair and a nearly full-grown beard. There were a few scabbed over lacerations on his face and neck. He didn't have a backpack, he wasn't wearing body armor, and not a single weapon was visible to her. Considering this and her current situation, she decided it was her best chance to act. She was going to break cover, confront him and attempt to find closure to the events of the day. If she had to, she would kill him. She didn't necessarily like the idea of taking a life, but she knew the consequences of inaction. She quickly closed the distance between herself and the man and his campsite. Using a large oak tree for cover, she lifted the rifle to her shoulder and placed the man's head on top of the front sight just as he turned to her. Startled, he lifted his hands in the air and a look of stark fear fell across his face.

"DO NOT FUCKING MOVE," Lauren's voice thundered breathily just as she flipped off the safety.

"Don't shoot! Please…don't shoot!" the man begged as his hands trembled.

"Are you alone?" Lauren demanded as her finger lay just off the trigger.

"Yes—yes. I'm alone."

"Do you mind telling me who the hell you are and what you're doing here?"

"It's a long story…please, don't shoot me…I mean you no harm. I'm unarmed and I'm injured," he said.

Lauren shuffled sideways. "These are not your woods. You have no right to be here," she asserted. "Your agency has no place here—do you understand that? We are a free people and we want to be left alone! I want to know right now, what the fuck you're doing here."

"Ok…OK," he said with a stutter in his voice, making sure to keep his hands up. "I know how this must look to you, and I promise you it's not what it looks like. I'm not really DHS. I mean, I am…but I'm not. This is just a uniform. I'm actually in a militia—local militia. A small group of us infiltrated the DHS and have been working security at the camp in Woodstock. That's the only reason I'm wearing this, I swear."

The man was breathing heavily and held his breath momentarily, in an attempt to control it. He looked Lauren up and down and noticed that she was unexpectedly calm and her weapon was steadily trained on him. He dared not to make any sudden moves.

"Are you certain that you are alone?" Lauren prodded.

"Yes—there's nobody else here, I swear."

"Go on, then," she said to him, "but don't you dare move." Lauren didn't believe anything the man had said and did her best to stay aware of her surroundings while listening to his explanation. He appeared truly scared to her, but she knew that appearances could be deceiving.

"One of our guys blew his cover…I'm not even sure how it happened. But they interrogated him and they executed him today. The rest of us stole a truck and broke the hell out of there…they gave chase and caught up to us just on the other side of that mountain," he said with a note of fear in his voice. He nodded his head backward, signifying the hill to the east of them where Lauren had just been. "We had to stop where the road ended and turned into trail. They blocked us in and opened fire on the truck. I swerved and hit a tree and we all jumped out. That's when the rocket…missile…or whatever it was hit the truck."

Lauren did not want to believe him, but she had just left a scene that resembled what he was describing. A burned truck, assorted debris and two dead bodies were right over hill just east of her, just off the wagon road. The bodies were burned so badly that she had no idea if they had been wearing the same uniform this man was wearing, but assumed they were.

"How many of you were in the truck you supposedly stole," she asked.

"Three of us total, including me," the man answered. "Two of my brothers died back there. There were four of us inside DHS. I'm the only one left."

"How did you end up being the only one who made it out of that mess I just saw back there?"

"You saw it? Good, then—" he began and then Lauren interrupted him.

"I saw it. But that doesn't prove you're telling me the truth," Lauren interjected. She began scanning him and the area around him closely. "I'm only going to ask you this one more time. Are you armed?"

"No. I'm not armed. I swear I'm not. None of us had a chance to get to our weapons before we left the camp, and the truck was empty when we stole it."

The man's nervousness was apparent now. His eyes were shifty, but never left Lauren. He was attempting to understand her predicament as much as he wanted her to understand his. She kept him in her sights at all times, her finger resting inside the trigger guard, a split second away from pulling the trigger. A moment of silence passed as the two observed one another curiously.

"Is that weapon—loaded?" he pondered humorlessly, making sure to keep his hands raised and in view.

"That's a pretty stupid question, in light of your situation," Lauren remarked sternly, "and before you waste time asking me if the safety is off, *it is.* "

"Sorry. I just don't like having a weapon pointed at me," he began, "especially with a finger so close to the trigger."

"Understandable—and I don't like being patronized," she countered.

The man nodded. "That's…understandable, too. I used to have an AR just like that. It's an M&P, isn't it?" he offered, as if trying to be friendly and de-escalate the situation. Lauren didn't budge, and kept him in her sights.

"Yes."

"It's a fine weapon," he said, and then paused. "Are you all alone out here, or do you have a family close by?"

Lauren was now officially spooked. As quick as she could while keeping the man in her sights, she backed up several paces. In her mind, she was beginning to feel as though approaching the man was a big mistake. She could feel the adrenaline begin to pump into her veins as her body prepared itself for fight or flight response. Where would she go? Heading back to the trail and back up the mountain would be a losing battle for her. The trail was all uphill from here and very steep, and she was physically drained already. She knew there was a farm and a couple homes just down the road near the old furnace ruins she could flee to, but she didn't know if those people were approachable, or even if they were still living there. She also had no idea what people in this area would think, seeing a young girl armed with an AR-15 asking for help or how they would react. They could take her in and protect her or they could just as easily kill her. The Cedar Creek Trail led the opposite way for several miles along the creek bed, but would take her to a much more remote location in the forest—a location that no one she knew had been in a very long time.

The look on the man's face changed quickly to one of disapproval when he saw her begin to disengage. As far as Lauren knew, he could be one of *them* in spite of his story. She didn't trust him, but something told her not to leave just yet. Lauren found a couple trees she was comfortable with for cover and got down on one knee, preparing herself for the possibility of an ambush. To her surprise, the man still did not lower his hands, even though he had plenty of opportunity to act while her guard was down.

"Whoa, wait," the man said, "I didn't mean to alarm you. I was only asking because—I just find it a little unusual that you'd be out here all by yourself."

"Why is that, exactly?" Lauren asked cynically.

"Well, for starters, we're in the middle of nowhere and you're a young girl. It's just weird that—" he said, just before Lauren cut him off again.

"Let me be clear," Lauren said authoritatively. "This is not a game and I'm not anywhere near ready to be this friendly with you. Stay right where you are, don't move, and answer *my* questions first, ok?"

"Easy there, kid. I told you, I'm militia. I'm not your enemy."

"I am not a child. You are wearing a DHS uniform and telling me you're not DHS. Forgive me if I'm not convinced," Lauren commanded. "I know who I am. Who you are and what you are, remains to be seen."

The man paused. "I'm sorry. I just don't want to get shot."

Lauren peered down at the man's leg. "Looks to me like it's a little too late for that," she said.

The man nodded and looked down at his leg and the blood-soaked pants. Lauren hated it but the fact was, she was beginning to trust his story. Knowing he was obviously hurt, she was also beginning to feel compassion for him. His story had some holes in it but so far, it was making sense to her, especially since it matched what she had seen. If he was truly a threat, he didn't appear to be. He had no weapon. Why wouldn't a DHS agent have a weapon or some gear with him? Nothing fully made sense to her. She kept telling herself to keep her guard up no matter what, and find out as much as she could from him. Her dad would want her to stay vigilant. Information was so rare in these times. She knew getting more meant continuing the conversation.

"How bad is it?" Lauren pondered quietly, her attitude with him quelled slightly.

"It's clean—looks like it slipped right through," the man replied. "I was hit while running away. I think it was a pistol round, probably a full metal jacket from the looks of the exit wound. If it was a rifle bullet or a hollow point, it would be a lot worse."

"I don't see any gear. I'm guessing you don't have a blow-out kit," Lauren said, not seeing a first aid kit on his person or anywhere around him.

Keeping her rifle to her cheek and finger just off the trigger, Lauren reached into her waist pack and pulled a wilderness first aid kit out. She tossed it over to the man who still kept his hands up, even as the kit landed beside him.

"Can I reach for it?" he asked, "without getting shot?"

Lauren placed her right hand back on the fore grip of her rifle.

"Yes. But do it slowly. I swear to God, if I lose sight of your hands for a second or if I think you are reaching for a weapon, your day will be over."

The man nodded and slowly reached for the first aid kit with his left hand while slowly lowering his right hand. He picked it up and unzipped the package, pulling out items, including a field dressing, some rolled gauze, cleansing wipes, and scissors. He began to cut the cuff of his pants leg with the scissors, in order to pull it over his knee.

"Thank you," he said as he began cleaning and dressing his wound. He cringed and gasped quite a bit while doing so. "I told you though, I'm not armed. If I was, you would've seen a few more dead bodies back there in black uniforms."

Lauren watched him closely and against her better judgement every so often, she turned her head to look around while he wasn't looking at her. Twilight had taken over the woods and it was getting much cooler. It had been an hour or so since the sun had set past the mountains to her west, shadowing her in the small hollow beside Cedar Creek near the historical area of Van Buren Furnace. It was usually warmer in the valleys but that was about to change as night set in. It wouldn't be very long before darkness would overcome and the only thing illuminating her field of view would be this stranger's fire pit. A few minutes of silence went by before her curiosity took over.

"How did you manage to get away?" she asked in a more humble, inquisitive tone. "I saw the truck. It was obliterated."

"I jumped out before the truck got hit by the rocket. I got about ten feet when it hit and the explosion threw me into the woods. I was airborne for twenty or thirty feet. I must've been knocked unconscious, but I have no idea for how long. When I came to, I was pretty well hidden in the bushes and I could hear the agents as they were looking for me. They kept calling me 'the third body'. They were pointing their rifles into the surrounding trees. I just laid there. Then, I saw the other guys. They had to have been in the truck when it exploded. They were pretty burned and torn up, and definitely were not moving."

The man continued to nurse his wound. Lauren's muscles were beginning to tire from holding the rifle at ready for so long, but she continued to aim it at the man. She wanted to trust what he was saying, but past experience told her not to. She knew that it was possible for anyone to be capable of lying and getting others to believe their story, especially now.

"So, how did you end up with a bullet hole in your leg?" Lauren pondered.

"When I saw them turn away from me for a cigarette break, I made a break for it," he said. "Before that, I heard them radioing in for a K9 to come search for me. Seemed like a good idea at the time." He smirked and shook his head in a show of mild disgust.

"Wait—they had working radios?" Lauren asked.

"Yes. Why?"

"I thought the EMP took out everything electronic," she said.

The man looked up at her. "For the most part it did—but there's always some exceptions. Around here, most radios and electronic devices were fried," the man said. "But government agencies like DHS prepared for this. They hardened some of their stock and placed quite a lot of electronic equipment inside shielded containers and metal buildings with elaborate grounding fields."

"Faraday cages," Lauren recounted. She could remember her father telling her about such things.

"Yep. It's not hard to do it, even with the slightest bit of ingenuity. So I guess you know what I'm talking about, then."

Lauren nodded. "Do you know how much of the country was affected?" she asked, her curiosity showing in the tone of her voice.

"From what I understand, it took out everything east of the Mississippi. The metro areas—the real population centers were hit the hardest. I have heard that there are parts of the country that weren't hit," he said. He paused and waited for another question from Lauren, and when enough time had passed, he continued. "Anyway, when I heard a dog was en route I knew I was screwed, so I took an opportunity when they weren't looking to make a run for it. I made it about fifty feet up the trail when one of them saw me and all of them opened fire at me. I thought for sure I was dead. When I felt the round hit my leg, I knew I was dead. Then, they just stopped. They didn't run after me and honestly, I have no idea why. I made it to the top of that mountain and hid under some rocks, hoping I could get the jump on them if they pursued me, but I never saw them. When I heard them drive away, I came down here to get some water and get warm. Just followed a blue-blazed trail and it led me to the creek, and then I followed that here."

"It's almost like they just let you go," Lauren went on, "and that makes no sense at all to me."

"I know. Me neither."

"If it was me, I would have wanted to make certain you were dead," Lauren said flippantly.

The man was taken aback at her response and his disapproval was obvious. Lauren's matter-of-fact attitude had normally caught those not used to her off-guard, and had ended more than several conversations with the recipient assuming she was a bitch. She began thinking how that might have sounded to someone who had just recently lost three of his closest friends. His expression matched what she was expecting to see. Wanting to get more information and keep the conversation civil, she decided to change her tune.

"I'm sorry. That was harsh," Lauren offered.

"It's ok," he said as he looked away again. "You're the one with the gun, so for now, its ok."

She paused. "I'm sorry, also—about your friends," she said with a glint of sympathy in her voice.

The man looked at her again, nodded and smiled grimly. "Brothers. They were my brothers," he said. "And thank you." He paused. "I need to bury them, but I don't think it's a good idea to go back there right now."

The man finished his handy work and placed the bandage over his wound. It was obvious to Lauren that he had some experience in emergency first aid. Tossing the wipes, bandage wrapper and bloody gauze in the fire pit, he placed the scissors back in the first aid kit and zipped it shut. He then held it up to her.

"Good as new," he said, as he motioned toward the camp with his head.

"You said you were in a militia?" Lauren asked.

"Yes. I'm a Corporal in the Shenandoah Valley Legionnaires."

"Never heard of them," she said.

"Not many people have. We were good at staying low on the radar. By the way, if you're cold, you can come closer to the fire. I don't bite."

"Oh, you're a fucking comedian, aren't you?" she quipped.

The man smiled and tossed her first aid kit back to her. Lauren let it lay on the ground, her instincts telling her that would have been an easy way to distract her, if that was what he intended to do. Appearing as though that was not his goal, he pushed some of the logs in the fire around with a stick. He then tossed a few more logs on top of it. He looked at Lauren again, then reached his right hand over to his left shoulder and ripped the DHS patch from his shoulder and tossed it into the fire. The patch that read "SECURITY" followed.

"Guess I don't need that anymore," he said. "A lot of good it did me."

With a slight grin, noticing his show of humility, Lauren chuckled through her nose and warmly asked, "What is your name?"

"Christian," he said, not missing a beat. "Christian Hartman."

"Well, Christian Hartman, I'm getting a little tired of standing here. I'm also getting hungry," Lauren said. "I'm going to put down this rifle and come a bit closer. Do *not* get any ideas."

"Guess my story makes sense then, huh?" Christian said.

"It does," Lauren said as she flipped the safety on her rifle and brought it down in front of her. She moved her hand from the grip and reached into her waist pack, pulling out her Glock. "But we are far from cozy, and I still have a lot of questions."

Lauren reached down and picked up her first aid kit, placing it back into her waist pack.

"I'll tell you anything you want to know," he said as he noticed the Glock in her hand. It was aimed in his direction, but not directly at him. "Can you tell me your name?"

Lauren nodded. "I can't see any harm in that. My name is Lauren," she said.

"Nice to meet you, Lauren," Christian said.

Lauren smiled. She walked closer to the camp and stood near a tree on the other side of the fire pit with her back facing Cedar Creek. She unslung her rifle and set it against the tree just behind her, then unsnapped the quick-disconnects on her backpack and slid it off near the rifle. Opening the top of her backpack, she dug around inside for a bit and pulled out a large bag of rice and beans and set it on the ground. She then pulled out a ditty bag containing her cook set and set it on the ground. She tossed both bags one at a time to Christian, who caught them easily as if he were expecting her to do just that.

"I guess I'm cooking," he said.

"Sorry, bud," Lauren said. "It's the only way I can keep an eye on your hands."

"And there, I thought you trusted me," he joked.

Lauren looked at him with raised eyebrows and cocked her head sassily. Christian quickly recanted.

"Kidding—only kidding," he said with a smile. He emptied the ditty bag and set the cook set near the fire pit. He then took the bag of rice and beans and poured what he guessed would feed both of them into the pot. Lauren pulled a bottle of water from the side pocket of her pack and tossed it to him, then took a seat on the ground. He poured the water into the pot and sat the pot on top of two new logs that spanned the fire pit. "You're pretty guarded, aren't you," he said.

"The times we are living in require it," Lauren said. "But, yes...I've always been very cautious."

"Yeah, I get it. Tough nut to crack and all that. But you seem like you know what you're doing, though. You handle a rifle pretty well. You've handled this whole situation well. Most people nowadays would've just shot me and moved on."

"I'm still contemplating doing just that," Lauren said, "if it's any consolation."

There was a pause before anything else was said. Christian turned his head to her and noticed Lauren's cynical, yet confident look. He offered her one of his own.

"It is, I guess," he said, then hesitated. "I mean, I know it's just a first impression, but you seem to really have your shit together," he continued, trying not to sound too presumptuous or flattering. "Have you had training?"

"More or less," Lauren replied.

"Military? Police academy?" Christian pondered, "Militia?"

Lauren drew back and gave him an anomalous look. "My father," she said. She then pursed her lips.

"Oh," he said with raised eyebrows, not expecting the answer.

A few minutes of silence followed. Lauren and Christian both just stared at the fire as it occasionally tossed a spark into the air.

"You said...that you and the others infiltrated DHS. Do you mind telling me how you were able to do that?" Lauren queried.

"Easy. We worked for them," Christian said, glancing at her.

Lauren's expression changed to one of apprehension once again. "What the hell does that mean exactly?" she asked as she gripped her pistol tightly.

"Calm down. It means just that. We were all government employees."

"So you—you actually worked for DHS?" Lauren demanded as her temper began to flare. "You lied to me?"

"Listen," Christian pleaded with a hand held up. "My brothers and I all landed jobs in Homeland Security and FEMA a few years ago. It was the only way to get vetted. We all knew some sort of fucked up scenario was coming a long time ago. The writing was on the wall. All the shady politics happening in Washington. All the corporate greed and fleecing of our country. All the race bating and all the violence and all the talk about gun control. They have been shitting on the Constitution for decades and suddenly, it just became the status quo. FEMA started building camps all over the country and stockpiling plastic coffins. Then, it became damn near a crime to be a patriot, and totally acceptable to be a criminal. People who took a stand and developed any type of following were silenced somehow or black-bagged. If you spoke out against an oath-breaking politician, owned guns or believed in the Bill of Rights, you were labeled a domestic terrorist. Patriots like me were shot in the back for abiding by the Constitution by some asshole federal agent, while terrorists were practically ushered into the country with a red fucking carpet rolled out for them. We the people lost the control of this country a long time ago, and it's all our fault. On top of it all, the government was spending our tax dollars, preparing for a war with us the whole time, while we were busy with sports and reality television." The disgust in his voice was clear.

Lauren couldn't speak. The look of apprehension left her face and one of enormous curiosity replaced it. A burst of wind blew through the trees and she pulled her jacket hood up and over her beanie-covered head. It was nearing dark and the lower temperatures in the valley could be sensed now.

"I joined the militia when I was out of high school," Christian continued. "My father was the County Sheriff here for several terms and he followed the oaths that he took to the letter. He lived it and breathed it and I wanted to be just like him. I didn't believe in joining the military and fighting wars that served corporate interests—and I didn't want to be a cop and serve the state, writing tickets all day. This region had a strong militia and it seemed like the best option. I could take the same oath, learn military tactics in my spare time, and live a normal life. So, that's what I did."

"Wait—your dad is Sheriff Hartman?" Lauren asked as Christian took a breath, "I think he and my grandparents knew each other."

"Yes. That's my dad," Christian said. "Who were your grandparents?"

"The Gallos—they lived in Woodstock. But if you don't mind, I don't want to talk about them right now."

Christian paused for a moment as if to gather his thoughts. "No problem. As I was saying, several of us militiamen had gotten some good espionage training from an ex-CIA agent who joined our team. We wanted a way in, so that we could provide intel and help as many people as we could prepare for what could or would eventually happen. Along the way, we learned that a group of elite oligarchs were planning for a new America, and they were arranging to turn the country completely upside-down, in order to get what they wanted."

"Wait," Lauren said, trying to put the puzzle in her mind together. "Are you saying that the collapse was actually precipitated by our own government? They are the ones responsible for all the shit that's happened?"

"Yes—but not exactly," he said. "I mean, they didn't do anything to prevent it or to stop it from happening. It was like they wanted it to happen—and why not? It fixes all their problems. Their new America can begin immediately. With the grid down, the elite and the rich still get fed. They get to enjoy things, like heavily armed security and underground bunkers to ride out the storm. They get to survive and repopulate. The poor peasants get to fight it out amongst themselves and deal with the tribulation. Of course, some decided not to fight it and just went along with everything—you know, people who actually trusted the government. They gave up whatever freedom they had left, in order to be fed and quartered. They're provided for in exchange for labor, but there's not room for everyone and not everyone can perform the tasks they're forced to do. At least fifty percent of our population nationwide is already dead for whatever reason I'm guessing, and it won't be long before we add another ten or twenty percent to that number. Most people weren't prepared for a nightmare like this and no one saw it coming because they refused to read the signs. I'm guessing the powers that be couldn't be happier. It fits their agenda for population control and they didn't even have to do a damn thing to force it to happen."

"Population control?" Lauren asked, completely taken aback.

"Of course. Can you think of a better way to rid the system of most—if not all of the people dependent on it?"

"I'm confused," Lauren said. "I'm sorry, but this is a lot to take in."

"It's always been about population control," Christian continued, "and natural resources. Earth only has so much to provide. If we keep populating at the rate we're going, the thought is that there won't be anything left. The elite believe this, and because of that, have done whatever's been needed over the years to kill off the population. I admit, their methods have always been much more subtle. Mass forced vaccinations, fluoride in the water, food additives that cause cancer and destroy reproductive organs. With less strain on the system, there's more for them and less for people like you and me. By limiting the population, there's less people like you and me around, and they can have even more than ever before. It's a world of haves and have-nots, and the *haves* play to win."

"So, it's greed then," Lauren concluded.

"Greed, power, and survival of the fittest," he said. Christian lifted the water bottle up and Lauren nodded to him, knowing he was asking if he could have a drink. He opened the top and took a large drink and another before twisting the top back on and continuing. "The government plays right into it—they're all puppets, especially our President. The Department of Homeland Security, FEMA, and all of the federal agencies who remain loyal have the same thing in common—plenty of power and next to zero accountability. They can pretty much do whatever they want and have no one to answer to." Quickly changing the subject as if it was natural to him, he said, "By the way, this is really good water."

"It's straight out of the mountain," Lauren replied as she gazed into the fire, not knowing what to think after what he had just told her. Her mind was in overdrive. Suddenly, she felt very alone in this world that Christian was describing to her. She had known it was bad—really bad, but she'd had no idea how bad it truly was. On top of everything, the last thing she wanted to believe was that there was an entire class of people literally getting off on it. People worse off than her and her family had suffered the worst of this catastrophe. Many had died, simply because the system that kept them alive had failed. Others were simply starving to death—or killing each other over food or other supplies. The country was in chaos, and the chaos was being aided and abetted by the government. She was just as angered as she was saddened by the news. She wanted to scream.

"I take it that you know these woods pretty well?" Christian pondered.

"Like my backyard," Lauren responded confidently with a nod.

"You must live close then—again, not pressing you for info, just an observation."

"Not really," she said as she shook her head. "It's about two or three miles as the crow flies...makes it ten miles or so on foot. Pretty treacherous in spots, too."

"Ah. So it *is* your backyard," Christian said.

"For about a year now," Lauren offered. "We used to live in Winchester. When things got bad in our neighborhood, we moved to Woodstock to be with my grandparents. Things got bad there, so we came here."

"What happened to make you leave home?" he probed, "if you don't mind me asking...my throat is drying out from all this talking. Need to take a break and hydrate."

"I don't mind at all, actually." Lauren paused, took a deep breath and exhaled. She decided to give in. "We got caught keeping to ourselves," she said with a sigh and raised eyebrows. "A few weeks into the event, a bunch of our neighbors were trying to start a socialist micro economy. They wanted everyone to join and combine resources for the 'greater good of the neighborhood'. We just ignored them and didn't budge. We had enough stored to go on our own for a while, and possibly ride it out. We stayed in our own yard, ate our own food, and drank our own water. We had stored food and we pulled water with a hand-crank well. We had a garden, a pantry full of food, and a chicken coop. We didn't ask for anything from anyone, and that wasn't cool with everyone. Before long, it became obvious that we had something that everyone else didn't." She paused. "My dad was one of those crazy conspiracy-theorist prepper types that everyone hated—that is, until the shit hit the fan...then everyone wanted a piece of what we had."

Christian nodded and stirred the rice and beans as the pot began to boil. "Sounds familiar. You were guilty because you were more prepared than they were," he said.

"Exactly. People who didn't prepare, suddenly thought we owed them something because we did. Absolute fucking bullshit progressive America." Lauren paused. "So one day, I guess about three months after the collapse, the pot boiled over. A huge group of people came to our house, looking like they were going to start a riot. They demanded to come inside or they were going to burn the house to the ground with us in it. They also had found out somehow, that my dad never made it home from work and it was just my mom, my older sister, and me. They took that to mean that we were defenseless. Well, they thought wrong."

Christian stopped stirring the rice and beans and looked at Lauren's eyes which were gazing deeply into the fire. A tear rolled out of her left eye and she quickly wiped it away. She looked up just as he looked away, not wanting for her to notice that he had seen the sudden emotion. Lauren composed herself quickly and continued.

"The self-appointed leader of the neighborhood was our next-door neighbor and believe me when I tell you, he was a total bastard," Lauren said. "He owned a wholesale restaurant supply store downtown and won everyone's loyalty when he delivered his food and drink stock to them, which I have to say was pretty substantial. But that of course, meant that they owed him, so people pretty much did whatever he asked them to. Take care of this for me and here's a six-pack of beer. Do this and here's some pasta or some beer. He managed to curry favor with just about everyone, except us because we weren't buying what he was selling. He also constantly made passes at my mom, in an effort to get inside our house. He figured since my dad wasn't there, she needed a man to help her. She wasn't having it, though."

"What happened?" Christian asked.

Lauren paused and swallowed over a lump in her throat. "I shot him," she uttered softly. "I shot him in the head."

"Wow," Christian said in a low, comforting tone allowing Lauren to pause. "I'm sorry. It's not easy taking a life."

"He deserved it. He forced his way into our house that day and went right after my mom. She was fighting him off, but he was bigger than her. She was yelling for help and no one would help her. The entire group stood outside our front door, watching him hit her and did nothing. My mom managed to push him off of her and that's when I turned the corner and shot him. Then, I went outside and told the crowd that if they didn't get off our property, I would kill every single one of them. They didn't believe me at first and started yelling that they were going to take us until my sister brought me this," Lauren said as she pointed at her AR-15 beside her. "Somehow, they got the picture and dispersed, but we knew that was only the beginning. We knew that eventually, whatever he had given them would run out, and when they got hungry they'd become more and more desperate. They would try anything to get what we had. So, we packed up and left that night. We met up with a few close family friends and booked it to my grandparents' house."

"Sorry to hear that happened," Christian offered, "but you made the right decision. There's no recovering normal again after something like that. It would have only led to more violence. Neighborhoods use to be the safest places."

"Yeah, they used to be. My dad used to preach about being the first to act in a life-or-death situation like that," she said. "He used to say reaction is always slower than action."

"Your father is a smart man," Christian said.

"Yes, he is." She paused with raised eyebrows. "I miss him," Lauren said quietly as she looked away with a sullen smile.

The two said nothing for a couple of minutes. The wind continued to pick up speed as it rushed through the valley. It was completely dark now and aside from the wind and occasional crackle of the fire, the water in Cedar Creek could be heard rushing over the rocks.

"Any idea where he is, or what happened?"

"He never came home, that's all I know. He was working at a job site in Washington DC on the day of the collapse. I know the cities were the first places that the craziness and panic would start—it was bad enough in our little hick town that day. People literally went nuts when they realized there wasn't any internet and their cell phones didn't work. The grocery store a mile away from our house was looted after the first day. People lost their minds when there wasn't any more food. I can't imagine what it was like in a big city."

"Maybe he made it out," Christian said. "Maybe he's still trying to get to you and your family."

"We've pretty much lost hope in that," she muttered. "We're all so spread out now. He would've had to make it here on foot and not knowing where we were, he'd have to make several stops—that's even if he made it out of Washington." She paused. "I don't want to talk about him anymore, ok? I've done enough crying."

"Ok," Christian relented. "So, your grandparents—you made it there and then what happened?"

"It was fine for a while, but people started acting shady and downright dangerous. My granddad had plenty of food and a lot of weapons. He was a prepper just like Dad. We could protect ourselves from most people, but it wasn't long before we started noticing federal agents in the streets. They were dressed in riot gear and they all were carrying weapons. It went from bad to worse. Signs started going up about the entire state of Virginia being under martial law because of the riots happening around DC, and the federal government came in and started taking over everything. A DHS agent came to our house one day and said they were empowered by executive order to search our house. He said they were going to impound our truck because it ran. Then, he said they were going confiscate guns, and anyone caught with large food supplies would be taken into custody and their food supplies would be seized."

"Yep," Christian said. "You'd be charged with hoarding. It's a crime against the state, punishable by incarceration. Possession of a firearm is even worse—it can be punishable by death now."

"Yeah. Suffice it to say, we were more than freaked out. My grandfather played dumb and the first chance we got, he sent us into the mountains in West Virginia to our family's cabin," she said. "We've been here ever since. I still don't know how we managed to get away, but I'm thankful we did."

"You were lucky. Woodstock has changed quite a bit. Massanutten Military Academy has been turned into a regional headquarters for FEMA and the DHS." Christian said.

"I didn't know that."

"And—the area that surrounds the three schools from Route 11 all the way to the Interstate is where the camp is," he said. "Fifteen foot high double fences with razor wire surrounds the entire compound."

"I guess they needed a place to put all those people," Lauren said.

"It's just a place where they can controlled—where they can be used for manual labor until they die," Christian said unapologetically. He placed the lid on the cook pot and set it off to the side of the fire. "That's where the town is now, well, what's left of it. Most people have been forced out of their homes and if they haven't, it won't be long before DHS gets to them. There's a barricade with heavily armed guards at the I81 bridge and at both ends of town on Route 11. They have automatic weapons and have been instructed to use lethal force, if they deem it necessary."

Lauren sat up and adjusted her posture. Her Glock was now laying on the ground beside her, no longer in her hand. Her guard was down at this point, whether she liked it or not. It was obvious now that this person was quite possibly someone she could indeed trust. He definitely was a wealth of information, which was scarce in the times they were living in.

"I guess, I just don't understand what all of this is about," Lauren said. "Why aren't they helping?"

"It's about control," Christian said. "It's the mantra of every totalitarian regime in history. Like I said—more for them and less for you. Control the population...make them reliant. Give them a little bit of something, provide for them, allow them to become dependent little worker bees. There's a lot of people out there who want to be told what to do. They'll do anything just to have a place to sleep and three squares a day—totally willing to give up their freedom to feel secure and taken care of."

"It's prison," Lauren offered. "People are working to be prisoners and calling it survival."

"Yes. And most are doing so willingly," Christian said. "We're talking about people who would probably even fight us if we tried to free them because they don't know how to take care of themselves on their own. I mean—can you imagine living the rest of your life in captivity for doing nothing wrong? I sure can't."

"That is so fucked up."

"I don't disagree," he said.

"What about the Police, Sheriff's Departments, and the damn military? Why aren't they doing anything?"

"Some of them did from what I gather," Christian said. "I know some officers were federalized into DHS agents and went directly to work for DHS. Others abandoned their posts to take care of their families, and most of those guys ended up being rounded up. They are now living in the camp with zero privileges. There's supposedly several citizen movements against the federal government out west that involves several companies of National Guard, Army and Marines, along with veterans, Oath Keepers and militia groups. The areas of the country that were unaffected by the EMP strikes are referred to as the *Promised Land*, or *the Redoubt*. They were letting in refugees for a while, but they had to stop because they couldn't support all of the people in need. It's rumored there's a civil war going on out there now because of it. We're so far away, it's not even worth considering or hoping for. Truth is, Lauren, we are all on our own here and could be for a long time."

Lauren closed her eyes and shook her head slowly in response to what was being said. She didn't want to believe this was really happening to her country. Once the rice and beans were ready to be eaten, Christian spooned out a portion of the food into a bowl that had been nestled inside of Lauren's cook pot. He handed her the bowl of steaming rice and beans. Lauren reached into her waist pack and pulled out the remainder of the deer jerky she had been snacking on all day and handed some to Christian. She also pulled out a titanium spork and placed it into the bowl along with the deer jerky.

"Is this what I think it is?" he asked.

"If you think it's deer jerky, then yes."

"Wow. I haven't had venison in a very long time."

"The valley we live in is full of deer. It makes up the majority of the meat we eat now," Lauren said.

Christian noticed she had mixed the jerky in with the rice and beans and did the same. He pushed his spork into the mixture and took a bite. Lauren was devouring her meal. The long day of hiking had had a profound effect on her appetite.

"Lauren, I don't want to continue being the bearer of bad news, but I have to tell you that life as you knew it, as I knew it—normal every day American life is just gone," Christian said grimly. "We aren't free anymore, and it looks like they've won. If you ever read books or saw movies about the concentration camps in Nazi Germany, that's the best visual I can offer you for the current conditions. It's authoritarian control. And it's like that in populated areas now, all over the state. Soon, it will come to the rural areas. No one is safe from it." He paused. "Every day, the camp sends out patrols that go out to an area of homes, looking for people who are holing up. If the inhabitants don't go peacefully, they are taken by force. Their homes are ransacked and anything martial law has deemed illegal is taken. If they find weapons that haven't been turned in, they take them and put the owner in solitary confinement."

"Unbelievable," Lauren said almost under her breath. "So, we really can never go back."

"It doesn't look like it," he said. "But if you could, would you?"

"That's an impossible question to answer for me," she said. "Living like this is hard, but at least we are free. I miss the world the way it was. I miss so many things about it I can't begin to think of them all. I just want to be free. I want my family to be free and I want them to leave us alone."

Christian paused. "I don't want to believe it any more than you do, but they will come for us. For you, me, and everyone you know that is living free right now. They won't allow it to happen for much longer."

"I don't want to hear that," Lauren said, "understand—my family and my neighbors mean everything to me. They are my entire world."

"You need to hear it. And you and your family and neighbors need to be ready," he said sternly.

"We don't have anywhere else to go, Christian," Lauren said. "We've moved twice already and we actually feel safe now where we are at. We have good neighbors who subsist along with us. We help each other and we watch each other's backs. There are people out there who try to take what we have, and they have yet to be successful because we stick together and fight. If that's what it takes to live in this world, then I'm all for it. But I'm not just going to bow down to what these men in black uniforms tell us we have to do. To hell with that. I'll fight them." She paused. "I would rather die than be a slave."

"I agree. I'm not interested in being told how I have to live either," Christian offered. "My problem now is…I don't have any other choice. Either I find a new way, or I'm dead. They know me and after what's happened, they will kill me if they catch me." He paused. "And I have no doubt, they will find the worst way possible to do so."

Lauren said nothing as the feeling of hopelessness overcame her. There was a pause before Christian asked, "How big is your group?" just before taking in a large bite of food.

Despite reaching a fair level of trust with him, Lauren cringed upon hearing his curiosity concerning her family. She began to think of how this encounter would end and what could happen if she brought this stranger home with her, and the possible repercussions not only from her own family, but from the community as a whole who did not take kindly to outsiders. Despite appearances, his true intentions remained hidden to her. He could easily be one of *them*. She knew that Christian could be an asset, but just as easily could be a Trojan horse for the DHS, and the next thing he infiltrated would be her community. Maybe that was his mission. Maybe it wasn't.

"Big enough," she said.

Christian paused and held a hand up in surrender. "Look, I'm not trying to join you. I just want to help if I can," Christian said slowly. "I think we can help each other."

"Joining us is impossible," Lauren said as she shook her head. "I have no idea if the community would accept you…they are leery of outsiders and the people in my group know each other and have for years. We are blood to one another. We have a trust built on longevity, something you and I do not have at the moment."

An uncomfortable silence befell the two as Lauren put her hand on the Glock handgun that had sat on the ground during the last part of the conversation. Her mind didn't know what to think or what to do, and on top of it all, she was exhausted. Christian had been through quite a lot as well in the past day. He placed both of his hands over the fire pit and shivered a bit. He wasn't dressed for the weather and wasn't wearing a jacket or even a hat.

"So, what happens now?" Christian asked as he stared into the fire with no visible emotion.

"I don't know," Lauren said. "This whole thing is a lot to take in. I don't know what to do about this or about you or about anything right now. I know that it's dark now, and my family will be worried that I'm not home with them. I shouldn't have stayed. I shouldn't have gone this far away from home. I don't know what the hell I was thinking."

Lauren reached into the top of her backpack again and pulled out a roll-top stuff sack that held her sleeping bag. She then pulled out a smaller stuff sack and tossed it to Christian. He picked it up off the ground and looked at it.

"It's my emergency bivy. It's waterproof and has a coating that reflects body heat. Get into it, it'll keep you warm," she said.

"I appreciate it," Christian said. "Guess I ran out without grabbing some gear. I was kinda in a hurry."

Lauren smiled slightly as she pulled out her down sleeping bag and slid off her hiking boots. She unzipped it and slipped herself inside of it, still leaning against the tree. She gladly welcomed the added warmth it provided and could feel it almost instantly. She reached for her rifle and laid it on the ground where her left leg rested in the sleeping bag, so she could feel it under her. Her hands went inside the bag along with her pistol, which she gripped firmly in her left hand. In a matter of minutes, she was asleep.

CHAPTER 8

"Without dignity, identity is erased. In its absence, men are defined not by themselves, but by their captors and the circumstances in which they are forced to live."

— Laura Hillenbrand

FEMA Resettlement Camp Bravo
Woodstock, Virginia
Several months earlier

FAITH SAT QUIETLY, READING HER Bible. It was all she could do to pass the time, and there was a lot of time to pass. She had lost count as to how many days she had been confined to the women's detention center, but she knew it had been a long time. She had also lost count as to how many days it had been since she had last seen her husband, Sam, who had accompanied her to the detention area of the FEMA camp long ago, only to be separated from her. She didn't like being separated from him, but had grown to accept it for what it was over time. Upon arrival to the camp and immediately following classification, he had been sent to the men's detention center, which used to a Holiday Inn Express. She was right next door, at what used to be the Hampton Inn, now repurposed as the women's detention center. Both buildings sat next to each other, but were separated by a tall razor wire fence, which also enclosed each building and kept them isolated from the surrounding grounds.

The yellow jumpsuit she wore was ragged and ugly and it made her skin itch. Even before she had come here, Faith had issues with excessively dry skin and had to ask special permission from the staff to be provided with skin lotion to help thwart her scratching. They had been surprisingly helpful to her. The room she was in had most of its amenities removed. It was relatively dark, but it was climate controlled and she was able to utilize indoor plumbing as needed, as well as a couple of the working incandescent light fixtures. She assumed there had to be an electrical generator somewhere in the camp that was providing their power, but never saw or heard one.

Despite being incarcerated, unable to move about or leave her domicile unless restrained and escorted by guards, she counted herself lucky in many ways. Being on the top floor, Faith had a window that she could use to see almost the entire camp eastward between the steel bars that secured her indoors. She used this window throughout the day to try and find people she knew, especially her Sam, but never saw him. A few months ago, they had been forcibly removed from their home by a team of DHS Security and relocated to the FEMA camp. Since they were found in possession of firearms and had a large food supply that they had not previously relinquished to DHS under the orders of martial law, they had been charged with the crimes of hoarding and possession of firearms. Hoarding had become illegal after martial law had been instituted statewide. She remembered the talks she'd had with her husband about giving up their provisions and arms and relocating willingly, but he had always been so steadfast to refuse. He was stubborn like that, possibly the most stubborn person she had ever known. She often wondered how much different her life would have been had they decided differently. Surely, it would have been better than solitary confinement.

She had been placed on the top floor which was considered a lower security area of the building, after displaying a fair amount of exceptionally good behavior, which came naturally to her. The accommodations here were an upgrade to what she'd had previously, which was little more than a room stripped of every comfort convenience up to and including the carpet. The floor was exposed concrete and the walls were bare hard plaster, which made it no more than a prison cell. Her accommodations now were, without a doubt, worlds better. It was, after all, a hotel room with a queen size bed, blankets, and pillows.

She had access to a shower that spit lukewarm water that she could use once a week at maximum. She also had her own toilet and valued that immensely. There was nothing worse than having to share a latrine with a large group of people. Her captors were strict but not unreasonable, and they had yet to harm her in any way. In light of her situation, things could always be better, but they could also be far much worse. She thanked God every day that they weren't, but she missed her husband and constantly worried about his welfare. She also thought often about her son and his family, and prayed for their safety in these strange times.

Placing a bookmark in her Bible, she set it down on the nightstand and walked to the window. Overlooking the barren trees in front of her, she could see the area outside of the detention center where the Elementary, Junior High and High Schools all sat beside each other. This was where the main residential complex of the camp existed. She could see people milling about outside on the football field, as well as on the running track that surrounded it. There were armed security guards in their signature black tactical uniforms all over the camp. There were several of them in the parking lot below her as well. All of them appeared to be carrying automatic weapons of some sort, but Faith couldn't tell what they were. They also were all wearing body armor.

The door opened suddenly behind her and a tall, red-haired woman with masculine features carrying a clipboard entered along with two other correctional officers that Faith didn't recognize. The woman was Officer Karen Mitchell, the Chief Correctional Officer of the women's detention center. Faith had been introduced to her on her upon arrival at the facility and had grown to know her to be a strict, but honest and somewhat fair person. She had even been allowed to call her by her first name, when not in the company of other guards. Officer Mitchell, or Karen, was an advocate and as well the primary reason that no one in the center had ever harmed Faith. She would never in a million years admit to favoritism, but it showed on occasion. In truth, she was not as fair to other inmates as she was to Faith, especially the new arrivals and anyone who attempted acts of disobedience. The young, the rebellious, and the new arrivals had to be indoctrinated, and Karen had no problem showing them who was boss. Faith had heard the late night muffled noises through the walls and floors that had disturbed her quite a bit, on more than one occasion. She knew that other women who were captive here were not all treated as well as she was. She thought at times, that maybe it was due to her being in her late sixties and that possibly Karen just had a soft spot for senior citizens, but wasn't sure. She took it for what it was—a blessing in an unkind world.

The two guards walked past Officer Mitchell and approached Faith with their arms crossed.

"Inmate 0710, turn around and face the wall," one of the guards said. Faith did exactly as they told her.

"Place both hands on the wall," the other said in a monotone voice.

Faith put both of her hands on the wall as one of the guards reached for her arm, and then the other, placing a set of loose-fitting handcuffs on her wrists behind her back. She could tell that the guard was being as gentle as he could be, but it still felt very uncomfortable to her.

"Good morning, Mrs. Gallo," Officer Mitchell said, lifting her clipboard up and jotting something down with her pen.

"Good morning, ma'am," Faith said to her. She nodded to the guard on each side of her and they nodded back to her in recognition. "I'm confused. Is something wrong? Is this an inspection?"

"Oh, no. We're here because you're being transferred out of the detention area today," Officer Mitchell said.

Once the guards backed away, Faith turned around and looked at her with surprise.

"Transfer? I don't understand," she said.

"We need the room," Officer Mitchell said with a smile. "We've received quite a few violators recently that have committed much more serious crimes against the state than what you're guilty of. So, we're transferring minor offenders out and moving them into the population."

Faith thought for a minute and looked around her room. This was very much unexpected and her mind suddenly filled with thoughts about what life would be like outside of these four walls that she had grown so accustomed to. She then thought about her safety and began to worry. She had been isolated from the dangers while here. Was she actually beginning to like solitary confinement in the detention center? Was this the Helsinki Syndrome she had heard about? Or was it that she had become institutionalized? She pushed the thought away.

"Are you talking about the schools?" Faith asked. "I'm being moved there?" She gestured out her window to the area she had just been observing.

"Yes."

Faith paused and looked out the window for a moment. "Is that a safe place to be for a woman such as myself?"

Officer Mitchell looked up at Faith and dropped her clipboard to her side. She looked back at the two guards standing behind her and motioned to them. "You two can wait outside, please," she said to them, "I can handle her." The guards both nodded and looked at each other, then turned and walked outside, closing the door behind them. Officer Mitchell set her clipboard on the bed and walked over to the window where Faith was now standing, and gently removed her handcuffs, placing them into her pocket. Faith looked at her appreciatively and they shared a smile.

"I thought that hoarding was a serious crime," Faith said. "Possession of a firearm—even worse. We were told when they came for us that our crimes were punishable by death."

"They are. But we make exceptions on occasion. There are crimes that are more serious—such as attacking a Federal Agent," Officer Mitchell replied, "or attacking a Federal Facility."

"Oh my—I didn't know that was happening."

"Yes. Lately, there have been quite a few attacks," Officer Mitchell explained. "We've been lucky, though. We haven't lost anyone. I've told you before it's pretty dangerous outside of the fence."

"I'm so used to it here, I'm not sure if I want to leave," Faith said with a frown.

"The decision has already been made. Don't worry, Faith," she said, "it'll be ok."

"Isn't it dangerous for older people in population?" Faith asked.

"It's not one-hundred percent safe by any means, mainly because there are so many different personalities grouped together. That's why we have security. No one will hurt you there, I promise. It's guarded twenty-four hours a day—plus, I'll look in on you from time to time," Karen said reassuringly.

"What can you do to help me there? I'll be there and you'll be here."

"I'll put a good word in for you with Security. I know a few of those guys. No one will bother you and if they do, they'll be dealt with," Officer Mitchell said.

Faith paused for a moment. "What's life like out there? I see people gathered together and walking south on occasion, but I can't see where they are going."

"In population, you live in group areas separated by gender and age for the most part, although there are some exceptions. Once there, you'll fill out a questionnaire and you'll be assigned a job based on your skills and physical condition. You work in exchange for food, room, and board. The groups you see heading south are going to either the farm or the gardens. There are two large fields on the south side of the camp where we have vegetable gardens and we also raise livestock."

"Karen, can't I just leave?" Faith asked, "If I'm technically not being held in detention any longer, can't I just go back home?"

"Unfortunately, Faith, no one can leave until we are ready to begin relocation and resettlement, and that cannot happen right now. There are too many unsecured areas outside of the camp—but we're working on it."

Faith took a seat at the foot of her bed, which she had made perfectly upon rising this morning. She had a habit of making her bed every morning, and had done so since childhood. She hardly ever allowed a wrinkle. Karen took a seat beside her and placed her hand on the back of Faith's neck.

"You'll get to wear your clothes again," she said. Faith looked up at her, astonished.

"Come again?" Faith said.

"Yep. All of your possessions that we had to take from you when you were placed in detention will be returned to you—with some exceptions. The clothes you had when you got here will be yours again."

"Wow," Faith said as she pulled on the pants leg of her jumpsuit. "That would be a Godsend." Karen smiled and patted Faith on her back. Faith continued, "I hope they still fit me."

"So, are you ready? I've got several transfers to do today and with that, quite a few new inmates I have to indoctrinate."

Faith paused. "Karen, do you have an idea where my husband is?" she asked. "I know I've asked you before and you've told me that you can't answer me—but I really need to know."

Karen stood up from the bed and walked over to the window. Turning to face Faith, she said, "Your husband is alive, Faith. He's still in detention, so that's really all I can tell you at the moment without chancing losing my job."

"At least that's something," Faith said with a sigh. "Knowing he is alive will keep me going for the time being."

Faith stood up from the bed and reached for her Bible.

"I'm taking this with me," she said as her eyes narrowed.

Karen smiled at her and picked up her clipboard.

"By all means," Karen said.

Once outside the room, the two other guards joined them and Karen led the group down the hallway to the elevator. A guard noticed that Faith's handcuffs had been removed and looked confused.

"My responsibility," Officer Mitchell said firmly. "Carry on, please."

The elevator brought them to the ground floor, they exited and walked through the lobby and to the double doors that led outside. One of the guards swiped a key fob onto a wall sensor, and the doors swung open. The four then walked outside. Faith immediately looked to the sky and smiled, feeling the sun hit her skin. It was a bit cool outside, but that didn't matter to her. The fresh air revitalized her and lifted her spirits.

As they approached a large four-seater Polaris ATV, Officer Mitchell nodded to Faith and she got into the back seat. Officer Mitchell sat beside her and both guards sat up front. Faith sat back in the seat once again and lifted both arms up, rubbing her wrists.

"Sorry about that," Karen whispered, "We had to follow protocol."

The driver started the engine and it roared to life. He backed it up out of its space, then moved forward to the end of the parking lot before turning right and reaching the gate. The driver waved to one of two armed guards on the other side of the fence, and the guard quickly unlocked and opened the gate to allow them to pass. Faith noticed a green street sign that said Motel Drive. She couldn't remember if she had seen it before. They turned right onto Warren Drive, and as they did, to her left Faith could see the remains of several old fast food restaurants out along Route 42. The buildings were beyond dilapidated, but she was able to recognize the McDonalds, the Wendy's, Pizza Hut and what was left of the old KFC. The KFC building was burned badly. As the old CVS Pharmacy with boarded windows came into view in front of them, Faith looked ahead and to her right, and noticed several residences that had been burned to the ground. She also noticed that the group of townhomes directly in front of her had a large number of ATVs and automobiles parked around the circular road that led to them.

She leaned over to Officer Mitchell and asked, "Do people still live there?" She nodded her head forward, indicating she was referring to the townhomes. Karen smiled.

"Staff residences," she uttered.

"Oh," Faith replied. She began to wonder what happened to the previous residents, but decided not to ask.

The Polaris turned right down Ox Road and the Woodstock water tower came into view, as did more residences. Faith could see two men on top of the tower walking around, and assumed they were DHS agents, helping to keep an eye on things. To her right and left were a row of several small homes, including some in a cul-de-sac.

"The higher ranking staff live in the single family homes," Karen added as she pointed. "The apartments and condos at the end of this road past the water tower are where the most of the lower ranking staff live."

"I assume you have your own home," Faith said.

"I do. I'm in one of the duplexes, just down the road from here," Karen replied.

"What about the assisted living facility?"

Karen turned to Faith and looked at her quizzically.

"Royal Harbor?"

"Yes," Faith replied.

Karen paused. "It's no longer in operation."

Not completely satisfied with the answer, but having a good idea what her response had meant and what it in turn, meant for the previous occupants, Faith turned her head and remained silent for the remainder of the trip. Something told her not to press for any more information. The Polaris took a left hand turn onto Falcon Drive and soon the high school came into view, followed by the elementary school. After passing a large parking lot to their left, which was full of old school buses that had been painted black, they took a final turn onto Susan Avenue and finally pulled into the parking lot in front of the elementary School. The sign out front that used to read "W.W. Robinson Elementary" had been replaced with a wooden sign that read, "FEMA Resettlement Camp Bravo - Senior Quarters."

"You're home," Karen said.

The four disembarked the Polaris and walked up to the front entrance of the old elementary school. Faith could immediately smell smoke in the air, but it wasn't like any other smell of smoke she had experienced before. It has a sweet smell to it, almost like smoke that came from a grill at a cookout, but not quite. Looking over the roofline of the school in front of her, she could see that something was smoldering a few hundred yards behind the building. One of the guards grabbed a fairly large duffel bag from the back of the ATV and slung it over his shoulder.

"Is something burning?" she asked. No one replied. In fact, no one even looked in her direction.

As they approached the front of the building, two members of DHS Security opened the steel doors in front of them which led to the lobby and the administration office. One was very tall and skinny, the other was a few inches shorter, but very stout and muscular. The skinny officer's name badge said Brown and the other's said Davis. The one named Brown looked at Officer Mitchell curiously. She handed him a sheet of paper from her clipboard and he took it, examining it.

"Morning, Karen. What do you got for us?" Officer Brown said.

"A transfer," Karen said.

"Oh, boy," the other Security Officer said, "from Women's Detention?"

"This is starting to become an everyday thing," Officer Brown said with a smirk.

"I'm just following orders, Mike," she said.

"Yeah, yeah," he said, switching his gaze to Faith. "Are we going to have problems out of you—" he looked at the paperwork again and continued, "—Mrs. Gallo?"

Faith shook her head and smiled. Karen held up her hand in a motion for Faith to not reply, which she didn't.

"Mike, I want you to make sure she's well taken care of. She's been no problem the whole time she's been in detention, and I don't expect that to change," Karen said assuredly. "She's not what you'd consider dangerous."

"Not dangerous? Then why were you in detention?" he asked, directing his question to Faith, still looking at her.

"Hoarding," Faith replied with a straight face and no expression. "And possession of firearms." She looked at the man and said nothing else.

Officer Brown smirked. "You had guns?"

"Yes. Quite a few of them," Faith responded.

"Ok, well—those days are over. Come on inside," Officer Brown said. "Welcome to Senior Quarters."

Officers Brown and Davis turned and walked back inside, holding the door open for Faith and Officer Mitchell to walk inside. The guard who carried the duffel bag pulled it off of his shoulder and handed it to Karen, who took it and slung it over her shoulder. Both guards from

Women's Detention remained outside, and began jawing back and forth as Karen and Faith walked inside. The doors closed behind them and they walked to the front desk where a somewhat overweight young woman, wearing the signature black DHS uniform seen all over the camp, was sitting. Her name badge said Hewlett.

"Transfer," Officer Brown said as he handed the sheet of paper Karen had given him to the woman behind the desk. The woman took it and looked it over, and then handed a clipboard to him with several sheets of paper clipped to it.

"Have her fill these out," Officer Hewlett said. "That's like the fourth one today."

Officer Brown handed the clipboard to Faith and motioned for her to take a seat in the lobby. Faith did and sat down in one of the hard plastic chairs that had most likely came from a classroom as it felt a bit too small for her.

"Mike, she has some property here," Karen said, taking the duffle bag off and handing it to him.

"We'll take care of it," he said. Looking back toward Faith, he said, "After you get this filled out, we'll take you to a private room to get changed, if you like. Then, we can take you to your new bunkroom and you can meet your roommates."

"I assume you'll want to burn that jumpsuit?" Officer Davis said sarcastically, finally speaking up. Karen gave him an evil glance and Faith looked up with a smile.

The sound of the words "bunkroom" and "roommates" made Faith shudder. She began looking through the paperwork on the clipboard as Karen began small-talking with Brown and Davis, overhearing the occasional bellow from Officer Hewlett. The first page looked similar to any document that had to be filled out when going to a doctor's office. The further she read, the more suspect it looked to her. Beyond the typical name, date of birth, previous address, known relatives, and social security number fields, were places that asked things like skills and hobbies, health considerations, and then a spot to fill in your religion and political affiliation. The thought of having to mandatorily offer this information, which used to be considered private was not an easy thing for her to swallow. This type of information, especially the latter two, she couldn't imagine would be used for anything other than to further classify and segregate her and others, and as well help identify potential troublemakers. Furthermore, she was a devout Pentecostal Christian and a Conservative Libertarian, both of which would most likely classify her as a dissident to the DHS and FEMA staff.

Casting her feelings aside, Faith decided not to jot down fabrications. She was proud of her faith in God and had been a Church-going Protestant her entire life, just like her mother before her. She had followed in the footsteps of her own father and had always voted Republican, even though she had little confidence in and detested standard politics. She filled in the religion block with "Christian" and the political block with "conservative." Neither were lies in her book. If they served to punish her in some way for her beliefs, she would simply accept the punishment. No one was going to tell her what to believe and she was used to turning the other cheek.

After completing her paperwork and turning it in to Officer Hewlett, Officer Brown did as he said and escorted her to a room near the front desk to allow her to change.

"Knock when you're done and we'll get you set up," Officer Brown said as he set the duffle bag on the floor near her. "Oh. I'm Officer Brown, by the way. Mr. talkative back there is Officer Davis."

"Thank you," Faith said gratefully "and it's a pleasure to meet you."

He smiled and nodded to her. The door shut and Faith immediately took a seat on the floor and began going through what appeared to be all of her belongings she'd had with her on the day that she and Sam had arrived at the camp, up to and including her Crocs. She picked them up and eyeballed them closely to make sure she wasn't dreaming. She then pulled out a pair of pants and a sweater and proceeded to change out of the jumpsuit that she was more than happy to get rid of.

Once finished, she zipped the duffle back up and then knocked on the door as instructed. It opened and Officer Brown peered in.

"All set?"

"Yes. I believe so," Faith replied.

"Let's go then."

Faith followed him down the hallway. As she passed what used to be classrooms, she looked into the open doors to see that they had all become bunkrooms with what appeared to be at least a dozen occupants, depending on the size of the classroom. After passing a few of the open doors, they turned right into one of the bunkrooms with a sign just outside that read 'B6'. Several of the room's occupants who were milling about, immediately looked in her direction. She noticed that there were some women who appeared in her age group, but there were a few younger women there too. The younger women seemed segregated from the older women, and she wasn't sure if it was by choice or if they had been instructed to do so.

Officer Brown walked Faith to an open bottom bunk in the rear of the room, the top bunk of which sat a younger woman who sported a haircut that was shaved on the sides and long in the back. She was a bit overweight and was smacking her gum. Faith did her best to not make eye contact with anyone in the room. She could feel their eyes on her however, and it made her very nervous.

"You'll be bunking here," Officer Brown said. "Get to know your roommates. You'll be housed together and you'll eat together every day." He pointed to a large plastic bin at the foot of the bed. "That's your footlocker. We keep them unlocked at all times and we haven't had a problem yet. Anyone caught stealing gets sent to detention."

"Ok," Faith said. "Thank you for your hospitality."

Officer Brown nodded, then turned and exited the room. Faith set her duffle bag down and then took a seat on her bed.

"Hospitality?" a young, short-haired woman who sat on the top bunk said. "Where in the fuck are you from, woman?"

Faith said nothing. She began emptying the contents of her duffle bag onto her bed and was sorting through them nervously. The woman jumped down off of the bed and knelt down beside where Faith sat. She smacked her gum even more loudly than she had been.

"I'm a lesbian," she said suddenly, as if trying to invoke a response. Faith ignored her. The woman giggled a bit, then stood up and said, "You know, if we're going to be bunkmates, you could at least introduce yourself. I'm Kat—short for Katherine."

Faith looked up at her and gave her a thin smile. Kat held out her hand for Faith to shake it, but Faith didn't.

"Pleasure to meet you, Katherine," she said. "I'm Faith."

Kat giggled as she pulled her hand back, realizing her gesture wasn't reciprocated. "Call me Kat," she said. "Everyone else does. Well, I take that back. Some people call me kitty-kat. Some people call me butch or butchie. I guess that's because I'm a lesbian."

Faith considered asking her why she had been housed with the seniors, but decided not to perpetuate the conversation. She turned away and continued going through her things. She picked up a makeup case and a smile extended across her face when she noticed it.

Kat looked her up and down. "Where'd you come from?" she asked.

"Detention," Faith asserted. "I've been in detention."

"OH, for real? For what?" Kat asked loudly.

"For a while," Faith said with her head turned.

Kat merely laughed and snorted. "You're funny, lady. I'll let you be for a little bit, I know you got shit going on." Kat then strutted away. She walked past a couple of the other women in the room and smacked a very distinguished-looking one on the butt. The lady turned to her and then turned back, with a somewhat annoyed look on her face, to continue the conversation she'd been having.

Faith sighed. This was what she was most worried about. At this point in time, being here made life in detention favorable to this. She lifted up her Bible and opened it back to where she had left off earlier this morning. Just as she began to read, she heard a familiar voice.

"Faith?" the voice said.

Faith immediately looked up to see a familiar face to match the voice. "Debbie?"

"Oh my gosh!" Debbie said as she advanced quickly to Faith. Faith put her Bible down and stood up as the two embraced. "It is so good to see you!" Debbie continued. "How have you been? How's your health? How's Sam?"

Faith pulled away from the embrace to see Debbie's immense smile. Faith was smiling too, almost ear to ear. She was elated to find someone she knew here, even more so that it had ended up being a close friend.

"I've been fine. Health's been ok. Sam is still in detention," Faith said.

Debbie pulled away as well and a sympathetic look covered her face. "What do you mean detention?" she asked.

"We were brought here by DHS," Faith said. "They kicked in our door, gave us five minutes to gather some things, and took us. They searched our house and found our guns and food, and then charged us with hoarding and firearm possession. Then, they brought us here. We've been in detention ever since. I was released today. Sammie is still there."

Debbie's look turned into sudden dismay.

"Oh, dear heart, I'm so sorry to hear that," she said. "I'm sure Sam is fine. God is taking good care of him."

"I pray that to be true," Faith said with a worried look.

"How did they treat you in detention?"

Faith went on and explained to her friend all that had happened since she had been incarcerated, including how bad the rooms were when she had first arrived and how she had been moved to much nicer accommodations due to her behavior. She told her about Officer Mitchell and how she had been exceptionally nice to her, despite the situation and the charges against her. Then, she went on to tell her about the noises she would hear at night and how it made it more than difficult for her to sleep through them. Although she had no proof of the cause of the noises, her imagination assumed the worst.

"Oh, my dear Lord," Debbie said.

"It really made me feel helpless," Faith said, "hearing that and being able to do nothing about it."

Debbie reached out and hugged Faith again.

"Well, you're here now and that is a blessing. Praise God," Debbie said.

"So, how did you get here?" Faith asked.

"Oh, Ben and I came here willingly," Debbie replied. "We were out of food and Ben was getting sick. When we came here, we found there was plenty of food and they gave Ben medicine. We've been here ever since."

"Is Ben here?" Faith asked. "In this building?"

"Oh yes. They keep the men on the A wing. We're on B wing."

"I see. Well, it's great to know you're here. Maybe you can help me get acclimated to all this," Faith said.

"It's pretty simple," Debbie began, "we get three squares a day and we work six days a week most times. It's better than starving to death. What did you put down for your skills?"

"Cooking, gardening, and sewing," Faith said. "I figured I couldn't go wrong with either of those."

"Perfect. So right after breakfast, you work until lunchtime. Then you eat and go back to work for a few hours. We get a few hours before dinner is called, so we have a bit of free time in the evenings. We're also off every Sunday and there's a church sermon in the common area."

"That is fantastic," Faith said sounding and feeling a bit more relieved. She paused for a moment, then asked, "Has anyone been allowed to leave?" Several other women in the room overheard her question and looked at her briefly.

"We keep hearing that once security is established outside the camp, we can all go home," Debbie said. "So in the meantime, we stay here where it's safe. People on the other side of the fence are dangerous--- killing each other over the last morsel of food and sip of clean water and what not. There's been rumors of an epidemic of typhoid and cholera, due to the unclean conditions out there. Trust me, it's safer for us to be here."

"Sorry, I can't see the allure," Faith said. "I'd rather be free to live my life as I please."

Debbie stepped closer to her and put her mouth to Faith's ear. "Faith, you can't say those types of things out loud. Don't let people know you feel that way. I've seen people taken from here because of the things they've said."

"Taken? What do you mean taken? Taken where?" Faith inquired with a whisper that matched Debbie's tone.

Debbie paused. She didn't know how to gently say what she needed to say. "People who are deemed to be subversive are taken and interrogated," she said. "And as much as it pains me to say this, there have been rumors of worse things."

"Such as?"

"There have been—executions," Debbie said quietly.

CHAPTER 9

"You must not lose faith in humanity. Humanity is like an ocean; if a few drops of the ocean are dirty, the ocean does not become dirty."
— Mahatma Gandhi

Tuscarora Trail
George Washington National Forest
Shenandoah County Virginia
Present day

LAUREN COULD FEEL SOMEONE SHAKING her. She could see nothing but blackness all around her. Nothing was visible to her and she could almost hear a voice calling her name. It sounded extremely subdued and was at times even completely inaudible. It came and went and then suddenly got louder. The fog in her head slowly lifted. Lauren opened her eyes and saw a bearded man with his hands on her shoulders, shaking her. She realized in her grogginess that she had just woken up, although she had no recollection of falling asleep. The man's voice was detectable now, and she kept hearing him saying her name and telling her to wake up. Lauren took a deep breath and pulled her left hand out of her sleeping bag, which was still grasping her Glock handgun. She placed the muzzle directly on the man's chin, pushing it into his lower jaw. The man immediately stopped shaking her and pulled his hands back and into the air, backing away. Lauren began to hear dogs barking in the distance.

"Easy—easy there," Christian said in a long, drawn-out tone. "It's me. It's Christian."

"What? What in the hell are you doing?" Lauren requested in a whisper, sounding more than very annoyed with him. She was noticing that the darkness around her was gone and the sky was starting to show signs that it was morning.

"Do you hear that?" Christian said urgently. "They're coming. We have to go. We have to go right now!"

"Oh shit—you've got to be kidding me," Lauren said as she turned her head from one side to the next, still hearing the dogs barking in the distance. Panic began to overtake her. She pulled her gun away from Christian's chin and he put his hands down and stood up. Lauren unzipped her sleeping bag. She placed her feet into her boots and laced them quickly. Standing up, she began stuffing her sleeping bag into the stuff sack, immediately noticing her rifle on the ground and remembering why she had put it there. She opened the top of her pack and shoved the stuff sack into it, seeing that her cook set and other items used for dinner last night had already been placed into it. Looking over to where the campfire had been, she saw that it had been filled in with dirt. She looked at Christian as she began cinching down her pack. "You've been busy," she said.

"For about the past ten minutes," he said. "As soon as I heard those dogs."

"How far away do you think they are?" Lauren queried as she busily began squaring herself away.

"I think they just cleared the hill to the east," Christian said.

Lauren shouldered her backpack and snapped it into place. She put on her waist pack and slid the Glock pistol into the concealment sleeve. She then reached down and picked up her rifle, slinging it over her head.

"Do you need me to help carry anything?" Christian asked.

Lauren looked down at his freshly bandaged calf and shook her head. "You're probably going to have a hard enough time dealing with that leg," she said.

"I'll manage," Christian began. "In spite of my pretty-boy appearance, I'm a pretty tough guy."

"That's good. Because we have a bitch of a trip to make up this hill." Lauren nodded to the west.

Christian looked at her in surprise. "I thought you said I couldn't go with you—"

"It's not my first choice—but do you see any other option right now? I can't just leave you behind."

Holding back a smile, Christian nodded humbly and said, "Guess I'm following you then."

Lauren led him out of the campsite and up toward the old forestry road that led along the banks of Cedar Creek. There was just enough daylight to lead their way and Lauren was more than comfortable with it, having hiked in early morning light numerous times. As they walked, she turned to watch Christian who was limping a bit, obviously in a bit of pain, but he didn't complain. As they approached the intersection where the Tuscarora Trail left the road and ascended, she turned around once again to see a confounded look on Christian's face. She stopped and turned to face him.

"What? What is it?"

"I don't know. I'm thinking that following this trail is a bad idea," he said.

Lauren sighed. "Why's that? This is the way back."

"That's what I'm worried about. I have a feeling they'd go this way even if they didn't have dogs, which they do have, by the way."

"Why?" Lauren asked.

"It's what I would do."

Lauren shrugged and sighed. "What do you suggest then?"

Christian looked down the road in both directions and thought for a moment.

"We need a detour," he said. "And some countermeasures to confuse the dogs. I guarantee that the handlers are using my scent to track us."

"What about the creek? Can't we just walk in the water for a while and then hike out?"

Christian shook his head. "That's a common misconception. The water will drip off of you and leave your scent all over the woods, and as it evaporates, it'll end up in the air as well."

Lauren stood still and thought for a minute, trying to come up with another option. "We can take this road just a bit north," she said, pointing to their right. "There's another forestry road that heads up the mountain a way. A trail on the left hand side leaves the road and leads through a hollow, rejoining this trail just south of the ridge. As far as losing the dogs, I'm not sure what you have in mind, but I'm all ears."

Christian pulled out the emergency bivy, that Lauren had given him the night before, from his pocket. He began ripping it into several large pieces as

Lauren watched him, giving him a strange look. Walking up the Tuscarora Trail, he tossed some of the pieces into the mountain laurel surrounding the trail. He then took a few pieces and rubbed them onto the trail. He picked up a couple rocks, wrapping them with pieces of the bivy, and tossed them as far as he could up the trail. "Let's go," Christian said taking the lead. "We can figure it out on the way. Do you have any Vaseline or mineral oil in your pack?

"No, why?"

"Dogs track you by following the scent of dead skin cells that your body is constantly shedding. Dandruff counts, too. It's believed that if you coat your skin with Vaseline, or something similar with a neutral scent, that it'll help you not to shed so much."

Listening as he spoke and understanding slowly that he seemed to know a bit about evasion, Lauren followed him down the forest road until they found the intersection with the road that she had mentioned to him. They turned left and began hiking up the road, soon crossing a steel forest service gate.

As they trudged uphill, Christian began, "It's much easier to evade the dog handler than it is the dog." He paused a moment to catch his breath, but kept pace with Lauren. "Every dog needs a handler who is capable of tracking and working the dog. But not all handlers are in the best of shape. They get tired just like we do."

"I'm listening," Lauren said as the road began to moderately ascend.

"The best strategy against them is distance. Since I'm not sure how much of that we have, we may need to find a way to confuse the dogs. Sending my scent up the trail back there is a start. Plus, once at our campsite, they'll spend a bit of time trying to figure out how long it's been since we left. Doubling back is out of the question—we're fighting an uphill battle and that's one we'll lose if we get too winded. Do you have any pepper spray by chance?"

Lauren thought for a moment and then answered, "I have bear spray."

"Perfect. We can spray that on the road every so often. The strength of bear spray will more than likely damage the dog's olfactory nerve. They'll have a hard time catching our scent again, if ever. Problem is, that's also a marker. If the handler sees that his dog is injured, he'll know we did it on purpose and with that, he'll know which route we took. You said the trail breaks off the road up here—does the road continue on?"

"Yes, for a mile or so—in the other direction," Lauren said.

"Let's hope they go a different way than we go, then."

"If they don't, we're screwed, aren't we?" Lauren blurted out, sounding frustrated.

"We just need to keep moving. Try to keep a better pace and get as much distance from them as we can. You said the trail rejoins the other one eventually. Worst case scenario—and I do mean worst case, we ambush them. You have guns. We can try to fight them off," Christian added.

Lauren thought about that for a moment and began mentally inventorying her ammunition supply. She then started to imagine what a firefight in the middle of the woods would look and sound like. Scenes from movies began popping up in her mind. She started to feel afraid. She felt like she had when her dad had to shoot two thugs in the National Park. "We don't know how many there are, Christian," she said solemnly, "and you know as well as I do, that they'll have guns, too. Big ones."

"You know these woods," he said. "It's your territory. We'd be above them and we'd have the advantage of high ground. We're also moving downwind which means they won't be able to pick up our scent in the air."

They continued up the road for a while before taking their first break. Lauren could easily tell that Christian was in relatively good shape. It seemed, at least for the moment, that the only thing truly holding him back was his injury. She was certain that without his gunshot wound, Christian would be able to keep a pace that she wouldn't be able to maintain. Then she smiled inside, remembering that she was carrying a forty-pound backpack, along with a rifle. She could still hear dogs in the distance, but they didn't sound any closer than they'd been earlier.

Still breathing deeply and sweating quite a bit, in spite of the cool morning air, Christian said, "If we get away from these people, I'm going to be a very happy guy."

Lauren smiled. "If you get me away from these people, so will I," she replied quickly almost not noticing her word fumble. "Well—happy girl, that is. This trail is about a mile longer than the other one and it's not very steep. We should be able to maintain a good pace."

"Fantastic," Christian said.

The two paced up the road for quite a while in silence. Lauren had pulled the bear spray from her pack and given it to Christian, who every so often would spray it across their path. They continued trudging along until the road began to level off and a trail appeared, veering into the woods to their left beside a small stream. The stream ran underneath the forest road through a culvert and a small dilapidated wooden sign that read 'Sulphur Springs Gap Trail' stood at the intersection. Lauren stopped and pointed to the trail as Christian stopped beside her.

"That's it. It'll take us up and through the gap and then to the ridge," she said, breathing heavily. "It's just over three miles."

"Are there any vantage points along the trail?" Christian asked still trying to catch his breath, "anywhere we can get a view of the group tracking us?"

"A couple, I think," she replied. "But it's been awhile since I've hiked this trail. I honestly can't remember."

"Ok," Christian said. "We'll play it by ear, then."

Lauren and Christian continued onto the trail, which ran alongside a small stream. Occasionally, Christian would stop to get a handful of water from the stream and splash it on his face. Lauren just kept moving when he did so. Christian, for some reason didn't appear to be bothered by the chilly air, in spite of the lack of outerwear he had on. Lauren was constantly maintaining her body heat by zipping and unzipping her jacket as she hiked on, like she always did during her hikes in cooler weather.

"I can't believe that you're not cold," she said as she huffed and puffed. "That water has to be frigid."

"I don't have time to be cold," Christian said, "I'll be cold once we get to where we're going."

"If we make it," Lauren added, not sounding convinced.

"We'll make it, I promise you," Christian said reassuringly.

Just as Lauren had described, the trail continued up and through a very narrow gap in the mountain and started moving away from the stream that it ran alongside. Lauren leaned up against a tree as the two, once again, took a break. She pulled a Nalgene bottle from a side pocket on her pack and handed it to Christian, who took it willingly.

"Thought you'd never ask," he said, trying to catch his breath. He opened the bottle and began gulping the liquid down. Lauren reached for the hose of her hydration bladder and stuck it in her mouth, sucking a large gulp of water down.

"Sorry about that," she said. "I'm used to hiking alone. My social skills need work."

Christian nodded in between gulps. He finished drinking and screwed the top back on the bottle, handing it back to Lauren. She took it and shoved it back into the side pocket of her pack. A moment of silence followed, as both listened for the barking dogs they had been hearing earlier, although nothing was heard.

"Can't hear the dogs anymore—but I'm not sure if that's a good thing or a bad thing," Christian said.

"Yeah," Lauren said as she spit the hydration hose from her mouth. "It's only about a mile to the intersection back to the Tuscarora. Let's go."

Christian nodded and followed her once again up the trail. It began steeply but once again leveled off, and they were able to cover the distance in a short amount of time. At about one hundred yards from the trail intersection, Christian looked to the left and noticed a rock outcropping surrounded by trees. When he stopped to take a look, Lauren noticed and turned to him.

"This might be the vantage point that we're looking for," he said as he began walking through the trees and mountain laurel toward the rocks.

"What?" Lauren asked rhetorically. "We haven't heard dogs in a long time—you don't think we've lost them?"

"Hell no, we haven't lost them," Christian affirmed. "And we're not going to. They're coming for me. They're not going to stop until they find me. If they find me, they find you."

"Shouldn't we continue on then?" Lauren asked.

"They'll just follow us and eventually end up where we end up," Christian said. "This has to end here."

Lauren sighed loudly and adjusted the pack on her sore shoulders. She was becoming irritated, but was also feeling very vulnerable at the moment, and she didn't like it. It was apparent to her that Christian had known the outcome of their predicament before they'd begun their trek. If that was the case, he had planned this whole thing out, up to and including an ambush and he hadn't let on to her his ultimate plan, other than it being a possibility. The contingency plan was appearing as the only plan, and she was beginning to feel a sensation of false hope.

"Christian, if you have a plan, I wish you would just fucking tell me already," she said, her irritation showing.

He looked back at her. Just as their eyes met, the sound of the dogs barking that they hadn't heard in a while became audible again, this time sounding closer to them than it had ever been. The proximity of the sounds got their attention almost as much as would a sudden gunshot. Lauren froze and her face turned pale. Very quickly, becoming increasingly uncomfortable with the situation, she turned away and began heading up the trail in haste. As she did, her foot became anchored under a tree root. She tripped and fell, her right hand and the rifle that hung in front of her, the only thing breaking her fall. She landed hard onto the cold ground with a grunt, her head hitting the dirt. Then, a sudden pain registered in her brain. It was a pain she had felt before and was all too familiar to her. She knew at that moment that she had sprained her ankle. She rolled over, tangled in her own gear and grabbed her foot.

"Son of a bitch!" she exclaimed under her breath, the anger in her voice only quelled by the pain.

Christian ran to her and tried to help her up. Lauren responded by pushing him away. She grimaced as she held her injured ankle in her hands.

"Are you ok?" he asked as he looked her over.

"No, dammit," she barked. "I sprained my fucking ankle!"

"Let me see it," Christian said, trying to offer some sort of help. She only pushed him away again.

"NO! It's sprained. I know what a sprained ankle feels like."

Christian gazed at her, feeling bad for what happened, but turned to look up to the rock every time he heard a dog bark or a spoken word, echoing from the men on the trail below. He was torn between trying to help a fallen friend and doing what was necessary to stop the enemies who were following them. At this point, he only knew one way out of this and therefore, there was only one thing left to do. He had no idea how Lauren would respond to what he intended to say to her, but he felt at this point; especially now, it didn't matter. Both of their lives depended on it. She was just going to have to understand. There were only minutes separating them from being discovered by their pursuers.

"Give me your rifle," he said as he stared into her hazel eyes.

Lauren's eyes met his. At first, her expression was of disbelief and quickly turned to anger. Then, it changed to outrage. *No fucking way*, she thought. Then she said it aloud, giving Christian a look that made him second guess his decision to say what he had just said to her. If looks could kill, he would've been dead two times over. He pushed away the thoughts and considered just taking it from her, which he was more than certain that he could do. He could just overpower her and do what was needed, and then they could move on. He then thought to himself that doing so, would most likely end with her Glock in his face, and a bullet in his brain. He decided that he wasn't above begging.

"Lauren, please, just give it to me," he said. "I know you don't trust me, but that's not important right now. If you don't let me do this, we will both die today. I promise you that."

"I'm not giving you my gun," she said as she looked back down at her injury and cursed profusely under her breath.

Christian took both of his hands and placed them on Lauren's cold, red cheeks. She became immediately furious and began to fight him, but the fight in her subsided quickly. The feeling of hopelessness that she had been holding back overcame her, and she let go. A tear rolled down her cheek, and Christian gently removed his hands from her face. She had become vulnerable again. She had hardened herself as best she could in the absence of her father, but this situation was nearing too much for her to bear. She needed someone to protect her. Trying to pretend she didn't was a losing battle for her.

"I will get you home," he said in a grave tone. "I promise you, I will get you back to your family, Lauren. But I can't do it without a gun. I can end this now, for both of us—I just need your rifle."

Lauren looked up at Christian and another feeling began to manifest inside of her that she couldn't help—one of faith. She felt as if she had no choice, other than to believe in this man whom she had just met only yesterday. She hadn't even known him a full day yet, and he had somehow managed to gain her trust. This wasn't supposed to happen. She was as vulnerable now as she had been when she was much younger. Her father had always had her back, but he wasn't here right now. All she had was herself, and the man kneeling in front of her. This new faith that she was feeling had to be tested. She reached down and unsnapped the quick-disconnect, separating her rifle from its sling. She then, slowly handed it to Christian. In that moment, she somewhat expected him to turn it on her. As she began to accept her possible fate, she noticed that it didn't happen. Instead, Christian pulled back on the charging handle to expose the reflection of brass in the chamber, indicating a loaded weapon, and verified the safety.

"Do you take care of this rifle?" he asked as he looked it over closely. "Do you keep it clean?"

"Yes," Lauren replied.

"When was the last time you fired it?

"A week or so ago. My neighbor has a range in his backyard that we train on," she replied again.

"What distance is this scope sighted in at?"

"One hundred yards," Lauren replied, "it's dead on at that range."

"Extra magazines?" Christian pondered yet again, his questions becoming nearly consecutive.

Lauren pulled off her waist pack and handed it to him. "There's two in there," she said, "and four more in my pack."

Christian removed the magazines from the waist pack and handed it back to Lauren. He then motioned for her to remove her backpack. She unsnapped it and laid it beside her, opening it up and reaching for the AR magazines that she kept inside it. Handing them to him, he placed all of the extra magazines in the cargo pockets in his ACUs. Lauren took off her rifle sling and set it aside. Christian helped her to her feet, placing Lauren's right arm around his neck and the two began walking to the rocks.

"Take out your pistol and get all of the spare mags that you have ready," he said. "This could end quickly or end up being a firefight. If they get past me, unload on them. Make every shot count, but be ready to empty all your magazines at them. I assume you can shoot..."

"Yes, I can shoot. What are you going to do?" Lauren asked as she began to see Christian for who he really was. He wasn't the enemy at all. His true intentions were revealing themselves to her, and it appeared that this man truly intended to protect her. He was going to help her get back home. She had placed her trust in him and given him a chance and was being rewarded for it, even though she had done so unwillingly. In this new world that they both lived in, this was truly a remarkable thing.

"I'm going to rain on their parade," he said. "Keep your head low."

Christian smiled as he took off with Lauren's M&P 15 and began climbing to the top of the rock outcropping. He nested in between two large sandstone boulders and lined the rifle up toward the noises he'd been hearing down the trail. It was as good a place as any to find some sort of ballistic cover. Lauren pulled the Glock from her waist pack, along with the two spare fifteen round magazines. She dropped the waist pack to the ground and pushed the spare magazines into her right jacket pocket. She then limped over to a rocky spot below him where she could not be seen, making sure not to put too much weight on her injured ankle. She lined her weapon up with the black uniform clad group, but they were still too far away for her to get a good sight picture. At this distance, her rifle was indeed, the only practical method of ending this conflict.

Christian placed the scope to his eye and brought the group of men on the trail below them into view. There were five of them total and as well two dogs, both German Shepherds. Two of the men were dog handlers and it appeared that they were each only carrying a sidearm. The other three were agents he recognized from the FEMA camp, and they each had a suppressed M4 rifle, a sidearm, and small backpack. They were also wearing chest rigs with several extra rifle magazines in pouches. As the men stopped to take a look around, Christian lined the crosshairs of the scope up with the lead agent, snapped off the safety and fired, immediately scoring a head shot. Skull fragments and tissue exploded as the bullet tore through his skull, and splattered onto the other two agents, who stood in close proximity. The agents were all stunned, but immediately raised their rifles as the dead agent's body fell to the ground. Christian lined the crosshairs again and fired two more shots back to back, dropping the second agent immediately as a burst of pink mist from the back of his head erupted. As the dog handlers turned to run away with their barking K9s in tow, the third agent began firing suppressed shots wildly into the woods in all directions, appearing to not know where the gunfire that had killed his two fellow agents was coming from. Just as the second body hit the ground, Christian fired a three-round burst that killed the last standing agent instantly. The agent's rifle fired a single shot as he went down backwards into the dirt and rolled down the steep embankment behind him. As the dog handlers struggled to control their flustered K9s in the chaos, Christian ended their lives, too. The dogs immediately began to whine and bark at their now dead handlers, who were laying in a lifeless heap almost on top of one another. The dogs sniffed around them and then took off running back down the trail, their leashes dragging behind them, occasionally getting caught on a root or some mountain laurel. Christian had hoped for this, as he had no intention of shooting the dogs.

Lauren didn't know what to think or what to say. Her mind was racing and her heart was pounding nearly out of her chest. She had seen men die from gunshot wounds before and had even killed before, but she had never seen anything quite like this. This was an ambush set up on the fly by the underdogs, and she was on the team who'd won. She gulped loudly as she could start to feel her adrenaline rush begin to lessen in intensity.

Christian hobbled down from his perch, being very careful to tread lightly on his injured leg. He walked over to Lauren who turned to him, her face white and expressionless. He pressed the magazine release on Lauren's rifle and pulled out the half-empty mag, then replaced it with a full one from his hip pocket.

"You ok?" Christian asked.

"Yeah," Lauren said with a blank stare, "I'm good, I guess. Just not used to seeing men die like that."

"I completely understand," he confirmed.

"I guess I should start getting used to it," Lauren uttered grimly.

"Don't lie to yourself. There's no getting used to it. I'm going to go down here and make sure these guys aren't moving," he said. Without waiting for Lauren to respond, he darted around the rocks and down the trail, surprisingly spry for having a hole in his calf.

As Christian approached the scene, he kept the rifle at low-ready and surveyed the area closely, looking for any signs of a reaction force. Even though the agent's shots had been suppressed, he knew that the ones he had fired from Lauren's rifle were not and therefore, could be heard for some distance. After a minute of looking around, he finally approached the first agent he had shot. Half of the man's head was missing. Christian placed Lauren's rifle on the ground and unsnapped the agent's rifle from its sling. It was a Larue suppressed M4 with a ten-and-a-half-inch barrel. He lifted it up to check the EOTech optic and magnifier and was pleased upon finding that they hadn't been damaged. When he saw that the selector switch had an "auto" setting, he grinned. He removed the sling from around the agent's neck and placed it over his own head. He then turned the body over and pulled off the agent's backpack by unsnapping the quick disconnects from the shoulder straps. Going through the backpack, he noticed that it was full of the same typical items that he would have packed on one of his own patrols, outside the confines of the FEMA camp. There was a Camelback hydration bladder full of water, several MREs, and other assorted comfort and survival gear. He removed the agent's belt accessories which included several pairs of zip-cuffs, a Spyderco folding knife, and an individual first-aid kit or IFAK, and placed them all in the backpack. He removed the agent's sidearm, a

Glock 19 9mm, as well as extra mag pouch which held two magazines, and snapped them both to his belt. Setting the backpack down, he then began removing the agent's chest rig, which had the spare M4 magazines attached to it. As he was doing so, he immediately felt the added weight of the rig which signified that it was indeed a plate carrier that held four plates of body armor. This made him grin as well. After removing the plate carrier, he slid it over his head and wrapped it around his body, securing it with the Velcro attachments. He attached the suppressed rifle to the sling around his neck and slung it behind his back. Picking up the backpack and Lauren's AR, he then walked over to the second agent he had shot and began going through his things in the same fashion.

Lauren watched Christian from above and noticed him going through the agent's belongings, but couldn't see anything in detail. She decided that it was time to do some work on her newly sprained ankle. Pulling out her wilderness first aid kit from her backpack, she removed the one-inch athletic tape and began tearing off strips in different lengths and sticking them to her jacket. She then removed her boot and both of her sock layers and could immediately see the swelling. She sighed and began placing the strips of tape on her foot, calf, and ankle until it was supported as best as she knew how. She then placed her liner sock on, an Ininji toe sock that her father had insisted she wear under thin hiking socks to prevent blisters. His insistence had paid off for her many times. She couldn't help but smile a bit, remembering how adamant he had been about it. She then put on her wool outer sock and slid her boot over her foot, remembering to loosen the laces around her swollen ankle.

Christian stood up after removing all of the second agent's belongings and placing them in his backpack. He immediately could feel that it had gotten much heavier, mostly due to the agent's body armor that he had stuffed into the pack, along with the other items. He was now carrying three rifles, after taking the second agent's suppressed M4 and slinging it over his shoulder. He looked down the embankment where the third agent had fallen after he had shot him. Not wanting to carry all of the gear with him to check on the third again, he removed everything and laid it all in a pile with the exception of the body armor, which he chose to keep on. Using trees to support himself, he reached the third agent. He reached for the agent's rifle and broke it open, separating the upper from the lower. Pulling out the bolt carrier group, Christian removed the firing pin and put it in his pocket, then reassembled the rifle, rendering it unfirable. Using an armorer's tool that he'd found in the second agent's backpack, he began working to remove the suppressor from the barrel. After a bit of effort, he unthreaded it and put it in his pocket. He could feel that it was still warm from the panic firing the agent had done before he'd died. He laid the rifle down beside the agent's body and tossed some leaves over it. He then removed all of the spare magazines and tossed them, one at a time, up the hill to where his pile of gear was.

Reaching into the agent's backpack, he dug around and pulled out a small nylon pack that felt very heavy. When he unsnapped and opened it, he smiled broadly.

"Oh, this is beautiful," he said to himself. "Beautiful."

Inside the pack were six hand grenades. He tossed the pack up to his pile of gear and spent a few more minutes digging around in the agent's backpack, before climbing back up the embankment.

Now on her feet, Lauren began to walk around on the trail, feeling out her ankle and the tape job she had completed. She could immediately tell that she couldn't put as much weight on it as usual, but this was to be expected. As she limped around, she began to think deeply about how much of a delay this would place on her getting home and with that, worry began to set in. She had already spent one unplanned night away from home and her family. She knew that they would already be worried, and if she had to spend another night away, they would most certainly come to look for her. She hated to admit it to herself, but that was undoubtedly exactly what was going to happen. She was about ten miles from home, on some very uneven and rocky trail. She could maybe make it half of that distance in her condition. She wondered about Christian and his injury, but after seeing how well he had moved on the trail this morning, she pushed the thought away. It was obvious to her that he either had a high tolerance for pain or he had decided that his injury wasn't going to get the best of him.

After a few minutes of pondering, Christian emerged around the rock outcropping that had provided them cover near the trail intersection. She noticed he had procured quite a bit of extra gear and with that, had two new black rifles hanging on him and a sidearm on his right side. He looked at her with an eerie grin. Lauren couldn't help herself and had to comment.

"Rambo, I presume?" she quipped.

"Not quite…but pretty damn close," Christian responded. "I got us some stuff."

He began laying the items on the ground in between them. He then handed Lauren back her rifle and her spare magazines. She took it from him, looking it over closely. Placing the magazines back into her backpack and waist pack, she then looked back at him and eyeballed his new outfit. Christian had taken one of the agent's field jackets, in addition to the body armor. Lauren noticed he had removed the DHS patches from it, like he had done with his uniform the previous night.

"Nice, digs," she said. "I take it, they're all dead?"

"Indeed," he said, "and since that's the case, I figured they wouldn't need any of this stuff."

"Glad to see you have a jacket now," she said, "but you could've used a hat, too."

Christian beamed at her sarcastically with a smirk. "I thought about that," he said, "for a second, until I remembered that I shot them all in the head."

"OH," Lauren said. She then smiled a bit, before the mental picture of what a hat would look like after the fact came to her. Her smile dissipated. "Gross."

Christian pulled out the other body armor vest he had taken from the second agent from his pack and went to hand it to Lauren. She looked at it quizzically. "Here. Put it on. If we're attacked, it will stop a rifle bullet," he said.

Lauren held up her hand at first and then went to take the vest, immediately noticing its weight. She cocked her head and raised her eyebrows. "You do remember that I just sprained my ankle, right?"

"Oh, shit—that's right," Christian said.

"Yeah. I don't think this is going to happen, as much as I would really like to stop a bullet with my body and all," Lauren poked.

Christian smiled and placed the armor back into his backpack. "Well, we'll keep it, in case we end up needing it," he said.

"Are those silencers?" Lauren asked, pointing to the two Larue M4s Christian had laid beside his pack.

"They are," he replied. "And both rifles are full-auto. True government issue."

"I've never even seen a suppressed rifle in person before," Lauren said. "Never fired a full-auto one, either."

"I may suggest that you take one of these," Christian said. "They are much quieter than yours, and full-auto may come in handy."

Lauren thought a moment and then looked at her rifle. It had belonged to her father before it had become hers. There was no way that she was going to replace it. It may be loud and it may not be a machine gun, but it had quite a lot of sentimental value to her. In fact, anything that was once her dad's had tremendous sentimental value to her. "I'll hang on to mine for now," she said. "Thanks, though."

"It's cool. It'll be here if you need it," Christian affirmed. "I did snag an extra suppressor, so let me know if you want it." Changing the subject, he said, "How bad is your ankle, by the way?"

"It's not the worst I've done to it, but it's definitely swollen," Lauren said. "I've got it wrapped in athletic tape so for now, it should be ok. I just can't put a lot of weight on it. It's going to take us a longer to get back now, though."

"We can take our time, Lauren," Christian said. "I'm in no hurry to get anywhere, and rushing will only increase the chance worsening our injuries."

"I'm glad you feel that way because we've got quite a trip," she said. "There is a locked cabin that was once owned by the trail club that maintained these trails before the collapse about half way back. That may be our destination tonight, if nothing else. It's made out of stone and the door is really thick wood, so it should provide us some protection."

"How do we get into it if it's locked?" Christian asked.

Lauren just looked at him with a smirk and said, "After what we've just been through, I think that's a minor issue. Besides, you've proven to be pretty handy so far today. I'm sure we'll figure out something."

After donning their gear, the two continued straight onto the Tuscarora Trail, this time, at a much slower pace. Lauren's sprained ankle was definitely taking a toll on the speed at which she could walk. Christian's wound wasn't helping him much either, especially now that he had taken on the added weight of the gear and rifles, and ammo he had acquired from the agents. The two took breaks often as the trail ascended gradually to the top of Little Sluice Mountain. Once there, they took a much longer break. Lauren needed to check on her ankle wrap; it felt like it was getting loose. Christian decided it would be a good time to put a fresh dressing on his calf. Now equipped with an IFAK, he had everything he needed to stay on top of it—minus antibiotics, if it got infected. Lauren re-wrapped her ankle and watched Christian as he navigated the military-style first aid kit, as if he knew exactly what everything was and what to do with it.

"Christian," she uttered.

"Yeah?"

"Thank you…for saving my life," she said with a modest tone.

Christian looked up at her for a second and smiled, then went back to re-dressing his wound. "You would've done the same for me, I'm sure," he said somewhat sarcastically, but with a tone that was still believable.

"That's just it," Lauren said, "I wouldn't have. That's why I feel it's more than necessary to tell you that I appreciate it."

"Why do you feel like you have to be such a hard-ass?" Christian asked. "I kinda like the humble Lauren."

Lauren leaned back onto her pack, brought her knees to her chest and didn't respond immediately. Christian occasionally looked up at her for a second at a time, as he was finishing his work. "It's completely involuntary. This is just who I am."

"So, you're telling me that none of what I've seen so far is a façade?" Christian asked.

"That's what I'm telling you," Lauren explained. "My dad taught me to be who I am. He always told me to be strong, even when I wanted to feel weak and to never give up, no matter what the odds were."

"Sounds familiar," Christian added.

Lauren smiled. "He used to tell me that I didn't need the world's approval. He always encouraged me to be myself—to not just blindly follow the so-called 'rules'. He was right about that and a lot of other things."

"And with him not here, you feel you need to honor him by adhering to what he's taught you."

Lauren nodded and said, "Yes. That's it exactly."

Christian repacked the IFAK and attached it to his vest. He didn't say much after Lauren's response and a peculiar look had swept over his face, as if something he hadn't thought about in a while suddenly entered his mind.

"Everything ok?" Lauren inquired. "Did I say something wrong?"

"No. You didn't say anything wrong," Christian responded almost immediately. "I don't blame you for wanting to honor your father. Lord knows, I try to do the same."

"I'm not sure I'm following," Lauren said. "Where's your dad now?"

Christian picked up a small rock. He looked it over and then tossed it at a tree. His expression turned into a combination of disgust and anger. "He's dead," Christian said abruptly.

Lauren was taken aback. She was not expecting this answer. The way that Christian had spoken of his father the day before had given no indication of this. "But, I thought he was the Sheriff. That's what you told me—"

"*Was* the Sheriff," Christian said. "Past tense."

Christian stood up and began picking up his gear without a word. Lauren did the same, as she didn't have anything to say to his response. Once they had donned their packs, Christian took the lead and Lauren followed up along the trail. Now that they had reached the ridge, the trail had flattened out and it was much easier to traverse. Lauren still took care not to worsen her injury. Christian's pace was easy to maintain for her. The two said nothing for the next half-mile or so. Lauren watched his limp and knew that she herself was limping. She smiled at the thought of what they two would look like, from another person's point of view. Two hikers with heavy backpacks, who were carrying guns and limping their way down the trail. She imagined it was quite a scene.

Christian stopped and placed the water hose from his backpack to his lips, taking a drink. He turned to look at Lauren who decided to do the same. "So, you know exactly where we are right now?" he asked.

"Yep," Lauren began, in between sips. "Just ahead is a side trail to the left that takes you over to White Rock Cliff. That's where I saw the smoke yesterday, which was the reason I decided to investigate."

"And how far are we from our destination?" he asked again.

"Four or so more miles until we get to Sugar Knob Cabin. Another six or so to get back home after that," she replied. "I think we're moving at about a half-mile an hour. We've got a steep ascent up to the next mountain that will slow us down considerably. Getting home is probably going to be out of the question today."

"Understood," Christian said. "Is not getting back today a bad thing?"

"Yes and no," Lauren began. "It's bad because I know they'll be worried and probably be looking for me. Good because it'll give me some time to decide how I'm going to explain everything to them."

Christian laughed. "You mean explain *me* to them."

"Yes, there's that. I think they will understand. I'm really hoping John will."

"John?" Christian pondered.

"My boyfriend," Lauren added.

Christian nodded. He was a bit surprised, as this was the first time she had mentioned anyone's name to him since they had met. Other than the mention of her grandparents' last name, she had been omitting quite a bit of personal information from him to protect herself and the people she cared about; and he didn't blame her. Deciding not to bring that fact up to her, he pushed the thought away. They both started walking again and it wasn't long before they reached the overgrown side trail to their left that led to White Rock Cliff. Christian stopped and looked up the trail. He noticed how treacherous it was and sighed loudly.

"Must be a tremendous view," Christian said. "If both of us weren't limping like a couple of geriatrics, it would be a nice spot for lunch."

"It'll be rice and beans again," Lauren said jokingly, trying to lighten the mood. Christian turned to face her.

"On the contrary, DHS was kind enough to provide me with some MREs," Christian joked back, "and I'm dying to lighten this backpack."

"Two MREs weigh at least a couple pounds, right?" Lauren poked.

"They feel like twenty pounds on the way out…"

Lauren squinted and pursed her lips, giving him a cross look. "Jeez, Christian. That is so gross," she said.

CHAPTER 10

"Coming together is a beginning; keeping together is progress; working together is success"

— Henry Ford

St James Church
Trout Run Valley
Hardy County West Virginia
Present day

ST. JAMES BAPTIST CHURCH WAS founded in the early 1800s and remained a local village staple ever since. It had seen many generations of parishioners over the years, mostly from the Rockland and Perry communities in Trout Run Valley, some of whom had been buried in the adjacent cemetery. In current times, the church served not only as a place of worship for all denominations, but as a common meeting place for the inhabitants of the valley. Like most churches constructed in those times, it had a thick stone foundation, stone steps that led to an entrance with large wooden double doors, and a steeple, complete with a church bell that would ring every Sunday morning to signify that a service was occurring. At full capacity, it could hold a congregation of about fifty. Michelle always thought it reminded her of the church from *Little House on the Prairie*. Norman concurred with her on this, although he pointed out that the church in *Little House* doubled as a schoolhouse and this one did not. Just about every Sunday, while walking to the church for the meetings and sometimes before the preceding sermon, which came earlier in the morning, they would converse about their memories of television shows that they used to enjoy. The little white church on *Little House* would eventually be brought up and the conversation would turn to how alike their lives were now, to those who lived in Walnut Grove. So many similarities. No electricity, no working indoor plumbing. No telephones. Neighbors had to meet and speak face to face because there was simply no other way to communicate and share information. Money didn't really matter anymore. The economy was based on hard labor and things that were liquid and tangible. Bartering was an everyday occurrence. People had to subsist, in order to survive. They had to practice skills again that people had practiced in the days before technology did most everything. The similarities were nearly endless.

Upon waking this morning, Michelle had torn through the cabin in a panic, looking for signs that Lauren had returned overnight, only to find that she hadn't. She had a short conversation with John about it, but had to end the talk not long after it had begun because John was completely exhausted. He had been on watch the previous night and hadn't gotten much sleep yesterday, due to the day's events. He had mentioned going out and looking for her after he got some sleep. That was a sign of how tired he really was. It was a marvel how he even managed to stay awake overnight, but Michelle easily deduced it was due to Lauren not being home. He was waiting for Lauren just like she was, and had a hard time sleeping last night because of it. Michelle did everything she could to keep her imagination from racing away with worst case scenarios of what had happened to her daughter.

With John getting some much needed sleep, Lee was guarding the cabin and Grace was to remain inside while they were separated. If they heard or saw trouble, they were to fire five consecutive shots into the air. The shots would be heard at the church and the entire community would be there to hear them. The church was a five-minute walk from the cabin, and it was a safe bet that help would be there promptly. If lethal force became necessary, they would use it to defend themselves and protect their property. Fred Mason's sons, Chad and Mark rarely left their homestead on meeting day and were only a few hundred yards away. Both of them were excellent shots. With the possibility of intruders in the valley, this gave added confidence. If a battle had to be fought, they wouldn't have to fight alone.

Walking side by side and nearing the church, Michelle and Norman were having yet another *Little House* conversation. This time it was being forced, in an effort to keep Michelle's mind from being preoccupied with her missing daughter. Michelle pointed out that Norman was like Charles Ingalls and she was most like Caroline, of course without the bonds of marriage between them. Norman disagreed and thought he was more like Almonzo Wilder, instead. Almonzo, in his opinion, had much nicer hair and was more attractive than Charles. He also pointed out to Michelle jokingly, that she reminded him more of Nellie Oleson, implying that she was an incorrigible troublemaker.

"No way in hell, am I like Nellie," Michelle said. "I'm definitely Caroline. I've become the quintessential mother hen. And with that, Grace has to be Mary—with the exception of her good vision. And Lauren is definitely Laura Ingalls."

Norman nodded. "I can see Lauren being Laura. I can even see Grace being Mary. But I am not Charles. I'm definitely 'Manly'," he said, referring to the nickname for Almonzo Wilder, who had married Laura Ingalls when she was seventeen years old. "Without the bonds of marriage, of course," he continued lightheartedly. "That just wouldn't be right."

"Damn right, it wouldn't," Michelle said.

Michelle's grin turned into a frown. Every time Lauren's name was mentioned, she felt a tingle on the back of her neck. She began to worry again. She tried not to, but she couldn't help it. She selfishly hoped that John would decide to go look for her, but she began to feel guilty and didn't want him to go alone. There was no certainty when this new danger in the community would manifest, and being alone was an altogether bad idea. There was safety in numbers and today, they had a job to do. They had to bring all of their neighbors up to speed on what had happened yesterday. After all, there was now a new threat that could affect everyone that lived there. After this meeting, the rest of her day would be about her daughter and nothing else.

Michelle and Norman walked up the stairs and stepped into the church through the double doors which were held-open. Immediately inside, they were welcomed by Michael Perry and his wife, Kristen. The Perrys lived near the northern boundary of the community, close to the old and now defunct animal petting zoo and general store. Although their last name had nothing to do with the town of Perry, they were often referred to jokingly as "the Perrys of Perry." Michael owned an excavation business and had a large lot of property full of equipment, including tractors, bobcats, dump trucks, backhoes, and the like. He was a generous person and had no problem occasionally using his equipment to clear Trout Run Road of snow when needed, in spite of the fact that fuel was as scarce as it was. He was a construction blasting engineer and had provided the explosives and expertise needed to barricade the road near Wolf Gap, when the community had decided it was needed to ensure their safety in the valley. Michael's wife, Kristen was a paramedic and had been one of the two non-volunteer professionals at Wardensville Fire Company before, and shortly after the collapse. Once Wardensville had become too dangerous for Kristen to remain there, she'd decided to pursue another career opportunity. Like so many of the other women in the valley, she'd become a homemaker. She also happened to be the only member of the community with experience in emergency medicine, and that made her a major asset.

Michelle and Norman shook hands with the Perrys and after a few words, continued into the church. Fred Mason was standing at the pulpit with his wife, where he usually ran the meetings. They were chatting with Bryan and Sarah Taylor who had their four-year-old daughter, Emily with them. This explained the bicycle that Michelle had seen outside the church that had a kid trailer attached to it. The Taylors were the youngest of all of the families in the valley and lived closest to what was considered the southern boundary of the community. Their property was therefore closest to the barricade, so if anyone had seen evidence of the intrusion, it would most likely be them. Bryan was a computer programmer by trade before the collapse. Sarah was an accountant. Since both professions were obsolete now, they had been able to escape their city commutes to become what they had always dreamed of becoming—farmers. The Taylors had the largest garden in the valley. In fact, just about all of their property was a garden of some sort. They harvested so many fruits, vegetables and herbs that even after bartering the majority, they were occasionally forced to give the excess away. Thanks to a large greenhouse that Bryan had built with the help of a couple other neighbors, they were able to garden pretty much year-round. They also had an assortment of chickens, goats, and hogs. Michelle often referred to Bryan and Sarah as the *newlyweds*, noting how extremely compassionate they were, as well as how affectionate they were with one another.

As Michelle and Norman took a seat on the second pew from the front of the church, which was their usual spot, they were greeted by Peter and Amy Saunders who sat just behind them in the third pew. Peter and Amy lived just north of the church on the opposite side of the road from the cabin with their sons, Jacob and Liam, both of whom were sitting beside their parents, playing with toy cars on the church pew. Jacob was thirteen and his brother was almost five years old, yet they always played together as if there wasn't an age difference. Jacob was very protective of his little brother and Liam looked up to him. The two were inseparable. Peter was a highly skilled carpenter and a welder. There was very little that he could not do with tools and wood or steel. He had worked for carpentry businesses in and around northern Virginia and had performed side work on his own before the collapse. Now, side work was all there was. Peter had helped the Taylors build their greenhouse and assisted his other neighbors with small tasks here and there, as it was needed. His wife Amy was an LPN and had worked at the Urgent Care center in Wardensville. Since the collapse, in addition to being a homemaker, she had become quite the cook. Cooking had been a hobby for her for years and in these new conditions, it offered her a chance to branch out from what was traditional. She became nothing short of extraordinary in the specialty of 'primitive culinary arts', as she preferred to call it.

"That's quite a beard you're growing there," Norman said, noting Peter's full-bodied facial hair.

"Jealous?" Peter said with a smile.

"Absolutely," Norman said as he ran his fingers through his goatee.

"My beard brings all the girls to the yard," Peter said jokingly. "I could teach you, but I'd have to charge." He turned to look at his wife with a goofy grin, and she immediately turned to look at him.

"There'd better not be any girls in our yard," Amy said. Peter laughed at her and she smiled.

Michelle tried to crack a smile, but she didn't have it in her. Amy noticed almost immediately that something was troubling her.

"Michelle, you ok?" Amy asked.

Michelle hesitated and then said, "Yes. I'm fine."

"That's a load of shit," Amy said.

Knowing that her friend would stop at nothing to find out what was bothering her, Michelle relented. "Lauren didn't come home last night," Michelle said in a solemn tone. "We have no idea where she is right now."

"Oh—shit," Amy said quietly. She placed her hand over her mouth, partially in an attempt to soften her voice, but also because she realized she was in a church.

"It couldn't have come at a worse time," Norman added. "We've got a security issue in the valley."

"Fred told us about what happened at the Ackermanns," Peter said with a nod. "He told us right after he talked with Mike and Kristen, and I'm guessing that's what he's talking to Bryan and Sarah about right now."

"Where are the Schmidts?" Michelle asked as she looked around the church.

"Those two would be late for their own funerals," Amy retorted. "They'll show up right after Fred calls the meeting and he'll give them both hell—I mean heck—for it, as usual."

The four looked up and saw that the Taylors had moved away from the pulpit and were now taking their seats. Kristen Perry walked to the front and took a seat in the pew in front of Michelle and Norman. Michael remained at the doors, looking around outside with his hand tapping the holster of his sidearm. Michelle glanced around the church and noticed that just about everyone indeed was carrying a gun, even the women. It was hard to believe just how much things had changed in the past year. At one time, open carrying a firearm was considered taboo and seemingly served only to frighten an uneducated populous. Now, it was the status quo. It was a necessity to ensure protection in uncertain times.

Fred cleared his throat as Kim took a seat just behind him.

"Let the meeting come to order," Fred announced in his usual flamboyant voice. "At this point, everyone is aware of the situation in our community. I've spoken with each of you. Norman, if you'd like to give us all of the details, we're all ears."

Norman nodded. Just as he stood up, the late arrivals Scott and Whitney Schmidt stormed into the church, huffing and puffing as if they had run the entire way from their house to the church.

"Sorry we're late," Scott said.

"We're used to it," Fred admonished with a smirk.

Scott and Whitney took a seat in the pew opposite of Michelle and Norman. They waved to them, smiled, whispered hellos under their breath, then waved to the other families and did the same. Fred crossed his arms and exhaled through his nostrils. The only thing that annoyed him more than people who were always late, were people who were oblivious to being always late and how it affected others. The Schmidts couldn't help themselves, it was just in their nature. They had both once been non-essential government employees who had enjoyed benefits such as flex-time and liberal leave policies. Scott was an IT professional and his wife was an analyst. Both had worked for a local FEMA office in Winchester, Virginia before the collapse. The home they enjoyed now, was once just a weekend getaway for them. When it had become too dangerous in their neighborhood, they'd bugged out to the valley.

Scott had been one of Michelle's husband's best friends since childhood. His parents had been Alan's parent's friends, even before Alan had been born. Scott's mother had even been a bridesmaid in Alan's mother's wedding to her first husband. The longevity of their relationship made them family to the Russells, and it was considered a miracle that a family that had been so close to them ended up in the same general location, after the collapse.

Once the Schmidts settled down and began realizing that the group was waiting for them to pay attention, Norman began filling in the group with all of the details about what had happened at the Ackermann farm, the day before. He wanted to be as specific and factual as possible but with children present, he left out a few of the gory details. As he talked, an assortment of looks were being exchanged among the group. Most of which showed extreme apprehension, others displayed looks of confusion. Scott Schmidt held up his hand. Norman paused and nodded to him.

"Wait a second," Scott began, "Sorry, I feel like everyone else already knew about this and we're just now finding out."

"That's because everyone else does know already," Fred interjected. "I took each family aside and gave them the rundown before the meeting. If you would have been here, you would've gotten the same information as I gave them."

Scott gave Fred a cockeyed cynical look. Fred was fuming, but kept his composure. Whitney Schmidt placed her hand on her husband's shoulder.

"Can we please not make this meeting about us?" she said. "It sounds like we have a real problem here."

"We do," Norman said. "I think what we found yesterday is just a sign of what's coming."

"We've dealt with people like this before and came out on top," Scott pointed out.

"Those people weren't true killers," Norman said. "These guys are."

Michael Perry closed the double doors to the church and walked closer to the group, so he could better hear the discussion. "We need to check on the barricade," he said. "In lieu of what happened, we need to find out how exactly they got into our valley."

"Is it is possible that they came from the north?" Whitney asked.

"Possible, but not likely," Michael said. "We certainly would have heard something."

"Agreed," Peter chimed in. "You said they were Harley Davidson motorcycles, Norm?"

"They were."

"Then we most definitely would have heard them going down the road," Peter said. "I seriously doubt they pushed their bikes all the way here from Wardensville, past everyone's house without anyone noticing. Also, I want to point out that even though I'm no expert by any means, what I've heard of the Marauders isn't good. Back in the day, rumor was they were gun and drug runners—similar to the Pagans or the Hell's Angels. Smaller in numbers, but just as deadly."

"Fantastic," Whitney said with a sigh.

"If the barricade is compromised, there's enough hill coming down from the gap that they could have drifted their bikes down here," Michael pointed out. Everyone nodded.

Bryan Taylor handed his daughter to his wife, and lifted his hand in the air.

"I just want to point out that Sarah and me haven't heard anything either," he said. "We live the closest to the barricade and it's been as quiet as it's always been."

"What about the abandoned houses over your way, Bryan?" Norman began, "any activity?"

"No, they're all still abandoned and locked up. I patrol that area often when I go squirrel hunting. By the way, we didn't hear any shots yesterday, otherwise I would've come running. I'm sorry that we weren't there to help. The Ackermann's farm is in that hollow, though—blocked from us by terrain."

"We didn't hear shots yesterday either," Scott said, "that I can remember. Sorry."

"Most likely it was because you were sleeping," Fred jeered.

"Well, we heard them plain as day," Michelle verified. "I'm glad we did, otherwise we wouldn't have any idea what had happened."

Several different conversations between the families began and went on for several minutes. Questions were brought up about Mr. Ackermann and his welfare, and some group members decided it would be a good idea to pay him a visit to see if he was all right or needed anything. After all, he was alone now with his wife gone. He had a small farm with livestock and he was the only one left to protect it. After the conversations died down, Fred once again regained control of the meeting.

"Our first order of business is to verify the barricade, then," Fred said. "Does everyone agree with that?"

Every head in the church nodded in recognition.

"We're going to need to step it up around here," Peter said. "If these guys have motorcycles, we aren't going to be able to respond riding bicycles."

"Pete is right," Fred said. "We have a little over four miles of valley between the barricade and Perry to patrol. It's going to be hard to do that with bicycles and damn near impossible to do on foot. My Humvees can help with that."

"We have four-wheelers," Norman began, "as well as my truck and Michelle's Suburban. We just don't have enough gas to justify using them on a daily basis."

"We have ATVs, too," Whitney offered as her husband looked on silently. "We also have our old Bronco we could use, if needed."

"I have my motorcycle and several jugs of gas," Peter said. "My old F-150 still runs. If the community needs what I have to keep safe, it's at your disposal." Amy smiled at her husband, noting his generosity and willingness to help.

"We have a Kawasaki Mule," Bryan began, "and enough gas to run it for a while, if needed. Unfortunately, both of our cars are junk—too many electronic control boards."

"I think everyone knows what we have," Kristen Perry finally spoke up. "Our property is virtually a graveyard of excavation equipment."

"Except most of what I own still runs, which makes it not a graveyard," her husband pointed out. He hesitated and smiled at his wife, then continued. "I'm a little reluctant to tell you all this, but I have two five-hundred-gallon unleaded fuel tanks behind my shop. One of them is full. The other about half. The gas is treated and will last a long time. I also have quite a lot of off-road diesel. If we need to be mobile, I can support our needs for a good while."

Everyone gave the Perrys looks of surprise. Every family had transportation but with fuel being as scarce as it was, no one had been willing to use what they had, unless it was absolutely necessary. Having fuel available would solve a lot of problems and give everyone more options. Michael Perry was known for his generosity as well as his resourcefulness, but no one had any idea the depths of it—with the exception of his wife. She gazed at him with a look of total approval.

"Michael, I'm blown away," Michelle said. "This is amazing news."

"I was going to hold out on informing the group for a while longer, but it seems to me like we have a real threat to our livelihood now and it's become necessary," he said.

"Well, since we're all cleaning out our closets now, I guess I can tell everyone that I have an underground gasoline tank, too," Fred said. "I don't have as much as Mike does, but its available if needed."

"After we check on the barricade, we can make a stop by everyone's place and gather all the empty fuel cans," Michael said. "I'll take them to my place, fill them, and distribute them."

"Sounds great," Norman said. The rest of the group showed their acceptance of the plan. "I don't know what I'm more excited about though—being able to use our vehicles or being able to use my chainsaw again."

The group laughed. Another conversation began, concerning how the group would need to begin patrolling the area on a regular basis. Norman brought up the fact that the barricade, regardless of its condition, needed to be guarded in order to maintain a level of security in the valley. The logistics of doing so would require two men to be present at the barricade at all times. Since the community was virtually unguarded on the northern end of the valley, options for barricading the road just past the old Perry Wildlife Zoo were discussed. The group also conferred about having roving patrols in the valley. With both ends of the valley guarded and patrolled twenty-four hours a day, all of the families could continue their daily routines in relative safety. The only thing that was left out was communication. In a world where everything electronic didn't work anymore, this was a touchy subject. Fred once again interjected.

"Everyone here knows I'm a prepper," Fred said. "Well, that being said, I do have some radios."

That got everyone's attention. It even stopped the incessant whispering between Scott Schmidt and his wife, which occurred normally when someone else was talking.

"You have radios that work?" Peter responded with a look of surprise.

"I do. Several of them. And I have rechargeable batteries for them and solar chargers," Fred explained.

"How did you manage to prevent them from getting fried?" Scott asked.

"I kept them all in ammo cans in my metal building," Fred said. "The EMP didn't affect them. I've checked them out and they all still work."

"What kind of range will we get out of them?" Peter asked.

"I'm no expert on radios, but they should work well in this valley," Fred said. "We'll keep a set of batteries in the solar charger and run a set in the radios. I have enough for all of us and some extra ones for the patrols."

"Maybe one for Lauren when she goes on walkabout," Michelle said under her breath to Norman.

Norman responded by tapping the top of her hand with his. He then whispered to her, "If we start patrolling the valley, she won't need to do it anymore."

Fred turned around and reached into a large plastic bin behind him. He pulled out some large mylar bags and handed a few of them to Kim. They both then began distributing them out to each family. When Norman opened his, he saw a small black radio, a few Ziplock bags of batteries, and a solar charger with a carry handle. He had once seen this same charger at Harbor Freight and remembered that they had gone on sale one Sunday for about fifteen dollars. That must've been when Fred had decided to stock up. The radios had the brand name Baofeng on them. That name sounded familiar to him. He wasn't certain, but he thought that maybe he and Alan had discussed this brand of radios before. He knew Alan was a licensed ham radio operator and it was very likely that he had one of these somewhere. Maybe two. Maybe more.

"They'll run on regular AA's too, so if you don't get a good charge from the solar, you can use regular batteries," Fred said.

Once they had finished handing out the radio kits, most of the men had pulled them out of the bags and had turned them on. Some were pressing the PTT button and saying things like *breaker breaker, over-and-out*, and *10-4 good buddy*. They were smiling like kids who had just gotten a new present on Christmas. Norman began cycling through the channels which were all quiet. He noticed the channels had names like FRS1, GMRS1, and MARINE1. He verified with Peter's radio that the channels and names were the same.

"Looks like they're all programmed with the same frequencies," Norman said.

"They are," Fred said. "No need to confuse anyone."

Fred did a small demonstration of how to operate the radio and did so, in a way that even a person who had zero knowledge of electronics could understand. Bryan and Scott picked up on their operation immediately, since they were the two most technologically inclined in the group. The others asked questions, but eventually got the idea. The group set up each of their radios on the exact same pair of frequencies.

After going over the radios, a small discussion was had about safety and the necessity for everyone in the community to be armed at all times. Some of the women who showed up to the meeting without a sidearm began looking at one another. Sarah Taylor had never been comfortable around guns. She never thought about it much until after the collapse but even then, she'd never considered carrying a weapon because her husband was an avid hunter and usually had a gun on him. She in turn, assumed she didn't need one. This conversation was causing her to feel differently, and she began a silent discussion with her husband. While Scott Schmidt always wore a weapon on his side, his wife had never been seen with one. Amy and Kristen always had on a sidearm. Kristen did so because it was just her and her husband on their property and they weren't always side by side. She had also seen the violence that had occurred in Wardensville the previous year, and knew the only way to truly protect one's self was to carry a firearm. Having a gun was the only reason she'd been able to escape the unrest and make it home safely. Amy had been brought up in a very conservative household where guns were just always present. Growing up around them and being educated about them, she'd never had an issue about carrying one wherever she went. It was empowering to her.

"I have a question, Fred," Whitney Schmidt said.

"Go ahead," Fred said.

"What if we don't have a sidearm?" she asked.

"If you don't have a sidearm, then you need to get one," Fred quipped.

"We don't have a lot of guns," Scott said. "I have the handgun I'm wearing now, a shotgun, and a hunting rifle."

"Scott, how long have you lived here?"

"For a while," Scott replied.

"And you're just now bringing this to my attention?" Fred asked as his temper began to flair.

"I didn't think we needed anything else," Scott said. "Sorry."

Fred shook his head in disgust. "I own a damn gun store," he said. "Come by today and pick something out. We can work out the payment details later."

Scott and Whitney both smiled. They knew that the two of them were not Fred's favorite people.

"Bring your kids with you," Fred said without looking at them, referring to their two teenage children, Brandon and Brooke, who had opted to stay home during today's meeting. "They'll need something, too."

After the meeting, all parties said their goodbyes and returned to their homes. They had decided to make a trip to check on the barricade about an hour after lunch, and it was nearing lunch time. Peter had offered to use his 1975 Ford F-150 to pick the others up. He insisted it would be the perfect choice because he could use it to pick up everyone's empty gas cans on the way back and drop off to be filled at Michael's house. In addition to Pete and Michael, Norman and Fred Mason decided they would join the party to check the barricade. Peter would pick them up on the way.

Michelle and Norman walked past Lee, who was standing guard, and entered the cabin. They could immediately smell that Grace was cooking something, and it smelled fantastic. Norman slipped off his boots and walked to the kitchen to see Grace tending to a large pot of what appeared to be some variety of noodle soup. Norman laid the Mylar bag that contained the radio kit on the table.

"Hey good lookin, whatcha got cookin?" he said to Grace.

Grace shook her head. "Chicken noodle soup," she replied. "And I hope it's good because everything in it was freeze dried."

Michelle walked past the two as Grace gave Norman a sample of the soup with a wooden spoon. His eyes opened wide and he nodded, signifying that Grace's concoction was palatable. She looked down the hallway and noticed that John's bedroom door was open, and he was not in his bed.

"Did John leave?" Michelle inquired.

"About a half-hour ago," Grace said. "He grabbed his shotgun, some gear from the gun safe, and left without saying much."

"He went to go look for Lauren, then," Michelle said quietly. "I wish he would have waited for me."

"You don't have any business out there right now," Norman said. "I'll be leaving soon to check the barricade. We need bodies here, not elsewhere."

"My daughter is out there somewhere, Norman," Michelle said firmly. "We need to find her and get her home."

"I'm aware of that, babes," he began, "and trust me when I say this—John will find her. He won't come back until he does."

"And if John doesn't come back?" Grace interjected.

No one spoke. Grace's outburst made everyone feel uncomfortable. Her attention turned back to her soup, which was nearing done. Michelle turned away and went to her bedroom where she picked up a pack of cigarettes and a lighter, and then walked back outside to the porch, mildly slamming the door behind her.

"I guess I shouldn't have said that," Grace offered, feeling sorry now that she had allowed her thoughts to be expressed verbally. "Honestly though, I just think it's stupid to keep dividing ourselves up like this."

"We get it, Grace. And don't worry, you're fine. We all just need to have a little faith," Norman said. He reached for a bowl on the counter and began spooning himself a large portion of soup. "It's delicious, by the way."

Outside, Michelle was puffing away at the cigarette she had just ignited. Her arms were crossed and she was shaking a bit, but it wasn't from the cold. Lee came around the corner and saw her.

"How did the meeting go?" he asked.

Michelle looked at him, but didn't say anything at first.

"Just like they all do, except this time we found out how resourceful people are here," she replied.

"Resourceful?"

"Let's just say, we are going to be using our Hondas a lot more now," Michelle said.

"That's great news," Lee said. "I am so sick of pedaling bikes all the time."

There was a moment of silence between the two as Lee could tell that Michelle was in a foul mood and didn't know exactly what to say. While Lee was feeling a bit uncomfortable with the silence, Michelle was completely content with the lack of conversation.

"Go inside and get yourself some soup," she said. "We have a radio now, too. Your dad can show it to you."

As Lee approached her, Michelle held out her hand and took Lee's AK-47. He smiled at her and walked inside. Michelle snapped the safety down and checked the bolt to make sure it was loaded, as she always did when handling someone else's weapon. She then placed the safety back on and cradled the rifle in her arms, continuing to take occasional puffs on her cigarette. As she looked around the property, all she could think about was Lauren. Even with the looming threat of an armed rogue biker gang infiltrating their community, nothing else mattered to her. Michelle prayed that Lauren was ok and this was just a fluke, but it was hard to find faith and have comfort in that thought. She couldn't help but imagine the worst. That was just her nature. She glanced down at the rifle she was holding and kept imagining what she would do if something had happened to her baby girl. If she found that someone was responsible for it, she would kill them without hesitation. If that someone had a family, she would kill them too out of pure vengeance. If anyone had harmed her daughter, she would end their existence and the existence of everything and everyone they held dear to them. It was non-negotiable. It was an eye for an eye, and completely justified in her book. No one fucked with her family.

With so many negative thoughts encircling her mind, she decided to smoke another cigarette. This wasn't something she normally did, since cigarettes were so scarce, but it was hard to fight the notion to smoke another, so she just did. Before she knew it, she had smoked three cigarettes back to back. After some time had gone by, Norman walked outside. He noticed that Michelle was shaking. Not knowing exactly what to say and at the same time knowing that something had to be said, Norman opened up.

"Lauren is a tough kid, Michelle," he said. "I remember when I first met her after Alan invited me over, just how headstrong and willful she was. She was just a kid but I always thought, damn, that kid has a fire inside her."

"She still does," she said with a half-smile. "I wish I could take the credit for it, but that is all Alan."

"That is a fact," Norman concurred. "Your husband got my respect a long time ago because of that. He never backed down to anyone or anything. He always said what needed to be said and didn't give two shits what anyone thought about him. He was a fighter, but he did it with his words more than with his fists."

Michelle put out her cigarette on the ground beside the other two and Norman noticed there were three butts on the ground just as he continued.

"Back when I knew Alan, before you two were together, we used to hang out at a bar together and shoot pool and drink tons of beer. The girl he was dating back then was a real stunner. She had guys ogling over her constantly, but it didn't bother him because he wasn't a jealous person. One night, a couple guys decided they were gonna mess with her. She did a good job standing up for herself, but Alan was watching the situation closely and didn't make a move until he needed to. He didn't do anything until he saw one of them touch her. When he approached them, he told them that she was with him and he didn't appreciate them disrespecting her. The two guys immediately challenged him and wanted to fight him. Alan just stood his ground. I walked up behind him a minute after, in case he needed some back up, but his mouth would not stop moving. He was a pitbull with his words. It took all of about five minutes for both of the guys to become disinterested and walk away. I don't know what all he said, but it worked. He was always like that. He could figure out a person in a second, and talk them down in another. He never went looking for trouble, and always managed to make the right decision when trouble came looking for him."

"Alan was my rock, Norman," Michelle said with a broken voice that signified she was on the verge of crying. "I cannot tell you how much I miss him."

"Well, he's my best friend. I can imagine somewhat, because I feel a bit of what you feel every day," Norman said. "I guess what I'm trying to say is…he has that fight inside him and Lauren inherited it. That's why I believe she's ok. I'm absolutely convinced of it. I've seen her dad handle quite a lot of situations where he was the underdog and still managed to come out on top. If he can do it, she can."

Norman reached out and gave Michelle a hug. Michelle let go for a moment and then quickly dried her eyes, just as a pickup truck pulled up to the gate and honked the horn.

"It's been awhile since I've heard that noise," Michelle pointed out.

"Yeah—looks like my ride is here," Norman said. He walked back inside to get his rifle and other gear, then started up the driveway, heading to the truck. He turned around and waved. "You guys keep it tight. The radio is on and Lee knows how to use it. Call us if you need us."

"Will do," Michelle said, "and Norman…"

"Yeah?"

"Thank you."

"Anytime, babes. Listen, for what it's worth, I still believe he's coming home to you," Norman said.

CHAPTER 11

Town of Edinburg
Shenandoah County Virginia
Present day

A
FTER SLAMMING HER NEAR-LIFELESS BODY to the floor, Damien Marcel climbed on top of her. Her eyes were beginning to roll into the back of her head. Pinning her arms beneath his legs, he began crashing his calloused fists mercilessly into her young face. What had once been muffled screams had turned into semi-audible whimpers, and had now become grunts. It wasn't clear to him, but she appeared to be knocked unconscious—he guessed it was possible she had been before he had started hitting her, but he didn't care. She had lost consciousness several times over the course of his assault on her, which had been ongoing since the previous evening. After the first few punches, damage was starting to show and it worsened every time additional contact was made. Her face began to show bruising, lacerations formed, and blood began to emerge from her eye sockets. Her tender skin was no match for his leathered, hardened knuckles that had been conditioned over the years for doing this kind of physical damage to another human being. His face showed no emotion as he relentlessly mutilated her, and it didn't take long before she began to choke on her own blood. Satisfied with his work, he stopped striking her and placed his right hand around her throat. He squeezed tightly and waited patiently until she took her last breath. His breathing had remained normal the entire time this had gone on. This was his normal.

Standing up, he adjusted his pants and then buckled his belt, upon noticing that it was unfastened. He took a look around the room, carefully admiring his work. The bed had been overturned and everything that had once hung on the walls was now on the floor, including a photograph of what appeared to be the girl and her best friends, enjoying a hot summer day at a waterpark. There were several holes in the wall, about the size of his victim's skull, where he had forcibly smashed her head through the drywall. Her belongings were scattered everywhere. She had put up quite a fight, but it had been all in vain. Damien was a large-framed, muscular man and had a mind fashioned for violence. This was all a part of the game to him. There were winners and losers; and she and her family had lost, just like so many other families before them. In this new world, the possibilities that it offered him it was just beginning. He felt like a god—like he could do whatever he wanted to anyone and had no one single person to answer to. Things like this that he done before the collapse were prosecutable. Now, in this new world, he was the law. The authorities had given him power over others. They had also provided him with total immunity and it felt extraordinary to him. The only edict that existed now was him. It was his world and there was no one who could stop him. He looked down at the body whose life he had just taken. He hocked up a large ball of snot and saliva and spit on the young girl's now unrecognizable face. Reaching down, he picked up the photo of the girl and her friends and pulled it from the broken frame. He eyed it for a few seconds while rubbing his chin, then folded it and shoved it into his back pocket.

As he walked out of the bedroom, he slammed the door behind him and stomped into the kitchen, walking past the two dead bodies in the living room, that belonged to the girl's parents, on the way. Both had their hands bound behind their backs with tie wraps and several bullet wounds in their chest, in addition to quite a few other noticeable injuries that he had inflicted on them. They had bled out overnight and the hardwood floor was a mess, with two separate puddles of blood that had become one big pool. He reached for a nicely folded dishtowel near the sink and began to wipe the blood off of his hands. He tried to turn on the water faucet out of habit and quickly remembered that the water probably hadn't worked here for quite a while. After wiping off what he could, he grabbed another clean dishtowel and walked to the bathroom. Lifting the top from the commode reservoir to check for water, he found there wasn't any and dropped the porcelain lid to the ground in disgust. Walking back toward the kitchen, he picked up a nickel-plated pistol off of the dining room table and shoved it in his waistband. He made his way to the front door and walked outside, taking a look around the yard. Noticing a bird feeder that had a good-sized puddle of water in it, he made his way over and began washing his hands off. The water quickly turned crimson as he did so. He dried his hands with the dish towel and stuffed it into the back pocket of his jeans.

Just a few doors down in the rural cul-de-sac, he watched as some other men he recognized, wearing black leather vests, dragged a helpless couple from their home as they struggled. The woman had her hands tied behind her back and was screaming for them to let her go. Her husband, who had been hog-tied was begging them to leave his wife alone while they laughed and kicked him. After a few minutes, the group began pummeling the man with their fists until he stopped moving, all while the wife watched in horror. One of the men pulled a revolver from his waist and shot the man in the back of the head. The wife screamed and sobbed—it was all she could do in her predicament. The group began pointing at her and laughing. One of the men yelled, "I'm going first!" and a short back-and-forth argument began between them. A life had been taken and another was about to be changed forever and it was all a joke to them. But it was all a part of the game.

Damien cleared his throat and said, "You assholes, take that crying bitch inside! Don't do that shit here—get her inside and shut her the fuck up, for crying out loud!"

As if they were all codependent children heeding an abusive father's warning, the men all nodded and began dragging the young woman past her dead husband as she cried and struggled, heading back toward the house. As they pulled her inside the front door and closed it behind them, a motorcycle approached and pulled into the driveway near where Damien stood. A tall man with long dark hair and a black leather vest covered in patches shut off his bike and approached him. The patches on his chest read *Marauders* and *Sgt. At Arms*. The man handed Damien a half-full bottle of Wild Turkey 101 bourbon.

"Here—found this at a house down the road," the man said. "Thought you might like a pull or two."

Damien took several gulps from it and then handed it back without even the slightest wince. He then pulled out a pack of cigarettes from the front pocket of his denim shirt, took out two, lit one and lit the other with the first and handed it to the tall man. Damien noticed the blood splatter on his shirt and shook his head in mild disgust. The tall man noticed and smiled.

"Looks like you might need another new shirt, boss," the tall man said as he placed the cigarette in his mouth. Grinning, he said, "What's that like, the third one this month?"

"Third one this week," Damien said gruffly. He pawed at his beard and spit on the ground.

"I suppose that's possible," the tall man said. "We've been busy."

"Yes, we have. Doing the lord's work," Damien said somewhat pompously.

"Did you learn anything?" the tall man asked.

Damien looked up at the sky and then back toward the house. "The girl didn't know much," he said as he took a puff from the cigarette. "She just took an awfully long and painful time to clue me in to that fact." He paused and took a couple more drags from the cigarette. "I figured killing her folks would have gotten her attention, but it took a little more than that."

"Maybe we should have tortured them a bit longer before we shot them," the tall man said, again with a grin.

"He told me everything I needed to know," Damien said. "Don't blame him—he was scared for his daughter's welfare." He paused. "Either way, I got what I wanted. When the boys get done whatever the fuck they're doing, bring them here and tell them to drag all the bodies out into the street. It needs a little cleaning inside, but this is the nicest house in the neighborhood I've seen so far. There's a bunch of food here. They got rations and canned goods in the basement. We can hole up here for a few days."

"Will do," the tall man said. "They're spread out now looking for supplies and whatever else. But I'll gather them up when they're done."

Damien took another puff on his cigarette and looked down to his shirt where a couple long blonde hairs hung. He brushed them off with the back of his hand and smiled. "I'll say something though, Danny, she sure was sweet," he began in a low, demented tone. "She had to be just a few days over eighteen. Just the way I like them."

The tall man laughed and soon, Damien chimed in with a sinister laugh of his own.

"Damn. Sounds appetizing. Next time, save some for me," Danny said.

Damien walked over to a black motorcycle and opened a saddle bag. Inside, he pulled out a pair of ratcheting pipe cutters and handed them to Danny. Danny gave him an emotionless stare. "Funny you would say that, Sarge," Damien said. "She's got a nice ring on her finger. It's a high school class ring, but it's definitely gold. It will make a nice addition."

Danny looked at the cutters which had specks of dried blood on the blades. He had used cutters just like these many times before and was more than familiar with them. "Oh, you're funny," he said as he took them from Damien. He looked them over for a bit before letting them fall to his side. "By the way, boss—the guys were wondering, what exactly is the plan?"

Damien sighed loudly. "Until we hear back from Jesse, Vance, and the others, we are staying put for a while," Damien said. "There should be plenty of provisions in this town for us—among other things. Something's happened to those two though, and we need to find out what. Hopefully, the guys who went looking for them will have something for us soon. If we have to send out more patrols to try to find them, that's what we'll do."

"Any idea where they went?"

"Jesse told me he was heading to the National Forest to see who was hiding about in the campsites," Damien said. "That's where we should be looking."

"So, if we find them and they're dead, then what?"

Damien gave Danny an infuriated look and severely squinted his eyes. After a pause, he said, "That's my VP you're talking about. No one takes that life but me. Jesse is my right hand. If he's dead, then we fucking kill who's responsible." He walked back over to his motorcycle and put on his vest, which he had laid across the seat. His vest was fairly weathered and had patches that said *Marauders* and *President* on it. He continued, "Another reason we're staying in this area is because that fuckhead DHS agent is supposed to meet me tomorrow to discuss terms. I'm fine with us being his hired muscle, but the price is gonna go up. I'm tired of being his bitch."

"If being his bitch means what I think it means, I have to agree with you," Danny said.

"What do you think it means, Danny?"

"Well—for starters, we shouldn't have to go looking for food while we're working for them," Danny asserted. "Not that I don't mind the work because it has its perks, but I'm tired of being hungry."

"If they want our help, they will give us whatever the hell we want, plain and simple," Damien said as he looked up and down the street. "If he refuses, then we'll move on—or maybe I'll just kill him."

Just as Damien finished his sentence, Danny pointed down the street. A man with a shotgun in his hands was walking steadily toward them. They didn't immediately recognize him and he wasn't wearing a vest, so they both knew it had to be one of the several people who still lived in the neighborhood. Danny immediately pulled his pistol and drew down on the man. The man saw the muzzle pointed at him and held his hands up.

"That's far enough," Danny said, "unless you want to meet your maker."

"What in the hell are you people doing here?" he questioned in a loud voice. "We didn't do anything to you!"

"Sure you did," Damien disagreed.

"What's that exactly?" the man huffed.

"Shit. Are you kidding? All you nice rich folks are sitting here in your pretty houses with lots of food and supplies," Damien began, "and you're not sharing it."

"What do you mean? We're doing what's necessary to survive!" the man exclaimed.

Danny looked at Damien, who smiled.

"That's exactly what we're doing," Damien said in a voice loud enough for the man to hear him.

"Well, it looks like you're doing the exact opposite, to me," the man said. He pointed to the house that Damien and Danny were just outside of. "Where are the Andersons? What have you done to them?"

"The Andersons are—indisposed at the moment," Damien said. His smile slowly disappeared, along with his patience.

"Who in the fuck are you supposed to be?" Danny asked, in the voice he preferred to use when talking down to someone. "Neighborhood security?"

The man lowered his hands and held his shotgun at low-ready. Damien placed his hand on his pistol.

"Maybe I am, maybe I'm not," the man said as screams had begun to be heard from the house to his right. "I cannot allow this! By God, I cannot allow this!"

Damien smiled and laughed at the man. The man did not seem amused. "Let me be the first to tell you," Damien said as he pulled his pistol and aimed at the man. "There is no God."

Damien pulled the trigger again and again, and emptied the entire magazine into the man as the man fell backwards to the ground. His Sergeant at Arms lowered his pistol and turned to look at him. Damien dropped the magazine into his other hand and replaced it with one that he had in his vest pocket. He pressed the slide release and slowly put the pistol back in his waist band.

"There's nothing like a little ethnic cleansing," Damien said. "Perhaps we need to step it up a notch. Let's finish this place off now. I don't want any more surprises. Bring all the food and supplies back to this house. Kill who you need to, burn what you want—you know the drill."

"What about the..." Danny began, holding up the pipe cutters.

Damien reached for them and said, "I'll take care of this one."

"10-4," Danny said. He mounted his motorcycle and backed it down the driveway, and then jetted off down the street.

A member of the group that had been instructed to take the screaming woman inside, walked out of the house and soon made his way over to Damien. He was holding a screaming infant in his arms. He approached his President and said, "Look, Prez—a baby." He laughed. "What should we name it?"

Damien was not amused. He flicked his cigarette into the yard and spit.

"How about we name it, *fuckin dumbass*," Damien jested, "After the idiot who found it."

The biker looked surprised. He backed away a bit, expecting some act of wrath by Damien to befall him.

"Get rid of it," Damien said. "Now. And I don't care how. It's just one more mouth to feed."

"We could get that bitch to feed him," the biker said, "once we're done with her, that is."

Damien pulled his pistol and placed the muzzle on the infant's chest. The biker gasped and looked at Damien fearfully.

"If I have to do this, believe me when I tell you, you'll be next," he assured.

"Brutal, boss. That's just brutal!"

The biker turned and ran back to the house quickly with the infant and Damien replaced his pistol.

"You ain't seen nothing yet," he said.

CHAPTER 12

Point Blank Weapons Training Center
Capon Bridge, West Virginia
Two years and six months earlier

A S HER DAD CONTINUED DRIVING further and further down the very narrow gravel road, Lauren was starting to feel apprehensive. They had been on it for the past fifteen minutes and still hadn't gotten to where they were going. Every time she would ask him how much longer, he would just look over to her and smile. It was annoying to her. The woods seemed to be closing in on them the further they went. The tree tops were hiding the sun. She felt lucky that she wasn't claustrophobic—she probably would have lost her mind a mile or so ago if she was.

"This is ridiculous," Lauren piped up. "The sign back there said Independence Drive. It should have said 'some random garden path', for the love of god."

Her father looked over to her lovingly and laughed.

"Will you please tell me where we are going, Dad?" Lauren asked.

"I told you—it's a surprise," he replied.

"I get it. You're taking me to the woods for my birthday," she said, giving him a cynical look.

"Something like that," he joked. "This place is different. I'm pretty sure you'll like it. If you do, we can come back as often as you like."

"You've taken me to the woods for just about every occasion I can think of," she reminded.

"That's not—completely true, but I'll agree somewhat."

"Will you at least tell me what it is?" she pleaded. "I can't stand waiting to find out."

He smiled. "I've been coming here off and on for the past few years," he said, evading her question. "I've been able to learn quite a lot of things here—useful things. I really enjoy my time out here."

"*DAD,*" Lauren said in an irritated voice.

"You'll see in a few minutes," he said. "I promise."

Turning around a corner, they pulled into an exposed field that was surrounded by the forest they had just driven through. In front of them was a sign that read, "*Point Blank Weapons Training Center – Lock and Load*". Lauren sat up in her seat.

"A shooting range?" she inquired. "Really, Dad…"

"It's much more than just a shooting range," he replied.

Lauren began to look around as her father drove them over to where the parking lot was located. She noticed groups of men and women walking around in tactical clothing. Some were fully dressed in camouflage military clothing. Almost all were carrying weapons of some sort. Some had on backpacks, some were wearing boonie hats or helmets. Some, even had their faces painted in camouflage paint. There were quite a few others walking around in black t-shirts, with the word INSTRUCTOR in large, white letters on the back.

"Dad, where in the hell have you taken me?" Lauren asked with a big smile on her face.

He smiled and parked the car, then said, "Point Blank is a tactical training range. The trainers here are nothing short of outstanding. They're all combat veterans. They teach marksmanship, proper firearm handling, group shooting, stack drills, patrols, and all kinds of stuff. I signed you up for the Intermediate Operator Course. The things I've taught you at the range were pretty basic. This weekend, you'll learn way more than I could ever teach you. It may come in handy for you someday. Happy Birthday."

Lauren looked stunned. She had been able to shoot her father's AR-15 every time he had taken her to the range, but had always wanted to learn more. She had watched videos many times, but was never able to learn much from them. This place appeared to be a haven for people who considered themselves devout members of American gun culture. She could feel the excitement building. She could barely contain herself.

"Dad, how'd you know I'd be interested in doing something like this?" she asked.

"Father's intuition," Alan said. "You're growing up like crazy, but I'd like to think I know you still—even if it's just a little bit."

"You know me more than just a little bit."

Alan smiled. "I truly hope it stays that way. Come on, let's go meet some people."

"This is absolutely amazing," Lauren blurted out enthusiastically. Her excitement getting the best of her, she allowed few choice curse words to escape.

Alan glared at her before getting out of the car. "Watch your mouth," he said.

They walked up to a small group of people that consisted several men and women, some of which were wearing solid color military-style clothing. They looked as normal as could be in a place like this. Lauren instantly noticed the lean, muscular man with very tanned skin, who wore a black shirt with the word INSTRUCTOR on the back in large, white letters. His skin looked like leather to her, and his arms were covered in tattoos. The instructor looked at them, nodded, and held out his hand, exposing his very muscular tattooed forearm.

"Alan Russell. Good to see you, sir," he said with a deep, raspy voice as he took Alan's hand. "I take it this is your lovely daughter that you've told me so much about."

They released their handshake and he turned to Lauren.

"Good to see you too, Dave," Alan said with a broad smile, "and yes, this is my youngest, Lauren. She just turned sixteen today. L, this is Dave Graham, he'll be your instructor this weekend."

Lauren began to blush a little. Dave reached out his rough hand to her and she took it.

"Pleasure to meet you, ma'am," he said, "and Happy Birthday to you."

"Thank you—and it's Lauren. Call me Lauren," she interjected.

"Fine. Pleasure to meet you—Lauren."

"Likewise," Lauren said, eyeing his tattoos and paying special attention to the one of a skull with a beret on its head. She paused and then asked, "Are you in the Army?"

"I was for a while, but not anymore. I retired several years ago. I'm what you'd call, 'career enlisted'. Spent most of my time on base as a firearms instructor. Now…I just hang out here, training fellow patriots how to shoot straight and not get killed."

Lauren nodded and pointed to the tattoo she had been eyeballing. "And that tattoo…what's it stand for?"

Dave looked down and twisted his arm outright to display his ink. "That, my dear, is from the Special Forces. *De oppresso liber* means 'to liberate the oppressed.' It's our motto. I retired from the Army. The Green Beret in me lives on."

Lauren was taken aback at his forwardness for a moment, but soon smiled. She had never met anyone like Instructor Dave before, but she was completely fascinated by him. She said nothing after his response. Feeling as though he may have frightened her, he digressed.

"Did your father tell you that he's one of my favorite students?" he pondered to Lauren. "He's been a regular visitor here for a while now."

Lauren looked up at her father with a confused look on her face. She knew he enjoyed his guns and loved going to the range, but she'd no idea that he'd been coming here and doing this "tactical shooting" thing. He was always so busy. She wondered how he was even able to find the time.

"I had no idea that he was a student, period," Lauren said.

"I appreciate the compliments, Dave," Alan said humbly. "You can stop anytime."

"Quit being so modest," Dave joked. "I'm not hitting on you…yet."

Lauren looked at her father curiously as he shook his head and waved her off. Dave made his way through the group while several other introductions were made around the circle. Alan seemed to know just about everyone. After Lauren had met the group members, she pulled her father aside with a worried look.

"They all have rifles, Dad," she whispered into his ear.

"My AR is in the car. Your Glock is in your backpack," he said, "or at least it should be."

"It is."

"Good. I brought your pistol belt and a spare magazine carrier, and there's about a thousand rounds of ammunition in the car. You're covered."

Lauren looked surprised, but pleased. "Thanks, Dad," she said in a very genuine tone.

"You're welcome, baby."

Instructor Dave motioned for everyone to follow him down to the range. Alan retrieved the weapons and ammunition from the car and locked it up, then followed the group with Lauren in tow. Once everyone had gathered on the range, Dave stood in front of the group and began to speak. Alan set their belongings on a large wooden table that stood just behind them.

"I'm seeing a lot of familiar faces," he began, "I'm also seeing some new ones. That's a good thing. Times are changing, folks. We need to change along with them. We live in a world today that isn't safe. It's a world where we are surrounded by our enemies everywhere we go. Decisions our government has made, have put every single one of us, along with our sons and daughters, in jeopardy. It's pretty obvious to me that we've been infiltrated. I hope all of you have chosen to not be oblivious. This isn't the America we knew during the Reagan years. You are here today because you have chosen to learn something that can't be learned anywhere else. Myself, along with the other instructors, are here to teach you that something. We are not here to teach you what you want to know—we're here to teach you what *need* to know. You're here because you have chosen a different life than most of the sheeple in our country. You're here because you've chosen not to be a sheep. You're here because you have chosen to live your life without blinders on. You want to be protectors. You want to be sheepdogs. You want to defend something worth defending, whether it's your family, your freedom, your lifestyle, or the country you love. Maybe it's all of those things. Either way, you're here because your way of thinking is different than what is typical." He paused. "That being said, welcome to the Intermediate Operator Course. This is the second course in our Civilian Warrior curriculum here at Point Blank. All of you know who I am and I know pretty much who all of you are. Some of you have been to my other classes, and to those I'd like to say, welcome back." He paused as he pranced in front of the group. "This is a two-day intermediate skill level course. When I say intermediate, I mean that we assume everyone taking this course already knows how to shoot and understands basic firearm and range safety—there shouldn't be any beginners here. All of the conditions we train for here are mirrored to conditions found in the field of combat. You will not see YouTube video tacticool shit here." He paused to allow some of the group's laughter to dissipate. "We will teach you weapon manipulations that you're not accustomed to. It may feel weird at first, but you will get the hang of it. We will shoot long distance and we will be performing CQC...or close quarters combat drills. We will train you to shorten your reaction time and help you develop advanced muscle memory. We will teach you how to transition from your primary weapon to your secondary weapon and do so under stress. We will practice firing from different types of cover. You will learn to shoot well on the move and you will learn to shoot from unconventional positions—in ways that are very, very effective. I know—I made them up myself."

He paused and allowed the group to finish another round of laughter. Lauren was smiling brightly, but was paying very close attention to him. He continued, "We will attempt to place you into several very realistic life-threatening scenarios to see how you think and react, and believe me when I tell you, we are going to do our best to make them feel real as hell to you. In fact, it may get a bit personal—but that is what is required. We will be doing lots of shooting this weekend, but any group exercises we do will not be live-fire. If you want to do that, you'll need to pass this class with flying colors, not shoot anyone, and live to take my advanced operator courses."

Lauren looked up at her father. He nodded to her. "I'll sign you up for it if you want," he whispered. Lauren began to glow.

"Ladies and gentlemen, this class has a moderate physical difficulty rating," Dave continued. "If you can't transition from standing to sitting, to kneeling and to prone in all combinations, you will have a hard time keeping up with those who can." He paused. "Today, we are graced with a member of the younger generation." He held out his hand and pointed at Lauren. She smiled and blushed slightly. "She will probably run rings around all of us. There will be quite a lot of tactical scenarios taught this weekend. I hope everyone knows how to take good notes. Good luck to all of you. Saddle up—we start the first exercise in five minutes."

After the introduction to the class, Alan took a seat behind the table and Lauren cocked her head with a confused look.

"You're not taking the class with me?" she asked.

"Oh no," he said. "I've taken it before. It's expensive, L. I had enough cash set aside for just you to take it. I do plan on taking some of the advanced courses with you though, so make sure and pass this one."

"Ok," she said sounding a little disappointed.

"Is something wrong?" Alan asked.

"I'm not sure I'm ready for this, Dad," she said. She took a long look around at the many shooting lanes and courses in her field of view. One in particular stood out to her and she didn't know why. It was a lane about one-hundred yards long, with a single grey steel silhouette that had an orange round circle on center-mass and on the portion which made up the head.

"You can do this, L. You are more than capable. I promise you that. I wouldn't have brought you here, if I didn't think you could handle it."

"Ok—if you say so," she said.

"I do say so. I want you to learn all you can this weekend. You'll be better prepared, should you ever need these skills. With the way things are going in this world, what you learn here will be a huge asset."

Lauren nodded and put on her pistol belt, which held her Glock 22, and a spare magazine carrier for both her handgun and the AR-15. Just a little way downrange, she could hear Instructor Dave exclaim that the first exercise would be dry-fire only. Dave made it clear that anyone caught with live rounds would receive an ass-kicking from him. She dumped the magazine from her Glock and placed it back into its holster. She then checked the chamber of the AR-15 and verified that it was indeed empty, then turned to join the members of the group who, one by one, were doing the same. She walked a few feet away from her father, then turned to him.

"Thank you, Dad—and, I love you," she said.

"I love you, too," he said with a humble smile. "Now, go show them what you're made of."

"Ok," she said, a bit unsure but confident nonetheless.

"Hey, L…"

"Yes…" Lauren said, sounding a little annoyed.

"You look beautiful…"

Lauren smiled and somewhat urgently said, "Dad, come on. I gotta go."

She turned away and joined her fellow classmates. Alan just looked at her with the eyes of a very proud father. The class moved further away down the range, following Instructor Dave as he did his thing. As his attention fixated on his daughter and the group, a man approached Alan from behind and poked him in the back. Alan turned around quickly and noticed his friend Fred Mason, standing behind him with a smile.

"She's come a long way," Fred's boisterous voice said to him as he took a seat beside him, pointing to Lauren and the group.

"Hey, Fred. I didn't know you'd be here this weekend," Alan said, a bit startled but otherwise happy to see his friend.

"I show up every so often to make sure Dave isn't making a fool out of himself," Fred said.

Alan smiled. "I never knew the Rangers and Green Berets were so close," he said, somewhat jokingly.

"Other than reporting to the same command at Bragg, we're not," Fred affirmed. "I overlook it though, seeing as how he's the wife's brother and all…"

"So, the fact that he speaks fluent Chinese doesn't bother you?" Alan jested.

"Not one damn bit," Fred said with raise eyebrows.

Alan laughed. Fred set a small olive green backpack on the table and pulled out a large stainless steel revolver. He extracted it from its holster and laid it on the table in front of Alan.

"Check out my new baby," Fred said with a grand smile.

"Whoa," Alan said as he palmed the enormous weapon. "Is this a .500 magnum?"

"Damn right. It'll blow some nice big holes in some deserving sonsabitches."

"It's a little too big for my taste," Alan said, as he palmed it. He opened the cylinder closed it, and then cocked the hammer back and tested the trigger pull.

"It's not a concealed carry weapon," Fred said matter-of-factly.

"Obviously. I just mean, my hands are a couple sizes too small for it," Alan said.

"Does that mean you don't want to shoot it?" Fred asked jokingly.

"Now—I didn't say that," Alan replied with a smile.

Later on that evening following class, Lauren joined her father along with Fred who were sitting in camp chairs at one of several primitive campsites within Point Blank's property boundaries. They were both sipping on beers and exchanging war stories while a pile of fresh firewood burned happily within the confines of the stone fire ring. As Lauren approached them, their collective laughter began to cease and the conversation started to die down when they noticed her presence. Lauren leaned the rifle she'd been carrying against a tree near her father's tent and set the rest of her gear on the ground beside it. She stretched and yawned. Noticing Fred had joined them, she waved to him and smiled. Fred nodded to her.

"Everything go ok?" Alan asked his daughter, his voice carrying a hint of a beer buzz.

"It's a lot to learn in a day," Lauren replied. "I think I did ok, though. I really suck at reloading."

"You'll figure it out—it just takes practice," Alan said.

"—And muscle memory. Want a beer?" Fred asked jokingly.

"Damn right, I do," Lauren affirmed.

Fred reached into a cooler beside his chair and pulled out a bottle of German wheat beer. He handed it to Lauren, who popped the top open with the bottle opener on her knife and took several large gulps. She burped loudly, a little unprepared for the flood of foam that followed. She wiped her mouth and soon finished the bottle, then dropped it on the ground near Fred's chair.

"Seriously, Lauren?" Alan said.

"Like father, like daughter," Fred said with a chuckle as he cocked his head toward Alan.

Alan looked at Lauren with slight disapproval. Lauren watched her father's gaze closely and dismissed it with a smile.

"Don't worry, Dad," she said. "That's the only one for me tonight."

"Going to bed already?" Alan asked.

"Yeah, I'm beat," Lauren answered. "Dave said we're starting at 0500."

"That's typical for Dave," Fred said as he reached for another beer. "He's usually up before the rooster crows."

"Sure you don't want to stay up and chat for a while?" Alan asked her.

"Yeah. I'm done for today," Lauren replied. She walked past Fred and patted his shoulder. She then gave her father a hug and a kiss on the cheek. She took off her shoes, and slid into the tent. "Goodnight, Dad. Goodnight, Fred."

Alan and Fred both told her goodnight, and continued their conversation, which was marked by consistent alcohol consumption.

"She's grown up so fast, Alan," Fred said.

"Way too fast, if you ask me."

"Megan is doing the same thing to me," Fred said. "I love her, but she's making me feel so old it ain't funny."

Alan lifted his beer, tipping the bottle toward his friend.

"My friend, I know exactly what you mean," he said. "They say that age ain't nothing but a number—but when you have a daughter, that's bullshit."

Fred nodded and smiled. Pausing for a moment before replying, his smile slowly went away. "I take it, you've been preparing her for what's coming."

Alan tipped his beer up, taking a long drink. He said, "I've got her on the right track. That's part of the reason that I brought her here." He paused. "She's taken it a few steps further, though. Lauren has always been like that. I teach her something and then she tangents off and teaches herself things. I just wanted to bring her here to learn the stuff that I don't know much about."

"You know plenty about it," Fred said. "But I get it. It's better sometimes to have an objective party do the teaching. You'd be too easy on her."

"Exactly," Alan said. "She's my baby girl. She needs to learn how to be hard. I can't teach her that on my own." He paused and took another sip of beer. "The writing is on the wall. It's only a matter of time now before the shit hits the fan."

Fred nodded. "I've been seeing your folks at the cabin lately quite a bit. Looks like they're stocking up. The last load was all five gallon buckets—must've been fifty of them."

"Yeah. Sam has been moving quite a bit of his preps there lately. He still keeps a lot at home, though. They plan to hold out there as long as possible just like us, but it's reassuring to know that we have a place to go if it gets crazy at home."

"He was smart to buy that property when he did," Fred said as he took a sip of beer. "The real estate guru that he is and all. He's done a good job making friends with the neighbors, too."

"You tipping him off that it was available had something to do with it, Fred," Alan said. "We owe you bigtime for that."

As the two continued talking, headlights could be seen approaching them from the road. The vehicle was moving at a very high rate speed. As it entered the parking area, the driver slammed on the brakes and the vehicle came to an abrupt stop, almost perfectly parked in a space between two other vehicles—one of which belonged to Fred. Fred set down his beer, stood up and unholstered his 1911 .45. Alan quickly stood up and reached forward, placing his hand on top of Fred's pistol. Fred's eyes darted at him.

"Whoa, don't shoot, Fred. He's a good guy," Alan said.

The driver's door opened and a somewhat skinny, muscular man stepped out. In one hand, he held a wide-mouth can of Coors Light beer, which he put to his mouth, finished, and dropped to the ground with a loud burp. He picked it up and tossed it into the car, then pushed the door shut. He pulled a flashlight from his belt and aimed it at Alan and Fred, and they shielded their eyes from the intense beam.

"Is that you, Alan?" the man said.

"Yeah. It's me. Where the hell have you been, Norm?" Alan said.

"Well—I would have been here a couple hours ago, but your directions suck," Norman said as he began walking toward Alan and Fred, aiming his flashlight toward the ground to their approval.

"My directions were perfect," Alan said with a smile as he started walking toward Norman.

"Maybe it's the beer then."

Alan approached him and shook his hand, giving him a half-hug. "What took you so long to get here?"

"Traffic," Norman joked.

Alan introduced Norman to Fred and three chatted for a few minutes about Norman's trip. All three went back to the campsite which was well illuminated by the fire. Alan and Norman took a seat and Fred remained standing.

"If you guys will excuse me, I'm going to go chat with Dave. It's almost nearing his bedtime," Fred said. He turned to Norman and held out his hand. "Very nice meeting you, Norman."

Norman shook Fred's hand. "Likewise, Fred. I'll be seeing you."

Fred nodded and walked off.

"So, what's so important that you had me come all the way out here?" Norman asked Alan as he reached into a cooler and pulled out an ice cold can of beer, handing it to Alan. He then took one for himself.

"Just some things I needed to talk to you about," Alan said.

"You sound serious," Norman said. "I'm not used to hearing serious things from you—unless you're drunk."

"I'm well on my way there, my friend," Alan said as he cracked open the beer and took a long sip.

Norman sat up and shifted in his camp chair. "That's cool. Well, you know me, I'm all ears."

Alan smiled and nodded. "You know that I've been spending most of my time working in the city lately," Alan said.

"Sure do," Norman responded. "I don't know how you can stand that commute every day."

"It pays the bills," Alan said. "I do it because it's necessary and I can't make money like this anywhere else."

"That's understandable," Norman said, taking a sip of his beer.

Alan paused and sat forward in his chair, feeling the heat of the fire on his face. Norman took another sip of beer and set the can in the holder on the camp chair. He took a closer look at Alan's contemplative expression.

"I can almost hear the gears turning in your head," Norman said.

"The gears in my head never stop turning," Alan said.

"Is this about what I think it's about?" Norman asked with a curious look.

"What do you think it's about?" Alan asked.

Norman chuckled. "What it's always about—the end of the world as we know it."

"Yeah—that's it," Alan said with a bit of a snicker.

"Shit," Norman said. "Well, I guess I'll get myself in the mood then. I hope you have plenty of beer."

"I do," Alan said. He turned his head to Norman and smiled, but the smile soon faded.

"Wow," Norman said, slowly losing the fun tone in his voice. "You really do think something's going to happen, don't you?"

Alan nodded in affirmation. "I do," he said.

"When?"

"Tomorrow, next week, next year," Alan said. "Sooner than we all think. I just know it's coming."

"Brother, ever since we started talking about this stuff awhile back, I've been buying guns, ammo, and food like a madman. You are the reason I started prepping," Norman said. "I have to admit though, it's been awhile and nothing has happened since. For me, it's like the urgency went away. But here we are again, and you're talking about it again, and now I'm getting scared again. It's like you have access to information that I don't or something. And that should not be the case at all, considering our choices of career."

Alan shook his head. "No, it's not that at all. It's just that—in a perfect world, when the shit hits the fan, I'd be home with my girls, Norm," Alan began, "but the problem is that I spend more time away from them now, than I do with them. With things becoming more and more unstable every day, that scares the hell out of me."

Norman took another sip of his beer. "I can see that, totally," he said. "If something happens, chances are you'll be separated from them, but not for long."

"Sure. If I'm able to drive out as if nothing's happened," Alan said. "But what if I'm not able to leave? What if I'm not allowed to leave? What if the car is disabled somehow and the only way out is to walk? What if there's so much civil unrest that it's too dangerous for me to walk alone on the street? You know as well as I do that some of the areas I work in, can and will get locked down in the event of a catastrophe. Cell phones networks will be so overloaded that texting will be the only option, and if the networks fail, I have no way to communicate my welfare."

"Jesus, Alan. You think too much," Norman said.

"I'm being serious, Norman," Alan said. "This is as serious as I've been in a long time. I think about it every day."

Norman leaned forward in his camp chair and placed the open palms of his hands toward the fire. "So, what's this got to do with me?" he asked.

"Brother, you are the only man on this planet that I trust with my family, other than me," Alan said. He turned to face Norman. Norman cocked his head sideways and stared back. "Michelle trusts you emphatically and she thinks the world of your boys. Lauren absolutely adores you—she's always considered you her second father." Alan paused and took a breath. "If this goes down, and I'm not there with them, I need *you* to be. My family will become your family. I know they'll be safe with you."

Norman turned away for a second and stared at the fire. He took a short amount of time to contemplate the conversation and then said, "Brother, your family has always been my family. Whatever you want me to do, I'll do it. I got you."

The next morning, Lauren geared up early and headed off to training. Alan, Fred, and Norman packed up the camp and went to the pistol range after enjoying a campfire breakfast. In addition to the .500 magnum, Fred brought a plethora of other handguns with him, some of them custom, as he usually did when he went to the range. The three took turns firing his full-automatic Glock 17 9mm, .44 magnum Desert Eagle, and a custom Smith and Wesson Model 29, which was the gun made famous by the *Dirty Harry* movies. The three spent some time blasting away with the .500 magnum until the hand cannon caused their hands to ache to the point that they couldn't fire another shot with it.

They eventually joined up with Lauren's group, following them through the many different ranges and watching the drills from a distance. Alan watched with pride as his daughter's performance was well above what even he had expected. She moved well and her shots were always on target. She was slow at reloading, just as she had admitted, and at one time, Instructor Dave had scolded her for it.

"You're out of ammo and the threat is still breathing," he said firmly. "Instead of spending time fumbling around learning to reload that rifle, transition to your sidearm and eliminate the threat."

Lauren was disappointed in herself, but she took the constructive criticism well. In subsequent exercises, she followed his instruction and performed well within expectations. On several occasions when they were out of earshot, Alan noticed Instructor Dave smiling and shaking his head after interacting with her. He could only imagine what was said, but had a pretty good idea.

During a drill later on in the day that involved Lauren moving through a short range rifle drill with multiple targets, she encountered a misfire. An empty casing had been placed in the magazine on purpose, to see how she responded to the weapon not doing what it was supposed to do. When the trigger was pulled and the rifle didn't fire, Lauren quickly moved to the left and hid behind cover. She charged the rifle quickly, and got back into the drill as fast as she could, hitting each remaining target with every trigger pull. Once finished, Instructor Dave came up behind her and told her to safety her weapon. She did and after allowing it to hang on the sling to her side, she moved her earmuffs from her ears. Dave walked up beside her and half-smiled. Lauren looked at him apprehensively.

"Did I do ok?" she asked.

"Absolutely. You've done pretty well all day. There's just one minor problem," Dave said slowly, with a smirk.

"What's that?" Lauren asked with an inquisitive look.

"Your head is on the wrong side of the rifle," Dave joked. "It's been like that all day."

Lauren sneered and looked back at her father, who was standing at the rear of the range with Norman and Fred Mason, all of whom had caught what Dave had said to her. Alan looked at Norman, who shrugged and smiled. Fred just shook his head.

"Give her a break, Dave," Fred said with a smile. "She can't help who her father is."

"Being left handed is a curse," Lauren said. "Blame him." She pointed at Alan, who smiled and took the blame willingly.

After a long day of mixed drills and various exercises with plenty of breaks in between, the group met at the head of a single-lane, one-hundred-yard range.

Instructor Dave pointed at Lauren. "Miss Lauren, would you step forward, please?" he said.

Lauren moved away from the group and approached him. She could feel that this was about to get serious because Instructor Dave was no longer smiling.

"Set your rifle on the bench behind you please," Dave instructed. "You won't need it for this particular exercise."

Lauren turned around and placed the AR-15 on the shooting bench, then walked back to him while the group looked on.

"Your dad told me about what happened on your hiking trip last year," Dave mentioned. "Do you still carry the gun he gave you?"

Lauren nodded. "Every day, unless I'm going to school. Otherwise, I never leave the house without it."

"Good girl," he said. Turning and looking at the group, Dave addressed them with a raised voice. "The reason I've chosen Miss Lauren to lead off this final exercise isn't because she's the youngest. It's because she and her family were involved in a shooting last year. They were attacked by a couple of men with very bad intentions, and they were forced to defend themselves. Without a firearm and the willingness to act, they could have easily become victims of a heinous crime. Even though she wasn't the one who shot them, she was a witness to it and since that day, has been carrying the same gun that put the men down, thanks to her father."

Members of the group nodded and smiled in approval. Some of them gave the thumbs up sign to Alan. Lauren looked at the ground as the memories of what happened to her and her family began flooding her brain.

"See that target downrange?" Dave asked, pointing to a grey steel silhouette target with two orange circles on it.

"Yes sir," Lauren replied as she looked up.

"Today, that target is an active shooter," Dave said, looking at her sternly. "He's in your neighborhood and he's going house to house. He's carrying a suppressed rifle with a one-hundred round drum magazine."

Lauren nodded and looked back and forth between Dave and the target, which was about one-hundred yards away. She was beginning to realize why this target had caught her attention yesterday.

"Do you have neighbors?" Dave asked her.

"Yes," Lauren replied.

"Tell me about them," Dave said as he crossed his arms. "I don't need to know everything, just some basics…if you don't mind."

Lauren thought for a second. "We live in a cul-de-sac. Most of our neighbors have kids. The Thompsons next door, work from home and have four kids. There's an older lady—Mrs. Randolph. She lives by herself across the street. There's also Mr. Hobson on the other side of us. He's an asshole, so if the shooter gets him it won't bother me."

Some members of the group behind them began to laugh at Lauren's words. Norman let out a snicker. Alan smiled and shook his head. Dave looked away and then back to Lauren with an emotionless stare.

"Mrs. Randolph is dead now. He shot her in the face. Are you close with the Thompsons?"

"Yeah, pretty close," Lauren said with a shudder. "Mom and Dad play cards with them on occasion and they always come to our parties."

"Well, they're dead now, too," Dave said. He pointed downrange. "The shooter knocked on their door and when they opened it, he fired into the house, killing everyone inside that he could see."

Lauren looked up at Instructor Dave as the words that he spoke gave her chills.

"He went inside and shot all four of the kids," Dave said. "He did it while they screamed and cried for their parents."

A lump began to form on the back of Lauren's throat and her body was shaking a bit. Dave looked at her and noticed, but didn't back down.

"It's Sunday, Lauren. Who's at home right now?"

Lauren paused. "Mom is home for sure. Dad is too. If I'm not at work, so am I."

"The shooter is on his way there, Lauren. He's about a minute away from walking into your house and killing your parents. You've gone for a walk and you just turned the corner to your street. You see a strange man walking toward your house with a rifle in his hands. He hasn't seen you yet. What do you do?"

Lauren looked at Dave and then stared hard at the target. She was beginning to imagine herself in the situation that was being told to her. The more he spoke, the more real it was. Dave walked away from her and stood near the bench. Lauren looked back at him expecting him to say more, but he didn't. She turned her body to face downrange and brought the silhouette into view, then turned to look at her rifle. She knew that with it, she could accurately hit the target with ease. Dave shook his head.

"Do you typically carry an AR-15 when you go on walks?" Dave said.

A bit unsure of what to do, Lauren fixated on the target. She began to realize that this exercise was all about action—the willingness to bring the fight to the enemy. If she acted, would the shooter see her? Would he open fire in her direction? Anything was possible. She knew that if she didn't act, her parents would be as good as dead. A feeling of responsibility overcame her and she knew then, what she had to do. Without further hesitation, Lauren drew the Glock from its holster, chambered a round and took off in a sprint toward the target, staying close to the dirt embankment on her right side. Jogging just behind her but giving her plenty of space, Instructor Dave followed. She raised the pistol upward and began firing at the target, seeing most of her shots hitting the ground just below it. She had never taken a shot this far out with a handgun before.

"He's spotted you, take cover!" Dave shouted.

Lauren dove to the ground and leaned sideways to her right, putting as much of the ground as she could between herself and the silhouette. With her pistol still pointed at the target, she aimed a bit higher and fired a quick double-tap, instantly hearing the report of the bullets hitting the steel. She then emptied the remainder of the magazine into it, hitting it with the majority of her shots. She stood up and proceeded closer. As she neared the target, she dropped the empty magazine from the Glock and replaced it with a full one. She raised the weapon, released the slide, and brought the target into her sight picture. Dave walked up behind her and carefully placed his hand on her shoulder. She shuddered a bit when she felt his hand.

"He's down," Dave said calmly.

CHAPTER 13

The barricade
Wolf Gap
Hardy County West Virginia
Present day

N ORMAN AND FRED BOUNCED AROUND in the bed of Peter's truck as it ran over some potholes on a very much unmaintained Trout Run Road. The weather always took a toll on the pavement each year and this was the first time ever it had gone this long without being repaired. As they passed slowly over the bridge that stretched across Trout Run, Norman looked back to see Bryan Taylor waving his hand to them from the end of his driveway. Norman waved back and Fred did the same. Bryan had a shotgun slung over his shoulder and a pistol on his hip. His daughter, Emily was with him, holding her father's hand. She looked up at her father and noticed him waving, and did the same.

"Guess they decided to take your advice," Norman said as Fred glanced at him.

"Yeah," Fred said, "I'm glad. Hopefully, he got his wife to carry a gun as well. I never see her with a gun. They need to keep a real close eye on that little girl, too."

Fred turned around and looked closely at the two homes that had been abandoned by their owners not long after the collapse. They had left without warning, presumably to join up with other family elsewhere. Due to their proximity to his own home, Bryan Taylor had been keeping a close eye on them, to make sure they weren't being vandalized or being used to quarter unauthorized occupants. No one knew if their owners would ever return, especially now with vehicle traffic and fuel being so scarce. The property was overrun with weeds and tall grass, but with all visible windows and doors appearing intact, Fred's attention turned back to the road and the forest around them.

Norman looked Fred over as he sat on the wheel well across from him and shook his head. Fred was wearing his multicam ACU fatigues and had on a body armor vest with extra magazines for his M1A rifle, which he took with him everywhere. He also had two Colt 1911 .45 automatic pistols, each in a drop-side holster on both legs. Pouches for extra pistol magazines adorned his belt, as did several other pouches that Norman had no idea what they were for. Fred looked like he was ready for combat. He was busy looking all around the woods as they drove, but had noticed Norman looking him over.

"What?" Fred asked with a grimace.

"Nothing," Norman replied. "It's just that, I wish I had known it was going to be this kind of party."

"This ain't no party," Fred asserted.

"What I meant was, I would've dressed for the occasion," Norman said, raising his voice a little as the truck began to ascend the hill and the engine, in turn got louder.

Fred nodded. "We all need to take this threat seriously," he said sternly, also with a raised voice in order to overcome the engine noise. He began to look around again, his attention fixated on the woods.

"Oh, I agree fully," Norman said.

Norman patted his AK-47 and adjusted his chest rig which carried three extra magazines. He realized this was the second time in two days that he had worn it. The incident at the Ackermanns was first time he had worn it since their run-in with a group of takers last summer. Fred looked at Norman, who was adjusting his gear to make it feel more comfortable. He could tell that Norman was not used to wearing load-bearing gear.

"I have a plate carrier and some body armor that will fit you, if you want to trade that thing in," Fred said.

Norman looked confused. "You don't think this is enough?" he asked. "I've always been told that three extra magazines is enough for most situations."

"Oh, what you've got on is fine for now, I think," Fred began, "but I'm willing to bet that if we end up in a firefight, you will want your internal organs protected a bit better."

Norman looked stunned. He had mentally prepared himself for such a thing, but hearing an Army veteran, who had seen combat and probably killed more than his fair share, say this was eye-opening for him. He turned to look forward and could see the crest of the hill ahead where the barricade would soon come into view. The barricade was nothing more than a large overhang of sandstone and quartzite that had been demolished and left to cover the entire road. The chunks that had fallen into the road varied in size, the smallest being compared to the size of a kitchen appliance with some as large as an automobile. The boulders were big enough that it would be quite an undertaking to remove them from the road. As the truck neared the barricade, Michael Perry stuck his head out of the passenger window.

"Son of a bitch!" he yelled in total disgust.

The truck came to a halt about ten yards from the barricade. Michael's door opened first and he ran to the pile of rocks. Fred wasn't far behind. He jumped out of the truck with his M1A and began scanning the woods around them. Norman hopped off the truck bed with his AK and stood beside the driver's door as Peter turned the ignition off and got out. Michael put his hands on his hips and cursed loudly.

"This is unbelievable!" he shouted.

Some of the stone chunks that made up the barricade had somehow been moved aside, creating a broken path right down the middle. It wasn't large enough for an automobile to pass through, but it looked like the right size for a motorcycle. Michael just shook his head in disbelief.

"You been up here moving rocks recently, Mike?" Fred asked.

"Hell, no," Michael replied. "This definitely wasn't my doing."

"Then how the hell did this happen?" Fred pondered.

"I have no idea," Michael said in disgust. "But it was done deliberately."

Norman and Peter approached him. Fred turned away and began scanning the woods again, especially the ones past the barricade near the curve in the road that kept the Wolf Gap campground hidden from view.

"Let's keep our voices down," Fred said. He walked through the path to get a view of the barricade from the other side, his rifle at ready.

Peter walked up to the barricade and pushed on some rocks with his hands while taking a look around. "This isn't good," he said.

"No, it isn't," Norman agreed. "But it explains some things."

Michael looked the work over, as if trying to imagine how it had happened. "One thing's for certain," he said, "with a path like this, they could have easily drifted their bikes down this hill and right to the Ackermann's farm."

"And it would have been the first place visible from the road this time of year," Norman pointed out.

The three just stood there, taking it all in for a moment. Fred stood just on the other side of the barricade from them. He said nothing and his head was literally on a swivel, looking into the trees.

"This is scary, guys. If someone has the ability to move these rocks, the barricade is no longer a viable option. The only way to make this completely impassable is to just blow the road up," Michael said.

"We're not blowing the damn road up," Fred declared. He lifted his rifle and began scanning the area with the scope. "You guys keep your eyes to the trees," he continued. "I don't like this shit."

Norman immediately lifted his rifle to low-ready and began to look around. While not formally trained in military combat maneuvers, he had received his fair share of tactical training during his tenure as a government contractor. Some of that training had been about how to know the signs of a possible ambush. To him, this was beginning to look like a perfect place for something like that to happen. It was apparent that Fred had had that impression since they'd arrived.

"You know, Fred, we're standing in a damn kill zone," Norman said.

"Yep," Fred uttered, seemingly not happy with their situation. "Nice of you to notice."

"For them? Or for us?" Peter said.

Michael pulled his pistol from its holster and also began to take a look around. Feeling a bit left out, Peter did the same.

"Us. I think," Michael said.

"Guess we picked a hell of a day to not bring more firepower," Peter said in an attempt to lighten the mood. It didn't seem to work.

Fred continued up the road toward the curve with his rifle ready. Not wanting him to be alone, Norman ran up to just behind him. He turned to Michael and Peter.

"Watch our backs," he said.

They both nodded, and then walked through the divide in the barricade and followed them, staying a short distance behind. The four moved forward as a team until they reached the curve in the road. Norman looked down at what appeared to be narrow tire marks on the road. He got Peter's attention and pointed to them.

"I'm no expert, but those look like motorcycle tracks," Peter said sarcastically in a low tone.

The group continued to walk slowly. As the campsite came into view to their left, Fred went into a crouch and motioned for the others to do the same. Norman did so immediately and Michael mimicked him, unsure of what exactly to do or what the plan was. Peter did his best to follow their lead, but soon found it wasn't the easiest stance to maintain. Norman brought his AK to his cheek and swiveled from one side of the camping area to the other. The camping area of Wolf Gap was a small roundabout with several numbered campsites for car camping. Some of the cars that had been left there by people fleeing populated areas after the collapse still remained, although their owners were long gone and had been for some time. The cars had since been vandalized with everything of value either having been removed or destroyed. Fred picked up his pace and Norman followed several yards behind him. Fred's M1A swept back and forth across the area. When he was satisfied that the area was secure, he stood up fully and lowered his rifle. Noticing this, Norman did the same. Michael took a deep breath and let it out audibly. Peter held onto his pistol with both hands and continued to look around.

"Sorry about that, guys," Fred said. "Force of habit. I could almost feel someone's eyes looking at me through all that cover."

"No need to apologize," Michael said. "I was getting spooked back there, too."

"Same here," Norman said.

"That's good. Fear is a tool. This is a great spot to get ambushed," Fred said. "There's no easy way in or out."

"I, for one, accept your apology," Peter said, once again in an attempt to make a joke.

Fred just looked at him and shook his head, partially in disgust and partially knowing that Peter just couldn't help himself. He took almost everything in stride—that was just his nature. Sometimes, it was nice to have a little comic relief.

"Well, there's no doubt in my mind about it now," Norman said, "those bikers definitely came through this way. They probably stopped here and looked around, then continued down the hill with their engines off."

"A sneak attack," Peter said.

"Well, in my mind, the big question is how in the hell those stones got moved," Michael pointed out. "It would have taken at least a bobcat or something similar. No way they did it by hand."

"There's also no way they chained up and towed them with a Harley," Peter pointed out, sounding serious for the first time since their arrival. He walked ahead of the group and into the gravel parking area near the campsite roundabout. Looking down at the gravel, he noticed some very large tire tracks. "Mike, take a look as these," he said.

Michael walked over to him and holstered his pistol. "Something's been unloaded off of a trailer here," he said and looked around some more. "With a dual-tire configuration like that, I can't imagine it could be anything else but an equipment trailer." He pointed to the end of the parking area at some other tracks. "There's plenty of room to maneuver in this parking lot."

"What came off the trailer?" Norman asked.

Michael shrugged. "I don't know. A backhoe, maybe. Wheeled excavator or something similar—maybe something bigger."

"Would that be enough to make that path?" Norman asked again.

"Oh hell, yeah," Michael said. "They could have cleared the entire road with either one of those."

"Then, why the hell didn't they?" Fred asked curiously. "Why do half the job when you could've just as easily cleared the entire road?"

"That would be the question of the day, Fred," Peter added.

"I agree, Pete," Michael said. "I got nothing."

Fred and the others began to ponder the possibilities, none of which they liked very much.

After a pause, Fred said, "Well, gents...let's not overthink this. Maybe it was something simple. Maybe their equipment malfunctioned before it could finish the job."

Michael began looking around for evidence of a more common equipment malfunction, such as oil or hydraulic fluid on the road or close beside it. "That sounds plausible, actually," he said. "Nothing else really makes much sense."

"Guys, we could stand here and ponder all day and it still wouldn't matter," Norman said, sounding a bit more annoyed than he normally allowed himself to be. "Someone's decided they want in, and this was the only thing keeping them out."

The group congregated in the middle of the road just outside the parking area and nodded in agreement with Norman, but none said a word.

Norman walked away from the group and then turned back to look at all of them. "We're going to have to secure this position now at all times," he said. "The plans we talked about at the meeting are going to have to be put into action—starting today."

The others nodded.

"How many guys in the valley can perform a task like that?" Peter asked. "The majority of us are laborers and homemakers. Being an armed guard isn't for everyone."

"It's going to have to be, Pete," Fred asserted. "We don't have a choice in the matter. We can't trust an inanimate barricade to do the job on its own. We tried that and look what we ended up with."

"If we're considering that, we should consider securing both borders—north as well as south," Michael said. "We need to think seriously about fashioning some sort of a blockade at the north end of the valley and guard it, too."

"I agree, Mike," Norman said. "We shouldn't half-ass this."

"Guys, I'm normally not the voice of reason and I really hate to be the one to point this out, but we don't have enough people for this," Peter said.

The others looked at him with mixed expressions.

"Pete's right," Michael agreed. "We'd need at least six able-bodied men working security at all times. Two here, two on the north end, and two for random road patrols. Bryan really shouldn't leave his wife and daughter alone, and I don't want to leave Kristen by herself either."

"Amy can handle herself, but I don't feel comfortable leaving her and the boys by themselves—especially with what's going on," Peter added.

"We could always go further north of Perry," Fred said, "and see if the Bradys would be interested in helping."

The other three men gave Fred a barrage of curious looks.

"Well, I've heard it all now. The Brady bunch?" Peter asked. "You're not serious…"

"Yeah, Fred. We tried that before," Michael pointed out. "It didn't work out very well from what I remember."

"The situation has changed, so maybe they'll reconsider," Norman said.

"Yeah, or maybe they'll just choose to cook us and eat us," Peter said. "They're barbarians."

"They're survivors, Pete," Fred asserted. "More so than you, or me, or anyone we know."

"Fred, the last time I checked, they preferred to keep to themselves and I'm happy to let it stay that way," Peter said. "Old man Brady is a raving lunatic and the rest of his family aren't much different—it's like they're inbred or something. I remember waving to him last time I saw him and all I got in return was his middle finger."

"You got off easy—it could've been the business end of his double-barrel shotgun," Michael said. "I've seen that myself a couple times."

"Did I mention he was naked?" Peter said.

Norman and the others got a good laugh. He sighed and said, "Inbred or not, there's enough Bradys to increase our numbers substantially if we can convince them. It's an option worth considering."

"Then let's consider it," Fred said. "As far as standing guard, my boys can handle the job. Those two are a couple of monkeys, but they can do it."

"Mine can as well," Norman said. "Both John and Lee are excellent shots and can handle themselves."

"Our immediate threat is here, though," Michael digressed, pointing to the ground. "We need to address this today. Do we all agree on that?"

As he finished his sentence, the sound of engines could be heard in the distance. Fred immediately turned around to face the Virginia side of the road, lifting his rifle to the ready position.

"Yeah…those would be motorcycles," Peter said with a wide-eyed look of surprise.

"Spread out and find some cover now!" Fred said in a loud whisper while waving his hand behind him. He moved to the right of the road and found cover behind a thicket-covered embankment beside a primitive campsite. Norman and Michael ran to the left of the road and dove into the drainage ditch. Peter turned to look behind him and remembered that his truck was sitting in view, just on the other side of the barricade. He took off in a sprint toward his truck. Fred turned to see him running as the sound of the motorcycle engines began to get louder.

"Get the fuck down, dumbass!" Fred yelled.

Hearing Fred and realizing he couldn't make it to the truck in time, Peter lunged forward over the embankment and landed behind a tree. He dropped his pistol somewhere in the leaves when he landed. He began rifling through them in an attempt to find it, making sure to stay as low as he could.

Remaining under the cover of the bank beside him, Norman got to his knees and lifted his AK-47 to his shoulder, laying the barrel in the leaves. He looked right and could almost see the muzzle of Fred's M1A protruding out near the roadside, but he could not see Fred and that didn't surprise him. He assumed a former Ranger probably knew quite a bit about camouflage. Michael laid prone behind Norman and had his pistol drawn. Norman looked back at him and placed his finger to his lips. Michael nodded and turned to see Peter desperately trying to find the pistol he had dropped. He snapped his fingers a couple of times to get Peter's attention. When Peter looked up, Michael repeated Norman's signal. Peter nodded and ducked down.

Three motorcycles approached the campsite entrance and turned into it. All of the drivers had guns in their hands resting on their handlebars. They each turned into the campsite parking lot. They circled through it and came to a stop beside one another, shutting off their engines. One of the drivers got off of his bike and pointed his gun in the direction of the car campsites.

"Mickey, check over there," he said. "See if they decided to have themselves a little camp out."

"10-4," Mickey said as he got off of his motorcycle with what appeared to be an H&K MP5 submachine gun in his hand. He walked bow-legged over to the entrance of the roundabout. "There's some cars over there… looks like they've been here a long time. I don't see any bikes."

The third biker walked to the edge of the parking lot and proceeded to relieve himself. "I hope we find those fuckers before it gets dark," he said. "I got shit to do."

"We will," the first biker said as he continued to look around, his own submachine gun at the ready. From the way he presented himself, he appeared to be the leader of the pack.

Norman looked back at Michael. He lifted his hand and held up three fingers. Michael nodded. Norman then made his hand look like a gun and began rapidly moving his thumb, trying to indicate to Michael that the bikers had machine guns. Michael nodded again, but it was unclear to Norman if he understood the specific information he was trying to get across. Neither one of them were as adept at hand signals as they would've liked to have been, at this very moment.

The bikers convened in the middle of the parking lot and each lit up a cigarette, one right after the other. Fred watched their movements and noticed they were constantly looking all around them. They never got complacent and never let their guard down and that indicated to him, they weren't amateurs by any means. He moved his scope's crosshairs to align with the leader's head.

"How much longer are we going to look for these guys?" the one that the others had called Mickey asked. "It's not like they can't take care of themselves. They probably found some bitches and decided to hole up with them."

"That's not the point, dumbass," the leader said. "You know what Damien will do to us if we come back empty handed."

"Yeah, I'm not trying to find out," the third biker said.

"Our instructions were clear. Find Jesse and find Vance, and don't bother coming back until we do," the leader asserted.

"That's what I heard too," the third biker said.

"Fine," Mickey said as he pulled on the crotch of his jeans. He then rubbed his belly. "Damn hell, I'm hungry. Let's find something to eat while we're doing this and let's find something soon."

"That's actually not a bad idea," the third biker said.

The leader nodded and took a long drag on his cigarette. He said, "All the houses we passed on the way here looked ransacked to me. Let's head on down this hill here and see what we can find. Who knows? Maybe they're not far. There should be some houses down there, so hopefully we can get some food."

"And maybe find us a little something-something while we're at it," Mickey said with a smile. "I like country girls."

The three bikers stood silent for a moment and finished their cigarettes, then mounted their motorcycles. Fred had heard everything they had said. In a moment, these three men, armed with machine guns, would be headed down and over the hill toward the barricade. They would quickly see Peter's truck and become alerted to their presence. This was not a good thing and he knew it. Fred was a man of action and knew that there was no way he could allow this to happen. He tried to signal Norman, but noticed that he wasn't looking in his direction. As the motorcycles began to exit the parking lot, Fred took aim and fired a single shot from his M1A. The tracer bullet grazed the gas tank of the bike belonging to the leader, causing it to rupture and catch fire. The rider yelped, laid the bike over and fell to the ground. He began rolling around on the gravel, in an attempt to put the fire out that had spread to his clothes, letting out cries as he did. He began barking orders to the other bikers to shoot back. And that, was when all hell broke loose.

The remaining two bikers began a hail of simultaneous full-automatic gunfire toward and around Fred's position. He pulled back and ducked under cover as best he could as dirt and debris flew all over him and bullets whizzed by his head. Norman slapped off his safety and immediately began firing his AK rapidly in the direction of the bikers, even though several trees were preventing him from having a perfect sight picture. The remaining two bikers laid their bikes down instinctively and fell behind them for cover. One of them began firing full-auto bursts in Norman's direction, forcing him to duck. Unable to aim his shots now, he pulled the trigger blindly, knowing that if he stopped, they would simply concentrate their fire at Fred's position and keep him pinned down. With their fully automatic weapons they had fire superiority. The only chance was to attack them from multiple locations and establish a crossfire.

Fred began firing his rifle from cover in their general direction, but his unaimed shots only managed to hit the ground near them. One of the bikers stopped shooting long enough to load a new magazine and he soon began another onslaught of rapid fire at Norman's position.

After several painstaking minutes of searching, Peter had finally managed to find his pistol. He remained under cover from the other side of the road, in between the gunfight and the barricade for a moment, then decided to break cover and try to move behind and hopefully flank the bikers. When he finally was able to see them, he laid down behind a large fallen tree and began to fire at them. His shots were aimed, but were out of range for his weapon and skillset. He had never practiced shooting his handgun at long distances before and quickly realized that having done so, would be very useful at this moment.

With the bikers being fired on from three different positions, one of which they had no cover from, they were beginning to get flustered. Sensing a break in the assault, Fred suddenly broke cover firing multiple shots at the bikers. As he ran, he took a well-placed single shot, killing the lead biker as he continued to roll around on the ground, half-covered in flames. When the bolt of his M1A held open, Fred realized he had emptied his magazine and went to the ground, simultaneously unholstering one of his 1911 .45 pistols. Upon seeing this, the third biker yelled, "To hell with this!" and hopped on his bike, tearing off through the woods behind him in a cloud of dust. Fred rolled to take a shot at him, but there were too many trees in the way. He then drew down on the remaining biker, the one the others had called Mickey. As Mickey aimed his gun in Fred's direction, Norman stood up with his AK at the ready. With a full magazine, he began to fire in the direction of the remaining biker. When one of the bullets darted past his head, Mickey dropped his gun and held his hands up. Seeing this, Norman stopped pulling the trigger. He wouldn't shoot an unarmed man.

"Stop shooting at me, dammit!" Mickey said. "I give up!"

Fred got up and ran over to him. He kicked his submachine gun out of his reach. He then brought the buttstock of his M1A down on Mickey's head, knocking him to the ground nearly unconscious. Norman approached soon after in an all-out sprint. He passed by rapidly, running in the direction of the biker who had escaped into the woods. Michael walked over with his pistol in hand as did Peter. Fred looked at Peter and smiled.

"Nice work," Fred said. "Your shooting really caught them off-guard."

"It was nothing," Peter said trying to brush off a very stressful situation. He was almost out of breath.

"Too bad you didn't hit a damn thing," Fred poked. Peter just offered a semi-shocked look and mocked him silently.

Fred rolled the man over and pulled a set of plastic zip cuffs from his vest pocket, then used them to secure the man's hands behind his back. He patted him down quickly and removed everything from his pockets, tossing the belongings on the ground near Michael's feet. Michael looked the items over and picked up a fairly new Spyderco folding knife.

A few minutes later Norman walked up to them, breathing heavily with his AK resting on his shoulder.

"Sorry, guys. He's long gone," Norman said in between breaths. "There's tracks leading down into the gulch and back onto the road. He was gone before I could even get a clear shot."

"Shit!" Fred exclaimed, showing his disgust. "That's just fucking great."

"I could go after them," Peter said, pointing at the last remaining undamaged motorcycle, "but you managed to shoot out all the tires, Fred."

Fred glared quickly at Peter and began to say something regarding his ability to hit a target, but only thought it for a moment and dismissed it. He figured he'd let Peter have his moment.

"This really changes things," Michael said as he pocketed the knife. "And I bet people heard that gunfire for miles."

Fred nodded and pulled his radio from a pouch on his vest and pressed the push-to-talk button. "All stations, this is Mason one. The gunfire was us. We are all OK, I repeat, we are all OK," he said into the microphone.

Fred's wife's voice came back over the speaker, a few seconds after he'd released the push-to-talk button. "Fred, what's going on up there?" Kim's voice said over the radio.

"We had a small firefight, but we're all ok, Kimmy," Fred replied.

"We heard the shots," Kim said. "We copy that you're ok."

"We'll be back soon," Fred said. "Out." Fred placed the radio back into its pouch and sighed.

"Well, one thing's for certain. They'll be coming for sure now," Norman uttered.

"You think?" Fred said, still sounding a bit disgusted.

"Who's this guy?" Norman asked.

Fred nudged Mickey the biker's vest a bit, exposing a patch that read, "ENFORCER."

"Enforcer, huh?" Fred said. He poked the muzzle of his rifle into Mickey's cheek, causing Mickey to cringe. "What exactly is it that you enforce?"

Mickey ignored him and said nothing.

"Wake up, dipshit! We got some questions for you," Fred said, sounding a bit perturbed.

Mickey opened his eyes and spit out a wad of blood on the ground. "I don't give a shit about your questions," he said. "You can fuck off."

"We'll see about that," Fred huffed.

Peter walked over to the lead biker and began kicking dirt over him, in order to douse the remaining flames. He then rolled him over with his foot.

"Oh, shit," Peter said, "You killed a club officer, Fred."

"What do you mean?" Michael asked.

"His patch says he's the Treasurer," Peter replied. "The money man. Wonder what he does now—now that money is obsolete."

"I should've killed all three of them," Fred said as he eyeballed Mickey, who was now sitting up, looking very rattled after getting his bell rung by the buttstock of Fred's rifle. Fred didn't take his eyes off of the man. He kept the muzzle of his weapon aimed directly at him.

Norman just shook his head. "That's great," he said. "Yesterday at the Ackermanns, it was the Vice President and today, it's the Treasurer."

Mickey looked up at Norman with a cold expression on his face. He said nothing.

"What the fuck are you talking about, Norman?" Fred asked. "You never said anything about that."

"Didn't really think it was relevant," Norman said. "One dead biker is the same as another, right?"

"Oh, it's relevant," Peter began, "if you know how these clubs work." Everyone paused.

"Do you mind elaborating, Pete?" Michael asked.

Peter nodded and said, "It takes a lot to become a member and these clubs take their membership seriously. Especially their officers. We know this dead guy today is—well, was the Treasurer. If one of the guys Mr. Ackermann shot was indeed the Vice President of the club, that's two dead club officers in as many days. The other members will not take kindly to losing two of their main guys."

"They were both killed in self-defense, though," Michael said.

"Sorry, Michael. Intent doesn't mean a damn thing to them," Peter said.

"No, it won't matter," Mickey said confidently, "not one goddamn bit."

"Shut the hell up, idiot," Fred said as he lifted his rifle to his shoulder.

"Go ahead, kill me. It won't change anything," Mickey said with a sinister smile, displaying his discolored teeth.

"Oh, it will change plenty," Fred said. "You see…it'll make you dead and not alive anymore—which is perfectly fine with me. I won't have to hear you talk and I won't have to drag your fat ass down this hill and tie your ass to a tree."

"It won't change the fact that all three of you walking dead men," Mickey said. "Damien will find you and he'll kill all of you. If y'all killed Jesse and Vance, you just started a shitstorm that can't be stopped."

"Who's Damien?" Fred asked. Mickey turned away and spat on the ground. Fred pushed the muzzle of his M1A into Mickey's temple. After a few more seconds of silence, Fred asked again with a much louder, gruff tone, "Talk, asshole. Who is Damien?"

"He's the President," Peter said. "The main man. Big cheese. Head honcho. Judge, jury, and executioner."

Mickey laughed. "Damien is more than that," he said. "He's your new god."

Norman, Fred, Peter, and Michael all looked at each other. The looks on their faces transitioned from dumbfounded to worried. Fred's expression was hard to calculate. He looked more annoyed than anything. Norman noticed Fred's finger was no longer alongside the trigger guard of his rifle. It was resting lightly on the trigger now. Fred wanted to kill this man. The biker didn't seem to care much that his life was now hanging by a thread. On top of everything else he had on his mind, this really made Norman nervous. If this guy wasn't afraid to die, it was certainly possible that every member of this gang viewed death in the same way.

"Are you afraid to die?" Norman asked the biker. "Because you're awfully close to finding out what a 7.62 to the brain feels like at point blank range."

Fred looked to Norman and smiled in approval. Mickey turned his head and looked up at Norman. Fred stepped back and pulled the muzzle away from Mickey's head a bit.

"I think the more appropriate question is—are *you* afraid to die?" Mickey deferred.

"I asked you first," Norman said.

Mickey spat again. He began to speak slowly and concisely. "You don't get it, do you, country boy? As I say this, he's coming for you. He's coming for all of you. Whoever and whatever you hold dear will soon be his and you'll all be dead. All of you. Every single one of you will be dead. If you have women, they will become his women. He will do things to them that will make torture look like a game of checkers. If you have kids, they will become his children. He will make them his slaves and force them to work like mules. Whatever possessions you have will become his. He'll kill you slowly and feast on your fucking dead corpses. He will burn your lives to the ground, and piss on the ashes."

Norman had begun to become enraged and was resisting the urge to kick Mickey in his mouth. Fred looked up at him and noticed that Norman was getting very flustered. He held up his hand to him and Norman turned away, sensing he was about to lose control.

"Don't let this peckerhead get to you, Norman," Fred said. "He's talking out of his ass."

"We'll see about that…won't we?" Mickey said with a grin and what sounded like a giggle.

"Yep," Fred said. "But for now, we are still alive and what's ours is still ours. And we even got ourselves a prisoner."

"You ain't got shit," Mickey said with a sinister chuckle. "You are all fucking dead men. FUCKING DEAD MEN!" Mickey's voice thundered as he began to breathe deeply and heavily.

"Ah, fuck it," Fred said. "Just hit him, Norman."

Norman handed his AK-47 to Peter, who took it and nodded. He then turned around in an instant, and in a burst of rage, drew back and slammed a right roundhouse punch to Mickey's chin, dropping him to the ground with a loud smack. Norman shook his hand a bit after the blow, immediately feeling the pain of a bare-knuckle punch in his hand. Mickey lay still. He was knocked out cold.

"Nice punch," Peter said, as he handed Norman back his AK.

Fred smiled and nodded. "Let's clean this stuff up and drag this dick cheese back to the truck. We need to have an emergency meeting when we get back. This situation just got real."

"Agreed," Michael said, sensing the urgency of the situation. "After we distribute fuel, I'll drive my front-loader up here and repair the barricade."

"Hey, Mike. Sorry, but I was just thinking. Don't you have one of them really big friggin bulldozers?" Peter asked.

"I've got a Caterpillar D9T," Michael replied. "It's pretty large. Why?"

"The blade on that thing—is it about as wide as the road?"

Michael looked down over the hill and turned back to Pete. "I'd imagine it's pretty close," Michael said.

"I was thinking—we could pull that sucker right up to the barricade. These guys could move stones around all day, but no one would be able to move that thing except us," Peter said.

"Damn, Pete," Fred said. "That gunfight must've jarred something. The shit that's coming out of your mouth is starting to make sense now."

Peter gave Fred a mocking half-smile and shrugged.

"Well, it does weigh about fifty tons," Michael said. "The blade is as wide as this road and it's tall enough to use for cover if needed. It would take a lot to penetrate it."

"Good idea, Pete. With that thing blocking the road, nothing would get by unless we wanted it to," Norman said. Grinning, he added, "You're not using it for anything at the moment, are you, Mike?"

"Nope," Michael said with a confident smile. "Not at the moment."

"If it'll keep a gang of pissed-off biker assholes from driving down this road into our valley, then that's what we need to make happen,"

Fred said firmly. "But we still need to set up camp here. I'll have Mark and Chad head up here and start working on digging us a foxhole up above the barricade in the woods. We'll be able to see anything coming down the road from there. It'll provide us plenty of cover."

After camouflaging the motorcycles and the dead biker's body deep in the woods on the Virginia side of the mountain, all four men returned to Peter's truck and began the ride back into the valley. On the way, they stopped first at Bryan and Sarah Taylor's house to gather their gas cans and delivered the news of what happened to them, informing them of the emergency meeting that would be held at Fred's house later that evening. The next stop was the Schmidt residence for the same reasons. After leaving the Schmidts, the truck turned down short gravel driveway that led to the Ackermann farm. Norman stood up in the back of the truck and was able to see Mr. Ackermann in his backyard with a shovel and a wheelbarrow, feeding his hogs. When the truck came to a halt, Peter turned off the engine and Norman jumped out of the bed, followed by Fred Mason. The hogs could be heard now as they squealed wildly. Both men decided to leave their rifles in the truck, to not appear threatening to Mr. Ackermann. Neither of them could estimate what his mental state would be.

"We'll go check on him," Norman said to Peter and to Michael through the open driver's side window. "Shouldn't take but a few minutes."

Peter and Michael both nodded. Fred followed Norman as he walked around the side of the house to where Mr. Ackermann was. Mr. Ackermann saw them approaching and threw one of his hands up to them in acknowledgement. As they got nearer to him, Norman noticed a wheelbarrow that was full of chunks of something covered, in what appeared to be blood. The hogs were squealing wildly and fighting over the food he had scooped into their pen. When Mr. Ackermann pulled the scoop shovel out of the wheelbarrow, Norman saw what appeared to be a human arm. Fred noticed it as well. Norman wasn't certain, but his imagination told him exactly what was going on here. When the contents of the wheelbarrow came into view, it became evident. Mr. Ackermann shoved the shovel back into the bloody contents of the wheelbarrow and nodded to Norman and Fred.

"How can I help you boys?" he asked calmly.

Norman, who was trying to hold back the feeling of suddenly

wanting to regurgitate said, "We just wanted to check on you and make sure you were all right, Mr. Ackermann."

"I'm fine, thanks for asking," Mr. Ackermann said quickly and firmly.

"Mr. Ackermann, is that what I think it is?" Fred asked him, not able to hold back his curiosity any longer. He knew the answer already, but needed to hear it for his edification.

"My hogs are hungry and need to eat," Mr. Ackermann replied in his half-Bavarian, half-West Virginian accent. "The good Lord blessed us with some fresh meat for them. No way in hell, I was going to let it go to waste." He pointed at Norman. "You and your boys drug these fellas off into the woods over yonder." He pointed to the woods where Norman, Lee, and John had taken the motorcycles and their deceased riders the day before. "Y'all should've just left them here so I didn't have to drag them back—but don't worry, I got it taken care of."

Norman covered his mouth and looked into the wheelbarrow and into the hog pen, and then back into the wheelbarrow. The feeling to throw up was almost unbearable and he could feel saliva building under his tongue. From what he could decipher, there was at least one body left in there. It had been cut up roughly with what he guessed had been a chainsaw.

"I imagine they were too big to just drag over here in one piece," Fred said, trying to relate to his neighbor's state of mind. "What did you use to cut them up with?"

"My Stihl, of course," he replied, his voice showing no remorse whatsoever. "Cut through them like a hot knife through butter."

There was an uncomfortable pause after his words.

"Mr. Ackermann, the community is having an emergency meeting this evening at Fred's house. We'd like you to come if you can," Norman said.

The old man shook his head. "I'm fine," he said.

"There's a threat to the community that we all need to discuss in depth," Fred said. "Things will be changing around here quite a bit now because of it. We'd like for you to be involved."

"I'm fine," he said again. "Whatever it is, I'm sure you'll be able to handle it without me. This farm needs me and I can't leave it alone to tend itself."

After a few minutes of near-pleading with him with no results, Norman and Fred both said their goodbyes and walked back to the truck. As they neared the truck, Norman noticed a new mound of dirt in the garden beside the house. He assumed the old man had buried his wife there.

"Everything ok?" Michael asked noticing their grim faces.

"Uh...yeah," Fred said. "Mr. Ackermann won't be attending the meeting tonight."

"Why not?" Peter asked, looking confused.

Fred didn't answer and Norman looked away with a distraught look on his face. Peter turned to look at Michael who shrugged, then looked back at Fred and Norman.

"Why are those hogs going crazy?" Peter asked.

"Blood," Fred said resolutely as he pulled himself into the bed of the truck.

"What?" Peter and Michael asked almost simultaneously, both with very confused looks.

Norman stood beside the driver's side door and explained the scene that he and Fred had just witnessed. Peter and Michael both were horrified at first, and both just shook their heads in disbelief. Peter started the truck and Norman hopped into the bed. Peter stuck his head out of the window, just as he began to back the truck up.

"I'm not trying to sound overly macabre, but can you guys think of a better way of disposing of a body?" he said.

CHAPTER 14

Sugar Knob Cabin
George Washington National Forest
Shenandoah County Virginia
Present day

IT HAD BEEN ONE OF the longest, most grueling hikes that Lauren could remember ever having taken in her life. She was beyond truly exhausted now, and each step she took made her just want to give up. Her ankle was throbbing badly. Every time she put any amount of body weight on it, the pain was nearly excruciating. She needed to rest and take her weight off of it. Her frustration was evident, both with herself and with her predicament. She was mad at herself for getting injured so far away from home. Faced with a petrifying situation of being stalked by dogs and men with guns, that she was certain had every intention of killing her, she had panicked and done something stupid. She had never trained or prepared herself for anything quite like this. The trails in these mountains were not forgiving and she'd known it. Now, she was paying the price.

The intersection with Little Stony Creek Trail was just ahead, and she yearned to at least just make it there. Sugar Knob Cabin was just a short way from that point. Without a doubt in her mind, that would be where she and Christian would have stay the night. Her day of hiking was nearly over, even though she was still several miles from home. She looked behind and saw that Christian's limp had gotten worse, due to the hole in his calf. He was bleeding under his bandage again and the wound needed to be re-dressed. Both of them just needed to call it a day.

Rounding the corner and hiking a little way down Little Stony Creek Trail, Sugar Knob Cabin came into view. It was a small primitive cabin with stone walls and a tin roof, with a short stone chimney and a thick solid wood door.

"Lauren, hang back a second," Christian said under his breath.

Lauren stopped walking and moved to the side of the trail to allow him to pass. He did so with his M4 at the ready and began scanning the area for threats. He moved past and around the cabin and then scanned the open camping area surrounding it. As he passed the stone fire ring, he held his hand over it to check for any heat which would be a distinct indicator of recent use, but didn't feel any. Reaching the door, he pulled on the thick padlock that secured it in place. The padlock didn't budge. The building was undisturbed as far as he could tell. He motioned to Lauren that all appeared to be clear.

"Is it locked?" Lauren asked as she began to slowly approach the cabin. She unsnapped all of the quick-release buckles on her pack and let it fall to the ground, then she placed her rifle on top of it.

"Oh, yeah," Christian said. "Like Fort Knox."

"Fantastic," Lauren said, her voice inundated with sarcasm and as well, showing signs that she was in some serious pain.

"There's got to be a spare key around here somewhere," Christian said. "I mean, if you reserved this place and hiked all the way up here and forgot your key, what the hell would you do?"

"Sleep outside," Lauren said passively. She took a seat on the ground and slowly removed her hiking boot to expose a very swollen ankle.

Christian looked down at her and noticed that her injury was looking much worse than it had been earlier. There were purple splotches all around her ankle, and it was so swollen that he had no idea how it'd even fit in her boot.

"You definitely need to stay off your feet," he said.

She nodded and pointed to his calf. "I'm well aware of what the protocol is for a sprained ankle. You, however, should consider taking your own advice," Lauren stated somewhat brashly.

Christian looked down at his dressing and noticed that it was indeed in pretty bad shape. He nodded and began looking around the building, in an attempt to find a hiding place for a key that may or may not exist.

"Now...if I were a key, where would I be hiding?" he asked rhetorically.

"You'd have a better chance crawling through one of those windows," Lauren jested, pointing to one of the three windows that weren't anywhere near large enough to fit a human body through. On top of it, they were covered in shutters made of wood that looked even thicker than the door.

"I haven't ruled that out yet," Christian joked.

Lauren began nursing her very much overworked sprained ankle. She had found small smooth stone and was rubbing her ankle with it, trying to massage and loosen the muscles. The underside of the stone was nice and cool, but nowhere near enough to sooth the pain or bring down the swelling. She pulled out her first aid kit and broke open an instant ice pack, then laid it on her ankle. As the pack got colder, the pain started to subside. She hoped it would last awhile since it was the only ice pack she had with her, and probably the only one left in her family's post-collapse supplies. While waiting for the ice pack to do its job, she popped a handful of ibuprofen.

Christian was overturning stones everywhere he walked. He looked underneath an old wooden picnic table that had been there for as long as Lauren could remember. He was relentless, checking every nook and cranny in the areas surrounding the cabin.

"Does anyone in your community have medical knowledge?" Christian asked, fully expecting Lauren to lay into him for asking personal questions again. He felt as though that bridge had been crossed already, but wasn't entirely sure.

"We don't have any doctors, but our neighbor, Kristen is a paramedic. She handles all the cuts and bruises—and the occasional gunshot wound," Lauren said in an attempt to make a joke. Christian looked over to her and grinned as Lauren continued. "My mom's friend, Amy was an LPN before the collapse so she knows some stuff, but Kristen is definitely our go-to."

"Gotcha," Christian said. "So, when we get back, we'll need to look her up."

"Yeah," Lauren said, not sounding very confident. She wasn't looking forward to being a cripple for a while, unable to move about and be active. She knew once her mother saw her condition, she would be confined to quarters. Kristen would probably tell her to keep off of her feet for a couple weeks to let the sprain heal. Just the thought of not being able to do anything for that long didn't sit well. A full day of doing nothing was enough to drive her crazy.

"HOLY SHIT!" Christian bellowed suddenly from the other side of the cabin where Lauren couldn't see him. Lauren looked up, somewhat startled as Christian hobbled around the corner of the cabin with a silver key held up between his finger and thumb.

"You've got to be shitting me!" Lauren said, both in surprise and disbelief.

"There was a hide-a-key in a knot in that tree over there," Christian said proudly.

He walked over to the door and inserted the key into the padlock. With a slow turn that required a bit of effort, the padlock pulled open. Christian pushed the door open with one hand while keeping the other hand on his newly acquired sidearm. The door moved inward, exposing the primitive interior of the cabin. Inside to the right was a table, a woodstove, and a host of simple cookware and utensils. To the left was a cot with a foam mattress, a pillow, and several wool blankets. A couple old chairs sat in the middle of the earthen floor and there were cobwebs everywhere. It appeared as though the cabin hadn't been used for a very long time.

"Have you ever been in this thing?" Christian asked as he knocked some of the thicker cobwebs from their moorings.

"Once, when I was very little," Lauren said. She pulled herself up to her feet and hopped on one foot over to where Christian was standing in the doorway. "Looks pretty much the same as it did then—minus the cobwebs." Lauren hopped past Christian over to the cot and pulled herself onto it. She laid back and put her head on the old pillow, crossing her hands over her stomach. She closed her eyes for a moment and said, "If you need me, I'll be right here."

"Sure, you just make yourself comfortable," Christian said. "I'll take care of everything else."

"I didn't mean it like that, Christian," Lauren said quietly. As she attempted to sit up, Christian held up a hand.

"I was kidding. Seriously, take a load off. I'll get all of our gear inside and get some food going," Christian assured her.

Lauren smiled. She truly felt now that she had managed to find a friend in Christian. He had saved her life and was now helping to take care of her in an injured state. It was endearing. It was almost like having an older brother around again. Her own older brother was a half-brother that she didn't see very often, due to their living situation. He was a year younger than her half-sister Grace and was a student at a local community college. He had been living with his mother and step-father several miles outside of Winchester on the day of the collapse. She hadn't seen him in at least a year before that day. She missed him because she grew up knowing him, and even though it pained her to lose touch with him, she knew there was nothing that could be done about it. She often wondered if she'd ever see him again. If she did, it would make her family all the more complete. She knew getting him back, and maybe someday seeing her dad again, would take nothing short of a miracle.

Christian dropped his backpack on the floor of the cabin and went to collect Lauren's pack and rifle. Once he'd brought everything inside, he began to look around a bit. He picked up Lauren's rifle and laid it beside her, moving her hand to the grip, so she knew it was there. He then placed her instant ice pack on her ankle and elevated it with some of the folded blankets at the foot of the cot. She didn't complain and her eyes were still closed, but he doubted she was asleep. In his own backpack, he pulled out two MREs, opened the boxes and dumped the contents out onto the table.

"I'm going to forgo making a fire here," he said. "I don't want to draw any attention to us."

"That's fine. I don't mind eating cold MRE stuff."

"Well, it's not exactly cold. My body heat took care of that for us," Christian said.

"And that's kinda gross," Lauren said.

Opening a packet of macaroni and cheese, he placed a plastic spork into it. He said, "Here you go," and handed it to Lauren. She sat up and began devouring its contents.

"My favorite," she said with a mouth full of food.

"I figured you for a mac and cheese girl," Christian said.

"I usually like mine with chopped up hot dogs, but in light of our situation, I can live without them," Lauren said amusingly.

"There's nothing more American than mac and cheese with cut up hot dogs," he said with a smile, then asked, "Question, though—is there a water source close by? My water situation is getting pretty desperate."

"Yeah, so is mine. There's an old spring about a tenth of a mile down the hill on the left," Lauren replied.

Christian nodded. He took a seat on one of the old wooden chairs and opened a packet of beef chili. "I have to say, I'm pretty worried about your ankle, Lauren."

Lauren paused before replying, in order to swallow a bite of food. "It's an old injury," she said. "I've hurt this ankle pretty bad before."

"Did it look like that?" he asked as he nodded toward her ankle, pointing out the purple blotches on her skin.

"Not that I remember," she replied quietly. "I'm hoping it looks worse than it really is."

"You might need to drop your pack entirely tomorrow and get some of that extra weight off of it. We can come back another time and retrieve it."

"No. Forget it. I'm not leaving this pack behind," Lauren said definitively.

"Ok," Christian accepted. "It was just a suggestion."

The two remained silent for a few minutes while they finished their entrees. Christian held up two more packets, one of mashed potatoes and one of rice. Lauren pointed to the potatoes and he handed the packet to her. He then tossed her a pack of crackers.

"This is almost like a gourmet meal," Lauren said with a grin.

"Not used to this five-star menu, I take it?" Christian jested.

Lauren snickered. "When we moved here, we had a trailer on the back of our truck with about a year's worth of food on it. My grandparents had another year of food already stored at our cabin—most of which was just rice and beans in five-gallon buckets. Dad was adamant about us having a long-term food storage system. He always said that if you control the food, you can control an entire population. He failed to mention how limited the options were."

Christian nodded. "He's right," he said. "It's astounding what a person is willing to do when they are starving. Even more so when someone they love is starving."

Lauren took a bite of her potatoes and stirred the packet. "Dad said that too all the time," she began. "He said that the best way to live free is to figure out how to live without technology, goods, and services. He also said having adequate firepower was absolutely vital to remain free."

"I have got to meet this guy," Christian said. He then looked at Lauren, who looked away. He remembered this was a touchy subject for her, so he decided to not to elaborate further.

"Christian, what happened to your dad?" Lauren asked after a long pause.

Christian sighed and nodded. "How did I know that question was coming…" he said.

"I'm sorry," Lauren said quietly. "If you don't want to talk about it, I understand. Lord knows, it hurts to talk about my dad, so if you want me to drop it, it's cool."

"My dad fought them and lost, Lauren," Christian said. "They wanted to federalize his department and he wasn't having it. It went from being handled diplomatically, to him being given no choice in the matter. When they came to dismantle the local government, he and all of his deputies tried to stop them from moving in. Homeland's storm troopers marched into downtown with riot gear and mine-resistant vehicles to put down any armed resistance. I was there that day—working for DHS, of course. Some of the local police force fought alongside of the sheriffs, but they were no match for what DHS had." He paused. "I watched my father get ripped apart by machine gun fire from one of those MRAPs. He died on the street in front of me and I couldn't do anything about it. If I'd blown my cover, I would've died right beside him."

"Oh my dear God," Lauren said. She placed her hand over her mouth as her face presented a look of total astonishment.

Christian looked up at her. "I was on the wrong side, Lauren…I was on the wrong fucking side," he said. "I should have fought with him. Instead, I was on the side that killed him."

"But you didn't kill him. They did," Lauren pointed out.

"I didn't do anything to stop it—" Christian began before he was interrupted.

"—Because it wasn't in your power to do so," Lauren said firmly. "You did what you did and saw what you saw for a reason, Christian. You can't take it back, so just stop it. My dad isn't here because of a lot of reasons—one being that he needed the overtime and was working when he normally wouldn't have been. I fought the notion for a long time that maybe if I didn't need so much stuff, he wouldn't have needed to work so hard and he would have been with us, instead of a hundred miles away. All the stuff we needed then is useless now. It's hard…trust me, I know. But I also know that you cannot blame yourself."

"I have to do something to honor him. I have to avenge him somehow. But now, with my cover blown with DHS, I honestly have no idea how to go about it."

Lauren scooted on the cot to get closer to Christian, who now looked very close to tears. She placed her hand on his shoulder. "He'd want you to live your life," Lauren said. "He'd want you to survive and keep moving forward—just like my dad would want me to do."

Christian looked down and then up again. He looked to Lauren, raised his eyebrows a bit and smiled at her gratefully. "I'm all alone now," he said matter-of-factly.

Lauren shook her head in disagreement. "You were alone. *Were*," she said. "You saved me. Now, I owe you something in return. Let me help you like you helped me."

Christian nodded and smiled. He stood up and helped Lauren lay back and get comfortable again. Knowing her ankle would need to be re-wrapped before they could move again, he pulled off the remaining pieces of athletic tape while she grimaced. He then placed the ice pack back on her ankle. He turned around and pulled the hydration bladder from Lauren's pack and stuffed it into his.

"I'm going to head down the hill and get us some water," he said. "After that, I'm going backtrack a bit and set up some booby traps."

Lauren gave Christian a peculiar look and asked, "Booby traps?"

Christian reached into his backpack and pulled out the grenade carrier that he had pulled off one of the agents earlier that day. He opened it and showed its contents to Lauren, who looked them over with profound interest.

"Are those what I think they are?"

Christian smiled. "Yep. It'll slow the bastards down when they come for us," Christian said. "Once they see what happened back there, they'll be coming for sure. Traps won't keep them out of your backyard forever, but it'll help. These little puppies will do quite a bit of damage."

Lauren began remembering her encounter with the woman and her daughter the day before. She then said, "Christian, we can't just set explosives in the woods. There's innocent people out there who might get hurt."

Christian looked at her, a bit confused. "You know this for a fact?"

"Yes. I met a mother and her daughter yesterday. They were foraging for food."

"You're sure they were friendly?"

"They didn't have weapons," Lauren replied.

"Fair enough, then. I'll save them for something else. Get some sleep and keep your gun ready. I'll call for you before coming back in. If anyone comes through this door but me, you know what to do."

Christian gathered his pack and his rifle and walked outside of the cabin. Before closing the door behind him, he looked down at his calf which he had completely forgotten about. Lauren watched as he humbly shrugged his shoulders, sat down again and began to re-dress his injury.

As she rested her head on the pillow and closed her eyes, she could hear her companion fiddling with his first aid kit and the occasional bird chirping outside of the cabin. After a few minutes, she heard Christian secure the door. Deciding it was the safest she had felt in a while, she allowed herself to drift off to sleep.

When Lauren woke up, she could see light peeking through the shuttered windows of the cabin. The rest of the cabin was very dark. As her eyes adjusted to the darkness, she looked around and noticed that Christian wasn't there with her. She hopped down from the cot, placing all of her weight on her good foot and reached for her rifle. With her right hand, she pulled the door open with her rifle at low-ready. When the door opened fully, the morning brightness quickly overtook her eyes. She looked to the right of the door and then to the left, where she saw him. Christian looked up at her with two very worn-out eyes. Lauren lowered her rifle and sighed in relief.

"Good morning, sunshine," he said with an early-morning raspy voice.

"You scared me," Lauren said. "Why didn't you come inside?"

"I can't see anything coming from in there," Christian replied.

"Have you been up all night?" she asked.

"Pretty much," he replied. "Even when I sleep, I don't really sleep."

"Well, you look exhausted," Lauren affirmed.

Christian nodded. "How's the ankle?"

Lauren looked down to her still swollen ankle that still had plenty of purple blotches covering it.

"It's not hurting right now," she said. "It still looks like hell, though."

Christian stood up and stretched, then reached into his pack and pulled out Lauren's water bladder and handed it to her. She smiled and took a few sips from the hose, then hopped over and placed it into her backpack.

"Ready to go home?" Christian asked her with a smile.

"You have no idea," Lauren said.

Lauren sat down on one of the wooden chairs inside the cabin and began contemplating what to do with her ankle. She'd loosened the laces as much as possible on her boot, but had found that she couldn't fit her foot into it, even with the thinnest sock she had.

"That's great…that's just great," she said with a tone of disgust.

"Did your boot shrink?" Christian joked.

"Now is not the time, Christian," she stated, not sounding the least bit amused.

Seeing that his attempts to add levity weren't going to be appreciated, he turned away and started squaring away all of his gear. Lauren reached inside her pack for her first aid kit and removed an ace bandage. She wrapped the entire thing loosely around her socked foot and ankle. She then pulled a hank of cordage from her pack and cut off several feet. She tied one end of it to her belt just about her hip, and secured the other end of it to her pants near her shin with her leg bent slightly. She wrapped the shin portion with some duct tape and went to stand up. Her foot was now being suspended by the cord, unable to touch the ground. She knew she could hold it up well on her own, but this would keep her from inadvertently dropping her injured foot to the ground. It might even give her hamstring a break.

Christian looked in on her to see what she was doing. Lauren looked up at him humbly.

"I'm going to need you to carry some stuff for me," she said, not wanting to admit that she needed help.

"Like what?"

"My rifle at least," Lauren said. "I'm going to have to use my trekking poles as makeshift crutches the whole way back today."

Christian looked confused and said, "You can do that?

"I've had to do it before—once before," Lauren confirmed. "I can't put any more weight on this thing and I can't get my boot on."

"I'll carry whatever you need me to. Let's just get you home, so you can rest for a while."

"Thank you," Lauren said gratefully.

After tying her unworn boot to her backpack, Lauren donned it and strapped on her waist pack. She then extended her trekking poles to a length that would make hiking this way as comfortable for her as possible. Christian had on his overloaded pack and had one of the suppressed M4s slung over his shoulder along with Lauren's rifle. The other M4 he had slung in front of him. After securing Sugar Knob Cabin as best as they could, the two began the short jaunt back to the Tuscarora Trail. Once at the intersection, they turned left and headed back in the direction of Mill Mountain where Lauren's adventure had begun two days ago. It was hard for her to believe that she had been away from home that long. She figured she had successfully scared her mother to death and guessed she'd never hear the end of it. As she hobbled along her mind went wild, making plans on how to explain everything to her and to the rest of her family. She also tried to imagine what her best option would be for how to explain this stranger that she was about to bring into the lives of everyone in her community. She knew it wouldn't be easy. The fact that Christian had saved her life would certainly have to be the selling point.

After a couple hours of trudging, Lauren and Christian came upon Sandstone Spring. They took a short break there and Lauren spent a few minutes telling him about the times she had camped there with her family. The hike continued and for the most part went well, in spite of their injuries. It was not an easy hike by any means for either of them, but the terrain along Mill Mountain trail was mostly a ridge-walk and easy to traverse, in comparison to where they had been. As the two came around a small turn in the trail, Lauren heard a distinctive sound that alerted her, but also caught her completely off-guard. Just as she realized what it was, she spotted the barrel of a shotgun protruding from behind a large oak tree, about twenty feet in front of her. Behind the shotgun, she saw a person with short blonde hair. She quickly turned around and noticed that Christian had heard what she had heard and was just now in the process of raising his rifle to the ready. Everything went to slow motion as her mind went into overdrive. The sound they had heard was the slide of a pump-action shotgun loading a round into the chamber. It was unmistakable. Lauren knew without a doubt that the man behind the oak tree was John. He had come to look for her, just as she had expected him to do. From his point of view, she knew that he could see that she was hiking with an injury and didn't have her gun. A man he didn't recognize was behind her in a black uniform with a government-issued M4 in his hands. That's when the disaster that was about to take place played out in her mind. She dropped her trekking poles to the ground, raised her hands, and began to scream.

"*JOHN, NO!*" she exclaimed just as Christian moved to overtake her and push her out of the line of fire. He pushed her down into a pile of leaves just as the shotgun went off. As Christian was struck in the chest with buckshot, his aim went high and his rifle went off twice just before he flew backwards to the ground, grimacing in pain. As Lauren did her best to get back to her feet, she heard John yell from behind the tree. He had been hit in the shoulder by one of Christian's shots and was reaching for the shotgun he had dropped to the ground after getting hit. Christian was in the process of rolling to his side with his rifle when he saw Lauren drop her backpack and move in between him and the other shooter. She turned to look at Christian with panic in her eyes, seeing that his body armor had taken the brunt of the damage that the buckshot had inflicted. He had seen this look before, but he was in too much pain to think clearly right now. She pulled his rifle away from him and he gave her a questioning look.

"Are you out of your damn mind?" Christian asked her with urgency. His voice was halved; the buckshot having knocked the wind out of him.

She turned away from him and held up her hand just as John strolled up to them both, with the muzzle of his shotgun pointed in Christian's direction. When John noticed that Lauren had moved into his sight picture, he lowered his weapon and gave her the most dumbfounded look she had ever seen from him.

"Lauren, what in the name of God is going on?" John yelled loudly. "Who the fuck is this?"

"His name is Christian," she responded in a panicked tone. "He's not the enemy, John, so stop aiming your gun at him."

"He's lucky that I didn't blow his fucking head off," John shouted in a very serious tone.

"You must be the boyfriend," Christian said, still writhing in pain but nonetheless, trying to be funny. "Nice to meet you."

"You shut your mouth," John instructed. He looked confused and was beyond completely pissed. "Lauren, you better start explaining things to me now," John said commandingly. "Where have you been? Your mother is losing her mind right now. I came to look for you, spent a cold night in the woods doing that, and the first sign of you I see is you being followed by some guy with a gun. How was I supposed to respond to that?"

"John, I got in over my head," Lauren said calmly in an attempt to persuade John to relax. She pulled herself up to her feet as John looked down at her ace bandage-wrapped ankle. "This man, the man you just shot—he saved my life yesterday."

John didn't know what to say. He knew that there was a story behind what she was saying, but he was too pissed to listen. He looked at his shoulder and noticed it was bleeding pretty badly. Lauren hopped to her backpack and dug around for her first aid kit.

Christian pulled off his IFAK and held it up to her. He then said, "Lauren, use this instead. There should be at least one dressing left inside. I'm not certain though—for some reason, I keep getting shot lately."

Lauren turned to him and took the IFAK from him. Christian sat up and dropped his backpack, then he pulled off his body armor which was starting to feel a little too confining for him.

"Are you ok?" she asked worriedly as she briefly looked him over.

"Just peachy," Christian responded sarcastically. "Nothing got through the plate, but damn, this hurts."

"Take off your shirt, John," Lauren said as she hopped over to him. John dropped his pack and removed his shirt. It appeared as though he was just now beginning to calm down.

"What happened to your ankle?" John asked her, showing some concern.

"It's a long story," she replied.

"We've got a long walk home," he said.

"I'll tell you everything, babe. I promise you, I will. For now, you are just going to have to trust me. This guy behind me is a good guy." Her voice changed to a whisper as she looked him in the eyes. "If it wasn't for him, I wouldn't be here right now."

John closed his eyes for a second. He nodded reluctantly and sighed. "Ok," he said. "I'm sorry for jumping your shit and I'm very glad that you're safe. But you have to understand what we've been going through. A lot has changed since you've been gone. Everyone is worried sick about you."

Lauren nodded and began to dress John's wound, which even though it wasn't as bad as it could've been, was bleeding rather heavily. Once she'd wrapped the dressing tightly, John put his shirt back on. He donned his backpack and slung his shotgun over his other shoulder. He gave Lauren a kiss on her cheek and she smiled oddly at him, turning away to hop back to where her pack was laying.

"Do you need help?" John asked her.

"I'll manage," Lauren said confidently.

"Can you walk or do I have to carry you, too?" John asked Christian rather coldly.

"Oh, I can walk just fine," Christian responded. "Breathing on the other hand, not so much."

"Well, I'm sorry for shooting you," John said.

"Now that's not something you hear every day," Christian said cynically. "But I do accept your apology. Think of it this way—you're lucky you got your shot off when you did, otherwise that 5.56 wouldn't have just grazed your shoulder."

John nodded. He was a humble person and knew the situation could've ended much worse that it had. Lauren bent over to pick up her pack and strapped it on once again, pulling up her trekking poles up to ready herself for the hike home. Christian somehow managed to shove his body armor into his already overstuffed pack and squared away all of his gear and weapons. The three began hiking down Mill Mountain Trail at a meager pace. John led the way with Lauren not too far behind.

Christian brought up the rear but kept his distance, feeling a bit out of place. He couldn't help but feel attached to Lauren, after their talks and what they had been through. He felt like he knew her as well as anyone could know her in such a short amount of time. They experienced a couple traumatic situations and even though he felt too humble to take credit for it, he had indeed saved her life. He had saved both of their lives. He decided even with this being true, she owed him nothing and he did not want to intrude in any way. If he had any chance of being accepted by her family and eventually by her entire community, he had to handle this with kid gloves, and he wasn't very good at doing that. He watched as every so often, John would look back to make sure she was close to him. How amazing it must be to know that kind of love in this horrible world, he thought.

Occasionally as they walked, Lauren would look back to Christian and smile. She gave him the thumbs up a few times to reassure him that this situation was all clear. It wouldn't be long before they would be descending the steep game trail back to her family's cabin. It would take a lot to explain to everyone why she had been gone for so long. She knew it, but she also knew they would eventually learn to trust Christian as she did. All they needed was to have a little faith.

As they neared the intersection to the game trail that led steeply for two miles down the mountain and into the valley below, John stopped and turned to face Lauren and Christian.

"Let's break here for a bit, guys," John said. He looked to Lauren who immediately, and without hesitation, dropped her pack and took a seat on the ground. "Now would be a good time to clue me in on what the hell happened to you," he said to her.

She sighed. "I hiked up to Big Schloss, just like I always do every day. When I was about to hike back down the mountain, I heard gunfire and explosions in the distance. I couldn't see anything, so I decided to hike further to get a better look. When I got to White Rock Cliff, that's when I was able to see the smoke." She paused.

Christian remained standing with his back turned to John and Lauren, looking down the trail as if to make sure that they weren't being followed. Lauren continued on with her explanation of what she had discovered and her eventual encounter with Christian. She told John everything she could remember, including the previous day's escape from the DHS agents and search dogs. When she told him about how she'd sprained her ankle, and the firefight that had followed, John's facial expression turned morose.

"I'm sorry that I wasn't with you," John said. "I probably would have come sooner, but I have had zero sleep lately."

"It's not your fault that any of this happened, John," Lauren assured him.

"I know. But I still feel like an ass," he said. He then turned his attention to Christian. "So, I take it that your agency is a threat to us now?"

Christian turned around to face John. "First of all, it's not *my agency*," he said firmly, "and yes, they are a threat."

Noticing the tension and wanting to eliminate any chance of further confrontation between John and Christian, Lauren interjected. "What's been going on at home since I left?" she asked John, curiously.

John stared at Christian for a few seconds before relenting. "On the day you left, Mrs. Ackermann was shot to death by some bikers," he said.

"What?" Lauren said in utter disbelief.

"They attacked her and Mr. Ackermann. He ended up killing them both. We heard the shots at the cabin and went to investigate. A couple of guys with some motorcycle club called the Marauders."

Lauren was shocked and deeply saddened by the news. She had nothing but fond memories of Mrs. Ackermann, and didn't say much for a few minutes. John allowed her to mourn and paused a moment before continuing.

"There's a lot more to it than that—but it goes without saying, we have a new threat in the valley now," he said. "Dad was supposed to get everyone on the same page yesterday at the church meeting. I'm not sure how all that went, but we can find out after we get back."

"That's just crazy," Lauren said. "How did they get into the valley?"

"We don't know that either," John said.

"Unbelievable," Lauren said as she began to worry. "Christian, do you know anything about a biker gang?"

Christian shook his head. "Unfortunately, I don't," he said. "But I can't imagine the rest of their buddies will take kindly to the news."

The three contemplated and made small talk for a few minutes, before gathering their gear and starting down the first set of switchbacks on the steep game trail that led down the mountain to the rear of Lauren's family's property. John made sure to keep a very slow pace, turning around to make sure that Lauren was able to maintain it while hiking on one foot. On the inside, Lauren was smiling. In spite of the new dangers that affected her, her family, and her community, it felt good to be back in familiar territory. It felt good to be with John again. In a matter of hours, she would finally be home, and that would feel just as good, if not better.

CHAPTER 15

The Cabin
Trout Run Valley
Hardy County West Virginia
Present day

ICHELLE HAD WOKEN TO THE sound of revving ATV engines coming from outside the cabin. The sound was unfamiliar to her, as it wasn't something she was used to hearing in the world she and the others now lived in. After getting dressed and gathering herself, she walked outside to the front porch and soon realized that she must've slept in a lot later than usual for some reason. Norman and Lee had pulled all three of their Honda Rancher four-wheelers to the driveway in front of the cabin, and were busy strapping gear to them. They had just finished topping off the tanks with the gasoline that Michael had given them. The entire community had been provided with enough fuel to operate their motorized vehicles and ATVs for the foreseeable future.

Today was to be the first day of a new strict security protocol that the entire community had to follow. The emergency meeting at Fred Mason's house the previous evening had been brief, but accomplished what it needed to. The barricade was now as secure as they could make it, after parking Michael's largest bulldozer there, using its enormous blade and sheer size to block the road. Fred's sons, Chad and Mark had driven one of their father's Humvees there not long after, and worked hard to dig a large foxhole in the embankment just above the barricade, which would be used to guard the barricade both day and night. The two of them worked the first overnight shift at the barricade and it had been a quiet one.

In order to keep the community as safe as humanly possible and maintain some semblance of normalcy in spite of the new threat, it was decided that there would be armed roving patrols along Trout Run Road. Every family who had an operating vehicle would need to participate at some point. The patrols would travel the road from the north end to the barricade roughly every hour at random intervals, so that their movements would not become predictable to anyone paying attention. The patrols would either be one or two-man, depending on availability of manpower, which was at a premium. Regardless of who was on duty, every able inhabitant of the valley was now, in one way or another, going to have to be an active part of community security. And that meant, that any borderline conscientious objectors would need to change their way of thinking.

With the help of the Baofeng radios that Fred had provided, the members of the community were now able to maintain contact with each other at all times, which was a true blessing. If anyone saw anything suspicious or threatening, they would be able to radio it in immediately, notifying everyone else who listened. Depending on the threat, a reaction force would be assembled to respond wherever they were needed. Since the meeting had been at the Mason house, Fred had been able to provide firearms and ammunition from the inventory in his shop to the members of the community that needed them. Every adult, both young and old, now had a semi-automatic, high-capacity rifle of some flavor and a reliable sidearm with ample ammunition. The teenagers in the community would be allowed to carry weapons on a case-by-case basis as decided by their parents, even though Fred insisted that in the case of community-wide defense, age was irrelevant. To his surprise, the Schmidts had been very interested in getting firearms for their children. Their daughter, Brooke was sixteen and had some experience with guns while their son, Brandon, who was fifteen, had no experience with firearms whatsoever. Scott and Whitney both wanted to have them involved in community security, in spite of their lack of experience. Fred Mason's daughter, Megan, whom he was extremely protective of and rarely allowed to leave their property, had been sent next door to the Schmidt home to teach them basic gun safety, as well as how to operate and shoot the weapons they'd been provided. She, just like her brothers, had been taught how to shoot from a very young age by their father, whose entire life was encapsulated with all things 'gun'.

Michelle walked around to the back of the cabin and took a long look around the foothills of North Mountain. She looked as far as she could up the steep game trail that Lauren used every morning on her hikes and didn't see anything. All she truly wanted to see was her daughter's smiling face as she traipsed down the hill and back home to her. Her mind was going crazy with not knowing where Lauren was. John had gone to look for her and hadn't returned last night, and that made her worry even more. It bothered her that Norman didn't seem worried in the least. Maybe he was—but he sure didn't show it. Grace walked outside and around the corner of the house. Her hair was pulled back into a ponytail today, and she was holding her rifle in both hands. She hardly went anywhere without it now. Today, she had a fierce look on her face.

"Are they back yet?" she asked with a tired voice and a yawn.

"No," Michelle said grimly.

"This shit is getting ridiculous, Michelle," Grace said.

Michelle nodded. "You don't have to tell me," she said. "I already know."

As Grace walked back inside, she slammed the door behind her. Michelle approached Norman, who looked at her curiously. He was getting ready to say something to her, when she reached outward to him with an open hand.

"Give me your rifle," Michelle demanded.

"What's that?" Norman asked.

"Give me your damn rifle," Michelle repeated. "I'm going to go find them. I've had enough of this shit."

Norman saw the look in her eye and knew she meant business. He slid the AK-47 off of his shoulder, checked the safety and handed it to Michelle.

"You want me to tag along?" he asked.

"Do what you want. I want my daughter back home right now," Michelle asserted.

"Ok," Norman said. "Let's go then." He turned to Lee. "Get this gear squared away and then get with Grace and see if she needs anything. You two watch the house."

"Ok, Dad," Lee said without protest.

Norman quickly closed the distance to Michelle as she literally bolted over the bridge and to the back of the property. He had never seen her move this quickly before and was nowhere near prepared. As she started marching up the first switchback of the game trail, Norman reached forward, grabbing her shoulder. She looked back at him quickly, just as he pointed his finger up the hill. She looked in the direction he pointed, and saw three figures moving slowly down the trail a few hundred yards away.

"There they are," he said confidently with somewhat of a grin, as if he'd known all along that they would be there.

"Dammit, it better be them," Michelle hissed as she squinted her eyes to get a better picture.

She pulled the AK-47 to her shoulder to take a look through the magnified optic. Norman quickly pushed the muzzle of the weapon down to the ground. Michelle turned to him with a stunned look.

"Girl, there's a round in the chamber," Norman said matter-of-factly, sounding somewhat bothered. "You want to accidentally shoot them?"

Michelle quickly realized her error and shook her head shamefully. As she pulled the magazine out, she slapped the safety off and pulled back on the bolt, ejecting the live round into the air. To her surprise, Norman caught it as it soared just over his head. Michelle's eyebrows raised.

"I'm sorry," she said sincerely as she began to look through the rifle's scope again.

"It's ok," Norman assured. "I know you're a little off-kilter. Just be careful—my son is up there too, along with your daughter."

Michelle brought the three figures into view through the scope. She immediately saw John, who was in front. Lauren followed just behind him. Michelle's heart skipped a beat and she could begin to feel a sense of relief sweep over her. She noticed that Lauren was limping and using her trekking poles as if they were crutches. Then, she noticed a person she didn't recognize in a black uniform who was bringing up the rear.

"Who the fuck is that?" Michelle queried.

"Huh?" Norman asked.

"There's a man in a black uniform following them," Michelle said with a slight hint of suspicion in her voice. "Who in the fuck is that?"

Norman reached for the rifle and pulled the scope to his eye to see what Michelle had seen. As he did so, Michelle pulled her Glock from its holster and press checked it, verifying that it was loaded. Norman saw John and noticed his shoulder had a wound dressing on it that looked nearly blood-soaked. He then brought Lauren into view and saw her struggling to move down the hill with one foot held off of the ground. Finally, he moved the scope to see the man that was bringing up the rear. The man was wearing body armor and a black uniform. His backpack was overflowing with gear and he was carrying a rifle with a suppressor mounted to the barrel. He had two other rifles slung over his back, including one that looked like Lauren's AR. Norman also noticed that he was limping as well. John was carrying his shotgun and had a slight grin on his face. Neither he nor Lauren looked frightened in any way. There were no signs that the man with them was a threat.

"Looks like three injured hikers to me," Norman joked.

Michelle punched him in the shoulder. "I'm not sure why you think this is funny, but I'm not laughing," Michelle said.

"Calm down, babes," Norman said. "If that man meant them harm, I certainly can't tell it by the looks on their faces."

After a few minutes, Lauren, John, and Christian were standing just in front of Michelle and Norman, along the lower portion of the trail. Michelle ran to Lauren, wrapping her arms around her daughter in a tight embrace. While she did, Michelle kept her eyes open, so she could glare hard at the stranger who stood just behind her daughter. In the black uniform he was wearing, he looked just like one of the DHS storm troopers that had paid a visit to her family in Woodstock before coming here. Christian paid no attention to her scowl and simply continued looking all around them, taking in a good view of his surroundings. Occasionally, his eyes met hers and when they did, he offered her a friendly smile.

"Thank God you're safe," Michelle said as the embrace ended. "Where in the hell have you been? What happened to your foot?"

"It's a long story, Mom. Please don't be mad," Lauren said, immediately noticing her mother staring at the man behind her, while her hand rested on top of her sidearm. Not wanting to postpone the pleasantries any longer, Lauren said, "Mom, Norman…this is Christian."

Norman placed both hands on John's shoulders as a sentiment to show he was pleased that his son was home. He was truly glad he had been right—that John would find Lauren and bring her back with him. As he touched John's right shoulder, John cringed and Norman quickly moved his hand upward to his neck.

"Damn, son," he said. "What happened to you?"

"I got shot," John said with a smile. He looked back at Christian, whose look of guilt was beginning to form. "But, I'm ok. It's just a flesh wound."

Norman then turned his attention to Christian and held out his hand, noticing the body armor the man was wearing, and the ripped up fabric and molle webbing on his chest. He looked down and noticed the dressing on Christian's calf.

"Looks like maybe you've taken a bullet or two as well. There must be something going around. It's nice to meet you, Christian," Norman said. "I'm Norman."

Christian shook his hand. "Pleasure to meet you, sir," he said.

"Don't give me that 'sir' shit," Norman said. "Call me Norman...or Norm. Anything, but sir."

"Ok," Christian said. "Pleasure to meet you, Norman."

Christian's attention turned to Michelle, who was still eyeballing him with her hand on her holstered pistol. Michelle finally took her hand off of it when she helped Lauren remove her backpack and set it down on the ground. She then looked back to her daughter and soon gazed down at her foot.

"Are you shot, too?" Michelle asked with a slight sense of urgency in her voice.

"Sprained," Lauren said. "It's just sprained, Mom."

Michelle turned to see Lee at the bottom of the hill, who had noticed the excitement and approached them with his rifle at low-ready. He nodded to John, who smirked and nodded back.

"Lee, get on the radio and call the Perrys," she told him. "Let Kristen know we have two gunshot wounds and a bad ankle sprain."

"Ok," Lee said with a nod. "Welcome home, Lauren." He turned away and slowly walked back to the ATVs where he had left the radio.

"It's good to be home. Thanks, Lee," Lauren said.

"Radio?" John asked. "What radio?"

"You left yesterday before we had a chance to tell you," Norman explained. "Everyone in the valley has a radio now. We met up with more of those bikers yesterday and ended up in a gunfight at the barricade. We need to fill you in."

"We need to fill Christian in, too," Lauren said as all eyes went to her. "He saved my life yesterday, Mom. He's lost everything and needs a place to live. I invited him here to stay with us."

Michelle's scrutinizing look slowly changed to one of compassion. She looked up at Christian, who seemed a bit embarrassed. "Is that true?" she asked Christian.

"I'm not one to take full credit, ma'am," he replied. "We ended up in a dangerous situation and I had a part in getting us both out of it."

Michelle's countenance began to show signs that she had finally started to relax. She smiled. Her daughter was back home and now she was being told that this man in the black uniform had had a hand in getting her here. "Well, you can tell us all about it when you're ready to. I'm Michelle," she said to Christian. "Lauren's mom."

Christian held out his hand to shake hers, but Michelle bypassed the gesture. She moved closer and gave him a hug, much to his surprise.

"Thank you for bringing her home," she said.

Christian didn't know what else to do but accept her hug and return it. Holding his rifle in one arm, he used the other to hug Michelle.

"So, how did you guys *both* get shot?" Norman asked curiously. "What did you do? Shoot each other?"

John and Christian looked at each other and shrugged, then exchanged grins.

"Funny you should say that…" Christian trailed off as John spoke.

"It's a long story," John said. He noticed the three Hondas sitting in the driveway, no longer housed in the shed. He began to wonder why, but decided not to ask.

As the group began to descend the final few yards of the trail back to the property, Grace noticed them from the porch and came running out to meet them. She hung her rifle over her shoulder and ran directly to Lauren, hugging her tightly with an enormous smile on her face. Lauren in turn, wrapped her arms around her sister.

"Holy shit, it's good to see you," Grace said excitedly. "We've been going nuts around here."

"I figured you guys were pretty pissed," Lauren said. "I'm sorry it took so long to get home."

"Not anymore—just glad you're home," Grace said as she looked at the tall bearded man behind her sister. "Who's this?"

"Oh. Grace, this is Christian," Lauren said as she pulled away from Grace and turned her body, so her sister could meet him. "Christian, this is my sister, Grace."

Grace flipped her hair and raised her eyebrows at Christian. He smiled at her. He moved a bit closer and held out his hand. Grace hesitated and then took it in hers. The two gazed at each other for a few seconds before saying anything as if they were instantly smitten. Michelle noticed and said nothing. The others noticed and offered sheepish grins.

"Are you the reason that my sister has been away for so long?" Grace prodded.

Christian smiled as he contemplated how to answer. "Yes," he said humbly. "She made me aware of her curfew, but there were extenuating circumstances."

"I see," Grace uttered. She nodded and pursed her lips.

"He's also the reason I made it back, Grace...so cut him some slack," Lauren said, smiling at her sister.

"Let's get you guys in the house and wait for Kristen to come and patch you all up," Norman suggested.

Grace picked up Lauren's backpack and shouldered it, realizing quickly that it was heavier than she had guessed. She then moved to Lauren's weak side and pulled Lauren's arm over her shoulder, to help her walk back to the cabin. The two took the lead with everyone else following not far behind. Grace shot a look at Lauren.

"Damn, girl," Grace said, "you sure know how to pick them."

"What's that supposed to mean?" Lauren asked.

"I mean...he's hot," Grace said. "Leave it to you to go out into the woods and find some hot guy to bring home to us."

Lauren shook her head and gave her sister a cynical look. "Really, Grace? I mean, seriously..."

"What? I can't help it. The guy is seriously good looking," Grace admitted.

Lauren sighed and shook her head again. She slowly began to remember when Grace had first started dating as a teenager and how 'boy crazy' she had always been. Some things never changed.

"I guess I've been too busy trying to get home to notice," Lauren said.

"Sorry, girl," Grace said, this time with sincerity. "I am truly glad you're back."

"Me too," Lauren agreed.

Once inside the cabin, Christian set his gear down on the living room floor and took a seat in the recliner. Leaning back, he set his feet on the footrest and put both hands behind his head, exhaling loudly. "I could definitely get used to this," he said with a grin.

Lauren took a seat on the couch and began unwrapping her ankle.

She looked around the cabin for a moment, realizing how truly good it felt to be home, and at the same time, realizing how close she had come to not making it back. Grace took Lauren's things and set them in her room. Walking back to the living room, she cocked her head at Christian, who was busy making himself at home.

"Glad you like it," Grace said to him, "because it's where you'll be sleeping for the time being—until we can set you up with other accommodations."

"I don't have a problem with that," Christian said. "I appreciate the hospitality."

Grace looked down at the huge pile of things that Christian had been carrying with him, including all three rifles, one of which she knew belonged to her sister. She shook her head at the disarray, which she wasn't fond of. John, Norman, and Michelle walked inside, with Lee following shortly after.

"I radioed the Perrys—Kristen should be here shortly," Lee said. "I told everyone that Lauren and John were home safe, too."

"Thanks, Lee," Michelle said.

Lee nodded and walked over to Christian. Holding out his hand, he said, "I'm Lee. John's brother."

Christian sat up with a slight grunt and took Lee's hand. "Christian," he said. "Nice to meet you."

"Likewise," Lee said. He then turned around and walked back outside, closing the door behind him.

Grace took a seat beside Lauren on the couch. John walked over to Lauren, put his hand on her shoulder and kissed her on the top of her head. Lauren smiled at him as his hand left her shoulder.

"Guys, I hate to be a party pooper, but I'm going to die if I don't get some shut-eye," John said.

"Don't you want Kristen to check your shoulder?" Michelle asked.

"It's not bleeding anymore," John admitted. "She'll just tell me to change the dressing daily and keep it clean. I already know that much."

"Go get some sleep then," Michelle said with a smile.

"We'll get you up later and fill you in on what happened yesterday," Norman said.

"See everyone at dinner," John said as he nodded to everyone and walked back down the hallway to his room, closing the door behind him.

"John told us about Mrs. Ackermann," Lauren said, then asked, "Did something else happen? Was it the bikers again?"

Norman nodded. "Yes. Things are going to be different around here for a while, but we'll talk about it later," Norman assured. "You two just relax for now. Let's get you and Christian patched up—we'll get everyone on the same page tonight at dinner."

"Are we in danger?" Lauren prodded.

"We've always been in danger, sweetie," Michelle said, "ever since day one."

"Mom, that's not what I mean and you know it," Lauren asserted. "Who are these biker guys? What do they want?"

Norman couldn't help himself. He wanted to wait, but he knew that Lauren would not stop persisting. It wasn't in her nature. He began divulging to Lauren and to Christian what he and his sons had found at the Ackermanns after they had been attacked. Lauren closed her eyes when he began explaining the details. Grace put her hand on Lauren's shoulder, in an effort to console her.

"For what it's worth, Sis, when they told me, I didn't take it well either," Grace said.

"What the fuck is wrong with people?" Lauren asked rhetorically in a highly irritated tone.

"When we told everyone at the meeting, we decided things had to change around here," Michelle said. "Our daily lives can't continue without security being increased."

"How did they get here, Norman?" Lauren asked.

"The barricade," Norman replied. "We went there yesterday after the meeting. Someone had moved the stones we'd put there to let them in. Fred and I, Peter and Michael got caught in a gunfight with three more of them. We killed one, one got away, and we took one prisoner. He's locked up at the Mason's house—probably tied to a tree or something."

Christian sat up in his chair as if to get closer to the conversation, although he had heard everything well.

"Is he cooperating?" Christian asked, looking at Norman.

Norman presented his knuckles to Christian, close enough so that Christian could see the mild bruising that had begun as a result of him punching the biker's lights out. "Not really," he said.

A vehicle horn was heard outside the house. Norman opened the door to see that Lee had opened the gate to allow an old white pickup truck to pull down the driveway.

"Kristen is here. Mike is with her," Norman said.

A few minutes later, Michael and Kristen Perry walked into the cabin. Kristen was carrying a large medical backpack and a paramedic's "tackle box." She looked around the room, as if visually triaging everyone there. She soon set her stuff down near the couch where Lauren was seated and gave Lauren a hug. Michael nodded to Norman who nodded back, and smiled at Lauren and Grace. He was carrying a small white bucket.

"We're glad you're home, Lauren," she said. She pulled away and looked down at Lauren's thickly wrapped ankle. "What have you done to yourself?"

"It's just a sprain," Lauren said.

Kristen removed the bandage from Lauren's swollen ankle. She said, "That's a pretty bad sprain." She turned to her husband. "Just set it down here."

Michael set the bucket on the floor near his wife and stepped back. Kristen opened the top to expose the contents.

"Instant ice packs are hard to come by and we don't have ice, so we'll have to improvise with cold water from the stream," Kristen said as she reached inside her backpack for a cloth. She dipped it into the bucket and wrung it out, then placed it on Lauren's ankle. Lauren jumped a bit, not realizing how cold it would be. "You'll need to keep this as cold as you can. Luckily, this time of year the water is pretty cold. There's not much we can do with this, other than keep it elevated and keep the swelling down."

"And you're going to have to stay off your feet," Michelle said to her daughter. "I know that will be hard for you."

"It'll be damn near impossible for her," Grace said jokingly.

"Do you guys have any ibuprofen?" Kristen asked Michelle.

"We do," Michelle replied. She then walked to the bathroom and pulled out a large bottle of Kirkland ibuprofen from the medicine cabinet. She plopped four of the brown pills into her hand and placed the bottle back into the medicine cabinet.

"Give her four of them every few hours or so for the pain and to help with the swelling," Kristen said, as Michelle handed the pills to Lauren. Lauren popped them into her mouth and swallowed them without needing to chase them down. Kristen continued, "It's imperative that you stay off this foot and keep it elevated, Lauren."

"Ok—I got it," Lauren said, not sounding convinced or happy with her situation.

Kristen looked up at Norman. "Where are the GSWs?"

Norman pointed at Christian, who was sitting up straight now in the recliner. Kristen peered at him, smiled uncomfortably, and then looked down at his calf.

"This man here has a hole in his leg," Norman explained. "John was shot too, but he said it wasn't serious."

"Lee made it sound a bit more urgent than this," Kristen said, sounding just a little bit annoyed. She crawled over and began assessing and working on Christian's injured leg. She introduced herself while she worked and Christian did the same.

"Looks like you've reinjured this," Kristen said. "There's a lot of damaged muscle here."

"We didn't exactly have a choice, ma'am," Christian said.

"You're going to have to stay off your feet for a while, too," Kristen said. "If this gets infected, you're going to be in a lot worse shape than you are already. You need time to heal."

Once done cleaning and redressing the wound, Kristen reached into her tackle box and pulled out a small bottle of prescription medication. She handed it to Christian, who read the label and smiled. She then handed him another bottle.

"The first bottle is Vicodin," she said. "Only take it if you need it—and honestly to me, it looks like you need it. The second bottle is Clindamycin. It's a pretty strong antibiotic. If it gets infected, you'll need to start a dose of these. Don't take them unless you're certain it's infected, though. We don't have a lot of these to go around."

"Yes, ma'am," Christian said. "I appreciate this. Thank you."

"You're welcome," Kristen said with a smile. Noticing that her patient seemed to be having a bit of trouble breathing, she placed her hand on his chest, causing him to immediately cringe. "What else is wrong with you?" Kristen asked.

Christian lifted up his shirt enough to expose what appeared to be several fairly well bruised ribs. Kristen looked around the room. Norman's eyebrows were raised. Michelle had a sudden look of concern on her face. Lauren quickly went on to explain what had happened earlier that morning as the room listened intently. Kristen began pushing around on Christian's ribs to verify if any were broken. He grimaced with every push.

"Guess that explains why your body armor looks like it took a round of buckshot," Norman said.

"Yeah," Christian said with a grin. "Because it did."

"I can't feel any broken ribs. You need rest. Manage your breathing and take deep breaths often. Take the Vicodin for the pain." Kristen looked up at Michelle. "Where is he staying?"

Michelle paused for a second as if to contemplate the answer to Kristen's question. She looked to Lauren who nodded to her. Looking at Christian, Michelle said, "He'll be staying with us."

"Ok, well, keep an eye on him and make sure he keeps this dressing clean," Kristen said. "He and John both need to change them daily."

"I can help with that," Grace said, a little more enthusiastically than necessary. Lauren turned to her and smacked her on the leg. She stared at Lauren, wide-eyed. Michelle looked at both sisters and smiled. Kristen did as well. She pulled some wound dressings from her med kit and laid them on the floor.

"I can't spare too many of these, so you'll need to boil them and reuse them," Kristen said.

"I think we can handle that," Michelle said. She was thrilled beyond words that her family was complete again—at least, as complete as it could be. Everyone in the room was now smiling in some way, for one reason or another. After chatting for a few minutes and leaving a small bag of assorted medical supplies, the Perrys left the cabin and returned home.

It wasn't long before Lauren stood up and hobbled to her bedroom, excusing herself. "Sorry guys, but I'm going to bed—for a week."

Later that evening, Norman answered a knock on the door. It was Fred Mason. Norman welcomed him inside and Fred immediately noticed the stranger sitting in the recliner, almost half asleep. Christian's eyes opened wide when he heard the door shut.

"Who's this?" Fred asked as he turned to Norman.

Before Norman could speak, Grace walked up to Fred impulsively and said, "This is Christian." She paused and turned to glance at Christian, then turned back to Fred and said, "Our new roommate." She handed Fred a cup of coffee which he took willingly, thanking her and almost immediately taking a sip.

Fred walked over to Christian, who sat up in the recliner, almost at attention.

"Do I know you from somewhere?" Fred asked.

"I don't think so, sir," Christian said.

"Where did you get the black uniform?" Fred curiously asked.

"Department of Homeland Security," Christian said with a grin.

"Is that some kind of joke?" Fred demanded. His drill sergeant-esque voice was beginning to come out.

"No sir, no joke," Christian answered confidently. "I'm an ex-employee."

"What exactly do you mean by ex-employee?"

"I was disavowed," Christian responded, not missing a beat. "They tried to terminate my employment with extreme prejudice, but were unsuccessful in their endeavors."

Fred turned to Norman, who shrugged. He then looked down at Christian's backpack which was overflowing with gear, his attention drawn immediately the body armor and the two Larue suppressed M4 carbines.

"Well, that explains the hardware," Fred said approvingly. He finally reached out his hand to Christian. "Sergeant Major Fred Mason, United States Army retired."

Christian smiled and shook Fred's hand. "Corporal Christian Hartman, Shenandoah Valley Legionnaires. Pleasure to meet you, sir."

Fred smiled and cocked his head to the side. "What is that exactly? Militia?" he asked.

"Yes, sir," Christian replied. "It's one of the oldest active militias in the Commonwealth." Pointing to Fred's Airborne Ranger Coat of Arms tattoo, he said, "We studied Ranger doctrine."

"No shit," Fred said with a smile.

"Not recently," Christian said.

Fred laughed slightly. "Well, I'll be damned. It's nice to meet you, Corporal."

"You as well, Sergeant Major," Christian said with a wide grin.

"Carry on."

Christian saluted and leaned the recliner back to where it'd been before, closing his eyes. Fred turned to Norman and Norman gave him a quizzical look.

"I suppose you're wondering why I'm here," Fred said as he took another sip of coffee.

"For good coffee?" Grace inserted as she took a seat on the couch.

"The thought had crossed my mind," Norman joked.

Michelle walked into the room from the hallway. She said hello to Fred and took a seat on the couch beside Grace.

"I wanted to see if you'd be willing to pay a visit to some neighbors in the morning," Fred said, almost uncomfortably.

"I take it, you're referring to the Bradys," Norman said.

"Yes, that's who I mean," Fred confirmed.

"If you think we can get through to them, I'm game," Norman said. "But I have my doubts."

"We all do," Fred said. "Some of us more than others—that's why I didn't bother asking Peter or Michael—and just came straight here."

Michelle cocked her head and raised her hand. "Guys, can I make a suggestion?" she asked.

"Be my guest," Fred replied.

Michelle adjusted herself in her seat. "If you two go there by yourselves, I'm pretty sure the Bradys won't hear you out."

"How do you figure?" Norman asked with a curious look.

"I imagine they are going to be on the defensive—seeing two men, from a community they alienated themselves from, showing up on their front yard from out of nowhere uninvited. It's just a thought, but I'm guessing you'll need something to divert their thoughts a bit."

"I'm not following you," Fred said.

"I suggest you take along some—eye candy," Michelle explained, nudging Grace with her elbow.

Norman and Fred looked at each other and then back at Michelle and Grace.

"What?" Norman asked.

Grace interjected. "Eye candy. Window dressing. Something attractive with other redeeming qualities," she said.

"Do you really think that will work?" Fred pondered.

"I think it will keep you both from getting shot," Michelle said jokingly.

Michelle and Grace laughed. It was a laugh that hadn't been heard in the cabin in a few days. With Lauren home and safe, Michelle was relaxed and her bubbly personality was finally able to show itself. She and Grace giggled and fed off of each other like two little girls. Norman smiled uncomfortably and Fred turned away, waving them off with an annoyed look on his face.

"All right, enough of that shit," Fred said. "Tomorrow morning, the four of us will go visit the Bradys—err Brady Bunch." He shook his head as he walked out the door, to the tune of the Brady Bunch theme song, which was now being sung by both Michelle and by Grace.

CHAPTER 16

FEMA Resettlement Camp Bravo
Woodstock, Virginia
Several months earlier

F AITH WALKED STEADILY FROM THE field on a hard dirt path
that ran alongside the road, following a large group of others. Her
friend Debbie and Debbie's husband Ben were walking with her, as
they had just finished the morning's work and were headed back to the
cafeteria for lunch. They had spent the morning planting seeds for lettuce,
spinach, and a host of other vegetables that were to be harvested in the
coming fall months. It wasn't the easiest work in the world, but they, and
other members of the older generation like them, were happy to have
something to keep themselves occupied. Most of them had had gardens of
their own that they'd cared for with pride and used to feed their families
before the collapse, just like their parents had done before them. Faith
had been chatting with Debbie all morning about the things that were
going on in the camp that worried her the most. Debbie was in the process
of explaining to her what she knew about the executions that had been
occurring there, almost since the first day that the DHS had taken over.

"They're calling it humane termination," Debbie said quietly.
"Anyone who is deemed a danger to the camp or themselves is humanely
terminated. We believe anyone who becomes an unnecessary strain on
their system is treated with the same consideration. The sick, elderly, and
even people who speak their minds a little too much have all disappeared."

"This isn't Nazi Germany," Faith said angrily. "Who do these people thing they are?"

"It doesn't matter, Faith. They are in charge," Debbie replied. "We have to do what they tell us to do, in order for everyone to be safe."

"It's only for now, anyway," Ben followed. "Before long it'll be safe, and we'll be allowed to go home."

Faith looked at Ben sternly. "Go home to what? What will be left of our homes, if and when we are allowed to go back, Ben?"

"I don't have all the answers," Ben said. "I just know what we're told. There's no other option right now, and we just need to make the best of it. We came here willingly and we just have to go along with the plan."

"You both have been desensitized and brainwashed by this," Faith said. "This is an autocracy under a humanitarian façade, and you both believe it's what's best for us."

"Anything is better than fighting to survive outside the fence," Debbie said. "Here, we have everything we need to continue our lives."

Faith wasn't convinced. She had spent her entire life a free person, able to do whatever she wanted. She followed the laws of the land and the laws set forth by God. She respected and honored her husband. To her, there was no other authority. Now, it seemed to her like this camp had become a small dictatorship, operating without any oversight, complete with corporal punishment and euthanasia. It ignored the Bill of Rights and was punishing normal everyday people for wanting the lives guaranteed to them by it.

"Who runs this place anyway?" Faith asked, her voice sounding more and more perturbed by the minute.

"His name is Bronson," Debbie replied. "He's a big wig in the DHS—something equivalent to a regional commander or something. He runs this camp and several others across the region."

"Is he stationed here?" Faith asked. "Where is his office?"

"His office is down the road at the old Massanutten Military Academy with the other higher-ups," Ben said. "DHS and FEMA took it over as their regional command center. He comes here sometimes and when he does, he brings quite the entourage."

"He's pretty well protected, Faith," Debbie added. "No one can touch him, so please don't get any ideas. Even bringing up his name could have consequences. I know you miss Sam—I don't want to see you do anything that you'd regret."

Faith thought for a moment. She agreed—she did miss her husband desperately. But she wasn't an idiot and had no intention of doing anything that would jeopardize the reputation she had in this place. She was known to be a genuine person by the staff. She wasn't a trouble-maker. She spoke matter-of-factly, but never insulted anyone. She followed directions even if she didn't agree with them. She had friends like Karen Mitchell who had been witness to her good behavior over her time spent in women's detention. Officer Mitchell had introduced her to Officer Mike Brown who, for all intents and purposes, was her advocate now in Senior Quarters and she was in the process of solidifying her relationship with him. Faith had been a good little conformist, even though every fiber of her being pulled her in the other direction. She wanted to resist, but what good would it do? Here in this place, like it or not she was powerless. With so many people following the status quo and believing it was best for them, not one thing she did as a single person would matter. For now, at least.

Faith, Debbie, and Ben walked into the cafeteria and were served trays of food, which they took to a table and found a seat.

"Is everyone who works here complicit?" Faith asked. "Do they all know?"

"Keep your voice down, Faith" Ben requested under his breath.

"Of course they know, Faith—they have to know," Debbie added, placing a hand on her husband's forearm.

"I don't understand how they can allow this to happen," Faith began. "They are putting free people to death for crimes invented by the terms of martial law—which is devised by oligarchs who want an easy way to suspend due process and control the people. They are creating kill lists just like the Nazis did—undesirables are put out of their misery, and no one even bats an eye. Is anyone even 'human' anymore?"

"They are following orders, just like us," Ben said passively.

"Ben is right. They're following orders. They're scared of consequences, just like us," Debbie said.

"It's funny that both of you say that," Faith said. "That's the excuse the Nazis used as a last-ditch effort for clemency during the Nuremberg trials." She paused and took a drink of water. "And for what it's worth, I'm not scared," Faith proclaimed. "These people are nothing to be afraid of. Death is nothing to be afraid of."

Ben took a bite of his sandwich and set it down on the tray in front of him. "So, what do you intend to do, Faith? Start an uprising? Are you going to rise up and fight the power all by yourself? It's too late for that now. Anything you do will be an exercise in futility. You might as well just bite the bullet and go along with things like the rest of us."

"I think God would want us to turn the other cheek," Debbie uttered.

"Exactly, Debbie," her husband agreed.

Faith sat quietly in her seat, appearing to have lost her appetite. She knew that any violent act would be dealt with harshly here, and the camp had more than enough security and firepower to cut down everyone if they needed to. She wasn't stupid—she knew they were prepared for just such a thing and possibly, were just waiting for the chance. Faith suddenly stood up and walked off toward the exit door that lead outside, while Debbie and Ben looked on surprised. The guard who stood by the door held his hand up to her.

"Let me pass, please," Faith requested. Her voice was soft, yet stern.

The guard looked at her, confused at first, and then peered up at his supervisor who stood near the breezeway that lead to the hall. His supervisor shrugged and then nodded to him and he let Faith pass through the door to the outside. Faith smiled and thanked the guard, and then proceeded through the doorway.

Once outside, Faith cleared the parking lot quickly. Before she knew it, she was back on Falcon Drive, passing the running track to her left and the parking lot full of black-painted school buses to her right. A couple vehicles carrying guards drove past her as she walked and they looked at her curiously, but didn't stop. As she turned right on Ox Road, she glanced up at the water tower and noticed that one of the guards there had his rifle aimed at her, possibly to get a look at her through his optic, but she wasn't sure. She waited for the sound of a gunshot that might seal her fate. Her breathing became heavier as she continued to walk at a brisk pace, now turning onto Warren Drive, where the old Holiday Inn Express building, that had been converted to the men's detention center, came into view directly in front of her. As she got closer, she could see the guards at the gate that led into it. Both had already eyeballed her, and were chatting with each other and pointing at her. Faith walked directly up to the two guards who stood at the gate. Both wore body armor and were carrying rifles which were slung over their shoulders. They looked at her quizzically for a moment, then at each other.

"Is there something we can help you with, ma'am?" the first guard asked.

Faith caught her breath. This was the most she had walked in a while. "Yes. I'd like to see my husband, please," she replied.

The guards smiled and looked at each other and then back at her.
"I'm sorry—it doesn't work that way, ma'am," the first guard said in a semi-jovial voice. He assumed she was kidding, or lost. Perhaps just old and senile.
"Sir, I haven't seen my husband in months. He's been cooped up in this building since we arrived here and they didn't allow me to see him. I miss him and I want to see him now," Faith explained. Seeing the disdainful looks she was getting, she changed her tone back to normal, and followed with, "Please?"

The guards shook their heads. "Ma'am, I'm afraid I can't help you," the first guard said while his partner remained silent. "Where are you supposed to be right now?"

Faith sighed. She turned away from the guards and began walking to the other gate in front of the women's detention center. As she walked away, the guards called to her, and she ignored them. Once she had reached the gate, the guards there—one man and one woman, eyeballed her curiously.

"Ma'am?" the male guard said. "Are you supposed to be here right now? Did you hear the other guards calling for you?"

"I'm really sorry to bother you," Faith began, "but is there any way you could get Officer Mitchell for me?"

The guards looked at each other and shrugged.

"You want to speak to Officer Mitchell?" the male guard asked.

"Yes I would like that very much," Faith replied with a comforting smile.

"What's this in reference to?" the female guard questioned.

"Well, I used to be here," Faith said as she pointed to the building, "and now I'm over there." She pointed behind her. "I just had a few questions, that's all. I won't take up much of her time."

The guards looked at each other and shrugged. The male guard smiled and said, "I'll go see if she's available. Can I tell her who's asking for her?"

"Faith Gallo," she said.

The guard walked away, leaving the female guard to stand with Faith. The two said nothing to each other. Faith just stood there confidently, occasionally crossing her arms and smiling. A few minutes had gone by before the male guard walked out of the building's front doors with Karen Mitchell following him. Just like she always did, she carried her clipboard close to her chest. When she saw Faith, she smiled and waved. Faith waved back. Karen told the female guard to open the gate. She then walked over to Faith and reached out, touching her on the shoulder.

"Is everything ok, dear?" Karen asked, showing signs of concern.

"No. Everything is not ok, Karen," Faith said sternly. "I want to see my husband."

Karen turned her head and smiled at the two guards behind her. She nodded to Faith and they walked a bit further away, her hand still on Faith's shoulder. "I've told you, I can't help you with that, Faith. I'm sorry—it's out of my power," she said.

"I know what's happening here, Karen," Faith said indignantly and she stopped in her tracks in the middle of the road. "You—and everyone that works here should be absolutely ashamed of yourselves."

"What are you talking about?" Karen asked, sounding somewhat annoyed. Her voice was several octaves lower than normal.

"Don't play stupid with me, Karen," Faith responded. "I'm too wise for that game and quite frankly too old. People are being put to death here—here in this camp. You know that it's happening and now I do, too. I want to see my husband now—before he becomes the next victim of your agency's humane termination policy."

Karen looked baffled. Her clipboard was now hanging by her fingers near her hip.

"Faith, I—" Karen began before being interrupted.

"I don't want to hear your explanation, Karen. Tell me though, if you can—what exactly is humane about putting someone to death for doing nothing wrong? Can you tell me that?"

Karen looked horrified. She turned around and nodded to the guards who were looking at them curiously. She put both hands on Faith's shoulders and turned to look her in the eyes. "Listen—I'll try to arrange a meeting with your husband, but you have to stop this talk right now, Faith," Karen pleaded. "There are things that go on here that even I don't understand or particularly agree with. Just because I wear the same uniform, doesn't mean I follow the same path."

"Prove it then," Faith said. "You go get Sam and let me speak to him, privately. Then, you'll prove to me that you care more than these animals do. You've been nothing but nice to me and I've always thought you were different, so if I'm coming across as judging, I apologize. I just cannot sit here and allow these things to go on in my own backyard."

Karen stood up straight, as if she was using her body language to assert her authority. Faith had seen her posture herself this way before, but she stood her ground and didn't falter. Karen's eyes zeroed on Faith's, then turned to the guards.

"We're good here. I'll be back shortly," she said to them as they nodded and waved. She turned back to Faith and offered a sullen grin. "Come on," she said.

Faith was dubiously surprised at Karen's willingness to help her— almost to the point that she didn't fully trust her but at this point, she really didn't care. If she had done something that had consequences, she would endure them. She was no stranger to accountability. Since her first day here, this was the first time she had overstepped, yet she felt— knew in her heart that it was absolutely necessary.

As they reached the front of the men's detention center, Karen motioned to the guards and they opened the chain-link gate, allowing her and Faith to pass through. A few confused nods were exchanged, but Faith didn't notice anything that would subvert her trust in Officer Mitchell at this point. She walked just behind her as they approached the front door to the old Holiday Inn Express, where Karen swiped a key fob, opening the door. They walked inside and Karen nodded to the guards at the front desk. One guard, a large-framed muscular man with a thick beard, stood up and held up a hand.

"Here to see Mr. Harden?" he asked her, referencing the chief of the men's detention center.

Karen shook her head. "Not today, thanks," she said.

"Anything I can help you with?" the guard asked again with a curious look on his face.

"No, thank you. I need to arrange a visit with one of your inmates. It won't take long," she assured.

"Roger that," the guard said. "I have to inform Chief Harden, ma'am."

"That's fine," Karen affirmed. "You can tell him now or I can tell him later."

Faith looked at her with an unsure gaze and Karen shook her head slightly at her dismissively.

"This isn't a conjugal visit, I assume?" the guard asked lightheartedly.

Faith, always the proper woman, and at times, to the point of appearing prudish, turned to him, her face aghast. "Absolutely not!" she said, her voice sounding mortified.

The guard chuckled and waved them off.

Karen looked over at Faith with a grin. "I don't think he was being presumptuous," she whispered, "I think that was his attempt at a joke."

"Doesn't matter," Faith concluded. "I don't want anyone to get the wrong impression of me—I don't care who it is."

The two turned around and walked toward the stairway.

"What did you mean when you said that you could tell him later?" Faith asked curiously.

"We have a bit of a relationship," Karen said. "I'm just hoping that he'll understand this."

Taking the stairway up to the second floor, Faith followed Karen down a hallway devoid of excessive lighting. The carpet had been removed long ago and all that was left was the bare concrete. They approached a door with a placard on it that displayed a serial number. Karen knocked hard on the door, simultaneously peering through the reversed peephole. She could see a slender man inside, his bare feet hanging off the bottom of the bed that he was laying on.

"Mr. Gallo, on your feet, please," Karen requested. She pulled a set of keys from her pocket and fiddled with them until she found the right one, and slid it into the lock.

Faith's anticipation was reaching an amazing level, having not seen her husband in a very long time. She could barely contain her excitement. She wondered why Karen had been so easy to convince, but decided to not look a gift horse in the mouth. In a few seconds, she would be reunited with her husband. Once near him, she would no longer fear anything. She could die right then and there. So long as she was with him, nothing else mattered. Karen opened the door and the two walked into the room, Faith following slightly behind. Inside, Faith's husband was standing up with his hands on his head, facing away from them. Faith couldn't help herself, and ran past Karen right up to him.

"Sam..." she said in a very satisfied voice.

Sam Gallo turned around with an extremely surprised look on his face which, in addition to the surprise, showed signs of wear and abuse. He looked like he had aged ten years since the last time she had seen him. Faith looked up to him and put her palm gently on his cheek, her eyes beginning to well up with emotion. Not known for being over-emotional or for being very affectionate, Sam stared down at his wife and a couple tears escaped his eyes. He reached around her and hugged her, not able to close his eyes. He was confused and a bit preoccupied with the red-haired guard standing behind his wife.

"Faithy," Sam said. "Oh baby, it is so good to see you."

The hug lasted all of about ten seconds but regardless, it felt good to Faith. She wiped her tears on her sleeve as they pulled away and said, "What happened to your face?"

"You look well," he said to her, ignoring her question.

"Honey, what happened to you?" Faith repeated.

"The same things that happen to anyone who is incarcerated and refuses to go along with the program," Sam said, his voice showing no emotion. He stared at Karen, who stood silently in full uniform.

"You've got five minutes," Karen said sternly. She turned around and walked to the door. "I'll wait outside."

"Ten," Faith dictated.

Karen nodded and walked outside, closing the door behind her.

"Sam, are you o—" Faith began before Sam hushed her.

"Honey, I'm fine, but we need to talk and it doesn't sound like we have much time," Sam said.

"Ok," she relented.

Sam took a seat on the bed and motioned for Faith to do the same. "Are they treating you fairly?" he asked.

Faith nodded. "Yes, surprisingly enough, they are. The lady outside—that's Karen Mitchell. She watched out for me while I was in women's detention."

"You're not there anymore?"

"No—they transferred me to the population," Faith replied. "They said they needed the room—people who were charged with more serious crimes are being moved in."

"I see," Sam uttered.

"Debbie and Ben are there. I've been palling around with them."

"Good," Sam said. "It's good to know there are other trustworthy people here."

"I've asked about you every day since we've been here," Faith said. "They've always told me they couldn't do anything and they wouldn't let me see you—until today."

Sam looked at her quizzically. "Why today?"

Faith looked down at the floor. "I found out about what goes on here," she said quietly. "I went to Karen—the only person who works here that I know has some sort of integrity. I told her to bring me to you and she did."

Same looked confused. "Let's pray that it is that and not something else. But I too am well aware of what goes on here," he said.

"You are?"

"Of course. They're purging the country of anyone who would stand up against them," Sam said.

"Purging?" Faith urged.

"The executions," Sam said firmly. "They're killing off all divergents. Anyone who doesn't go along with their plan to fundamentally change this country. People who love the country, like oath-keeping law enforcement and veterans, survivalists, preppers, etcetera. Patriots. People like me."

"Sam, please don't say that," Faith pleaded with a sorrowed look. "I don't want to hear you talk like something is going to happen to you."

"It's too late, Faithy," he moaned and shuffled his body on the bed. "I already have a bullseye on my head."

"What? What in the hell is that supposed to mean?" Faith shrieked. She hadn't uttered a word that even remotely sounded like vulgarity in years. It was probably the fourth or fifth time that she had done so in her entire life. It caught Sam's attention immediately, and he turned to her, holding both of her hands.

"You listen to me, and you listen to me like you never have before," he began, "we all have to die. All of us. Our birthdates and the day we die is written in the Book of Life, long before any of us were ever put on this earth. Faith, I'm not afraid to die—and neither should you be. This is all in God's hands how—this is God's will. If He wants me there with him instead of here, then I must accept that. So should you."

Faith began to cry; it couldn't be helped. She couldn't believe what she was hearing. Never in a million years would she have ever guessed that she'd be here right now, having this conversation with her husband. He squeezed her hands and allowed her to deal with her emotions naturally. He was a stubborn man but this was his wife of many years, and he loved her more than anything in the world. If this was the last time he'd see her, he wanted to take it all in, good and bad.

"I don't want to lose you," Faith said in between her sobs.

"We will be together no matter what," he assured. "You will never lose me."

"What should I do? How do we get you out of this mess? Should I try to fight them?"

"Absolutely not," Sam said. "You should know the futility of something like that. These people are more than ready for an uprising. I'm actually surprised that they haven't incited one already, in order to expedite their agenda."

"Then what? Tell me—I'll do anything," Faith whispered, now aware she was making more noise than she intended.

"You being here right now, tells me that you've earned some high opinion from these people—perhaps a bit of clout?"

"I suppose," Faith said.

"That's a fantastic beginning for something much greater," Sam said. "You've always been a born leader. People have always been drawn to you—the words you say and the way you say them."

Faith nodded. "My mother was the same way," she said. "People just loved her and she could never explain why."

"Faithy, you need to keep doing what you're doing. You need to continue gaining their trust and as well, find a way to gain the trust of the people, too. You need to find a way to unite them. There's a lot of strength in numbers, Faith. The problem is, just as it was before the world changed, that we are too busy fighting amongst ourselves to realize who the real enemy is. Sun Tzu said that an enemy divided is easily defeated—now look at us. If you can find a way to unite everyone here, you may be able to end the suffering that goes on here. I'm not saying it will be easy or even possible, but who knows? You've been known to be very persuasive."

"Gallos don't give up easily," Faith said.

"No, we don't," Sam agreed.

A smile broke across his face and he ran his fingers across Faith's aging hair. Faith kissed him on his cheek and they embraced, just as they heard a few loud voices from outside the door.

"I think our time is up," Faith said with a grave smile.

"Be strong," Sam said. "Do not let these people get the best of you. This is our tribulation—and the only thing left on the other side of it is salvation. You can do this, Faith. I know you can."

"I will pray for you," Faith said.

"And I you," Sam responded. "There's one last thing…"

Faith looked up and into the eyes that she had fallen in love with so long ago. "What?"

"If something does happen to me…I want you to avenge me…"

The door burst open and two armed guards walked in with Karen Mitchell walking beside them, her arms raised in deep protest. Pushing Karen aside, one of them grabbed Faith by her arm and pulled her to her feet. Sam reached forward in an attempt to remove the guard's hand from his wife, but was met with a punch to his face that knocked him to the ground. Faith shrieked.

"Be easy on her, you bastard!" Karen exclaimed. "She hasn't done anything wrong!"

"She shouldn't be here and you know it, Mitchell," the guard who had punched Sam said.

Faith looked down at her husband, who was already recovering from the blow and was beginning to sit up. He was bloodied, but he looked at her with a visage that showed no fear. He was as steadfast and as strong-willed as she had always seen him be. These people didn't scare him—she hadn't been sure at first, but now she knew it.

Faith's head was pushed down onto the bed as the guard who restrained her placed his zip cuffs onto her wrists. He pulled her upright and escorted her out the door with Karen following behind. The second guard followed.

As the door was being closed, Sam exclaimed, "You know what to do, Faith! You know what to do!" until the closed door muffled his voice to the point it couldn't be heard.

Faith closed her eyes as she was led down the hallway and began to pray. She could no longer hear her husband's voice. All she could hear now was Karen arguing with the guards. Under her breath, she prayed, "Lord God, comfort my husband. Place your hands on him and comfort him. He needs you now, Father. We all need you. Guide us, and protect us. Amen."

CHAPTER 17

Trout Run Valley
Hardy County West Virginia
Present day

NORMAN PULLED HIS DODGE UP to the long hardened dirt driveway, but didn't enter it. He instead, parked on the edge of the road just beside several rusty mailboxes, all of which had the name Brady stenciled on them in faded black paint. The driveway beside the mailboxes led through some trees to a cluster of small houses which seemed to all share the same yard. The houses, either had painted wood or well-weathered cedar siding, and looked fairly dilapidated with rusty tin roofs. There were old rusted bicycles in the yard, as well as a host of other children's toys, including a couple metal swing sets which themselves, showed signs of weathering. Fred, who sat in the cab seat behind Norman was the first to get out of the truck. As he got out, he placed his M1A gently on the floorboard and removed his pistol belt, setting it down beside his rifle. Norman got out of the truck, shortly followed by Michelle and Grace, who both had been sitting in the front seat with him.

"Leave your weapons in the truck," Fred instructed.

"You really think that's a good idea?" Norman inquired.

"I think if we step foot on their property with firearms, it will give old man Brady a damn good reason to cut us to pieces with his shotgun," Fred said firmly. "So yes, I think it's a good idea."

Norman nodded and set his AK inside the truck, then removed his pistol belt and set it on the floorboard. Michelle turned around and did the same with her pistol belt. Making sure that no one noticed, she unholstered her Glock and slid it into her waistband, pulling her t-shirt and hoodie down over it to hide the protruding grip. Grace stood still, her AR still slung over her shoulder. She didn't budge. Fred noticed and snapped his fingers at her, a notion she ignored. Michelle tapped her on the shoulder and Grace quickly turned to her. The evening before this meeting had been a bit of a joke to them—now, it had become serious.

"Grace—you awake?" Fred asked.

"I'm not putting this gun down," Grace asserted. "Sorry."

Michelle looked at Norman who stood emotionless and then glanced at Fred, who appeared both a bit nervous and annoyed. She said, "Grace, we can't appear as a threat to them."

"What about them being a threat to us?" Grace quipped. "Sorry. I feel safer this way."

"Stay in the truck then, and cover us," Fred quickly inserted. Grace looked to him, then nodded and got into the rear passenger seat. She closed the door and rolled down the window, setting the barrel of her rifle on the door frame. Her eyes were darting all around her.

Norman, Fred, and Michelle began walking down the dirt driveway to the cluster of houses, each holding their hands outward to signify to whomever was watching them that they were unarmed. No one was outside that they could see. They walked cautiously up to the first house which had a long wooden front porch. From inside the house, an older man's gravelly voice called to them, "That's far enough!"

They stopped in their tracks. Norman and Fred stood side by side in front of Michelle.

"Who are you? What do you want?" the voiced called. The sound of someone stirring inside the house was heard.

"It's Fred Mason from down the road," Fred said in a voice loud enough for the person to hear, but careful to not sound threatening. "Norman Boyce is with me, and so is Michelle Russell. Her daughter Grace is in the truck. We just want to talk."

"Talk about what?" the voice asked, sounding somewhat exasperated. "We don't want to be bothered." The door opened and an old man stepped outside of the house, letting the wooden screen door slap shut behind him. He was a tall, skinny man with a thick white beard and long, thin white hair. He wore denim overalls and in his hands was a very large double-barrel shotgun. Norman looked him over and then took a long glance at his weapon, which wasn't pointed in their direction, but just as easily could be in a split second. The man's skin was wrinkled, but he didn't appear anywhere near as decrepit as the house he'd just walked out of, which was little more than a shack with a metal roof. Norman had never seen a shotgun that size before and guessed that it was maybe a 10-gauge, which was a rare sight even in normal times.

"Mr. Brady, we wanted to talk to you and your family about helping us tighten security in the valley," Norman said in a calm tone. "We've encountered some new threats recently and we need your help."

"If you're talkin about them damn raiders like the ones we had last summer, we got that covered," Mr. Brady said. "I seem to remember us talking about this before, back then. Nothing's changed on our end." He spat a wad of what appeared to be tobacco juice onto the wooden floor of the front porch.

"Mr. Brady, a lot has changed since then," Fred spoke up. "We have a new problem now. We had a run-in with two members of an outlaw biker gang a few days ago. They attacked the Ackermanns at their home, and Mrs. Ackerman was killed in the attack."

Mr. Brady said nothing at first as he looked away from his visitors and took a look around his property. Norman and Fred glanced at one another. They wondered if any of what they had said was getting through to the man. It was impossible to tell.

"Sorry to hear that," Mr. Brady said in the most sincere voice he was capable of, which was still very gruff. "Erika was a sweet lady." He paused and continued looking around. "Well—did you kill 'em?"

"Mr. Ackermann did," Norman said. "He didn't have any choice."

"Good then," Mr. Brady grunted, "Problem solved."

"Not exactly, sir," Norman said. "We had another run-in with them at our barricade near Wolf Gap. We exchanged fire and were lucky to live through it. We killed one, captured one, and one managed to escape. We're certain he'll go back and tell the others what happened, and they will be looking for some vengeance."

"What makes you think there's others?" Mr. Brady questioned. "Seems to me, in light of what's going on in the world, a group like that would've starved to death already."

Fred looked at Norman and then to Mr. Brady. He stepped forward and began to elaborate on Norman's story. After a few sentences that Fred was sure he had ignored, Mr. Brady held up his hand and Fred stopped talking.

"I said that's far enough," Mr. Brady said as he lifted his shotgun slightly. Fred held his hands in the air and retreated slowly backward.

"I'd like you all to get off my property—now," Mr. Brady commanded. "I didn't invite you here—you're trespassing."

A middle-aged man exited the front door of an adjacent house. He cradled a scoped hunting rifle in his arms. As he walked outside, two young girls wearing tattered dresses ran outside, one chasing the other. They laughed as they ran around to the rear of the house, periodically moving in and out of sight. Michelle peered over Norman's shoulder to get a better look at the girls. She knew that the Bradys had grandchildren, but had never actually seen them. One of the girls was about eight years old, the other a bit younger. Both had long, unkempt blond hair and a skin tone that told of how much time they'd spent outdoors. They were beautiful.

"Everything alright, paw?" the man asked.

"Everything's fine, Bo," Mr. Brady answered. "These folks were just leaving."

Bo Brady looked at Fred and Norman and nodded to them. He then nodded and tipped his hat at Michelle. "Ma'am," Bo said to her.

Michelle smiled at the gesture and lifted her hand slightly to wave. Despite appearances, she knew that these people weren't as much dangerous, as they were misunderstood. They were as country as anyone could be—the modern definition of hillbillies. But they were also simple, old-fashioned family men that loved their children and respected their hard-working women. Chivalry wasn't dead, even in the woods of West Virginia.

"Mr. Brady, good morning," Michelle said. While introducing herself, she felt it was time to stop hiding behind Fred and Norman. She pushed between them to stand in front, facing Mr. Brady. Upon seeing this, Mr. Brady lifted the barrel of his shotgun into the air, so as to not aim it at her.

"Sorry, ma'am. Didn't mean to aim this here boomstick at you like that," he said. "My apologies."

Fred and Norman were both astonished at how quickly the situation had changed. The looks on their faces were priceless.

"Mr. Brady," she began, "I know us coming here like this looks bad, but we don't believe this situation is anywhere near being over. That's why we decided to enlist your help. We wouldn't be here right now if this wasn't serious. None of us will be safe here until we can all cooperate and secure our lands. We are already doing all we can, but we need your help."

"We can handle ourselves, ma'am," Mr. Brady said. "I'm not sure what else we can do."

"Please, just humor me for a moment," Michelle pleaded. "These people that we are dealing with—they have no morals. They are the kind of people that will sneak up on you in the middle of the night and rape and kill your granddaughters, Mr. Brady." She paused. "We found some items in their possession that would indicate they are very much capable of that type of behavior," Michelle said grimly. "We aren't taking it lightly down the road. Neither should you or the rest of your family."

For some reason, her words seemed to get Mr. Brady's attention somewhat. His eyes grew wide and he turned around to see his granddaughters playing what appeared to be a game of tag. After a minute, he turned to Michelle again and asked, "What do you want from us?"

"For starters, we need you to guard your end of the valley," Michelle said. "We are already guarding the other end. There's other needs but for now, just getting your family onboard with us will be enough."

"We don't have the manpower, George," Fred stated, feeling that with Michelle taking the lead, the situation had calmed down enough to be informal. "We have the southern border secured and we're patrolling the road hourly—but we can't sustain this level of security without the help of you and your family."

"We need more people," Michelle added. "People we can trust."

"How do you know that you can trust us?" Mr. Brady asked. "How do we know if we can trust you?"

Michelle looked away and sighed, then looked into Mr. Brady's grey eyes.

"That's not an easy question to answer," she said. "We took a chance coming here today. Past experience had us second guessing doing that. We want to build a trust with you and your family. We want to survive and protect ourselves and our children. Life is tough enough for us already— we don't need any more enemies." Old man Brady coughed. He leaned his shotgun against the wall behind him. He turned around to face the group as Bo Brady walked from his porch to his father's, his rifle now slung over his shoulder. He occasionally looked over his shoulder at his two young daughters, who were laughing and playing behind his home.

"What do we get...in exchange for helping you?" Bo Brady asked.

"By helping us, you help yourselves. There's safety in numbers," Norman said. "With the valley under constant guard, with some obvious exceptions, life for the others can go on."

"My sons and I aren't soldiers," Mr. Brady said.

"We're defending our way of life now, George," Fred said. "Fighting for survival makes us all soldiers, whether we like it or not."

Mr. Brady nodded, seemingly beginning to understand the situation for what it was. He then said, "We want our children to be safe as much as any man does. This land is ours and ain't no one gonna come down here and take it from us. Give us some time to think about it."

"That sounds fair," Michelle said, trying to pretend like she wasn't amazed with the results of their encounter. "Let us know as soon as you can."

Michelle motioned to Fred and to Norman to turn and walk away, and they did. She could hear Mr. Brady and Bo mumbling back and forth between each other. She turned back and saw that another one of Mr. Brady's sons had joined them, also with a scoped rifle in his arms. As the three were nearing Norman's Dodge, Mr. Brady called to them. Michelle, Fred, and Norman stopped and turned around, seeing Mr. Brady and his sons walking up to them in the middle of the driveway.

"We'll help," Mr. Brady presented. "But we want something in return."

"What's that?" Fred asked.

"We need gas," Mr. Brady's other son said. "Looks to me like you guys might have some." He pointed to Norman's Dodge. "We have some old trucks, some mopeds, and a few other things that I'd like to get going, and some other equipment I'd like to be able to use again—like my chainsaw."

Norman nodded and smiled. "I can understand that," he said.

"We don't have an unlimited supply, but we can help you with gas," Fred said. "In exchange for a secure northern border and the additional manpower, that is."

"Surely," Bo Brady said. "We can set up a blockade at the bridge up the road and we can take turns guarding it. Once we get some gas, we can help patrol the road. We have quite a few able-bodied men here. All of us are farmers, hunters, and fishermen. We can all shoot."

"What about the women?" Michelle asked curiously.

"Our wives stay here at all times with the children, no exceptions," Mr. Brady growled. "That's our policy."

Fred held out his hand and shook with Bo and Mr. Brady's other son who'd introduced himself as George Junior, but told them all to call him 'Junior'. Mr. Brady seemed reluctant at first, but extended his hand. Norman shook their hands as well. When Michelle shook with them, all three men smiled at her and lowered their heads reverently while saying, "Ma'am." The gesture, once again made Michelle smile.

As the group exchanged smiles and pleasantries after reaching what appeared to be a successful detente, Grace began shouting from the truck and everyone snapped to attention. They heard her door slam shut as she ran to them up the driveway, her AR in one hand and a radio in the other. Confused transmissions, that included lots of raised, panicked voices, could be heard coming from the radio's speaker. Fred grabbed the radio from Grace and put it to his ear. He immediately could tell that the voices belonged to his wife Kim and daughter Megan. He went to press the PTT but before he could, she called for him, asking if he could hear her.

Fred mashed down the PTT. "Meg, it's Dad. What is going on?"

"Dad—we're under attack," Megan voice whimpered over the speaker. "They're coming out of the woods—the Schmidt's house is on fire!"

"Megan, where are you exactly? Are you safe?" Fred asked his daughter frantically. He was trying to remain calm, but couldn't find a way.

"I'm ok, Dad. I'm with Brooke and Brandon and their parents. We're staying low—hiding in the woods. Their house is burning down, Dad! They started shooting into the house before they set it on fire."

"Do you have your gun with you?"

"Yes. We all do. I'm locked and loaded and Mom is on the way. Dad—the guys who attacked us are heading across the road now. It looks like they're going to attack the Russell's cabin next."

Fred began sprinting toward Norman's Dodge. Michelle, Norman and Grace all followed.

Michelle was frantic. "Fred—call Lee and make sure he's getting everyone up—they were all still sleeping when we left," she said anxiously.

Fred tried to contact Lee over the radio a few times, but Lee never responded. He then called his daughter. "Meg—listen to me. Stay where you are and shoot anyone that comes near you. You kill anyone you don't know. Stay on the radio. We're on the way…" A bullet whizzed over his head, causing him to dive to the ground in a cloud of profanities just as several ATVs and two old pickup trucks approached on the road at a high rate of speed. As they closed in, they began firing their weapons at Norman's truck, scoring hits in the radiator and both front tires. The windshield was the next target as pieces of glass shattered all over the hood as well as the road.

"Son of a bitch!" Norman yelled as he instinctively grabbed Michelle and tossed her to the ground behind a tree and then dove in front of her. Michelle pulled the hidden Glock from her waistband and emptied the magazine at the attackers while Norman covered his ears with his hands after the first couple shots. Grace fell to the ground beside them and began firing her AR back at the ATVs that had already sped past the Brady's houses. As the pickup trucks sped past, Bo Brady ran behind his house and quickly gathered his daughters, sending them indoors. Junior stood beside his father with his rifle raised in the air, but didn't fire. Mr. Brady, surprisingly didn't move an inch, in spite of what was going on around them.

Norman got up and ran to his truck, immediately noticing its condition. "Oh, that's just great!" he yelled, slamming his fist against the hood. "Just fucking great!"

As Grace and Michelle rose to their feet and joined Norman at the truck, Fred turned to look at Mr. Brady who stood silently with his son, seemingly unfazed. They said nothing to each other, the looks on their faces signifying that they didn't seem interested in helping for whatever reason. Fred yelled into the radio for someone to come pick them up and Peter quickly responded, telling him that he would be on his way to get them after he took Amy and their sons to the Perrys, where he knew they'd be safe. After gathering their weapons from Norman's Dodge, they all began running down the road as fast as their feet could carry them.

"We'll be waiting on that gas," Mr. Brady proclaimed with a raised voice.

Christian awoke suddenly to the sounds of gunfire in the distance. He jumped up from the recliner and pushed the drapes away to look out the window, instantly seeing several armed men running down the driveway toward the cabin a couple hundred yards away. The front door opened and Lee appeared, inhaling and exhaling loudly as he fell inside, slamming the door shut behind him with his foot.

"They're coming!" Lee shouted as he ran down the hallway in the direction of the gun safe.

Christian turned around and quickly ran down the hallway, turning into to Lauren's room to wake her. She jumped up from the bed when she felt him nudge her shoulder.

"Get up," Christian said. "There's a group of people coming down the driveway with guns. We're under attack."

"Takers—get John," Lauren said as she rubbed her eyes.

Christian nodded and ran to John's room. He walked inside and woke up John, who was very surprised to see him. All four gathered gear, weapons, and ammunition and met in the living room. Lauren moved more slowly than usual, keeping in mind her injured ankle. Her heart was beating a mile a minute. As quickly as she could, she put on a pistol belt and slung her AR in front of her. John put on a chest rig full of AK magazines and slung his Mossberg across his body. He then picked up his AK and eyeballed his brother, who was beyond flustered and completely out of breath, barely keeping his composure enough to properly seat a magazine into his AK. He then looked to Christian.

"You want to back me up?" John asked.

"I thought you'd never ask," Christian said as he finished sliding his body armor on and checked his rifle.

John stepped forward and put his arm around Lauren, then kissed her forehead.

"No warning shots, John," Lauren said as she charged the bolt on her AR. John nodded and said, "Guard the fort."

John burst out the door with Christian in tow. Lee finally got up and walked to the window, leaning his large body against the wall. Several shots were heard from outside, the bullets impacting the cabin's outer wall. Several more shots were heard, including a burst of full-auto suppressed fire that Lauren assumed belonged to Christian and one of his government issued M4s. Lee and Lauren both got down as low as they could.

"If we make it through this, I swear—I'm going on a diet," Lee said in a huff. He crawled through the kitchen to the rear door of the cabin which lead to a small porch, opening the door just enough to see outside.

Lauren wanted to smile at Lee's resolution, but couldn't. She crawled over to the door and cracked it open, allowing her rifle's barrel to lead the way. She couldn't see John or Christian anywhere, but could definitely smell that something was burning outside. She heard an occasional yell and thought she could hear screaming in the distance. As she peered left, the driveway came into view, where three men in ragged clothing lay dead. She peered through the magnified reticle of her rifle's scope, just to verify that she didn't recognize the men, and let out a sigh of relief when she didn't. She then began to wonder where her mother, Grace, and Norman were.

"Where's our radio?" Lauren asked Lee.

"I left it outside—I think the batteries are dead," he replied.

"That's perfect," Lauren retorted in disgust, keeping her rifle ready. As she continued scanning to the left past the driveway, two men came into view on the edge of the woods, both moving low and slow toward the family's ATVs which were parked out front. The men were carrying high-capacity rifles of some sort and she didn't recognize them. If the three men that lay dead were members of their group, she couldn't tell. The approaching men paid them no mind.

"Contact front," Lauren said under her breath.

Lee turned to her. "How many?"

"Two," she whispered.

The two men began to closely check out the ATVs as Lauren watched. One of the men pointed to the house and the other nodded. He broke away from his companion and began walking toward the house with his rifle ready. Lauren closed her eyes and took a deep breath. She opened her eyes and lined the up the crosshairs of her scope with the man's torso. Just as she clicked off the safety and prepared to fire, she heard a suppressed shot. The man's head exploded and he went down, falling just in front of the porch. Lauren quickly lined up her sights on the second man, who had begun firing wildly into the woods, at where he thought the shot that killed his friend had come from. Lauren pulled the trigger twice, hitting the man center-mass and sending him screaming to the ground. She followed with a single shot to his head, ending him. Her body began to shake. Killing the man reminded her of the first time she had ever pulled the trigger on someone—a moment in her life that she would never forget. She had killed that man for a reason. She kept telling herself that this one was no different. Lauren tried hard to gather herself.

Turn it into something else.

"Multiple contacts—rear!" Lee shouted as he began firing his AK-47 wildly out the back door. "They're coming out of the woods!"

"How many?" Lauren asked, as she began to regain her composure. Looking over her shoulder at him, she could hear bullets smacking the cabin in between Lee's shots.

"Ten or twenty," Lee bellowed as he continued to fire his rifle. "I can't tell—it's too many!"

Lauren reluctantly pulled back from her position in the doorway and closed the door, locking the deadbolt. She didn't want to leave the front of the cabin unguarded, but didn't know what else to do. She crawled to John's bedroom and slowly peered through the window, immediately noticing what had gotten Lee so rattled. A large group of armed men, along with several women were standing near the shed, some of them attempting to gain access to it with hatchets, a crowbar, and other tools. Others were standing near them and firing occasionally at the house, using the shed as cover. Lauren reached up and unlocked the window, sliding it upward as fast as she could without being seen. She then lifted her rifle up and pressed the muzzle against the screen. Bringing the targets into view, she noticed that every time Lee would shoot, his shots were either too low or too high, many of them smacking the ground in front of the men, merely covering them with dirt.

"Lee, you need to calm down and aim your shots!" Lauren exclaimed out the door of the bedroom.

"I'm trying!" Lee yelled back from the kitchen.

Lauren adjusted the magnification of her scope and lined up her crosshairs on a man's head who was shooting at them from behind the cover of the shed. She fired and his head snapped back as he switched off, the ejected brass from her rifle making an audible "clink" as it hit the floor beside her. A man beside him dropped to his knees and began pulling the dead man's gear off. Lauren drew down on him and fired two rounds into his neck. His body leaned sideways and fell to the ground. After seeing their comrades do down, three other men began yelling loudly and started running toward the cabin.

"Go over there and kill that bitch!" another one of them said as he pointed to the cabin.

One of the men headed to the cabin had a crossbow and the other two only had baseball bats. The man with the crossbow fired a bolt at the cabin, which imbedded itself in the door that Lee was hiding behind. Lauren shot the man holding the crossbow just as he made it across the bridge, his body falling down into the ravine. She then put two rounds into the man with the baseball bat that was closing in fast on the cabin, and after he went down she fired two more shots, ending the life of the third. Her heart was racing now as the adrenaline inside her began to boil over.

When Lee noticed that their attackers had taken some damage, his composure returned and he began aiming his shots again, taking down several of the armed men near the shed. Seeing the fallen members of their group, most of the remaining men and women began retreating back into the woods. They had either dropped their weapons or didn't have weapons to begin with—but it didn't matter. He and Lauren both let them run away. The firefight seemingly over, Lee noticed one man left, who had crawled beneath the shed. Lauren noticed as well from the other room.

"You got him?" she asked Lee. "The one under the shed?"

"Yep," Lee said confidently.

"Ok. I'm moving to the front," Lauren said. She dropped the magazine from her rifle and replaced it with a fresh one, then crawled to the front door. Opening it, she saw John and Christian, who had found cover in the front yard. John was kneeling behind a tree and Christian was on his knees behind one of the ATVs. Both were unhurt and were scanning the area for additional threats. Lee's rifle went off from behind her. She turned to him and he held up his hand.

"He's down," Lee said proudly. "The rear is clear."

"Good job, buddy," Lauren responded.

John turned to see Lauren peering out the front door when he heard the door creak open. He lifted his thumb into the air and Lauren responded with the same, signifying that everything was ok. Christian snapped his fingers and John turned suddenly to him, seeing him point to the gate. John nodded. Christian turned to Lauren and gave her an exigent but concerned look, but didn't say anything. He didn't have to. It was obvious to Lauren that he had somewhere to go, but didn't want to leave her defenseless.

"Go," Lauren said to Christian in a voice just loud enough for him to hear. "We're good here." As she finished, the sound of multiple engines became audible from the road. She knew then, that Christian had heard the engines before she had.

Christian nodded and began quickly walking up the driveway, staying fairly low to the ground. John followed him. This time, with his shotgun at the ready and the AK-47 slung over his shoulder. He began loading the Mossberg with slugs, figuring they'd be more effective at disabling moving vehicles. Their walking soon became running as they leapfrogged from cover toward the gate. As several hostile ATVs came into view, John began to unload his shotgun in their direction, attempting to take out the vehicles. Hitting the ATVs first, the riders were forced to jump off and the trucks behind them came to a sudden stop. Not all of the riders had guns, but those that did began firing wildly at John and Christian. Christian returned fire in full-auto, sending thirty rounds in their direction in no time, hitting a few and stifling the others' shots. He reloaded quickly, dropping the empty magazine to the ground and sending the bolt home after inserting a fresh one. He switched to semi-auto and began taking aimed shots as John finished off the ATVs before reloading with buckshot.

"They came from the woods behind our house," Bryan Taylor's voice said over the radio.

Fred pressed the PTT from the passenger seat of Peter's truck, which was speeding south down Trout Run Road. "From one of the abandoned houses?"

"Negative," Bryan said. "From the old logger road at the edge of our property. I saw a bunch of them running through the woods on foot."

Fred shook his head and cursed under his breath. "Keep those girls safe, Bryan. My sons are on the way from the barricade to help you guys out."

"10-4," Bryan said. "We're in the cellar."

"Chad, Mark, what's your ETA?" Fred inquired to his sons.

"Two minutes," Chad's voice said over the radio.

Grace sat in between Peter and Fred, her rifle against her chest. She was shaking. "'Two minutes' sounds like a lifetime," she said.

Peter stopped his truck in the middle of the road beside St. James Church. He pointed to the vehicles that sat in the road about a hundred yards in front of them, all of which were surrounded by bodies. All of which weren't moving.

"Slowly," Fred said. "Very slowly, Pete."

Peter nodded. Fred knocked on the window to get Norman and Michelle's attention, who were seated in the back of the truck. Norman was already standing up, his AK-47 resting on the roof of the truck. Michelle had her Glock at the ready. As they pulled forward, two figures emerged from the woods on the left side of the road. At first, they had their guns aimed at Peter's truck, but disengaged soon after.

Norman tapped on the roof. "Don't shoot—it's John and Christian," he said.

"Who's Christian?" Peter asked. As they began waving to him, he pulled forward to them and stopped the truck.

"Our new neighbor," Fred said, "and from the looks of it, someone we could definitely benefit from having around."

"Come here often?" Peter said to John and Christian, his head hanging out the window.

"Is the area secured?" Fred asked urgently, stopping Peter's goofiness in its tracks. There was no time for jokes today.

"All hostiles have been neutralized," Christian said grimly, slinging his rifle over his shoulder and pointing to the smoke that rose from the woods nearby. "We were heading over there now to check that out."

"Where's Lauren?" Michelle asked urgently, looking at Norman, "—and Lee?"

"Back at the cabin," John said. "We had a bunch of takers attack the house. They're all dead. Lauren and Lee are fine." He spit on the ground. "Any idea what's burning?"

"The Schmidt's house," Fred said angrily. "Get in the truck."

John and Christian hopped into the back of Peter's truck and continued down the road. Peter pulled the truck into the Schmidt's driveway and the house, which was now fully engulfed in flames, came into view. Fred jumped out and began calling for Megan and Kim on the radio. He then ran over to the woods where his wife and daughter emerged and ran to him. They embraced as the Schmidt family slowly stepped out of the woods. Whitney and Scott both looked devastated. Their hands covered their mouths while they watched their home burn completely out of control with no way to stop it. Their teenage children, Brooke and Brandon, were hysterical. Grace walked over to them and put her arms around them, trying her best to calm them down. Michelle joined Whitney and Scott and began offering whatever comforts she could, although she knew it wouldn't do much good. Norman stood beside Scott, placing his hand on his shoulder.

After everyone else had gotten out of the truck, Peter stepped out with a radio in his hand. "Guys, I'm sorry, but I have to go. I told Amy what's going on and she wants me to come back," Peter said in a rare serious tone.

"Get out of here, Pete. Give us a yell on the radio if you need anything. Thanks for the ride," Norman said as Peter waved to everyone and soon sped off down Trout Run Road.

A few moments of silence followed as the Schmidt's once beautiful, split-level home began to collapse in places where the fire had consumed it fully.

"Why would anyone do something like this?" Whitney said in a choked-up voice, tears covering her cheeks. "Why would you just set fire to someone's house?"

"Maybe to scare us off," Michelle guessed.

"Well, it makes no sense," Whitney uttered. "Not one damn bit of sense."

"They got what they deserved, babe. We're alive and well, and we can always rebuild," Scott said, trying to muster something positive out of it.

Fred, Kim, and Megan walked over to the group. After a pause, Norman got Fred's attention.

"They attacked at dawn from two different directions," Norman said, trying to keep his voice down.

"I know. Goes to show that you should never underestimate your enemies," Fred said.

Christian walked up to the group with John. He broke away and went to stand beside Grace, who was still consoling the children. She smiled at him and he winked at her.

Scott turned around and noticed Christian, but didn't recognize him. All he saw was the black uniform, body armor, and suppressed M4. Seeing how close he was standing to Grace, he motioned to her and said, "Friend of yours?"

She nodded and introduced Christian to the Schmidts and to the others who had yet to meet him.

Seeing all the distraught faces and helpless looks, Kim had become uncomfortable with the situation. "Let's get you guys out of here," she spoke up. "We can clean this up tomorrow after the fire has died down." She stepped in front of Whitney and embraced her. "We have plenty of room. For the time being, you all can stay with us."

The Schmidts were overcome with what Kim had offered them and thanked her, deciding to take her up on her offer, after discussing it amongst themselves for a bit. It came as a surprise to them, especially knowing that they were not Fred's favorite people. Regardless, the events of the day had them emotionally exhausted. There wasn't any point in watching their home, and everything they had held dear, go up in flames any longer.

Lauren held her rifle at low-ready as she hopped on one foot from the front of the cabin to the rear. She took a quick look at the ATVs that sat in the driveway and was glad to see that they hadn't been damaged. The cabin had taken a few hits, both on the front and rear. The logs prevented the bullets from penetrating, but had nonetheless been damaged. There were bodies scattered all over the property. Lee was outside in the driveway, investigating the ones that had been the first to go down.

"Takers?" Lauren inquired.

"Yeah," Lee uttered. "No one special that I can see—and no bikers."

"I'm going to go check out the shed," Lauren said.

Lee acknowledged her and she made her way to the rear of the property. Lauren moved slowly over the wooden bridge that crossed Trout Run and out to the shed. When she got to the front door, she noticed that the group had actually managed to break into it, and the door was just sitting there cracked open. She began to feel like she had a few days ago, when the feeling of curiosity had overwhelmed her. She stepped forward and lifted her rifle to her cheek, and then forced the door open with her right hand.

"Don't shoot us," a voice in the darkness said. "We don't want any trouble."

Lauren was startled. She had heard that voice before, but couldn't place it. She stepped back and took cover behind the shed wall. She kneeled down instinctively with her rifle's barrel aimed into the darkness. In an authoritative voice, Lauren said, "Come out of there slowly, with your hands where I can see them, and I won't shoot you."

Two figures began to emerge from the darkness. The first figure that came into view was a little girl. Lauren immediately noticed her shoes—they were dimly flashing with each step. At that point, even before the woman came into view, she knew exactly who they were. Lauren backed away slowly. She lifted the rifle up and aimed it at the woman—immediately noticing that she had a revolver in her right hand.

"Drop the gun!" Lauren exclaimed. She continued putting distance in between herself and them.

The woman smiled. "I can't do that," she said.

"Lady, I'm telling you right now, I will shoot you if you don't put down that gun!" Lauren warned.

"I'm not afraid of death," the woman said with an emotionless stare. She patted her daughter's shoulder. "Neither is she. We deal with the prospect of death every day—therefore, we don't fear it. We embrace it."

"You don't have to die today," Lauren said slowly. "We can live in peace with each other. It doesn't have to be this way."

"You're wrong," the woman began, "this is how it is. This is our reality. This is how we survive."

"By taking things from others?" Lauren indignantly asked. "By killing other people? There are a million other ways to survive that don't involve taking someone else's things from them or killing them."

The woman smiled deviously. "Are we so different? You say these things, but look what you've done," she said as she pointed around the shed to the corpses. "You murdered these men without any regard for who they were, or why they were here."

"We didn't murder anyone," Lauren asserted firmly. "You attacked us. We defended ourselves. Self-defense is not murder."

"Our opinions differ because we are truly different," the woman said with a devious grin. "Look at all that you have—look at all these things. You have food, shelter, water, everything you need. We have none of this. Just with what you have stored in this building here, could keep us alive for months. Why is it that you have these things and we do not? Who made you people the lords of the land?"

"We didn't take this land using eminent domain," Lauren explained. "The people who live here bought the property from previous owners. The only reason we have what we have is because we planned ahead and now, we utilize what the land provides—same as you do. We don't lay claim to anything that doesn't already belong to us."

The woman's emotions began to escalate as her cheeks filled with color. The little girl looked up at her mother often, but didn't say a word. It was almost as if she had been programmed not to.

"And how did the original owners of the land acquire it? How did the original settlers of this country get their lands and other things they needed? That's right—they took it. They took it by force," the woman argued.

"You and your people made a choice to live this way. We made a choice to live our way. We work hard to have what we have—and we don't go out and kill people to get what we want. That's the only difference between you and me." Lauren paused. "Aside from that, we're just two people trying to survive."

The woman laughed slightly, seemingly amused at the exchange. Lauren began remembering things that her dad had told her over the years. She remembered him telling her that some people were just impossible to get through to. The oblivious ones, as he called them. They only saw things from one perspective and were devoid of compassion. This person was just one of those people.

Lauren said, "You can make another choice right here, right now— to live in peace with us, and us with you. If you can do that, you and your daughter are free to leave."

The woman coughed and lifted the revolver into the air slightly, but didn't point it at Lauren. Lauren's finger was nested on the trigger of her rifle, ready to shoot her down if necessary. She truly did not want it to become necessary. She had done enough killing today.

"Look around you, girl!" the woman shouted as she began to become enraged, "look what you have done to us today! And now you ask for peace between our people?" She paused and shook her head violently. "No! There can be no peace—after this day, there will be no peace!" she announced with a maniacal grin. "We have just as much right to all of this as you do. We are sovereign citizens of this land. The only choice to be made is yours. You can give us what we want or we will take it. And, every single one of you, I assure you—will die."

The woman raised the revolver, this time aiming it directly at Lauren. Lauren fired two quick shots at her without taking a second to aim. Both shots went unintentionally low and hit her in the stomach. The woman dropped the gun to the ground as her body bowed over, landing face first in the dirt outside the shed. Her daughter screamed and ran to her. The woman groaned loudly and rolled over, blood running from her wounds. When the little girl approached her, she grabbed her head and whispered something into her ear. Her daughter looked at Lauren with tears rolling from her eyes and then, slowly and methodically reached for the revolver.

"Sweetie, don't do that," Lauren pleaded as she aimed her rifle at the little girl. "I'm serious—don't pick up that gun."

The little girl did so anyway and Lauren began preparing herself to shoot her, even though every fiber in her soul told her not to. The little girl slowly handed the gun to her mother who took it, with her very weak and shaky hand. Lauren watched her diligently. She put the woman's head in her sights and waited for what she was sure was going to happen. With narrowed eyes and a devious grin, the woman then took the revolver, deliberately placed it to the base of her daughter's head, and pulled the trigger. Lauren shrieked as she watched the young girl's lifeless body fall to the ground amidst a pink mist of blood. The revolver recoiled and caused the woman's weakened grip to release it and it fell just behind her into the dirt and leaves. She closed her eyes and let her arm drop to the ground, not making an attempt to retrieve it.

"WHY?" Lauren screamed amongst a storm of emotional obscenities. "WHY?" she screamed again in a thundering voice as she walked up to them, her rifle at the ready. Her ankle stung her when she inadvertently put weight on it, but she didn't care. It didn't seem important to her now. She was numb—both emotionally and physically. A fire was burning out of control in her soul and she could feel an uncomfortable rage inside her begin to grow. Lauren was ready to empty the entire magazine of her rifle into the woman's face after watching her senselessly murder her own child—having done so with a smile on her face.

"We do what we have to do," the woman groaned, blood beginning to roll and bubble from her mouth.

Lauren began shaking uncontrollably. The anger inside her was exploding now. She flipped the safety on her rifle, screamed and soon, just dropped it to the ground. She fell to her knees and began to cry, almost hysterically. Tears began streaming down her face. She couldn't help it anymore and just let herself go. Over the course of the past year's events, she had grown so much and gotten so strong, but this was just too much to take right now.

Turn it into something else

"I can't!" she wailed, in an attempt to answer her father's haunting voice.

Her sobs had overtaken her. There had been so much killing today. She herself had done so because it'd been necessary. If she hadn't killed them, they would have killed her and her family today. She didn't like taking lives, but she knew she could eventually find a way to live with herself because of that fact. In these times, death was something she knew she had to learn to get used to, but a woman killing her own daughter in cold blood was different and too much to comprehend. It was the vilest thing Lauren had ever seen in her life. Through her sobs, she began hating this place. She hated what her world had become. The woman was right, there wasn't any peace. There seemed to be no end to the horrors of this new world. They were free, but at what price? Would things always be this way? She wasn't sure that she wanted to live in a world like this, if it meant seeing these things.

Hearing Lauren scream, Lee ran up to just behind her and gasped when he saw the scene. He put a hand to his mouth. He turned away, not able to process with what he was seeing. At first, he thought that maybe Lauren had shot the little girl, but the exit wound and the shiny revolver that laid near the shed told a different story. He tried to look back, but couldn't. "Lauren, are you ok?" he asked, not knowing anything else to say.

Lauren hesitated through her tears and managed to utter the word, "No," as she rose slowly to her feet.

Seeing that there wasn't any danger and sensing Lauren needed her space, Lee decided to walk away. He was never very good at situations like this. He would go tell his brother what he had seen and let John handle it.

Lauren stood there for a while alone, her eyes darting back and forth from the dead little girl just a few feet away from her and her mother, whom she had shot twice but was still alive, taking painful breaths. One of her wounds oozed blood that was nearly black in color. Lauren had heard before that this meant the bullet had hit her liver, but wasn't sure. The only thing Lauren was sure of was that this person would die soon and she wasn't bothered in the least about letting the woman bleed out in front of her, no matter how long it took. Blood oozed from the woman's mouth occasionally as she coughed. Her glassy eyes stared at the sky and she said nothing as she gasped for air. Lauren wanted her to suffer.

A few minutes had gone by and John walked up to Lauren, placing a concerned hand on her shoulder. Lauren didn't even look at him. She didn't want him to see her eyes right now. He unfolded a white sheet that he had brought with him and laid it gently over the little girl's body. He closed her eyelids reverently before covering her face. John wasn't known for letting his emotions get the best of him, but after seeing this, it couldn't be helped. He allowed himself to cry briefly. Noticing that the woman was still alive, after hearing her death rattle, he said, "Lauren, we need to put her out of her misery."

Lauren, who had managed to gather herself to just sniffles, shook her head in refusal. "No," she uttered. "Fuck her. Let her die slowly. I want her to feel every second of it."

John pleaded with her, but Lauren wouldn't budge. After a few minutes of trying to get through to her, John relented and said, "I'll be inside if you need me."

After John walked away, Lauren looked to the sky as if to find answers there. She felt so lost right now in this horrible place. "I can't do this, Dad," she whispered. "Please hear me—wherever you are. I need you.

Please come home. Can you just do that? I know you would want me to be tougher than this, but I just can't and I'm sorry. I'm not a soldier..."

"No, you're not," Christian's voice said as he appeared behind her. "But you are a warrior."

Lauren turned to him, somewhat surprised to see him, and then turned away quickly. "I thought I was alone," she said.

Christian walked up behind her and surveyed the scene. He counted at least twelve dead bodies before seeing the sheet that John had placed over the lifeless little girl. He looked at Lauren's pale face, and then looked down at the woman who had been gut shot and was bleeding out. Without any hesitation, he pulled out his Glock 19 and fired two shots into the woman's chest, and one shot into her head. Lauren jumped at the sound of the abrupt gunshots, and then looked at him angrily. She began to shake again.

"This...isn't who you are, Lauren," Christian said softly. "You're not an animal." He paused and pointed to the dead bodies that lay near the shed. "These people—the people who attacked you...they're animals. They lost what was left of their humanity a long time ago. Don't let the fact that they lost theirs, influence you to lose yours. If you do, you'll have nothing left truly worth fighting for."

Lauren was taken aback by Christian's actions as well as his words, but soon calmed herself down and began to take what he was saying to heart. She didn't understand why, but he had a way of speaking to her that was calming and reassuring. He was like no one she had ever met before—almost. Christian moved beside her and patted her on the back as she began to cry again. As soon as the first tear fell from her cheek, she heard her dad's voice from inside her once again.

Turn that shit into something else, L.

She wanted to heed his advice, but really felt like this situation more than warranted the tears. After all, wasn't sadness, compassion, and sorrow a part of the humanity that Christian had just mentioned? After allowing herself to mourn for a couple more minutes, she wiped the tears from her cheeks and took a deep breath, exhaling slowly as her shaking subsided.

"There you go," Christian said. "That's more like it."

Lauren smiled at him genuinely through her tears. It wasn't so much a happy smile; it was more of an appreciative one. "I never even knew her name," she said, barely able to get the words out.

Christian smiled and looked down at the sheet that covered the little girl. "Then we'll call her Angel," he said. "Her innocent life was taken from her too soon, but her pain is over. I'm sure she's in heaven now—looking down at us."

Lauren smiled slightly. "That sounds like something my grandmother would say," she said quietly. As the seconds passed, an overwhelming feeling of comfort befell her, in spite of the gruesome scene that surrounded her. "Rest in peace, Angel," she said.

Christian took another look around them, taking in the entire scene. He looked to the cabin and saw Norman and Michelle, pointing around the property and talking. Amidst the talking, he heard them laugh and saw them hug each other. John and Lee were standing near them, and he saw the brothers shake hands and give each other a one-armed hug. Grace soon walked over to them and began hugging each of them with a broad smile. At one time, she peered over her shoulder to the rear of the property with a concerned look but once she saw Christian and Lauren, she looked relieved. She smiled happily at him and waved. Christian nodded his head and smiled back at her, offering her a wave of his own. Amazingly enough, no one on their side had gotten hurt during this attack and he was thankful for that. He didn't know if it would always be this way—in fact, he doubted it. But it was a good feeling to know that these people, his new family, had come out on top and unscathed.

In spite of what had taken place, Christian felt good being here. These people were Lauren's family and friends, but they felt like they were now his family, too. They were members of a community that he was beginning to feel a part of. They had successfully defended themselves against an invading force. Today, they were *survivors*; in the complete sense of the word. They had won this battle and he was proud to know that he had helped them win it. He would do it again, if he had to.

Taking it all in with a feeling of pride, he turned to Lauren, who was staring off into the woods. He placed his hand on her shoulder and said, "I know you weren't comfortable giving me information about your family and this place, Lauren. I guessed, from the words you used and the tone of your voice, how much you loved them and what you were willing to do to protect them. Looks like I was right. All things being equal, thank you for letting me come with you."

"You're welcome," Lauren said with a grim smile. "Just don't let me down, ok?"

"I won't, I promise you," Christian said. After a pause, he continued, "Up until the other day, I didn't have a place to call home. I had no family. For some reason now, today, I feel I have both. And I have you to thank for that."

Lauren nodded, but didn't respond. This was as sincere as she had ever heard him. Christian, sensing something more needed to be said, gathered his thoughts quickly.

"I know that none of this is easy for you...but the things you did today were great things, Lauren. You protected your family today and defended your home. Your world is safer now because of what you did."

"I guess," she said humbly.

Taking his hand off of her shoulder, he pointed to the cabin and the others standing outside. Her eyes followed his finger while he looked at her eyes. "Your family, this place—all of this around us, this is your world now, isn't it..."

Lauren glanced over at Christian briefly with a blank look before turning around, picking up her rifle, and hopping carefully back toward the cabin. As she reached the bridge, she stopped and turned to him.

"Yeah, this is it. What's left of it."

EPILOGUE

L
AUREN TOOK A DEEP DRAG on the menthol cigarette she had lit
a few minutes before. She still had the mini BIC lighter in her left
hand and was rolling it in between her fingers while she breathed in
the smoke and exhaled. She attempted to blow a couple smoke rings, but
wasn't quite able as she had never learned the art of doing so. Smoking
wasn't one of her favorite habits, but it provided her with a way to
decompress, during one of her two fifteen minute breaks that she was
allowed for every eight hours that she worked. It was quite warm outside,
probably near eighty degrees and the sun shone brightly on the parking lot
in front of her that was about half full of customer vehicles. It had been
a very warm autumn Saturday and Toys R Us had been fairly busy that
day; she guessed primarily due to the weather. Lauren had gotten the job a
year before, and worked all summer long when school was not in session.
She had just begun her junior year of high school. She had her driver's
license, a decent car, and a vision of what she wanted for her future. Her
grades were remarkable, and even though academics came easy to her
she worked hard, and felt that she was well on her way to a life of fun and
independence. This part of her life was simply a stepping stone.

Not allowed to stand outside the front of the building while on the clock,
per company policy, Lauren's smoke breaks occurred on the east side of the
building, where the trucks that kept the shelves filled with product backed
up to the loading dock. Her view was not quite a notable one, just the side
parking lot and a guard rail overlooking the road below. She inhaled a long
drag and blew out the smoke from her nostrils, flicking the dead ash from

her cigarette onto the ground. Pulling out her smartphone, she checked for messages and sighed loudly when she saw that there were none. Nothing from her school friends or even the boyfriend. She fumbled through the phone instinctively, opening a couple different social media apps to see if there were any waiting messages for her, and upon finding out there were none, pressed the button that turned the screen off and put the phone back into her pocket. She shook her head slowly and sighed in relative disgust.

The blue security door behind her opened. Lauren turned her head and noticed her best friend and coworker Madison had walked out. She smiled and Madison smiled back.

"Hey, hooker. Enjoying that cancer stick?" Madison asked.

"You know me, if it's not one habit, it's another," Lauren replied, "It's about all the pleasure I can get out of life at the moment."

"It's not that bad is it?"

"I'm not saying it is. But this working on weekends shit is for the birds, " Lauren said, taking another drag from her cigarette.

"I guess you're right about that, but we do need the money," Madison pointed out.

"It would just be nice to have more to look forward to," Lauren said.

"Please. I would love to be in your position right now, Mrs. Honor student," Madison began, "One of these days, you'll be a college grad and you'll have the entire world at your feet. Me, on the other hand…who knows? I'll probably end up cutting grass and shoveling snow with my old man."

Lauren dropped her cigarette on the ground and stomped it out. She turned to look at her friend with a stern eye. Madison curiously looked back, waiting for what was to come out of her best friend's mouth.

"Your dad is a terrific guy and he'd do anything for you. You're lucky to have him, Maddie. And so what, if you end up cutting grass. It's a proud family business and there's nothing wrong with working hard for a living. At least, that's what my dad says."

"Sure, Lolo. Coming from a man that doesn't work hard," Madison rebutted using her favorite nickname for her friend, "He's got a great job."

"Um… he used to when I was younger. Dad always had problems making money. He's not educated. He's just smart. He worked for himself and it was feast or famine those days. Yeah, he ended up getting a great career later on in life, but we were damn near dirt poor for a very long time," Lauren said.

"I guess," Madison said unconvinced. "I'm bored. Ready to go back inside?"

"Aren't you going to take a break?" Lauren asked.

"Nope. Don't need one."

"Well...let's get back to the grind then."

Lauren put her arm around her friend and they walked back inside the store together. Once inside, they walked back to the stockroom and resumed pulling boxes of merchandise from the store room shelves and placing them onto a cart to be taken out onto the sales floor and fronted.

After diligently filling the cart, Lauren walked to the front of the cart and began pulling it out of the stockroom while Madison followed her, aiding her by pushing the near overloaded cart from behind. As they reached the double doors that led to the sales floor, all of the lights in the building went out. The rooftop air conditioners that normally could be heard rumbling above ambient noise levels were no longer operating. It was total silence, other than the customers talking quietly and scurrying about, with the occasional child's voice asking questions. Surprised at this and the sudden darkness and silence that surrounded them, they stopped the cart and stood there for a second, as if waiting for the situation to return to normal, and lights to come back on.

"Any time now..." Madison said rather loudly, ignoring nearby customers and assuming the tone of her voice was justified by the current situation.

"The generator should kick on in a minute," Lauren said. "I didn't have a chance to see the western sky when I was outside—maybe there's a storm coming in," Lauren suggested.

"Um...I didn't hear any thunder, Lolo," Madison added.

"Good point."

"Well, what else could've cause this?" Maddie asked.

"Really, Maddie? It could be anything. Maybe a drunk driver hit a damn electric pole or something," Lauren retorted.

Madison began digging in her pockets. She pulled out her keys and her cellphone. "Got a flashlight?" she asked.

"Yeah. In my backpack that's in my locker," Lauren said.

"Well, that's a good place for it," Maddie snidely commented.

"Shut up. What is this, 'give Lauren shit' day? How the fuck was I supposed to know we'd have a power outage today?" Lauren inquired, slightly toning down as she could almost hear her dad's voice in her head. He would be irritated with her as well right now, for not being prepared. He'd be reminding her of the importance of always keeping her EDC, or every day carry, on her person at all times.

Madison clicked the screen of her cellphone a few times and turned on the flashlight application, which enabled the camera flash LED as a flashlight. She had an older flip phone that predated the smartphone that Lauren had in her pocket by a few years. "Got it," she said, feeling proud of herself that she had an answer to the darkness around them.

"My hero," Lauren said sarcastically, even though she was happy that they at least had an option in the current situation.

As the two began shining the flashlight around, they heard a familiar voice walking through the store. It was Sally, the store director, and she was walking through the store with a bright flashlight and speaking loudly to all of the customers in the store, assuring them that it was a temporary situation and that the lights would be back on shortly, in spite of the fact that people were becoming increasingly uncomfortable with the darkness. Sally walked the isles and after giving orders to a few other employees, eventually ended up walking directly up to the two girls. Her expression turned to one of slight irritation.

"Ladies, the two of you are needed up front. We have a line of customers trying to check out and they need paperwork done on their purchases so they can leave," Sally said, shining the flashlight into Lauren and Madison's eyes. "The POS system is down, so everything has to be done on paper."

Lauren smirked and readied herself for a conflict. She absolutely hated running a register, and any other job associated with the front-end of the store. She had chosen a stockroom position because of her disdain for dealing directly with people. With many clashes with Sally under her belt, she was not a fan of her boss and had next to zero respect for her. "Sally, we were just on our way to my locker to get flashlights," she said.

"We have flashlights up front, miss. Plus, the sun is shining through the front windows up there, so come on. Let's go," Sally demanded. "Now."

"Have it your way," Lauren said reluctantly. She made a face and Madison looked at her and shrugged in acceptance.

They both half-heartedly followed their manager to the front of the store where in fact, there was a long line of customers waiting to pay for their purchases, and the current situation was making them nervous, as well as unhappy. Maddie turned off her phone's flashlight and put it back into her pocket, the sun shining through the front window providing adequate light for her to see. Lauren immediately noticed that all of the register screens were off. She peered over to the customer service desk and saw that the computer monitors were off as well. She began to notice, in the silence, that the battery backup UPSs that usually kept the registers and other computers in the building running during an outage were not beeping annoyingly, as they would have been doing ordinarily. Thinking this was especially strange, thoughts started coming together in her mind and she could feel her heart beginning to beat faster. She pulled her smartphone from her pocket and went to turn on the screen, noticing that it would not respond when she pressed the power button. She thumbed it several times with the same result.

"Dude, what the hell?" Lauren said. Sally, who was still standing close enough to hear Lauren's expression, turned to her.

"Lauren, as I've asked you time and time again, please watch your mouth."

"Sally, the UPSs aren't beeping," Lauren proposed. "My phone isn't working either."

"AND?" Sally retorted.

Lauren's attitude, responding to Sally's comeback, switched gears quickly and jumped beyond exasperation. She became indignant with her boss. This was not the first time it had happened. "Sally, the UPSs aren't beeping. Meaning that this isn't a typical power outage. It's *more* than that," Lauren interjected.

"Lauren, honestly, I don't need your lip right now. We have a ton of work to do with the POS system down, so please assist the cashiers," Sally said as she stomped off to her office.

Madison, who was beyond belief once again, that her best friend had been involved in another confrontation with her boss, looked at Lauren with cross eyes. "Lo, what the hell? Are you nuts? Do you want to get fired?"

Lauren took one final look at her smartphone before pushing it back into her pocket. She stepped toward her friend and pulled Madison's cellphone from her front jeans pocket, flipping it open and thumbing the buttons. Madison lifted both of her arms with her hands outward, in an unknowing gesture.

"Why in the hell is your phone working?" Lauren asked rhetorically.

"Huh?" Madison enquired. "What do you mean?"

"I mean your phone works, dipshit." Lauren held it up to Madison's face. "It doesn't have any service, but it works. What the hell?" Lauren exclaimed, again, not caring that customers were near her. Some of them turned to her only to look away seconds later. Most were beginning to check their own phones, most of which had screens that were as blank as Lauren's.

"Maybe my phone is smarter than your smartphone," Madison joked with a grin.

Lauren didn't respond. She just kept looking around her, watching the actions of every single person who was gathered tightly in the front of the store. After a minute of silence from her friend, Madison was becoming increasingly paranoid. Her expression went from confusion to utter fear. She reached out and grabbed her phone from Lauren's grasp. Looking at it, she noticed the screen worked and the phone reacted when she pressed buttons.

"Lo, level with me. Just what in the hell is going on?" Madison asked insistently.

Lauren shrugged. "I don't know exactly. But we need to get out of here and go home," Lauren replied.

"What? Are you serious? I..."

"Now, Maddie," Lauren said with an extremely stern tone of voice.

"What about work? What about Sally?"

Lauren grabbed her best friend's hand and started walking to the back of the store, literally dragging her behind. Madison allowed it, even though she was second guessing the entire situation and was unsure as to what to do. They neared the dark hallway that led to the break room and Madison pulled out her flip phone and turned on the LED light. With the way illuminated, Lauren pushed the door to the break room open and walked up to her locker as Madison's light led the way. She began rolling the combination lock back and forth. Madison typed a phone number into her phone and hit the send button, putting the phone to her ear. The phone refused to connect and only remained silent. She tried again with the same result.

"Lo, what the hell is going on? I can't call home," Madison said.

Lauren opened her locker and pulled her backpack out. She grabbed a few individual personal items that were laying loose in her locker and stuffed them into her pack, then zipped the top pocket shut.

"Try sending a text message. Dad says sometimes they'll go through, even when you can't make a call," Lauren offered.

Madison began typing into her phone's keypad tediously. After a moment, she sent the message that she had typed to her mother. Seconds later, an error message was displayed on her phone, saying the service was unavailable.

"No dice," Madison said. "I literally have no connection. This is getting weirder by the minute."

"I wish I knew the answer, but I honestly don't know what to tell you. All I know is that when something like this happens, there is only one place to be."

"What? Where's that?" Maddie asked.

"Home," Lauren said. "We just need to go home—and we need to get there as fast as we can."

"Ok. Let's go home then," Maddie said, now sounding very satisfied with that answer.

Lauren slung her backpack and they left the break room. They walked to the front of the store, past their jeering co-workers, and out the front door, which they had to force open, since the automatic motors than ran on electricity were not working. Walking toward the lower front parking lot, Lauren pulled her keys from her pocket and pushed the unlock button on her car keyfob. She pushed it again and again, but the doors never unlocked. Lauren and Madison approached the car.

"Is your remote broken?" Madison asked.

"No. It worked fine this morning," Lauren replied.

"Ok. First, the lights go out. Then, the generator doesn't start. Then, the computers are dead and no one's cellphone works except mine. Now, your keyfob isn't working? What does all this mean?"

"It means we're in deep shit, girl. You're right—it's like nothing electronic works anymore," Lauren replied. "Except your cellphone, which is a little confusing."

"Yeah. But it's old. I don't have service. But at least the light works," Madison said.

Lauren pushed the unlock button on her keyfob several times before tossing her car keys onto the ground in disgust. "Dammit!" Lauren exclaimed. She then reached into her backpack and pulled out a Kershaw EMT folding knife. The knife had a tungsten glass breaking bezel point on the bottom. Lauren palmed the knife, and slammed the bottom against the driver's side window. The window quickly spider webbed, and the safety glass reacted and quickly crumpled and soon fell into the driver's seat and floorboard. Lauren reached inside and unlocked the car's doors. She then opened the driver's door and got inside, sitting on the now glass-covered seat. Madison reached down and grabbed the keys that were laying on the ground and handed them to her friend. Lauren placed them into the ignition and turned the key. Nothing happened. The car was dead.

Lauren began shouting a barrage of obscenities. She angrily punched the steering wheel repeatedly and Madison began to panic. She placed her hands on her head and had almost started to cry. The abnormality was beginning to really get to her and it showed.

"Lo, how are we going to get home? I'm getting scared."

Lauren stepped out of the now lifeless car which was, up until recently, her favorite thing in the entire world. It marked the beginning of her independence. It was a level-up in her coming of age, a stepping stone to her eventually becoming an adult. "I guess we're walking," Lauren said. She stepped out of the car slowly. "It's not that far. We can do it."

Madison's crying stopped almost as soon as it started when an idea hit her. "Can't we just take some of the bicycles from the store?" she said.

Lauren looked at her friend and smiled. She walked to the back of the car and opened the trunk with her keys. Inside, she grabbed a few small bags of belongings and another medium-sized backpack. She pulled the backpack out and opened it, unshouldering the smaller pack she'd had on her back and began shoving items from the smaller pack into the bigger pack. She then rolled the smaller backpack tightly and stuffed it in the larger pack as well.

"How many backpacks do you have?" Madison asked.

"The one I keep in my locker is just for my every day carry items. I keep my GHB in my car," Lauren answered as she adjusted the straps on her pack.

"Why do you call it that?"

"It's a get-home backpack. It has everything in it that I need to get me home," Lauren affirmed. "My dad made me start carrying one around when I got this car."

"That makes me feel fucking stupid," Madison offered somberly. "I have a purse. That's about it. I think there's a knife in there."

"But you have it on you, right?"

"Yeah," Madison replied.

"Then you're ahead of most people in our situation," Lauren said.

Madison looked around and noticed an exodus of people leaving the store. "And exactly what is our situation?" she asked.

Lauren slammed the trunk shut and shouldered her now full get-home backpack, which was little more than a typical nylon military 3-day pack with MOLLE webbing. "Fucked," Lauren said. "I'd say at this point, completely fucked."

Lauren pointed to the streets where cars had seemingly stopped in their tracks in the middle of the road, and passengers were outside of their vehicles, looking about in confusion. Many of them had their hoods up, toying around their vehicle's engine compartment. Others were talking in groups, all were holding a cellphone of some sort, and it was more than obvious that everyone was confused. "Do you see that shit?" she asked her best friend.

"Yeah. I do. What in the hell is going on?" Maddie asked, trying to get a grip on what was happening, partially in an effort to convince her best friend that she wasn't completely ignorant, and partly in an effort to convince herself. "It's like the beginning of some bad movie."

"Maddie, babe—haven't you ever read any books about shit like this?" Lauren asked.

"Um, no. I read novels, mostly novels. Nothing like this ever happened in books I've read," Madison said.

Lauren unshouldered her pack and placed it on the ground beside her now non-functioning car. She approached her best friend, who was looking low to the ground in front of her. She was shaking and seemed lost, rifling through the items in her purse. Lauren was scared too, but had learned skills that had helped her develop confidence over the years. She pulled the rolled up smaller backpack out of her GHB, and placed her hands on Madison's shoulders.

"Maddie, we have to get home. It's important. We can't call our family and we can't text them. We can't communicate to them what's going on or where we're at. They don't know if we are safe. Let's just concentrate on getting home," Lauren said confidently.

"Yeah. You're right. Let's go home," Maddie agreed.

Lauren reached down and grabbed her backpack, slinging it over her shoulders. She then handed her smaller backpack, which was now empty, to her friend. Madison smiled and placed her purse and cellphone into the bag, zipped it up and shouldered it.

"Now. Let's go inside and grab a couple of these bikes," she said.

ABOUT THE AUTHOR

C.A.Rudolph is a God-fearing Conservative who lives, works, eats, and occasionally sleeps in Northern Virginia. In his spare time he has been known to visit the gym, hike mountains, engage in the occasional QSO on the amateur bands, shoot guns, write books and short stories, enjoy an adult beverage or two, shoot pool, and spend time with his loving, very supportive, and very German wife, and amazing children. He can be found online on Facebook, Instagram, and via his website at

www.carudolph.com

Made in the USA
San Bernardino, CA
20 March 2017